THE
GUILTY
SLEEP

A THRILLER

THE GUILTY SLEEP

JEREMY D. BAKER

DIVERSION
BOOKS

Diversion Books

A division of Diversion Publishing Corp.

www.diversionbooks.com

Copyright © 2025 by Jeremy D. Baker

All rights reserved, including the right to reproduce this book or portions thereof in any form whatsoever. No part of this publication may be reproduced or transmitted in any form or by any means, electronic or mechanical, including photocopying, recording, or any other information storage and retrieval, without the written permission of the publisher.

Diversion Books and colophon are registered trademarks of Diversion Publishing Corp.

For more information, email info@diversionbooks.com

First Diversion Books Edition: May 2025

Hardcover ISBN: 9798895150290

e-ISBN: 9798895150221

Cover design by Anthony Morais

Design by Neuwirth & Associates, Inc.

Printed in the United States of America

1 3 5 7 9 10 8 6 4 2

Diversion books are available at special discounts for bulk purchases in the US by corporations, institutions, and other organizations.

For more information, please contact admin@diversionbooks.com.

The publisher does not have any control over and does not assume any responsibility for author or third-party websites or their content.

To Sarah and Charlotte, who told me to keep going.

THE GUILTY SLEEP

MONDAY

THE BLACK RIVER

DEX

Dexter Grant's life fell to pieces on the pitted moonscape of Thievery Collective's parking lot. More accurately, it detonated extravagantly, like reactive armor under an RPG strike. The bar was ten blocks from work and a half-step up from a dive. It was Dex's usual spot if he was looking to tie one on but avoid drinking alone in his apartment, solo binge drinking being a key indicator of alcoholism. He wasn't ready to look into *that* cracked mirror quite yet, thank you very much. Indicators. Signs and portents, his stock-in-trade as an Army counterintelligence grunt. The training, like the nightmares, never went away. It was flash-baked into his blood. Maybe this time the booze would help.

And while he was deluding himself, maybe the sun would rise in the west, his family would take him back, and he'd get out from under . . . everything.

A decent day's work at the bank used to make him feel better. But lately all it had done, especially Freddy's usual nonsense, was make him want to get drunk. Forget who he was, what had happened, what it had done to him and his family. Soon as Freddy locked the doors behind them, Dex was on his way, following his feet to that hollow promise before he even knew it was his destination.

He texted Daria as he walked.

Saw I had a missed call from you last night?

The three cycling dots of her reply appeared, vanished. He could picture his wife—he couldn't think of her as his ex, not until it was *over*—brows drawn together in thought, mulling her response.

He looked at the phone every ten steps. The dots came and went.

Five minutes later he glanced up, realized where he was headed, and decided his subconscious was on the money. There was a rumble of thunder in the distance and he quickened his pace, dragging a sleeve through the beading sweat on his forehead.

Dex walked past a liquor store and its next-door neighbor, a fast-food joint. Two surefire prospects in this town along with the bar, the pain clinic, and the funeral home. The booze shop and the restaurant shared a row of rusty dumpsters. A trio of skells burrowed industriously through the one on the end. He wondered if they'd jump him, and slowed down to give them a chance, but they never looked up. Disappointing.

Those shambolic wrecks were his future. The thought hit him like falling into freezing water. The black river, pulling him down.

Once, the future—The Plan—had looked like a stable contracting gig, maybe even working for his former team lead, Sergeant Saenz, in a civvy job at Golden Oak. Full medical to cover Ro's eye surgery, since military Tricare only kicked in when you were on active orders or retired in good standing and Dex was none of the above. Good corporate money, to pay down Daria's j-school loans and to carve away at their mortgage until they weren't drowning.

The Plan was smoke on the wind as soon as he'd washed out of the National Guard. No military contractor was going to hire a vet with an OTH discharge, especially when said other-than-honorable disposition was due to repeated absences without leave after returning from a war zone. And—*allegedly*, since there were no witnesses—striking his commanding officer during his first debrief following the incident outside Kandahar. Didn't exactly speak to a stable candidate. It spoke

THE GUILTY SLEEP

to a guy with a short fuse, prone to benders, likely to disappear into himself when needed most. Just like he'd done with his girls.

Forget the surgery, the student loans. Forget the mortgage and a new home, somewhere safer for Ro. Away from their narrow, cracked street, its gutters sanded with broken glass. Away from the front yards that were all high grass and sun-bleached toys and cars on blocks, neighbors prone to fire off shotguns to celebrate holidays. Their neighborhood was a microcosm, a symptom of the sickness eating the rest of the town, and Dex was the physical manifestation of the place. Rotting from the inside, the things that made it once useful now shuttered, shattered.

He floated on the black river. Ahead, the carnivorous roar of a waterfall, and after that the endless dark sea.

The phone buzzed in his hand and he almost dropped it in a puddle.

Why didn't you answer? Daria replied.

Wasn't feeling well.

It was true enough. Last night, like most nights, he'd been in no condition to have a conversation. He added:

Is Rowan ok?

She's fine, but we need to talk.

About what?

You need to sign, ok? It's dragging on
too long. Things need to get settled.

Dex stared at the blue bubble. His thumb hovered over the screen, looking for the right letter to start with. There was no right letter to start with.

I want to see her.

Let me think about it.

He cycled through potential responses. He could say he had a right to see his daughter. To check on the house, make sure his wife and kid were safe. Get an update on Rowan's eye. And Daria could say he was in no condition to have any input into her or their daughter's life. She wasn't wrong.

Dex swallowed hard. Almost threw the phone across the street. The rage rose in him, the desire to lash out.

And then he remembered how it was after he'd gotten back from Afghanistan. When everything was all fresh and sharp, before it curdled and set in his veins like concrete, a chittering homunculus latched across the folds of his brain. The screaming, the cursing, the flashes of fury he couldn't control. The exhaustion of sleepless nights and feeling forever nine meters off the mark. Trying to get somewhere close to good, and never even smelling it.

He remembered New Year's Eve. The neighbors and their stupid shotgun. The look of terror on his little girl's face.

The plate and the wall and the blood.

Dex shook his head, tugged at his collar. At least Daria hadn't said no. The black double doors of Thievery Collective loomed in front of him, an obvious ambush.

He looked over his shoulder. The sun was setting and the clouds, dark and thick as black sheep's wool, spread across the horizon, trailing tendrils of silvery rain-smoke. He didn't want to look at something so beautiful. He heaved the doors open and let the air-conditioning and the hum of television and conversation wash across his senses before plunging into the dim interior.

It was a mistake and he knew it instantly. A trap, one he set and baited for himself. He still went and stuck his face into it.

2

TWO-THIRDS OF A HALF-BAD SONG

DEX

A couple of stools were open at the end of the bar. Prime real estate, but it was under the television. On-screen, a blonde in a jewel-tone dress and a guy with massive, shellacked hair were having an animated conversation. The chyron read "Afghanistan Retreat Disaster."

"Hey, Dex," said Tempest. "Usual for you?" She was the weeknight bartender. Cool as anything, all tattoos and piercings and distant affect. Polite and efficient, but God help anyone who pressed their luck. No way her name was really Tempest—probably Lisa or Jennifer or something—but he respected her vibe enough not to ask.

"Sounds good."

Behind Tempest, the wall was a long mirror fronted by glass shelves of bottles lined up in soldier-neat ranks. He scanned the reflection. A practice ingrained from his days in CI training at Fort Huachuca, he could no more turn it off than he could still his own pulse. If you're not facing the door, you need to be able to keep tabs on your surroundings. He skimmed past his own face: pale, two days' growth, crosshatched scar above his left eye half-concealed by too-long hair. There was a couple at a high top near the front window, but they'd picked the one that was partially obscured, and they were both angled so they could see the door. He had a ring on; she didn't. A late afternoon sneak-away. Other end of the bar, a UPS driver sipped an end-of-shift beer. Between the driver and Dex, three elderly drunks nursed inveterate highballs and traded susurrant murmurs. In the back room, a mismatched quartet of guys was shooting pool at the single table. Place was quiet, but it would pick up once the sun went down.

"Start a tab?" Tempest half-asked, setting the glasses in front of him with a professional smile. She already knew the answer. He nodded in thanks and sipped his bourbon. Once she turned away, he swallowed half of it, holding the burn in the back of his throat until he couldn't take it anymore, then followed it up with a sip of the lager. The usual: one bourbon, one beer. Like a blues song, and not one of the good ones.

His eyes flicked to the television, and by the act of looking at it, the volume fell into place and he could hear what the jewel-tone dress lady and bouffanted dude were saying.

"Isn't this a huge indictment of the administration's foreign policy, Jarrett?" the woman asked, her voice sopping with scripted credulity.

"Absolutely, Ashleigh," the high-haired chump responded. "A *complete* disgrace, if you ask me."

"Well, don't just take our word for it, folks," Ashleigh said, turning to face the camera and crossing her legs. "Stay tuned for retired U.S. Army Major Curt Slicker, who's going to break it all down for us." The screen split, showing a puffy, red-cheeked guy with a wispy buzz cut glowering at the camera.

"We'll be . . . right back," Jarrett intoned.

Dex nearly threw his tumbler at the television, but instead he downed the rest of the bourbon and thumped the empty glass on the bar. If he'd stopped there, at the one beer and the one bourbon, two-thirds of a half-bad song, what came next would have shaken out into a typical week. Go to work, go to the bar, go home, try to sleep, nightmares, go on a long run, text Daria, try to see Rowan, hate his own reflection, rinse and repeat. But, as Ol' Dirty Le Batard had once said back in K-town, "If wishes and ifs were dried shrimp and grits, I'd have myself a fine-ass brunch."

THE GUILTY SLEEP

He caught Tempest's dry-ice gaze and she drifted over for a refill. The hour melted into the next. Sip, swallow, repeat. Avoid the TV. The guys from the pool table crowded up next to him, squeezing around one stool that had remained miraculously empty. They hooted at Tempest, which was a strike against them, and they hollered at the next batch of airbrushed jack-wagons on the television, which would have balanced it out except the things they were saying were even more insipid than the bobbleheads of the small screen commentariat.

Dex finished the third bourbon and turned his fuzzed attention to the quartet. Put on his CI hat and studied them in the mirror across the counter. An odd set. The loudest mouth of the bunch was wearing shiny suit pants, a fitted white dress shirt, and a narrow tie. His hair was hard and slick-looking. Another, a guy with a bull's neck and a beard that flowed over his chest like a bib, was wearing work pants with oil stains at the knees. The third was in ripped jeans and a black T-shirt for a hardcore band, and looked like he subsisted on Mountain Dew and cigarettes. The last guy was right out of a commercial for a mattress store, khaki pants and white sneakers, polo shirt tucked in tight around a spreading paunch.

Dex couldn't make them fit at first, but they were a set for sure. Lots of laughing and clapping each other on the back, finishing each other's sentences. Inside jokes and innuendos. He landed on former high school teammates. Football. They had an easy camaraderie, the kind that would hold on for a decade after graduation as life took them in different directions. Probably got together once a month to slam beers and reminisce. Linebacking crew, maybe.

"Put us on a plane and we'll clean 'at mess up right quick," said the biggest guy, the one with the stained knees and beard.

"ARs and a few grenades, some a' them rocket launchers," put in the metal fan, his voice rattling with a speed un-slurred by the Natty Bohs he'd been chugging.

"Buncha primitive monkeys," muttered the one who looked like he managed a mattress store. His eyebrows made a knot of anger at the bridge of his nose.

"You want to keep it down a bit?" asked Tempest, delivering their boilermakers.

"It don't piss you off, sweetheart?" asked the businessman in the tight shirt, nodding at the TV. It was replaying images of Taliban technicals swarming the streets of Kabul, interspersed with chaotic evacuation scenes at the airport. "We cut and run an' let those raghead camel-humpers take over? Makes us look like a bunch of cowards."

"What'll piss me off is if you guys break another glass."

"Said I was sorry, hon," said Metalhead. "It slipped."

"G'head and start us another round, OK?" said Big Beard. "Put it on his tab." He jerked his head at Businessman, who mouthed something unpleasant at his friend, smiling all the while.

"Ah, just look at them," Mattress Guy grumbled, still staring at the screen.

"I think," said Businessman, "we went too easy. Only way to go is scorched earth." His three pals chorused agreement. "Do 'em up like Connery said in that movie. 'They pull a knife, you pull a gun. They put one of your guys in the hospital, you put one of theirs in the morgue.' Like that."

"Yeah," said Big Beard. "They set up an IED, we nuke their ass. Glass parking lot. Scorched earth, like you said. Shoulda wiped out every one a them sand nig—"

"Excuse me," Dex said.

3

A FRANK EXCHANGE OF VIEWS

DEX

"What's up, bruh?" asked Businessman. The leader of the group. Probably the defensive captain. Still in good shape: tall and lean, but broad across the shoulders and thighs. Middle linebacker for sure.

"Just wanted to thank you guys for your service," Dex replied.

"What?" said Metalhead, his face slack.

"You got all these expert takes, I figure you did some time in the sandbox," Dex said. He willed himself to shut up, but his mouth kept going. His temper was like the thunderstorm that had chased him into the bar. It spread across the horizon, inevitable as the flash before the boom. "So . . . you know . . . thank you for your bravery and sacrifice and all that. Shame the administration hasn't retained you as consultants."

"You tryin' to be funny?" Big Beard asked.

"Hey," said Tempest, her voice low and urgent.

Dex waved at her gently but kept his eyes on the group. His body followed his mouth, betraying the desire to slouch on his stool and drink until the night was hazy around the edges. He slid to his feet.

"What's funny," Dex asked, "about a humble private citizen wanting to buy a round for a group of such . . . distinguished war heroes?"

In addition to being the leader, Businessman was clearly the smartest—or soberest—of the group. "This guy," he said, looking over his shoulder at his buddies, "thinks we ought to shut up about Afghanistan because we weren't there."

"What, and you were?" sneered Big Beard.

"Who says I was?" said Dex, same time as Tempest said, "Why doesn't everyone just chill?"

"Ah," said Businessman. His eyes drifted to the faint X of scars above Dex's left eye, then down to the inside of Dex's left forearm, where the unit crest—raven in profile sinister on mantled shield, *296 MI BN* stamped above, *BLACKBIRDS* scripted below—took up a wide swath of skin. Dex fought the urge to tug his sleeve down. "Ah," said Businessman again, drawing it out to three syllables.

"No way," said Metalhead. "This skinny-ass hipster?"

"So, you're qualified to talk about it and the rest of us should shut up?" said Mattress Guy.

"No and yes," said Dex. "In that order, in case you weren't following—don't strain your brainpans." He couldn't stop. There was a smell in the air, might have been ozone. "I can ask Tempest for a box of crayons and construction paper if you think it would help. Make you a little presentation for clarity."

"Wait, what?" This from Metalhead, clearly the driest marker in the pack.

Dex sniffed, scenting like a hound. "You smell that? This guy's cerebellum just started smoking."

"This prick thinks he's better'n us, fellas," Businessman said. "Just 'cause he was over there."

"No," said Dex, whispering through his teeth. "I'm no better than you. I'm worse, if such a thing is remotely conceivable. And you doorknobs look about as collectively beneficial to society as an unsalted pretzel."

Mattress Guy snarled a curse under his breath and cracked his neck.

THE GUILTY SLEEP

"Gentlemen," Dex said, rolling his shoulders and spreading his hands wide in faux apology, "if I've said anything to offend you, I can assure you it was completely intentional."

"Wait, what?" This from Metalhead. Again. Dex thought it might make a good chorus in a heavy metal song.

"Y'ask me," grunted Businessman, "losers like *you* are why things look like *that* right now." He waved at the screen, which showed a frantic woman trying to pass a little girl over the barbed wire fence that ringed the airport. The girl was Rowan's age. A teenager in Marine Corps fatigues reached for her, his face tight.

"Be back to settle up in five, Tempest," Dex said, and shouldered his way through the foursome. He reached the door and looked back. "You guys coming or what? Don't keep me waiting. I'll get all lonely."

Businessman slammed his glass down, sloshing his drink across the bar. "Let's go, boys. This guy needs his ass beat."

"Thought you were never gonna take the hint," Dex said. He stepped out into the night.

TC was at the end of a strip mall, with a narrow extrusion of parking lot stretching between its side wall and the scrub field beyond. He moved into the shadows of the lot. Stood in the middle of the space and faced the way he'd come—bar on the left and the field to his right. Only a couple cars in this section, up near the bar entrance. Plenty of room. The fresh air sharpened some of the blurry edges. He breathed deep.

The football team followed thirty seconds later, walking like they'd done this before. Surely they had. Dex scrolled back through a dozen fights, realizing belatedly just how stupid this was. He'd never, even on his wildest day, been dumb enough to take on four guys.

"Oh man, we are gonna kick the *shit* out of you," said Big Beard.

The four chuckleheads formed themselves into a semicircle, from left to right: Metalhead, Businessman, Big Beard, Mattress Guy.

Before Afghanistan, during his first combat tour in northern Iraq teaching the Kurds to interrogate people without using a car battery and kiddie pool full of water, Dex'd been teamed with a Romanian corporal who'd trained as a cage fighter for fun. Thickset guy with hands like ham hocks and a dry sense of humor. He used to spar with Dex at the base gym. The Romanian would never touch gloves; he'd just explode into attack mode right from the jump. He told Dex he didn't believe in wasting time with niceties. When you're there to touch gloves and smile, touch gloves and smile. When you're there to talk, talk. When you're there to fight, bloody fight.

Dex figured two things: He'd done enough talking, and Big Beard was the most dangerous member of the group. He was thick, with bulging arms and the rough hands of a guy who worked with them every day. Looked like he could take a sledgehammer to the gut and shrug it off. The rest of the crew probably figured Dex would want no part of him. Metalhead and Mattress Guy each took a shuffling step forward. Any second, they'd move in, either driving him back or pinning him for Businessman and Big Beard.

Dex danced forward, grabbed a fistful of Big Beard's big beard with each hand, and yanked the guy's face down as hard as he could. Same time, he pistoned his knee into Big Beard's chin. The guy snapped straight back and kept going. His feet went slapstick high, and he slammed into the parking lot on his back, legs dropping like a pair of felled timbers.

Dex spread his fingers. A dusting of wiry hair drifted down, and he blew it in Mattress Guy's face, laughing. He whipped toward Businessman, planning a right into the guy's face and then a spinning elbow strike into the side of Metalhead's . . . well . . . head. Then he could take his time with pudgy Mattress Guy, who was clearly the lowest threat of the bunch. It was a perfect mental choreograph and he was already flowing into it when Mattress Guy ruined everything by being, in fact, the highest threat of the bunch. Businessman was still gaping at Big Beard's prone form, Metalhead was beginning to shout something (probably "Wait, what?"), and Dex was winding up for a beautiful cross into Businessman's jaw when Mattress Guy flowed like water and planted a hard left into Dex's side. Pain shot up his back and down his right leg, which suddenly didn't want to hold his weight. He staggered and Mattress Guy grabbed Dex around the waist and dumped him to the ground.

Businessman and Metalhead crowded in, bouncing off each other in their haste to reach him. Mattress Guy rained blows at Dex's head and Dex mostly took them on the forearms, but one caught him with a glancing swipe on the ear and his head rang with the hot sting of it. Dex got a hand around Mattress Guy's heel and twisted, rolling them over. Now on top, Dex sent a left-right combo into the guy's double chins, but then the other two were dragging him off.

Businessman threw a sharp left into Dex's cheek, snapping his head back. "Hold still and take what you got coming," he snarled. Metalhead seized Dex's arms, pinning them behind his back.

Dex felt a trail of blood flow over his upper lip, tasted it with the tip of his tongue. And then Mattress Guy was on his feet, pushing Businessman aside. He worked Dex's chest and midsection like a heavy bag. Metalhead whooped, which was at least better than "Wait, what?"

Three, four heavy punches to the body. Mattress Guy grinned at Dex and Dex found himself grinning back into the guy's face. The pain wasn't real yet—that would come later—but the promise of it was there, thick and rich as each blow landed.

"What—are you—so—happy—about?" Mattress Guy grunted, winded from the effort.

"When—are you—gonna—*really*—hit me?" Dex gasped, but what he meant was, *Keep it coming. This is what I deserve.* The smell of ozone had become the lightning strike, and the thunder was right behind. The black river waited.

"Switch out," said Businessman, and Mattress Guy gave a grateful nod and grabbed Dex's arm as Dex sagged against him. Businessman stepped in front of Dex and started rolling his sleeves up his forearms. "My boy worked the body, but I think I'll rearrange your pretty face some more—what do you think about that?"

There was a flare of light from the main road, headlights across rain-slicked pavement. The shadows behind Businessman coalesced and suddenly the guy disappeared in a gray billowing cloud. There was a hollow thump and Dex blinked and Businessman was crumpled on the ground, unmoving. There was someone standing where the guy had been, haloed by the streetlights and traffic. Fair hair and a long gray raincoat.

"Wait, what?" mumbled Metalhead.

"You ever say anything else?" Dex groaned, and whipped his head back as hard as he could, smacking into Metalhead's face with a satisfying thump.

Metalhead let him go with a screech, and Mattress Guy stepped to the side. Dex slumped to his knees. There was a *snick* and a gleam in the reflected light and suddenly Mattress Guy was holding a carpet knife, blade angled toward the new guy. There was a rustle and the sound of metal on leather and the new guy had a pistol, held out and away from his body so its outline would be clearly visible against the variable-light background.

"Hey, man," Metalhead said, holding his streaming nose.

"Uh," said Mattress Guy, dropping the knife and putting his hands up.

"Go away," the silhouette said in a harsh whisper. "Come back for your friends in five minutes."

The two scampered, cutting a wide berth around Raincoat Guy, who stepped forward and held out his hand. The gun was gone. Dex looked up and the man's face came into focus.

"Sarnt Saenz," he managed. "Long time no see."

Saenz waved his hand in front of Dex's face. In the shadows, his expression was unreadable. "Come on, Frogger. On your feet."

4

TÊTE-À-TÊTE

SAENZ

Frogger moved like a tenderized slice of veal about to be deep fried and topped with marinara. He was unsteady on his feet, navigating the narrow hallway of the crappy apartment building like a ship of the line trying to cross Cape Horn. His nose was swollen from where the guy in the dress shirt had gotten in that one good shot before Saenz materialized. A mess, in other words. Just what Saenz was looking for.

Grant reached his apartment door, crashed against the jamb, staggered back, then leaned in slowly and scraped his key ineffectually against the lock.

Saenz slipped an arm around his waist. "I gotcha."

A door opened down the hall, and a guy poked his head out. He was small and wiry. Square face punctuated by a wisp of a mustache. "OK, Dexter?" he stage whispered.

"Dawit, hi. I'm all right, thanks. Sorry." Frogger waved at him, hand fluttering like a hummingbird who'd had too much sugar water. The man waved back and started to duck back inside, when Dex called out, "Hey, Dawit!" Saenz clenched his teeth, hand on Dex's elbow.

"Yeah, Dexter?"

"Thank Mariam for me, OK? She was right—the tsebhi was delicious."

Dawit smiled. "I will tell her." He started to duck back inside and Frogger called his name again. Saenz thought his jaw muscles might cramp.

"I . . . I—why are you guys so nice to me?"

"The Lord tells us to be kind to our fellow travelers, Dexter. Says we might be entertaining angels."

"I'm no angel."

The man smiled, puffing his mustache. "You never know, man." He waved and disappeared, his door closing gently.

"Nice neighbor." Saenz gently extracted the key from Dex's fingers. "Here, let me." He slid the key home and opened the door.

"The nicest," Frogger said, flipping the lights. "His wife made me some Eritrean stew."

Saenz stood in the doorway and watched as Grant sloped unsteadily to the kitchen table. On the way, he tried to casually swipe a stack of bills and a manila envelope from the rickety table, but fumbled it. The envelope, Saenz already knew, was labeled *Dean and Morris, Family Law.* Frogger got the papers under control and tossed everything on top of the refrigerator.

"Something to drink, Sarnt?"

"Got anything that's not booze?" Saenz said it softly and smiled when he did, trying to keep the rebuke soft, but Grant staggered like he'd taken a fresh kidney shot. Kid was more fragile than Saenz realized. He was going to have to be careful. Saenz closed the hallway door behind him, pulling it until the lock clicked.

"Um, probably some OJ in the fridge. Maybe."

"No Diet Pepsi?" Saenz said, half-kidding, half-hopeful.

"Sorry, Sarnt. Never my drink."

"No worries. Bad for me anyway, all that fake sweetener. Sit down. I'll scope it out." Saenz pulled out one of the mismatched chairs. Dex sank into it and hunched over the table, staring at the cheap, pitted pressboard. Saenz opened the fridge, saw what wasn't inside, and sighed.

THE GUILTY SLEEP

"You sound like a disappointed mother hen."

"Not disappointed. Concerned."

"Not that I'm complaining, Sarnt," Frogger said to the tabletop, "but what were you doing at Thievery Collective tonight?"

"Let's get some food in you. Few eggs in the carton here. And a Tupperware of . . . something?"

"That's the tsebhi Mariam made. It's good. Little spicy for this time of night."

"Eggs, then. Assuming you have a pan or something."

"Under the oven."

"Coffee, too, I think. Clear your head."

"Sounds good, Sarnt."

Saenz let the conversation ravel out like an untangling skein, in the time-honored tradition of the American male. Limited eye contact, words carried across a proximity never closer than arm's length, and at least one of the participants engaged in some sort of activity with their hands. The way of fathers and sons having The Talk under the open hood of Dad's Chevelle. A young man asking his best friend to stand up with him at the altar over the tees on eighteen. A grandfather and grandson musing over life's vagaries and fortunes while faced opposite in the canoe, lines in the water, ripples slowly spreading.

"Don't need that Sergeant stuff anymore. Not since you got out."

"I'll try, but old habits and all. You still in?"

"Yeah. Picked up First Class last year."

"Congrats, man," Frogger said. Seemed like he meant it. "SFC is a big deal. They give you a platoon?"

"Indeed. Worse gig, though. Don't get to operate quite like I used to. More politics. Still, better for retirement when I pull the plug."

"How long you got?"

"'Bout a year, then sunsets and six-packs."

Grant whistled, then grimaced at the pain and rubbed at his cheek. "Unit deploying anytime soon?"

"Off the hook for now," Saenz said, cracking four eggs into the small cast iron skillet, dropping the spent shells back into the carton, and then stuffing the box in the trash. He gave his hands a desultory rinse, shook them dry, and put the skillet on the burner. "No need to activate Maryland's finest military intelligence National Guard battalion with the drawdown going. Peace breaking out all over."

"Except for the Afghans."

Saenz nodded. Exactly what he wanted to hear. "'Cept for the Afghans."

"And except for whatever comes next."

"Always something else," Saenz agreed. "Seen anyone from the team recently?"

"Sully. About a year ago. He was down from Boston, had a conference in DC. We grabbed a beer." Saenz suspected it had been more like a dozen and the night was a diaphanous ghost in Frogger's memory. "It was good to see him." Saenz let the pause hang until Grant continued. "They did a good job on his ear."

"You know, I ran into ol' Sullivan a few months ago myself," he replied. "Same deal—he was down for some business thing. He did mention he'd caught up with you a bit."

"Still didn't answer my question, Sar—sorry—Stu," Dex said.

"I didn't. Don't suppose you'd believe it was a happy accident?"

"You always said believing in coincidences was a great way to get killed."

"Coffee?" Saenz said, looking up from the stove and meeting Frogger's eyes for the first time. Dex nodded to the cabinet next to the fridge. Saenz pulled out a tin of grounds, the cheap stuff, and shook out a quarter of the can into the paper filter. He inserted the filter, filled the pot from the tap, topped up the machine's tank from the pot, and pushed the button, which lit up with an apologetic orange glow.

Ritual complete, Saenz leaned against the counter, facing the table but looking over Dex's head at the far wall.

"These are . . . slightly more humble circumstances than those in which I hoped to find you, Frogger."

Dex grimaced.

"Forgot you hated the nickname." He hadn't. "Sorry."

"Not that. The circumstances. Humble's . . . too kind a word for it."

THE GUILTY SLEEP

"What happened?" Saenz's eyes flicked, meeting Grant's for a split second. "You were married, right? With a kid, a little girl?"

"All due respect—"

"—technically none due at all," Saenz interrupted, smiling. He turned back to the eggs, giving Frogger a sliver of psychological space.

"Yeah, OK, then: You still haven't answered my question about what you were doing at the bar tonight."

Saenz grabbed mugs and plates from the cabinet where he'd gotten the coffee. He dished the eggs, poured the joe, and set everything on the table. He pulled out the other chair and threw one leg over the top and dropped into it. He nodded at the mug.

"If I recall, you take yours like I do, black as Sergeant Major Pereda's heart. And eat your eggs. Get some food and caffeine in you. Make a world of difference." He illustrated the point by forking a huge mouthful, hissing around the bite to cool it, then taking a dangerously large sip of coffee.

Frogger stared at him. Flaunting the rules, defying convention. Daring the eye contact and making the silence work for him. Saenz smiled at him over the rim of the mug.

"I taught you that look—I'm immune. But fair's fair. Eat something, drink something, and I'll spill." He mimed crossing his heart, then stabbed another bite of eggs.

Dex took a sip, made a face like it was almost too strong. Took a bite of eggs and paused, then another.

"Good," said Saenz. He looked at the far wall and ran a hand through his hair. Time to put the line in the water, see if he could get a nibble. "I was looking for you."

"Why?" The direct questioning technique. Another piece of his training holding on. Saenz suppressed a smile. Vast majority of interrogations you don't need to use fear up, fear down, omniscience, or any of the other variants. Ninety-five percent of the time, you get what you need with direct, simple questions. No subterfuge needed, and *thus endeth the lesson*. 'Course, this wasn't an interrogation. Just a conversation between a couple guys who hadn't seen each other in three years. A couple guys bound by gunfire and blood and loss. By darkness.

"I need your help."

"For what?"

Saenz took a beat. Let the silence do the work, build the connective tissue to Frogger's interest. Kept his tone firm, sincere.

"To save Jalal Hamidzai's life."

5

WE NEED TO TALK ABOUT JALAL

SAENZ

"Say again?"

"Jalal," Saenz repeated. "His family too. I need your help."

Saenz watched Frogger start to put the pieces together. Jalal had been one of their interpreters in Kandahar. A great one. He would've been high on the Taliban payback list for that alone. And if word had gotten out about what he'd done during the incident at the compound, he'd be in their top ten.

"What happened?"

"Yeah, I started at a bad place," Saenz said. "I was going for dramatic effect to get your attention."

"It worked. You have it. But how about reframing the scenario for me?"

"Listen to you. 'Reframing the scenario.' You really did pay attention."

"You made us smarter. Better. So, help me understand the problem."

"Fair enough," Saenz said, holding up his hands in mock surrender. He laid out the tale carefully. Setting the stage for Frogger's eventual capitulation, piece by microscopic piece. It was a masterwork, equal parts horror, Kafka-esque bureaucratic nightmare, and tragedy. And like all deception ops, it was a perfect blend of lies and truth. It was a long story, and they ended up polishing off the neighbor's tsebhi after all. Frogger was right: It was spicy as a demon's tongue, but delicious. Restorative.

After what happened at the compound, it was all over for their team in Afghanistan. The Blackbirds flew home on broken wings. But Jalal decided to stay in Afghanistan. Keep fighting the fight. Moved his family out of K-town and up to the capital and, with Saenz as a reference, landed as a terp for the Defense Intelligence Agency's clandestine HUMINT program operating out of the embassy in Kabul. Another two and a half years of service to the U.S. flag, knowing there was a new life for him and his family on the other end.

When the Americans decided to pull out, turn the security of the country over to its capable Afghan allies, Jalal—always savvy as a vacuum cleaner salesman at a dust convention—read the chay leaves. He was a target, and his family would be greenlit as well. Accordingly, he was first in line for an SIV, *the* promised benefit for Afghans who'd helped the U.S. during the war.

Only there was a problem with the Special Immigrant Visa. A hiccup. The State Department factotum reviewing Jalal's bona fides and family tree noted a troubling relation. A second cousin by marriage to an individual of concern, that person being Kamaluddin Haqqani, the youngest son of Sirajuddin Haqqani. And even though Jalal himself had disclosed the relationship on his background forms when he first applied to work with the Americans, it was suddenly enough derog to kibosh the issuance of the SIV. A connection to the infamous and sprawling Haqqani Network—half mafia, half terrorist, all bad juju— even one as tenuous as Jalal's, was a no-go for State. It painted unpleasant pictures: A family of sleeper agents burrowing into American society, waiting for activation. Suicide bombings. School shootings. Poisoned reservoirs. Sniper attacks. A nightmare on home soil, one we invited in ourselves? Thank you for your service, but no thank you.

All nonsense, of course. Jalal had proven himself loyal a dozen times over, but especially at the compound. He should have been given a medal and a first-class flight to the States. When he'd exhausted the

THE GUILTY SLEEP

appeals process, working his way through the bureaucratic chain and getting a *no* all the way up to the chief of staff to the ambassador himself, who relayed yet another *no* (but at least this time with regrets), Jalal reached out to Saenz.

And Saenz, in his capacity as the finest counterintelligence mind in a generation and rising junior partner at the military-adjacent contracting multinational Golden Oak, broke out all the paraphernalia in his considerable toolbox. He reached out to every single military, paramilitary, and contract partner in the company portfolio, going off the books when needed, making promises he'd never be able to keep. Might cost him his job when everything unraveled, he said with a gentle shrug calculated to the razor's edge of self-deprecation and fatalistic acceptance. Next, he leveraged the network of sources, informants, and officials in Afghanistan he and Jalal had built in-country. Pulled every thread, called in every favor, read everyone the same chay leaves.

Upshot was, he managed to arrange for Jalal and his family to travel north by jingle truck from Kabul to Mazar-i-Sharif, then across the border into Uzbekistan. Along the old silk road to Samarkand, then on a series of decreasingly rickety airframes to Baku, Ankara, Addis Ababa, and Nairobi. There, Jalal picked up the reference chits Saenz'd laid in with a bent Merchant Marine loadmaster, and the family boarded a cross-continental flight to Dakar. Six hours after landing, they were on the Panamanian-flagged cargo ship *Antares*, bound for the Americas. Two days later, Kabul fell. Almost couldn't have cut it any closer.

"Ship docks at the Port of Baltimore on Saturday," Saenz said, draining the last of his coffee. He stood and stretched, cracking his back. Poured a fresh cup. He raised the pot and his eyebrows. Frogger nodded. Saenz topped him up and set the pot back on the burner. It gave off a soft hiss.

"You've been *busy*."

"You're telling me." Saenz chuckled. "Had all my hair last month. But I had help. Sunny Porter and Winkowski are at Golden Oak with me, and they pitched in."

"Anyone else from the old team involved?" Frogger was curious, and how could he not be? It was a good sign.

"No. Keeping the circle small on this."

"I understand that. You've basically coordinated an international human smuggling operation."

Saenz gave him a vestige of an interrogator's stare, and it was Frogger's turn to put up his hands. "Not saying it was wrong. State should have processed the SIV and put him and his family on a private jet out of Hamid Karzai International."

"We agree."

"You did the right thing."

"We agree," Saenz repeated.

"It also sounds like you have things under control. You were the best op planner I ever served under."

Saenz fed him a grateful smile, then said, "But since I was keeping the circle small, why am I expanding it now?"

Dex nodded and sipped his coffee.

"Hit a snag. Bad one."

"I'm listening."

"OK. Jalal's on the boat—"

"—the *Antares*—"

"Right. Due in on Saturday. With his family."

"How many?"

"Four others. His oldest son, just turned nineteen. Younger son, seventeen, I think." That much was true. And now another lie: "His wife and their little girl too. She's, like, five? A little older than your daughter."

"Full house. Or shipping container, I'm assuming."

Saenz tapped the tip of his nose. "In one."

"The snag?"

"World runs on money, Dex."

"As they say."

"And we ran out. I played fast and loose with the Golden Oaks books, changed up some contract terms, and called in those favors in-country to move a few suitcases of dinars, rupees, and afghanis

THE GUILTY SLEEP

around. Hell, I wiped out my own personal savings, cashed in my 401(k), everything. Porter too. Even Winkowski, that maniac."

"Not enough?"

"It *was*. That's the problem. My guy in Nairobi called."

"Not a good sign."

"The worst," Saenz said, nodding. "He said we have to pay a skinner fee on arrival."

"Skinner fee?"

"COD payout. To the port director in Baltimore."

"Ah," Frogger said. "I've heard of those guys. They run security at the cargo ports, right?"

"Exactly," Saenz said, and doled out the rest of the breadcrumbs. "And the Baltimore bubba is bent—main reason we chose the place."

"Home turf doesn't hurt," Frogger added, and Saenz nodded because he saw the wheels turning, and it would be better if Frogger worked the next part out himself. "And your Nairobi coordinator told you the port boss changed the terms on you?"

Saenz allowed a proud-papa smile. "Got it in one again."

"Let me guess, he raised the price because it was Afghans. Like an import duty. I read a thing, said Mexican smuggling groups do the same when they move South Asians and Middle Easterners over the Texas border."

"That's it."

"Shoot, your guy in Nairobi's probably the one who gave the port boss the heads-up."

"Cynical—big surprise—but you're righter than you know. This port director is the law enforcement and inspection chief, head bureaucrat, and senior oversight presence for Uncle Sam, all rolled into one. Responsible for everything that comes in and out, and he's got a couple dozen badge-and-gun toters crawling all over the port on any given day. Maryland Port Authority dances to whatever tune he's playing. Basically, dictator-god-for-life. Gatekeeper for all cargo, licit and illicit, moving through the port. Drugs and money coming in; cars, guns, and money going out."

"People."

"Say again?"

"And people. Coming in," Frogger said.

"Uh-huh. And the port director doubled his rate."

"Call me cynical again, but I would have expected that, Sarnt."

Saenz sighed heavily. Ran his hands through his hair again. Rubbed his face. Let himself look defeated. "I did," he said, after a long pause. "But I hoped for the best, that I'd have time to pull more cash together just in case. I was wrong."

"And if he waits until your precious cargo is halfway across the Atlantic, you can't exactly pull out of the deal while they extract the rest of the blood from the stone."

Saenz nodded, letting his face go hard.

"Only problem is," Frogger continued, following the last of the breadcrumbs, "if I'm hearing you right, there's no blood left in the collective stones."

"Exactly."

"And you're hoping I can help."

"I know you, Fro—Grant. You were always one of the good troops. Stand-up guy, wanted to serve his country, do the right thing. That . . . thing at the compound hosed you up." Saenz cast a look around the dim kitchen. "Got you twisted so much when we got back to the world you didn't know your head from your fourth point of contact. Missing duty weekends. Or showing up smelling like a bottle. Taking a swing at the CO." Frogger's eyes flicked up for a second, caught his own, then sheared away. Saenz thought he'd gone right up to the line, so he pulled back, softened his voice with an injection of sympathy. "I get it. I disagreed with the OTH discharge—I would've tried to get you right—but Battalion made the call, not me. I say there's no shame in it. The thing that happened . . . it messed with all of us."

"Where you going with this, Stu?"

"You're still the guy who wants to do the right thing. I can see it. And you know as well as I do Jalal saved us. Any of us who made it through that day, it was because of him. And if we don't come up with $240,000, the port director's going to call the captain of the cargo

THE GUILTY SLEEP

ship and have him slit Jalal's throat and throw him overboard. His sons too. Probably give the crew the wife and daughter as *payment*," Saenz finished, disgust coloring his tone.

Frogger stared at him. Saenz saw him focus inward, like he was studying his own breathing. In and out. Slow. Trying to take in the enormity of it. He was almost there. Right on the precipice, ready to take the leap. Saenz focused on his own breathing, subtly matching Dex's. Amazing how after all these years in the game, the approach to closing the deal still got his blood up. What a *rush*.

Dex straightened.

"I'd like to help. It's righteous, and God knows I'm trying to do right these days. But look around you, man," Frogger said, spreading his arms to take in the kitchen, dimly lit by the stuttering fluorescents; the wobbly table, the mismatched chairs, the battered fridge. Then he pointed at his own battered face. "I look like I'm in any position to help?" He laughed bitterly. "I have nothing. My wife kicked me out. Filed for divorce and primary custody. I'm not making a hundred grand a year at Booz Allen or Golden Oak like you—got a mountain of bills crushing my spine instead. Top of that, I drink too much. Even sold my beater of a car so I wouldn't end up with a DUI. I have *nothing*," he repeated. "I'm no help to anyone right now."

"It doesn't have to be that way," Saenz said.

"What?"

Saenz paused, hands wrapped around the coffee mug. He looked up, his eyes boring into Frogger's own. Time to land him.

"You still work at the bank?"

6

INTERLUDE:
KANDAHAR, THREE YEARS AGO

DEX

"Babe, you look amazing."

"Shut up," Daria says. But she does that thing where she self-consciously bites her lip and tucks a loose strand of her fire-red hair behind an ear.

"I mean it. The connection's all fuzzy, but I can tell."

"We haven't been apart that long."

"Twenty-two days, six hours, nine minutes."

"You're full of it, Grant."

"And you love it, Grant."

"I do," she says.

"Did I miss Ro?"

"Yeah, she tried to wait up but she's been out for an hour."

"Can you peek in?"

"Sure," Daria says. "Just keep quiet."

The screen goes even fuzzier as Daria climbs the steps—she skips the creaky fourth—and tiptoes to the door of the tiny corner bedroom. His view stabilizes as the door cracks open slowly, slowly, and the picture zooms in and adjusts to the dimness. Rowan is on her side, one hand on her cheek, covers bunched around her little feet. Brownie the stuffed sloth is clutched tight against her belly. His

THE GUILTY SLEEP

31

daughter's hair floats around her face, wafting gently with each breath. Dex drinks her in and time stops.

The screen tips, and he hears his wife creep back down the steps. Half a minute later her laptop is back on the kitchen table and he's staring at his wife again, trying to count the freckles on her cheeks, watching her watch him. She blinks and smiles, raises her mug of tea, and toasts him.

"Say something, husband."

"You look amazing."

"You already said that."

"Can't help it, it's true. I miss you."

"Enough. Don't start something you can't finish," she says.

Dex winks. "You remember that house?"

"The Airbnb?"

"Yeah, white with black shutters—"

"—and the red front door," they finish together.

"How could I forget?" Daria says. "It's the dream."

"I think we should go again, once I get home," Dex says. "Get away from the neighborhood for a weekend."

Daria laughs in agreement. "That was a lucky place, Dex."

"Rowan's origin story. Let's do it again, same as before."

"My mom can watch Rowan," Daria says, giving him that look again, the one that just isn't fair. "She owes us an overnight at least, for the spare room."

"Look at you. My idea, but you've already gamed it out."

"Who, me?" Her smile is soft and wry, but somehow blazes through the screen.

"You'd be a hell of a counterintelligence agent. Besides, it's all part of the plan."

"Ah, The Plan," Daria intones, capitalizing the words in her inflection. "Tell me once more of The Plan, Specialist Grant."

Dex chugs the last of his Rip It and tosses the empty can into the trash bin across the room.

"I'll give you the abbreviated version because we're rolling in like five minutes, OK?"

"You can give me whatever you want."

"Unfair. OK, The Plan. This is combat tour number two, right? Six, seven months side by side with the snake eaters, doing the real work."

Daria nods, her face grave.

"Do my job, make a good impression," Dex continues. "Build the resume. When we demob back to the world, I start pounding the virtual pavement. Between this and the Iraq tour, too much experience to turn down. I'm too good a fit. Place like Booz Allen or Harding or, shoot, even Golden Oak. You know our team lead, Saenz, is a Golden Oak guy?"

"For his day job?"

"Yeah. Some sort of project manager. It's lucky he picked me to replace Russo. If I make a good impression with him, I bet he'd vouch for me."

"How is this guy? Any good?"

"He's a *legend*, Dare." Dex lowers his voice, glancing over his shoulder to make sure he's still alone in the bunkroom. "Story goes, he came up in a family of redneck gangsters outside Frederick. They say he could steal a car before he knew how to walk. Tractors and combines too. Only got caught once, just before he turned eighteen, and they gave him the old join-the-Army-or-join-the-chain-gang ultimatum."

"Doesn't inspire a ton of confidence, Dex."

"Here's the thing—guy goes hardcore hooah: Army infantry, then gets his Ranger tab. After his first enlistment, he cross-designates to CI, and nineteen years ago he parachutes into northern Afghanistan in the first wave after 9/11. Spends the next decade doing the work. Crosses over into the National Guard, takes the killer day gig making *bank*, and still mobilizes whenever he gets the chance. Guys at the unit say there's never been a better CI operator."

"Good to work for?"

"So far, he's awesome. And if I do well, next thing you know I'm riding a desk somewhere outside D.C. on an intel community or DOD support contract."

"Somewhere safe."

THE GUILTY SLEEP

"If you can call driving the Beltway safer than Kandahar. And pulling down a hundred Gs a year, easy. We pay down your loans. Get ahead on the mortgage, look at selling the place, get out of that neighborhood. Maybe find our own black-and-white Colonial out in the country somewhere. And your mom can come too."

"I love The Plan, Dex. And I love talking about it. And now that we *have* talked about it, I want you to file it away. Focus on being safe, coming back to us. Not the bills."

"Well, the combat pay's coming. Should see it hit next week. Make a couple extra payments, OK? Get the principal down?"

"Yeah, or . . ."

"Your face just did that thing, babe. What happened?"

"It's probably nothing. I shouldn't even say anything until I know."

"Until you know what?"

She pauses so long he thinks the screen has glitched. "I'm taking Ro to the doctor on Friday."

"What are you telling me right now?"

"I don't want to scare you. It's just . . . when she woke up yesterday, I noticed her right eye had crossed in."

"Crossed in?"

"Just a little. But, like, that happened to me when I was her age."

"Your eye thing."

"Right. Strabismus, caused by amblyopia. It's genetic, so I'm thinking that might be what this is."

"And you needed surgery, right?"

"Eventually, yes. When I was four."

"So," Dex says, "Doc on Friday to confirm?"

"Yes. But don't worry," Daria replies. "I've got this. And it's not dangerous if caught early, not painful. We'll figure it out. You've got enough on your plate. Focus on staying safe and coming home to us, OK?"

"You got it."

"Frogger!" Ahn sticks his head in the door and twirls his finger. "We 'bout to be wheels out, hey?" Dex waves at him and PFC Ahn Jun-Seo, who will choke to death on his own blood in three hours, ducks out of sight.

"Dare, I gotta go."

"I heard. Everything OK?"

"Yeah. Easy meet-and-greet. Back before nightfall."

"We're gonna have to talk about 'Frogger.' But for now: Be safe, babe. I love you."

"Love you more."

"Not possible."

"Possible."

TUESDAY

7

THE RAVENING DARK

DEX

The night spit him out like he was Jonah and the whale had a burning stomach full of rotgut. Dex clawed free of the funeral shroud of his covers with a gasp that would've been a scream if he'd had any air. His chest heaved like a cracked bellows. His eyes burned and there was salt on his lips. The dark bedroom was unfamiliar, its angles strange and haunted. He lasered in on the blackest corners, the lightless void behind the closet door. Nothing moved. Everything moved. The darkness pulsed like a swallowing throat. The waves of the black river lapped against his skin, trying to pull him back under.

He had to get out.

His legs tangled in the sweat-slicked sheets and he tumbled to the floor, cracking the side of his face against the bedside table on his way. An empty glass shimmied off the table and thumped into the carpet a few inches from his nose. His phone followed, popping him above the ear before tumbling to rest against the glass with a soft *clink*. Insult to mocking injury.

Dex lay on his side, one foot still in the bed, covers holding him like the web of some insane, vengeful spider. He finally captured a breath and held it until his lungs turned to fire. He released it grudgingly and it caught, somewhere between a sigh and a sob. There was a soft light on the other side of his eyelids and he cracked them open, squinting. The phone.

Rowan stared back at him, half-smiling, all tousled brown hair and eyes that seemed too big for her face. Ever so slightly cross-eyed. The pitiless screen claimed it was four twenty-seven in the morning. Dirty dark thirty.

Dex pulled his foot out of the sheets slowly, extricating himself from the web without waking the spider. Kept his eyes locked on Rowan's until he couldn't take it anymore. Once, the sight of his daughter's face would have calmed him, holding him steady and grounded until the black waters receded. Now it was just another red-hot poker tearing at his guts. He clawed at the phone and clicked the sleep button.

He sat with his back against the bed and drew knees to chest, going fetal. Clenched his eyes. Saenz. Jalal. The bank, and what Saenz had asked him to do. He could have sworn he heard the tap-tap-tapping of a fly somewhere, trapped against a window, trying to get out.

Dex focused on the physical, mechanical act of simply *breathing*, until the last of the shakes passed. Until the imagined sound of black waves on stony banks faded. The bruises on his torso and face throbbed in time with his heartbeat. His tongue sat heavy in his mouth, bourbon-bloated, like a rotten slug. He could suddenly taste his own breath, the booze and cigarettes.

He staggered to his feet and stumbled to the bathroom and reached the toilet in time to get most of the sick into it. He rested his head on the cool porcelain for a few minutes until he was sure everything was out. Then he cleaned the mess, brushed his teeth, and held his face under the faucet and gulped water. He was desiccated as a January corn furrow. He did it all in the dark, much as he hated it. Couldn't look in the mirror.

He cupped his hands together underneath the faucet and then stuck his face into the shallow pool of his fingers. Exhaled forcefully through his nose, sending bubbles cascading over his fingers. He jolted upright and flung his hands apart, scattering the remaining water across the mirror and wall. Rowan used to belly laugh over that

THE GUILTY SLEEP

move. He leaned over the sink, gripping its edges so hard he thought it might break into pieces in his hands. Willing it to happen.

No going back to sleep now.

He pulled a pair of running shorts and a T-shirt from the rickety dresser. Dragged his hair back into a short ponytail. Socks and shoes, then out the door, not looking at the pile of *urgent* and *final notice* envelopes on top of the fridge. Definitely not looking at the thick manila folder from *Dean and Morris, Family Law,* on top of the mail, a supine dragon guarding its hoard.

Down the hall with its threadbare industrial carpet, across the dusty lobby that always smelled of fish sauce, outside into the early morning.

Dex's building was half a block north of the run-down county hospital on Old Washington Road. South to the community college and back, it was a tidy four-and-a-half-mile run. He set the timer on his watch and ran for all he was worth. Lost himself in the filling and emptying of his lungs, the whiskey-pepper tang of his sweat, and the damp stillness of the air. With every step, his face and torso pulsed. He was a semi-mobile bruise.

No earbuds, no music. Only the beat of heart, the whoosh of breath, the slap of feet on asphalt, the plainsong of early-rising August crickets. Fueled by the hatred of himself, his weakness. His retreat to the bar and the booze, picking a fight with the four jack-wagons of the apocalypse, then Saenz—no, he wasn't ready to think about *that* yet. Another cannonball leap into the black river, washing farther downstream with each dip. The roar of a waterfall somewhere in the distance.

He pumped his legs, driving himself forward. Starting to unlimber and unclench.

The therapy hadn't helped, though he'd given it a year with the rumpled little VA shrink who kept forgetting his name. He'd cycled through the antidepressants, the first of which turned him into an emotionless, fuzzy zombie, while the next filled him with hair-trigger, white-hot rage. Terrence's veterans support group, where he didn't share anymore, though he still went every week.

Picturing his daughter's face and white-knuckling it worked better than most things, but it made his shame all the deeper that he couldn't keep the nightmares and flashbacks at bay.

No sidewalk, so he ran on the cracked shoulder in the direction of oncoming traffic, dodging broken bottles and fast-food wrappers. Past the abandoned car lot, weeds poking up through breaks in the vast field of empty asphalt. *LABOR DAY SALE*, wheezed the sun-faded, sagging banner. Past two rueful strip malls, each with more than half their storefronts empty—rotten teeth in failing gums. Past the empty gravel lots, cracked plywood signs promising shiny developments long abandoned. Past the gutted tire factory, where Daria's mom, Carleen, had sunk twenty-five years of her life, with nothing to show for it but a husk of a body and a gutted pension plan. Past the funeral parlor and its faltering front porch, black windows gaping like hollowed eye sockets. Past the spanking new pain clinic, all glowing blues and reds and opioid promise.

The streets were leaky veins full of old, sick blood. The town was a skull.

Halfway to the college, a county blue-and-white slowed as it passed him. The deputy gave him a quick once-over, and for a second, Dex thought the car was going to coast to a stop on the shoulder and the guy was going to roust him. Dex gave him a little head nod. *'Sup, champ, nothing better to do?* The cruiser accelerated toward the college. Guess a tall white guy with too-long hair, a scar on his forehead, and a scruffy beard wasn't on the BOLO sheet. Dex sent a little wave after the deputy, tossing his head. Sweat flew into the morning dark.

He pushed himself like he was running from a literal, physical pack of demons and not just the ones in his head. It wouldn't matter. No matter how fast, how far, they'd be waiting when he was done. When he closed his eyes.

The blue shrouds. The sound of the fly. Tapping, tapping at the window.

He'd tried everything, and nothing helped. Grief and guilt, cursed lovers dancing hand in hand. The insomnia. The uncontrollable fury

THE GUILTY SLEEP

that appeared without warning. He was being washed downstream to a sea of darkness, and the only question was if the black river was going to drown him before he reached the delta.

Dex pressed even harder. He leaped a curb, cut a corner, and accelerated into a sprint. He kept coming back to the night before, couldn't push it away. What Saenz had asked him.

"You were always the smartest guy in the room, Stu," Dex had said, staring across the table at his former team leader. Stu's sandy hair was thinning, his short reddish beard shot through with ash-gray threads. But he didn't look *old*, worn out, like Dex felt. He was still trim, keeping it together, his pressed slacks and crisp shirt no worse for the parking lot tussle with the football team. "It's why you were so easy to follow. We never doubted you knew what you were doing. But come on, man, you want me to help you rob my own bank? That's a federal crime—and federal time." His voice rose. "I'm a mess. You got me pegged, no surprise. But I'm not ready to go to prison. I don't owe you that." *Or Jalal*, he almost said, but stopped. If he said it, he'd have to look at it.

"Take a breath," Stu had said, his voice gentle. Then he went there anyway. "You don't owe me anything. We owe Jalal. And his family. He saved your life, Dex."

"Even if that's true, it doesn't change —"

"And we don't want to rob the bank."

"—anyth—wait . . . What exactly are you asking?"

"You remember"—Saenz paused, searching for the right word—"after the thing at the compound? The airbase in Oman. Waiting for the flight back to Bagram."

Dex nodded reluctantly. "Pieces. Blurry at the edges."

"For all of us, courtesy of the Air Force morale tent."

"The cider," Dex said. He could almost taste it.

"The cider," Saenz agreed. "'Cause the dang Air Force pukes had drunk all the beer already. We were talking about real life—"

"—back in the world, yeah—"

"—and you were talking about your day job. Remember?"

"If you say so."

"Few times a week, you said, some biker-looking guy brings a fat bag of cash. Your boss always handles it personally. Puts it in safety deposit boxes. And once a month, your boss goes to a casino for an overnight, always with a suitcase, right?"

"I don't like where this is going."

"You know what you were describing. You're too smart, too well-trained, not to know."

"Speculation's worth a fart in a wind tunnel, quoting you. As for me, too much Air Force cider and I go wagging my mouth. Always did get me into trouble." Stu smiled at that, his eyes crinkling deeply around the edges. "Not my business, though," Dex continued. "Freddy's never included me or anyone else in it. He's always treated me right, kept me on, even when . . ." Dex trailed off and waved at the kitchen. It said what he needed it to.

"You know what it is."

The silence stretched for half a minute while Dex studied his hands, the bottom of his coffee mug, anything but Stu's face. "I *suspect* what it is. Quite a flyer to take, though, that it would still be going on three years later."

"When I caught up with Sully earlier this year, he said you were still at the bank. Thing like you described, when it's over—when it winds up—you either walk away rich or go down hard and everything burns to the studs. You're still there—it tells me the bank's still there and your boss is still at it."

Dex turned the mug in his hands. Saenz waited, wiping at his nose with a napkin. The tsebhi's berbere spice had gotten to him.

"It's still happening. Regular as a clockwork outhouse."

Saenz sighed in relief. "A money laundering operation happening under the nose of a guy best positioned to help exploit it. Right when we need it the most."

"Destiny, huh?" Dex laughed disbelievingly. "Ripping off a criminal enterprise is not exactly better than robbing a bank."

"'Course it is. Destiny—your word, not mine—and better, too. Hosing a bad guy to help a good guy. The bad guy's not calling 911."

THE GUILTY SLEEP

43

"We're not Robin Hood and his band of merry dipsticks."

Saenz ignored him and pressed on. "No cops, no FBI, no prison. A clean op, doing the right thing." He met Dex's eyes and didn't look away.

"And some cartel boss harvests our skulls for beer steins. No thanks."

"Come on, man, you've got a chance here to—"

"No." Then louder, "No. I'm trying to get my family *back*, not lose them forever. Something like this goes bad, I'm locked up or dissolving in a barrel of acid in some murder-shed somewhere."

"We can do this."

"Sarnt," Dex said, low and quiet now, gripping his mug with fingers gone white at the joints, "you need to leave."

Saenz stood up, deflated. "Take a breath, Grant. Think about it, at least."

"Get. Out." He didn't look up. Just stared down at his mug, shoulders hunched.

"OK," Saenz said, then from the doorway: "I blipped our numbers, back at the bar. Call me if you want to talk." He left, pulling the door until the lock caught. Dex stumbled the four steps to his bedroom and collapsed on the bed, trying to do anything but think. Sleep finally came, and of course the nightmare was waiting. The compound and what happened behind the blue door. It was inevitable, sure as night following day, death following life, and another lost Orioles season.

By the time he finished his run, Dex's T-shirt was soaked and steam wreathed his head. He checked his timer, saw he'd made the run in 32:45. Three minutes slower than his best per-mile time, but faster than he'd managed in six months living here. Maybe it was the nightmare. Maybe it was the bar fight, or Saenz's insane proposal. Whatever it was had put wings on his feet.

The adrenaline dump faded. He leaned over and braced himself against a brick awning pillar.

The front door jostled open and Mariam came out. She had the early shift on the custodial staff at the college.

"Hiya, Dexter." Her voice was too bright for the ass-crack of dawn.

"Hi, Mariam," Dex managed, hands still on his knees.

"You OK? You run too hard, looks like."

"I'm all right."

"If you say." The little woman paused, looking at him with equal parts concern and curiosity. Dex straightened, gasping.

"Mariam, the tsebhi . . ."

"Good, huh?"

"It was the best. I didn't think anything could top your tihlo, but I was wrong."

"I'm glad you liked it. I'm bring you another batch next time I make it."

"I won't turn it down. I'm serious, it was the best thing to happen to me in months. I'll bring the Tupperware by later, OK?"

"OK, Dexter. See you later!" Mariam turned with a wave.

Dex was heading inside, but then he remembered the thing with his front door. His first day in the apartment six month ago, he'd made the mistake of not pulling it closed until the lock clicked, then came home to find it cracked. He'd made a point to double-check it ever since, but he'd found it slightly ajar again last week. It was probably the bourbon, but still.

Mariam was getting into her car, a dinged-up white Toyota. It had a large sticker for the local Tewahedo Orthodox church plastered over a crack in the bumper.

"Hey, Mariam?"

"What's up, Dexter?"

"Last week, I think . . . Friday morning about this time, did you see anyone in the hallway?"

"Oh, I can't remember, honey. Maybe just you, coming back from your run like today. Everything's OK?"

Had he locked the door when he left? It's not like everything was squared away in his headspace right now. He shook his head.

"Yeah, everything's OK. Thanks."

8

FOUNDATIONS

TURNER

The access road wasn't paved yet, and the El Camino bounced and scraped through the ruts even though Turner kept his speed just above a walk. The branches overhead reached out from either side to almost-but-not-quite touch, like lovers separated by a stream. On the radio, Stevie Winwood sang about higher love, with that perfect five-beat horn hit punctuating the hook.

The rising sun snuck through the wall of trees to his right, periodically catching the corner of his eye and strobing the El Camino's cream leather interior orange-red, the warning klaxon color of a construction safety vest.

The trees retreated, pitted track giving way to grassy field. He'd been here on a windy day once, and the waist-high grass flowed and waved like a green sea pulled by the tides of a dozen greedy moons. Today the grass drooped motionless in the still air. A plywood sign half the size of a highway billboard proudly proclaimed he was entering the future site of Sunrise Vista Assisted Living, another Cooke Construction Solutions project. The earth movers were parked around the edge of the clearing, but they'd be back in action later, tearing apart the sea of grass, delving and smoothing the earth in turn. Dead center, the meadow had been flattened and the basement dug. Foundation boundaries blocked in, waiting on a concrete pour from the cement mixer backed up to the edge of the pit. There was a rough oval about twenty-five feet around the open hole of the dig where the sticky Maryland red clay lay bare to the sky. A promissory scar. It made him feel something he didn't like, so he pushed it down.

Turner parked next to the mixer. There was a picture taped to his dash. Two-by-three. One of those third-week-of-school pictures, faded by the sun. Little blonde girl with a gap-toothed smile. Turner touched her chin with his thumb, then turned the key. The rumble of the V8 gave way to what felt like quiet, until he hauled himself out of the car (the springs giving a grateful sigh) and picked up the low grinding churn of the cement truck's rotating tub. He left the satchel of money—the night's collected take—on the seat.

Angie was at the back of the mixer. She was dressed for the construction site in battered work boots, carpenter's pants, and a flannel work shirt gone soft and fuzzy from a thousand washings. The discharge chute was unfolded, angled over the pit. She leaned against the chute casually, watching Turner approach. Her eyes were brown and warm, with deep laugh lines laying a delicate tracery across the tops of her full cheeks. Turner wished he'd put on his sunglasses after all. He glanced around as he approached, just for something to do with his eyes. He didn't see the Kaibiles, but it didn't mean they weren't there. Probably in the grass or trees, watching him.

It was a typical August morning, the thick air prophesying afternoon storms, but Turner felt a chill like someone was pressing the tip of an ice-cold knife to the base of his skull.

"Melchizedek," she said, drawing it out, her face bunching up in a smile that showed white, even teeth. She was the only one who ever used his first name, and she seemed to derive some kind of pleasure in the taste of the word, the choppy construction of its syllables. Probably because it was biblical. Her evangelical roots ran deep, all the way to the soil of her native Guatemala.

"Mornin', boss." Turner didn't know what to do with his hands, so he sank them into his pockets.

"Yes, a good one." She took a deep breath, lifting her shoulders and turning to the sun. "A *great* day to be alive. Are you well?"

"Yes, ma'am."

She tilted her head a millimeter to the right and looked back at him. The rumble of the concrete mixer lay an undertone across the space. It somehow emphasized the quiet, and Turner thought maybe he heard something else. A muffled cry. Probably a bird.

"Slade texted. Said you wanted to see me."

"Did he now?"

"Yes, ma'am."

Thing about working for Angelita Cooke—his perceptions always warred with reality. She was a short woman, chubby, dark hair threaded generously with gray. A face made for smiling and a body for comforting hugs. She could have been someone's sweet, religious abuelita if he didn't know better.

She'd been in Maryland since she was ten, long enough to start seasoning her empanadas with Old Bay. Long enough to grow up, marry into Charles Cooke's low-rent contracting business-slash-crime family, and transform it by sheer will and natural acumen into central Maryland's most successful mid-sized construction company *and* its most ubiquitous and profitable criminal network. And, after Motherchucker stroked out three years ago, she expanded like an amoeba, pushing out to Baltimore, Wheaton, and Frederick, with designs on southern Pennsylvania. She knew her way around a construction yard and could run a worksite with the best of them. But she was equally comfortable behind an abandoned strip mall with a Glock tucked in her waistband, overseeing the transfer of merchandise from the back of a box truck to a row of waiting sedans. She had a knack and she had a knife and she wasn't afraid to stick that knife in your neck if you needed a good sticking.

Cognitive dissonance, that was the term. During Turner's bit at Lompoc, the well-meaning social worker had used it a bunch. With Angie, it kept him wrong-footed. He was always worried he'd chosen his words badly, had taken an off step. Next thing, she'd climb a stepstool and stick that knife in his neck and never mind that Motherchucker had recruited him personally, never mind the years of valuable service. He told himself for the thousandth time it was no way to live.

"My nephew's right," Angie said, turning her eyes briefly to the woods. They flicked back to his, and he imagined he heard a click when they did. Like one of those paper twists filled with cap powder he'd played with as a kid. Throw it on the ground and it gives a little snap. She cocked her head a millimeter to the left, like a small, fluffy bird waiting for a worm to poke its ass out of the ground. Turner waited. It was the safe thing.

"Melchizedek. I need your help with something."

"What I'm here for, boss."

"What are my priorities?"

She was fond of spot checks. This was an easy one. If you'd worked for Angelita Cooke for more than a week, you'd heard the list. "Business, Bible, Blood."

"Yes. The work, the Word, and the family. I've got a problem with number three."

After Motherchucker donked off, there was only one branch of the Cooke family tree left, given she never mentioned her side.

"Slade?"

"I'm worried about him."

And with good reason, Turner thought. Boy had a reputation.

"He's been running his little crew down in Baltimore," Angie continued, "rolling tourists, jacking cars, petty stuff."

"I've heard."

"You know he had to go away before, right? When he was fifteen?"

"A year in juvie camp, wasn't it?" He didn't ask what for. No one knew, and Angie never said.

"Sixteen months. And for a while I thought maybe that would get . . . things . . . out of his system. Maybe keep him out of the life. A wake-up call."

THE GUILTY SLEEP

He heard the sound again. Something like a bird, but he couldn't place the location because it almost sounded like it was coming from the foundation pit.

"Once you been inside, it feels like only a matter of time 'fore you're back in," Turner said. "Starts to feel like home."

Angie grimaced, and Turner felt that freezing prick at the base of his skull again.

"And he's a Cooke, so it was foolish of me to think he wouldn't follow the rest of us into this world. I've been watching. He's taking too many risks. Escalating. Last week, he ripped a Fells Point corner boss for half a key. He's going to get pinched or killed, or he's going to kill someone and get pinched for that."

"What can I do to help?"

"I won't lose him. I want you to bring him on under you."

"Ma'am?"

"Apprenticeship."

Turner didn't like the sound of that. He'd been with the Cookes a decade, and Slade had been around a lot, except for that juvie stint. Angie's nephew had grown from a pissant little bully to a young man who seemed like he was all sharp edges and shadow, swinging between moods like a sprung jack-in-the-box. Intense.

"Ma'am, I'm worried this might not be the time."

She cocked her head at him again, that warm and bright bird-stare, then raised her hand, palm up, waiting for him to drop his words into it.

"Friday, I was making the drop at Pine Hill—"

"Freddy House," Angie said.

"Yep. And, ah, I got kind of a weird vibe."

"From him?"

"Everything at the bank seemed copacetic. But outside, I had a feeling. Like somebody was watching me."

"Law?"

"I don't think. Weren't obvious, no blue-and-whites or clean-side plumber's vans. I'd been driving crooked as a Paraguayan goat track from stop to stop and nothin' shook out obvious, but the notion wouldn't leave me. You know I get these feelings." It was one of the reasons Motherchucker had kept him on, promoted him up. Turner had a reputation of his own, borne out over the years. A man of good instincts, honed by his time inside, and by his time as a prison wildfire volunteer out of Lompoc. A man who could scent a changing wind, feel the fire turn at your back. "I wanted to let you know," he finished.

"You did the right thing, telling me."

Turner briefly felt a wash of relief, a lightening of imaginary weight, but then that muffled bird (maybe not-a-bird) sounded its call again. Angelita's eyes flashed with annoyance and flicked briefly toward the foundation before snapping back to his, and the weight came back twice as heavy. Not a bird, then.

"You're bedrock, Melchizedek. You don't spook."

"Like to think so."

She turned toward the pit, beckoned him with a nod, and walked to the edge. He followed like he was wearing cinderblock boots. She looked into the foundation.

There were two guys down there, wearing jeans and hoodies and purple bandanas. Hands zip-tied behind their backs, mouths stuffed with balled rags and wrapped with duct tape. Angie waved at them like she was saying hello to long-lost friends at church. She had the cross necklace in her hand. The only one Turner had ever seen her with. She never wore it around her neck, just carried in her pocket, almost like a rosary. It was black, made of stone. Hematite and onyx.

"Pinche coños were trying to sell down in Finksburg, pushing up from Baltimore. Florencio and Lael found them. They wanted to cut their heads off, hang them from an overpass as a narcomensaje. Like we do back home." She raised a hand above her shoulder, the necklace darkling in the hazy sun. Turner looked back at the cement mixer.

Florencio, one of her Kaibiles, was there, standing by the discharge chute. Turner had no idea where he'd come from. The man's hands were on the control panel.

THE GUILTY SLEEP

"Do not lie in wait, oh wicked men," Angie whispered, "against the kingdom of the righteous. Do not plunder their resting place."

Turner kept his mouth shut. Angie was always quick with a Bible verse, especially at moments like these. Never anything from the Gospels, mind you, none of that peace and love. Always the Old Testament. Thunder and judgment. Imprecation.

"For a righteous one may stumble seven times and rise again," she continued, "but the wicked shall fall by calamity."

Her arm came down with *fall*. Turner looked at the bangers. Their eyes were wide, showing whites all around. They pleaded through the rags. There was a short, happy double beep from the back of the truck and the slurry flap slid into its housing with a dusty crunch. The concrete cascaded down the discharge chute and waterfalled into the foundation pit.

The guys screamed, the rags in their mouths barely muffling the terror. They rolled around, away from each other and back again, trying to find refuge from the gray, heavy liquid splattering over them. They were coated in it. They looked like animated statues.

It was quick, but not quick enough. Three minutes, maybe. Probably felt like eternity to the kids in the pit. Toward the end, when they were almost covered, they nestled together. Face to face, forehead touching forehead. Taking comfort in each other as the inevitable stone tide rose around them.

Angie waited until they were buried, then waited some more. There were bubbles in the wet concrete, big around as a beer can. They rose and formed shiny domes, popping with obscene, sensual slowness. She waited until the surface was smooth and flat. Then she turned away and walked Turner back to his El Camino.

"You did the right thing, telling me about the bank."

"Thank you, ma'am."

"It's the perfect time to bring Slade in."

Turner's gut clenched, but he forced himself to nod.

"Take him on your rounds," Angie continued. "Starting tomorrow morning. Make sure the collect is secure. Show him the ropes. If he's going to be in the life, he's going to learn to do it right. With us."

"Yes, ma'am, the family business."

"Just so. And follow Mister House to his next casino adventure."

"This Friday."

Angie nodded, once. Efficiency of movement, bird darting for worm. "Make sure he gets my cargo there safely."

"Will do, boss," Turner said. He climbed into the El Camino, cranked the key, and reversed toward the trees, resisting the urge to bury the accelerator. Angie stood at the edge of the shadows, watching him go.

9

FIDUCIARY INSTRUMENTS

DEX

The bus was on time for once, so Dex was ten minutes early to work. It was already muggy enough that he almost wished he hadn't sold his car. Freddy wasn't there yet. The boss liked to arrive and unlock the front doors just as the clock tower across the street at Saint Patrick's chimed the last bong of nine o'clock. It was a routine he'd turned into an art form.

Dex paced in front of the bank's glass doors, avoiding his reflection. He didn't recognize himself anymore, and the blurry image looked like a stranger's ghost. He pulled at the collar of his blue button-down. It wasn't new—he had five rotating work shirts, two blue and three white—but it felt stiff and overstarched against his throat. The top button was already undone, but it still felt like strangulation.

Marty provided welcome distraction, strolling up with a paper sack and two huge coffees in a cardboard tray.

"Broheim," she said, grinning at Dex's scowl. His headache was back. "Who ate your bowl of sunshine this morning, little thundercloud?"

"One of those for me?" he asked.

"Oh yeah. And one of these too." Marty jiggled open the sack, exposing a pair of monstrous breakfast burritos. Dex took the coffee in one hand and a burrito in the other with something approaching reverence.

"To what do I owe this beneficence?"

"It's Tuesday."

"So?"

"You've, um, developed a bit of a habit."

"I have?"

"Thievery Collective on Monday nights," Marty said. "I'm guessing it's because you've gone a whole weekend Freddy-free, so Monday comes around and it feels like a double-dose."

"You may not be wrong, partner."

Marty tipped the mouth of her coffee cup against his. "Hence, my bestowal of these most bounteous blessings." She was wearing a turquoise shirt and paisley tie, her clear-framed eyeglasses perched on her head, keeping her hair out of her eyes.

"How do *you* manage to look so fresh-faced?"

"For one, Black don't crack. For another, I don't get blitzed on a Monday night. When it comes to an evening's entertainment, 'Manda and I prefer board games and a glass of wine as opposed to blasting our brains to space dust on bottom-shelf hooch like a couple of dumbasses. No offense."

"Assuming I'm the dumbass in question, offense extremely taken."

"Drink your coffee and eat your abomination of a breakfast so I don't have to deal with Grumpy-Pants Dex the rest of the morning."

He tried to queue a scathing retort, but his brain was still grinding gears and his mouth was full of burrito. By the time he'd finished chewing and taken as deep a sip as the scalding coffee allowed, the Saint Pat's bell was tolling.

There was a deep, woeful blatting. Freddy had installed an air horn in his otherwise innocuous gray F-150, and the boss liked to advertise his arrival. Broadcast to the entire shopping center that Freddy House was on the scene. The truck hove into view with one more blast of the horn and a squeal of tires.

"One of these days he's gonna lose it right into one of the light posts," Marty mumbled.

THE GUILTY SLEEP

"A boy can dream."

"No serious injuries, mind you. Maybe a broken toe."

"His horn finger?"

"Oh yes." Marty grinned.

"Break the horn while we're at it?"

"At least. Total the truck, if we're lucky."

"*Complete* loss. A life lesson about loud noises on hungover mornings."

"Replace it with a Prius, while we're fantasizing."

"A wish too far, Brohette." Dex smiled in spite of himself. The coffee and carbs were working. Marty was working, bless her.

Freddy slashed into his reserved space (right in front of the bank, natch) and stood on the brakes.

"What's shakin', you two?" their boss said, climbing from the cab with some effort. He smoothed his thinning salt and pepper hair back into place.

"Waiting for you, boss-man," Marty replied. "Gonna make it by last bell?"

"Don't you start on me, not wearing *that* tie," Freddy said. He strutted past them, jingling his keys.

"And a good morning t'you too, Mister Grant," he sang over his shoulder. "*You* ever gonna put on a tie again?"

"Not if I can help it, Fred." Freddy felt about Fred like Dex felt about Frogger, so it was all Dex ever called him.

The Saint Pat's bell hit six chimes and Freddy quickstepped to the bank's double doors, unlimbering the master key, sliding it home, and opening the doors in one smooth motion. He disappeared inside and around the corner, deactivated the alarm, then popped his head out.

"Whatcha two want, an engraved invitation? Work ain't gonna wait for yas."

Marty rolled her eyes and scanned the mostly empty parking lot.

"They're really lining up this morning. We'd better get in there," Dex whispered, loud as he could.

"I heard that!"

Freddy House was a vintage Maryland redneck. In other words, a conundrum. Called the big city to the south "Warshington" and thought it was politically correct nonsense when the 'Skins changed their name, but happily voted in consecutive elections for that RINO Hogan for governor. Gadsden flag right next to the Maryland flag on his bumper. Big yellow ribbon sticker in the bank's front window, proudly putting his combat vet front and center. But he also had no issues hiring an out-and-proud biracial woman for the other teller position in a rural county, where the Stars and Bars might flap from a porch nearly as often as the Stars and Stripes.

"Ya know, Miz Higgins, I'm never sure what your hair's gonna do on a given day, but I'm diggin' the vibe. Can I touch it?"

"Inappropriate, Freddy. How many times I have to tell you?" Marty said.

"Wait, what'd I say? Was that offensive, Dex?"

"Wasn't great. You ever heard the term *microaggression*?"

"Can't say nothin' to nobody anymore."

"Forget it, you two," Marty said, staring deliberately around the empty lobby. "We got work to do. Let's not keep all these customers waiting."

Freddy huffed an elaborate sigh. "Sorry, Marty. I'll make it up to you. It's a casino weekend, you know . . ."

"Not on your life."

"I mean, maybe you just ain't met the right guy yet?"

"Fred, you know that's not appropriate either, right?"

Freddy threw his hands up. "I can't win with you two. It's a wonder I schedule you for the same shift. Inviting a gang up on myself."

"You love it," Marty said, powering up her CPU. She'd been with Freddy almost as long as Dex and was inured to his nonsense. And she gave better than she got.

"Yeah, I must be a, whaddayacallit, sadist."

Marty was in the process of correcting him when Dex's phone chirped. A text from Daria.

THE GUILTY SLEEP

> Call me.

"Can I get a quick minute?" Dex asked.

"Ya just *got* here," Freddy complained. But he got a look at Dex's face and nodded.

Dex walked past Freddy's office and the vault, down the hall to the small break room. He leaned against Billy Ripken, the massive printer-scanner-copier that dominated the space.

> I just got to work, what's up?

> If you want to see Ro, I need you to
> sign the papers.

He stared at the bubble around her words, refusing to read them again. Took a deep breath, tapped the screen, and waited while the phone rang.

"Dex." His wife's voice was soft, frayed around the edges.

"I—are you OK?" He couldn't help himself.

"Long day yesterday. I was out on interviews most of the evening, and Rowan didn't sleep well."

Dex felt a huge, invisible fist squeeze the back of his throat. He couldn't say Ro's name, not without breaking down.

"What are you working on?" he asked instead, hunting for a salient into a conversation fragile as spun glass.

Daria was a crusty old reporter trapped in a twenty-eight-year-old's body. Newspapers and police scanners and waking up early to chase a story. Her life goal was working her way from culture reporter for the local paper to a feature writer for the *Washington Post* or *Baltimore Sun*. She was well on her way, because she was smart, persistent, and good at what she did.

"New brewery's opening in Sykesville next week, and I was meeting the owners. Nice place. All renewable energy. Piece'll run Sunday."

"They let you try anything?"

"The stout's great, but the IPA needs some work. Musty. Better angle's gonna be the sense I got from the front-of-house staff."

Even now, after everything they'd been through, the old patterns wanted to assert themselves. He felt a tug of pride trying to start up. He fought the urge to trade, to tell her what had happened with Saenz the night before. He sat on it, partly because he almost couldn't believe it hadn't been part of his nightmares.

"Bad vibes?"

"They don't like the owner very much. He seemed like a bit of a perv. Worth digging into."

She'd kept her voice neutral, but Dex could tell she was excited. He used to love that about her—he still loved that about her. He swept the feeling away before it could spread, let the anger flow over the dry ground of their conversation.

"Dare, I want to talk to Rowan. I want her to hear my voice, and . . . I need—"

"Dex, you're not in a good place. I don't know if it'd be good for her."

"That's not fair. You don't get to unilaterally make those calls."

"Until you sign the papers and we get custody ironed out, I *do* get to make those calls, because she's living with me—"

"—with your mom as in-house enforcer. I called the house line last week, asked her to talk to Rowan, and she told me to pound sand. Did you know?"

"She told me."

"What's up with that, Dare?"

"What's up with that is my mother is paying room and board by graciously helping out with the babysitting so I can work. So I can pay some of these bills—"

"I asked Freddy for another shift."

"Another shift isn't going to pay for Rowan's surgery, Dex, unless the going rate's thirteen grand per."

He thought of the picture on his phone's lock screen. Rowan's tousled hair and half smile. Big brown eyes, just like her mom's. Ever so slightly crossed. On top of the mortgage, Dex's apartment, Daria's

THE GUILTY SLEEP

j-school loans. Carleen's medications, now that her tire factory pension was toast. All of it piled up, a rockfall they'd never get out from under. He ran a hand across his forehead, feeling the scars. The money, the damn money on top of everything else.

"We'd be saving more if I was still living at home."

"Don't go there, Dex." Her voice was windswept, sere as a salt flat. He was losing the thread. In CI school, they'd trained him how to get a sideways source debrief back on track. But they didn't teach what to do when you were in love with the source, and had a kid with the source, and it was all collapsing under its own weight like a neutron star.

In his frustration, he lashed out: "Since when do you get to tell me what kind of place I'm in, anyway?"

"Since I can tell from your voice you're an absolute mess right now."

She wasn't wrong. He was falling apart, and they'd known each other too long—loved each other too long—to hide it. The anger blew away as quickly as it had come.

"Dex?"

"I'm here."

"Listen to yourself. I can hear your voice shaking. It's hard for me too. And as hard as this is for you, for me? It's a thousand times worse for Ro because she still can't understand why you're not with us. Why you're not coming home."

"I could . . ."

"I won't pretend to understand what you're going through. What's happening over there right now is probably making it worse. Bringing up a lot of stuff. I'm not sure I want you spending time with Ro when you're feeling like this. You know how sensitive she is. She'll pick up on it."

"You won't let me talk to her? Phone, FaceTime, nothing?"

"When was the last time you talked to someone?"

"I've talked to three people today already."

"The patented Dexter Grant sarcasm shield. This is what I'm talking about. When was the last time you went to Terrence's group?"

Dex blinked. Another thing they'd never taught at Fort Huachuca: When you make yourself vulnerable, truly open to another person, that doesn't go away because the relationship explodes. They don't stop understanding you. He pulled the phone away for a second, looked at the time. "Dare, I've got to get back to work."

"Dexter." She paused, choosing her words. "This darkness in you, it's a riptide. It's going to pull you under. And I am not going to let Rowan be dragged under too. You have to deal with this or . . . or it's going to destroy you."

"I'm trying, Daria. I've been at T's group every week since—" he didn't say *since the thing with the plate* "—since I left. Haven't missed." He didn't say, *But I just sit there, because I can't bring myself to say anything.* "And I'm back on the waiting list with the VA. To, you know . . . talk to someone. Again. I'll ask for meds, better ones. I'm trying, I promise." He didn't say, *It's just that nothing is working.* "You've got to let me talk to Rowan. See her."

"Are you going to group this week?"

"Tomorrow night, like always."

There was a long silence. "I don't want to be cruel, Dex. I want you to be in Rowan's life. I want you to be OK. For her."

"I do too." He dug a knuckle into the corner of his eye and blinked rapidly. "Dare, I have to go. Will you let me see my daughter?"

"Text me after group. Let me know how it goes." She ended the call.

Dex thumbed the sleep button and shoved the phone into his pocket. It vibrated and dinged with another text, but he ignored it with willpower he didn't know he could muster at a quarter past nine, hungover, with the taste of burnt coffee in his mouth. With his chest feeling like a raw crater. He fought the urge to slam his fists against Billy Ripken's faded beige cladding. Tear it to pieces. The thing was years past its prime and constantly breaking down. Might be good for Freddy, once he stopped mourning. It sure as cherry pie would make Dex feel better, if only for a minute.

He remembered the plate. The cheap white thing, from their wedding registry. The feeling of raw, animal joy as it left his hand. The

THE GUILTY SLEEP

way exhilaration transmuted into curdled sewage before it even hit the wall. Reverse alchemy.

He gave Billy Ripken a soft pat on the corner, and could have sworn he heard it pop a spring deep in its innards in grateful response. He walked out of the break room, rubbing his eyes, and almost ran right into Freddy.

"You look like you want to burn something down or crawl into a dark hole, maybe at the same time. Talkin' to your baby-momma?"

Dex didn't even have the energy to be annoyed at him. "Just . . . stop, Fred."

Freddy put a hand on Dexter's arm. His windburned face went soft around the eyes. "Divorce sucks, don't it? I should know; I've had two."

"Yeah. Sucks hard."

"Whyontcha come with me this weekend? Little party time, little gambling, some booze, a little blow. Maybe meet someone?" The man was trying to help in his own way, but nothing sounded worse than a weekend at a casino with Freddy House.

"I, ah, actually appreciate the offer, Fred. But no thanks. Can't afford to lose any cash right now."

"Fine. In that case, you know what'll make you feel better? Getting back out there and making *me* some money."

As Dex rounded the corner into the Pine Hill lobby, the front doors were closing and a tall guy with sandy hair and sunglasses disappeared down the sidewalk. Definitely not part of his nightmare, unless he was having them while wide awake now.

"Dex?" Marty called as he walked past his station and out the doors. He followed the man with the sunglasses down the sidewalk, waited until he turned a corner, then darted forward and grabbed him by the arm, spinning him around.

"Frogger. I just texted you."

"What are you doing here, Stu?"

"I wanted to drop by. Check on you."

"Are you insane? After what you asked me to do, you come here?"

"Lower your voice." Saenz's face flashed hard, then smoothed so quickly it was like a strobe. "I made like I was interested in opening an account, took a brochure. Kept my sunglasses on, head down. Easy, Frogger. Remember who you're talking to."

"You know I hate that nickname."

"Sorry. Look, I just wanted to make sure you were OK after we left things the way we did last night. And to say sorry for pushing so hard."

"It's over?"

Saenz shrugged. "Not for me it isn't. Not for Porter or Winkowski, either. Not so long as Jalal and his family are on that boat."

"What are you going to do, Sarnt?"

Saenz smiled gently. "You don't exactly have a stake in what comes next."

Stu patted Dex on the shoulder and walked away. Dex watched him go. Thinking of Jalal. Of the little girl Dex had never seen, the one Stu said was about Rowan's age.

"What was that all about?" Freddy asked, holding the door for him as he came back inside. Dex stepped into the shadows of the bank. The cool air was stirred to life by the big overhead fans.

"He wasn't one of our regulars, and it looked like he hadn't been in here long enough to open an account. Thought I'd introduce myself, give him a bit of the hard sell," Dex said.

"That's what I'm talking about," Freddy crowed. Marty rolled her eyes. "I'm always telling you guys, you gotta give 'em the hard sell!"

Freddy stayed in the vestibule, holding the door open for the guy who came in after. He was huge, easily six-and-a-half feet, pushing three bills. Blond mullet going to gray, handlebar stache, mirrored shades on the back of his neck, tight black T-shirt with *Sunshine Vending* in big yellow letters across the front. Full sleeve tats covering some gnarly scars on his forearms. He looked like gasoline and cheap beer and iron free weights somehow coalesced into sentience.

"Afternoon, everyone," the man said in a surprisingly high and gentle voice. He was carrying a nylon satchel so pregnant the zipper looked likely to give up its teeth any moment.

"Hey, Turn'," Freddy said. "That time already?"

THE GUILTY SLEEP

"That time all the time, my dude."

"Let's head on back, then."

Freddy pulled out his safety deposit keys and jangled them like he was trying to entertain the world's largest baby. He led the mobile mountain through the side door and into the vault. There was the sound of keys turning, locks clicking, and zipper unzipping. Turner said something and their boss laughed.

Freddy claimed Turner represented a local conglomerate of cash-heavy businesses from across the triple counties: laundromats, vending machines, lawncare outfits, food trucks, that sort of thing. Few times a week he'd bring in their collected take. Freddy always handled Turner's visits personally. He put the cash into a safety deposit box until Fridays, when he'd tag and sift the deposits into three umbrella accounts—overhead, growth, and miscellany—collectively shared by the conglomerate's various branches. It was all smoke and mirrors, of course. Parlor tricks. Dex knew better.

10

INTERLUDE: KANDAHAR, THREE YEARS AGO

DEX

A simple op. Easy in, easy out. A local unit of Afghan National Army halfway between K-town and Spin Buldak found an abandoned Taliban weapons cache in their compound, and the Blackbirds are heading out. They'll chat up the ANA company commander and anyone else with a wagging tongue, inventory the ordnance, make sure the ANA set it aside for a controlled demo, make a quick push out to the Pakistani border to sniff the air. Write up the reports, listen for the boom. Simple.

Dex is thrilled that Staff Sergeant Saenz has him back in the mix, especially after that disastrous first time outside the wire, the thing with the kid and the bike. He's still trying to put it out of his mind. He's been in-country three weeks, a late addition to the team when Russo caught dysentery and had to be medevaced to Landstuhl. It's only his second combat tour, and the first hardly counted: six months in the relatively restful northeast of Iraq two years ago, training the Kurds on the finer points of elicitation—adjusting their standard practice from a rubber hose smashed across the base of the feet to building rapport with coffee and cigarettes.

Now he gets a chance to reset his in-country vibe, maybe earn a better nickname if he can swing it. He hasn't been out to Spin Buldak

THE GUILTY SLEEP

yet, much less the border with Pakistan. To hear the rest of the team talk, it's not a bad trip. Get out of the oppressive heat of the city and see a horizon not marked with smoke and haze. Mountain views, higher elevation. Breathable air. Meet with the various local allies, mingle with the border guards, visit the bazaar just over the line of demarcation and pick up a few cartons of decent smokes and a few flats of Diet Pepsi to feed Saenz's four-can-a-day habit.

Allegedly the ANA people have some women at their compound, wives and daughters of the higher-ranking soldiers, maybe a few domestics. Saenz thinks there's a chance one or two of the women might've been at the compound when the Taliban were still in control. A wife or daughter left behind when they cut and ran. A girl who'd been in a forced marriage. Someone with an inside track on who buried the cache and if they planned to come back for it. Dex's beard is still in that awkward patchy stage, marking him as a junior member of the team in the eyes of their allies. He'll be a less offensive presence to the ANA and their women than a more respectably hirsute soldier. Not as unthreatening as a woman, but Battalion still isn't assigning female soldiers to the southeast. And Fatima is, according to Saenz, adept at smoothing over potentially rough intros. The terp will provide enough female chaperone presence to assuage the Afghans.

Dex stows a trio of extra magazines in his chest pouches. The second one slides past the folded photo of Daria and Rowan. He follows Ahn down the steps. Fatima falls in beside them with a nod and a smile.

Saenz is waiting at the first pickup with his deputy team lead, Sergeant Porter, and a thickset Spec Four named Winkowski. Jalal, the male half of their interpreter team, is there too. They're deep in a conclave, heads inclined together. Jalal, a head shorter than the other three and built like a fire hydrant, is gesticulating wildly, a lit cigarette in his hand. He's not angry, just animated. It's his way. Saenz sees them coming.

"'Bout time, Frogger. What you waiting on?" His tone is gruff, but he throws a wink to soften it. Saenz is tall, whipcord thin. The start of crow's feet around his eyes, windburned cheeks. With his sandy hair and beard, cargo pants and rugby shirt, he looks like a modern-day Lawrence of Arabia.

"Sorry, Sarnt," Dex replies, smiling. "Must've missed the signal flare."

"Better keep that sass out of your voice, Specialist Grant," says Sergeant Porter. "Being downrange does not mean I will refrain from smoking your tail in front of God and everyone."

Winkowski grins over Porter's shoulder and wiggles his eyebrows provocatively. "Won't be nothin' left but a stain and a faint smell if Sarnt Porter has his way," he adds.

"Sorry, Sarnt," Dex says again, this time to Porter. "Just ready to . . . um . . . hop to it is all." If he can't swing a new nickname, maybe he can roll with this one.

Saenz chuckles, but Porter only grunts and stares, massive arms crossed over massive chest. The Army quartermaster never dispensed Sergeant Porter a sense of humor. It's still sitting on the *non-issued* shelf of the personality supply cage, right next to contractions and slang and foul language. What they did issue Saenz's deputy, in the usual Army vein of sarcastic nicknames, was the moniker Sunny.

Saenz claps his hands to get everyone's attention, keeping the easy, wry smile on his face. Dex gets the feeling he likes being the good guy and doesn't mind Sunny Porter being the heavy.

"Frogger, you and Fatima ride in Bravo with Ahn and Chonk. Ahn drives, Chonk's payload," Saenz says. "Sunny, Wink, Jalal, you're with me in Alpha."

The order rolls off laconically, like he's never second-guessed himself. The guy's got enough combat experience that he probably hasn't. "Rest of you chuckleheads," Saenz continues, waving at Ol' Dirty Le Batard, Sully, and Schoepe-Dogg, "you're in Charlie. Watch our six. You remember why."

There's a chorus of nods and *hooahs*. Cigarettes are thrown down, ground to streaks of ash under heels. Slides are racked, rounds chambered, caps adjusted, sunglasses donned. Vests tightened, armor plates resettled. They look like a modern version of an old west posse getting ready to go hunt some dang rustlers and hang 'em *high*, baby.

THE GUILTY SLEEP

Dex pops open the dual passenger doors of the second Hilux in line, and Fatima climbs into the jump seat behind PFC Ahn. He starts to get in and Ahn leans over and looks at him over his sunglasses. "Lock 'n' load, eh, Frogger?"

Dex grimaces, embarrassed. He pulls the charging handle of the M4. It slides home with the satisfying clack of a chambered round. The governor's palace where they're based is in the middle of Kandahar, and from time to time the occasional Taliban or Al Qaeda remnant like to remind the allied forces they're still viable. Just last week, a convoy of Aussie SAS took an RPG on their way out to recon the site of a proposed water treatment plant at Musakhan.

Dex climbs in, rolls down the window, and braces the barrel of the M4 across the bottom. He'll be shooting left-handed if the fecal matter hits the rotary impeller, but he'll make up for accuracy with volume.

The massive gatehouse door grinds open, groaning like rust given voice. They drive through an entryway so narrow it nearly scrapes the side mirrors, moving from shadow into sun. They merge into the crowded street in front of the palace, passing the Shrine of Muhammad's Shirt. Dex keeps his head on a swivel ahead and to the right, knowing Chonk is doing the same in the bed, scanning the 180 degrees behind them, SAW at the ready.

Basing them at the governor's palace—little more than a glorified three-story mud hut with a single working toilet and shower—was the idea of some bright boy at Battalion HQ. Put a counterintelligence team, the eponymous Blackbirds, right in the heart of K-town. Leaven it with psyops and civil affairs groups, then add a Special Forces A-Team for extra spice, and you have a multi-mission intelligence and kinetic ops crew smack where the action is, not clumped at the airfield outside of town, behind miles of barbed wire and minefields. Great in theory and outstanding in practice—someone was going to be promoted ahead of zone for the idea.

You put a group like that together and you're talking major successes on the operational *and* intel sides. Go out, hit up a source, find out about an AQ safe house on the outskirts of town. Send up a report, but by the time Battalion messages you back with a request for further information, the SF guys have already gone out and hit the house, taken out the tangos, and blown their weapons cache. The civil affairs guys and psyops team come in right behind to drill a new well and broadcast messages of goodwill and offers of payment for additional information about local muj or foreign fighters. New intel comes in, new target gets hit, new batch of weapons and bombs gets taken off the board, a new well gets dug or a schoolhouse gets built, new friends get made, new intel comes in. Rinse and repeat, with the CI guys serving as the hub inside the circle of kinetic operations.

The Blackbird way.

What it means is they're the most successful combined ops team in the history of the theater, for both intelligence collected and tangos scrubbed from the board. It also means they're a high-profile target, something Saenz and Porter drill into them at every opportunity.

As they leave the outskirts of Kandahar, dust rising behind them like a long comet's tail, Dex starts to relax. The wind roars through the open windows, driving away the smell of raw sewage, burning trash, and cooking oil. The heat eases in the open where there's room for the air to move, though it's relative—sweat runs down the nape of his neck and under his vest. *Makin' the K-town soup*, Winkowski calls it. Ahn hums to himself tunelessly.

They reach the ANA compound in another half hour; there's a wooden sign outside the gate in Dari and Pashto.

"What's it say, Fatima?" Dex asks. She leans forward, bracing on the seatbacks.

"'Welcome to Fort Kumal, home of the 26th Airborne Regiment of the Afghan National Army.'"

"What?" grunts Ahn. "ANA has airborne units now?"

"Not anymore. They did, though, under the Soviets. They keep it as an honorific."

Fatima is a tiny woman with huge dark brown eyes under thick brows. Her family left Afghanistan in the '90s after the fall of the Soviet puppet government. She's reserved, unless you get her talking about the Yankees, at which point she'll launch into a detailed, profane discourse in the thickest Bronx accent Dex has ever heard.

THE GUILTY SLEEP

There's a gaggle waiting for them inside the gate. A massive, bearded bear of a man stands at the fore. He's in olive green fatigues with the crossed-swords-and-two-star insignia of a dagarman on his collars and a jauntily cocked pakol atop his mass of wild hair. He raises his hand in greeting, and this is when the first hint, the first feeling something is off, slides like a whisper of cold air across the backs of Dex's ears. He shivers and blinks and chalks it up to nerves.

The dagarman is flanked by half a dozen men in a mix of fatigues and traditional perahan tunban, all armed. The sunlight catches on the dagarman's rank pins, refracting into lances of fire that stab Dex's eyes. It's like hot sand in his tear ducts. Dex shakes his head and pushes his fingers behind his sunglasses and scrapes his fingernails against the corners of his eyes. He takes a breath, drawing in the hot dusty air and holding it as long as he can.

There's a problem with those simple in-and-out ops.

The bad guys get a say too.

WEDNESDAY

COLLECTIONS AND DEPOSITS

TURNER

Any self-respecting narcotics and firearms trafficking business runs on two peak cycles. There's the midmorning to early-afternoon crest, when day-jobbers need their pick-me-ups and late-rising stoners come out of hibernation to pick up their evening supply. Second peak's midnight to five, a time of lighter but more lucrative traffic. Serious customers—the subset of felon interested in moving weight for profit and iron for worse. It's the ideal time for that type of transaction, when the streets are clear enough to see the constabulary coming, and when the badges on night shift are there due to some combination of laziness, incompetence, and unpopularity.

The best time to make your money pickup is morning, after second peak and before the cycle restarts. You sweep through between six and nine. Let the corner guys scrape the bottom of the barrel customers between five and six, then work your way through the town in a narrowing spiral. Start at the outskirts. The all-night diner on 97, where the tired-looking waitress with the red-to-gray hair keeps trade in more than good coffee and better pie. The apartment complex out near Lutheran Village, where the local crew was steadily growing a customer base equal parts nouveau riche bougie types from Union Bridge, local farmers looking for an extra pep in their step, and residents of the complex themselves. The abandoned shopping mall on 140, where the seemingly empty tire shop in the rear parking lot held a secret vault that looked like an army arsenal, presided over by a shaven-headed ogre even bigger than Turner. You work your way toward the center of town. Finish with two adjacent stops. The twenty-four-hour pain clinic on Old Washington, where the night-shift medico's been in Cooke's pocket since before they graduated pharmacy school. Next, the high-end coffee stand across the street, where the first-shift barista will throw a little something extra in your to-go bag if you ask for a "gold stamp card" with your order and slip him a folded twenty.

Do all that, you'll find yourself with a full bag, three blocks from and immediately before Pine Hill Bank opens. Somewhere between twelve and fifteen thousand a day.

You make the bank drop three times a week but you always change the days. Sometimes you space them out, sometimes you do them back-to-back. You vary your drop-off time. Keep things irregular in case anyone's watching. Regardless, you're dropping a hundred K a week of pure profit, give or take, setting up your bank boy's monthly trip to the casino at National Harbor or Maryland Live.

Turner tried to explain it all to Angelita's nephew, Slade Cooke, as they made their way through the spiral. Talked about the need to vary the pickup order by starting the spiral at different points of the compass each time, but always finishing near the bank at opening time. He talked about the finer points of identifying potential tails, and the danger of relying only on old-school thinking when it came to cell phones and GPS trackers.

But the man—no, the boy, even if he was twenty-two—gave Turner nothing back. Spent the night on his phone, alternating between a dating app and some other thing that looked like he was building a castle and mining for gold. He kept the obnoxious sound effects turned on at full volume to compete with the radio. Turner thought Slade was doing it on purpose. Testing him. That maybe he wasn't actually bored with it all. He caught Slade glancing up from the phone now and then, peering at his surroundings with quick looks, like he was trying to lock the route in. The kid didn't seem to blink much.

And the testing had started from the beginning. First thing Slade did after shimmying his narrow ass into the passenger seat was look at the picture of the little blonde girl taped to the dash and run his finger over her face. "Cute kid," he'd said, still stroking the picture. "You'll have to introduce us."

Turner glanced at him from the corner of his eye, but Slade was already looking at his phone.

The rest of the night, Slade looked up from his screen only to complain about being hungry or thirsty or needing to piss. Turner explained the need to stay contained, stay mobile. No stops for food or drink, which is why you pack a snack and a reusable water bottle. No stops to pee, which is why the water bottle is only half full when you start out. Most of all, never bring your cell. Too tempting, too distracting, too easy for a rival or the law to track your movements.

So, when Slade finally put his phone away, squinting against the sunlight pouring through the windscreen, and asked a question, Turner was relieved the kid was finally showing interest.

"The gun guy at the tire place. What was his name?"

"Don't worry about it."

"Fine. Think he'd give me a family discount? Want to upgrade my piece," he said, patting his waistband where it bulged with the blocky shape of a Glock. "Maybe something in a .45, you know? Bigger boom and all."

"Listen, kid. You have to pull a heater on this job, you've already failed."

"Come *on*, man." Slade flipped the sun visor, studying his reflection in the mirror. He scratched at the pencil-thin beard he clearly spent a lot of his free time manicuring. "I seen that piece you keep strapped under the steering wheel. Good spot, easy to reach. Sawed-off, double-barrel jobber. Argument ender."

"You haven't been paying attention."

"It's *boring*. Bunch of driving around, taking bags through the window, listening to your terrible old-ass music. Mandolin Storm or whatever. Didn't hear no mandolin."

Turner set aside his wonderment the kid even knew what a mandolin was.

"Boring is good, kid. Boring is safe. And from your aunt's perspective, most importantly—boring is *profitable*. You think of anything less in the black than dropping a body that comes back to her business?"

"Whatever, man," Slade sneered. "And don't call me kid."

Turner grasped the kid at the back of the neck and bounced his face off the dashboard. He took a little force off at the last second. No permanent damage, just send a message. The hula dancer glued to the center of the dash shimmied provocatively.

Slade screeched, holding his forehead. With his other hand, he scrabbled at his beltline, pushing himself up in his seat for leverage. Turner clamped his left hand over Slade's right, trapping the gun in place.

"Dang, son," Turner said. "Acting like you got two brain cells and they're both fighting for third place. Keep struggling, you're gonna blow your nuts off." Slade froze. "Never carry your gun stuffed down around your tenders. Recipe for disaster. Now," Turner said, grinding Slade's wrist bones in his fist, "do I have your attention?"

12

THE NEXT RIGHT THING

DEX

Dex did three things right the night before. First two were actually things he *didn't* do: He stayed away from the news and he stayed away from the bar. The former directly precipitated the latter. He didn't want to watch the talking heads bloviate about the speed with which Afghanistan had collapsed like a wet sock back into Taliban control.

Staying in his apartment had started to feel wrong too. It was a disaster of a self-inflicted wound: dim and dingy, made worse because he hadn't finished unpacking the dozen boxes he'd brought. They made haphazard, tilting stacks in the corners, mocking his inaction. A monument to his stubborn refusal to settle into his new life.

He ditched his work clothes, pulled on his running gear, and hit Old Washington Road. Again. South to the community college and back. That tidy four-and-a-half-mile run. The abandoned dealership. The strip malls and the funeral home. The pain clinic. The corpse of a town that lacked the good sense to know it was dead.

When he got back, he did the third right thing and washed the remains of the tsebhi from the Tupperware and left it outside Mariam and Dawit's door. Showered and laid in his coffin-sized bed and tried to sleep.

It all should have made for a marginally better night. Instead, he tossed and turned, thinking about the bottle of Catoctin Rye on the top shelf of the broom closet that passed for a pantry in his tiny kitchen. Thinking about Jalal and his family, their throats slit, dumped over the side of the cargo ship like so much trash.

When sleep came at last, the nightmare waited, like a bad old friend you can't shake.

Fatima pulls him into the dark as bullets slam into the mud bricks above the door. He falls down the trio of rickety wooden steps, tripping over someone's feet. The women are huddled in the far corner, seven of them, three in burqas and the rest in hijabs. His ears ring with a continuous, whistling hum. Someone crashes through the door behind him, manages not to fall down the steps, and returns fire in the direction they came. The light is dim, but flares bright as the door slams open every time someone else makes it to the room. Even in the high, naked gunfire aftertone he can somehow hear the tap-tap-tapping of the fly. He crawls away from the steps but the door flings open again and there's a juddering tangle of limbs and the sound of grunts and cursing and Jalal falls across his hips. The stocky terp gnashes his teeth and scrambles toward the steps. Dex grabs him by the belt and heaves him back. Jalal fights madly against his grasp, pulls away.

The room blooms bright. Shadows sharpen into knives.

Saenz bellows something. This was when it happened. Dex is looking at the body. Ahn, his sunglasses askew, staring at nothing. Skin the gray of wet dust in the blade-edged light. There's the ghost of another sound, the dead man gasping for his mother.

This was when it happened. The blood paints Ahn's neck and chest an impossible shade.

This was when it happened. The fly tapping, the razor brightness, Saenz's shout, Ahn's blood.

This was when it happened. Dex pushes to his knees, turning. Reaching for his rifle, but not in time. Never in time.

This is when it happens.

THE GUILTY SLEEP

Dex screamed himself awake, throat shredded, face buried in his pillow. He tore at it with his teeth and thrashed upright, gasping. Came to himself, staring into the corners and searching the darkness. The sounds of the tap-tap-tapping fly, the slinking flow of the black river. He threw his pillow across the room and it plopped against the wall and slid to the floor, a defeated hump. He tapped his phone, stared at Rowan's face until his eyes blurred. Almost six. Three hours of bad sleep.

He staggered upright. Took a couple steps, leaned against the doorjamb for a minute until his breathing was under control. His ribs and lower back and face throbbed in competing rhythm.

He was in a spiral, spinning in circles on the shore of that black river, the lapping brack calling him to wade on in—the water's *fine*, hon.

He couldn't stop thinking about Jalal's wife and little girl, just a little older than Rowan, given to the cargo ship crew as payment for the unsettled debt. He couldn't stop thinking about Rowan and Daria and about how exhausted he was. And how tired of being exhausted. Tired of the bank and its warm wood and potted succulents and overstuffed chairs. Tired of Freddy's constantly running mouth. Tired of himself: A failure of a husband and father. A failure of a person. Tired of feeling like he'd tried everything and couldn't pull himself up, couldn't pull himself out.

A camping trip with his father, an annual event. The one when he was eleven, an unexpected rainstorm had come through at midnight, sending an impromptu creek through the middle of their tent. They'd bagged it, packed everything up in the darkness, and then sat dripping in an all-night diner in Cumberland, drinking hot chocolate and eating pancakes. It was his best childhood memory, because sitting there in the bright lights and tasting the whipped cream, his father had talked to him—really *talked* to him, like he was a man. He remembered almost nothing about the conversation, just the feeling of it and his father's rough plumber's hands clasped around his steaming mug and his father's tired blue eyes, and the one thing he said Dex could remember was this: "Dexter, when you don't know what to do with yourself, when you don't know where you're going or what you're going to be, just focus on figuring out one simple idea—the next right thing. You do that, you'll be OK."

Two years later, the old man was dead, felled by a widowmaker in a widow's kitchen, a length of PVC in one hand and a tube of caulk in the other. But Dex remembered that one thing, that one perfect moment he'd had with this father, that one piece of advice.

He skipped the run since he'd gone the night before. He showered, wondering what it would be like to feel clean again. He thought about the next right thing, wondered what the next right thing could possibly be.

The next pair of khakis in the drawer, the one with the pinprick hole in the back pocket. The next button-down in the closet. White shirt day.

Picked up coffee for two and a pair of apple fritters from the Safeway and had them ready in front of the bank before Marty arrived. Returning the favor. She grinned at him.

"Look at you, broheim, almost making an effort."

"Let's not get carried away."

"Whatever, I appreciate it anyway," Marty said, toasting him. "Popped in to Thievery Collective last night for a quick drink with Timanda. Didn't see you there."

"Maybe I'm turning over a new leaf."

"Yeah, and maybe Freddy's leaving me the bank in his will."

"Not too late to marry into the family, you know."

"Shut up, loser," she said, elbowing him as he was about to take a sip. She pulled it at the last second, saving his shirt and his skin, but winked to let him know she knew it.

Not quite nine and the air already had the dusty granite taste that meant summer storms in the afternoon. Freddy's dull gray truck breached the parking lot on cue, preceded by three quick blurts of his air horn, the echoes warring with the scratchy tolling of Saint Patrick's prerecorded bells.

Pine Hill Bank had been in Freddy House's family four generations, which Dex well knew thanks to untold repetitions of the story. There were neither pines nor a hill within miles, Freddy pronounced, nor had there been in the bank's history, far as anyone knew. Freddy'd been running the place since his uncle Martin Luther House (named for the theses-nailer, not that *other* one, mind you, and no offense) died two decades ago. And when ol' skinflint ML had passed on, young Fred made it his mission to shed the chintzy, small-town image of Pine Hill Bank. Got a huge boost when the city held a bid-auction to build a shopping center right off the central intersection of the town, where Pine Hill held sole command. The winning developer, Cooke Construction Solutions, had been required to compensate the bank for the disruptions caused by the construction, and Freddy carpe'd that diem like a dog to a T-bone. Complete gut-job of the place, refreshed with wood and brass and big overhead fans. Billboards from Frederick to Taneytown. Radio spots, too, even on powerhouse WTOP (traffic and weather together on the eights, hon).

Dex had worked at Pine Hill for seven years, a shade longer than he'd been in the Guard. He thought Freddy liked having a National Guard guy, a combat veteran, on the rolls. An imaginary feather in his imaginary green plastic visor. Companion to the big yellow ribbon sticker plastered on the front window.

Seven years was plenty long enough for a guy with Dex's CI training to figure out Turner's weekly deposits were from a cash business all right, but not from a bunch of food trucks and soda machines. Freddy wouldn't let him or Marty touch Turner's money. He handled the processing and disbursements personally, even though he took little interest in any other customer. Neither Turner nor anyone else from his supposed conglomerate had ever made a cash withdrawal, yet they never ran out of room in the vault. The stacks of bills had to be going somewhere.

That mystery was solved by Freddy's regular casino trips. Every few weeks, always on a Friday, always after Turner's last deposit of the week, Freddy would wheel a hard-sided suitcase out to his truck and head off to Annapolis or Charlestown or National Harbor or even, if he was feeling especially fortuitous, Atlantic City. Dex figured the hard-sided rolling suitcase wasn't for Freddy's nightwear and toothbrush, but rather the cash Turner brought in, and Freddy's casino trips were probably the midpoint of a money-washing operation.

He tried not to think about it too hard. He suspected but he didn't *know*. So long as Freddy didn't involve him, he could keep his head down, put in his hours, try to gather the emotional energy to look for something better. Not that his chances were good, not with that *other than honorable* discharge categorization on his DD-214.

Thinking of his father, dead on a widow's floor with a tube of caulk in his hand. "*The next right thing, Dex. Find that and you'll be OK.*" Tired of trying to find the next right thing but not being able to see what it was.

At 9:12 a.m., Turner walked in. Six-and-a-half feet of old beef, with that soft smile and gentle voice, nodding at everyone. El Camino idling out front, a new silhouette in the passenger seat. Turner had the usual nylon satchel over one shoulder. Dex had never seen inside the bag, but he knew. He knew. Freddy jingled his keys and led the big man to the vault.

At 9:19 a.m., his phone buzzed. He dug it out, not caring if Fred came out of the vault and saw, chewed him out. It was Daria.

Are you ok? I can't stop thinking about
our last conversation.

For this, at least, he knew the next right thing.

Yeah, me too. You're right about everything.
I'm going to group tonight.
And I'm calling the VA again tomorrow.

I don't care how long they keep me on hold.

I'm glad.

Any chance I could see you and Ro today?
This afternoon, when I get off?

THE GUILTY SLEEP

Not today, we have an appt w Dr.
Feuchtbaum.

Everything ok??

Normal consult to check Ro's
strabisbus, see if the eyepatch is
working, finalize surgery plans.

He could've said he wanted to be there for it. Demanded it as a
father. But he'd pushed too hard already. He didn't want to drive her
away.

How about tomorrow? Community Pond?

I'll think about it.

At least it wasn't a no. Dex smiled, and ignored Marty's raised
eyebrows.

Let me know how group goes.

I will. Promise. Kiss Ro for me?

Ok. Got to go.

He started to put his phone away, but it buzzed before he got it in
his pocket. Marty whispered, "C'mon, Dex, at least try to be subtle."
It was Saenz.

Hey man, sorry about yesterday.

Buy you a cup of coffee?

Sunny and Wink want to catch up. How
about tonight?

Dex knew what it was, and Saenz wasn't really trying to hide it.
Another piece of the Saenz legend went that he'd pitched one potential source, an Iraqi Baathist militia captain, fourteen times before the
guy cracked and came over to the side of the light.

The only way to win was to not play. He stuffed the phone away. It didn't buzz again.

He tried to lose himself in the minutiae of the job. The numbers swam, the keyboard was too loud, the mouse buttons clicked annoyingly. He looked out the windows. The sun hit the windscreen of Freddy's pickup, reflecting back and stabbing into his eyes.

When it did, he saw the dinner plate, plain white ceramic. He had hurled it across the room. Away from his wife, but needing to—compelled to—heave it, give an outlet to the inexplicable eruption of fury. It flew in slow motion, taunting him as he tried to claw it back. A clump of roast chicken and a dozen peas scattered in a slow-falling constellation. The plate hit the far wall with the sound of a gunshot, which made everything infinitely worse. It exploded, shattering into a thousand sharp pieces and leaving a dent in the drywall. But that wasn't the worst part.

"Dex." It was Marty. Her hand on his shoulder. "You OK, man?"

"Yeah. What's up?"

"Going on break. I told you like three times but you weren't hearing me."

"Sorry. Just tired."

She looked at his face, taking in the bruises and abrasions. "Sure," she said, unconvinced. "Going to CVS. You want anything?"

"I'm OK. Thanks."

"Tylenol in my drawer. Help yourself, OK?"

The next right thing. Saenz would tell him the next right thing was easy, was right in front of his face. Help someone who needed—deserved—help more than anyone. Dex's father might have said the same. Was it truly that simple? Dex turned the idea around in his brain, examining it like he used to do with a nugget of intelligence gleaned from a particularly unreliable source. Levers and fulcrums. The next right thing. He'd tried everything else—Terrence's meetings, the VA shrink, the antidepressants, the bottle. It was a wild, insane risk, and if it went wrong, he'd be dead or in prison, with no chance of winning his family back. He still had a chance there, maybe, if he

THE GUILTY SLEEP

could figure things out, get stable, find a better job, start helping with the bills, pay for Rowan's surgery.

At his lunch break, he pulled out his phone. He texted Daria.

> Hope Doc F visit goes well. I'd love to see you guys at the park tomorrow.

> I'll be there either way.

Then he opened Saenz's text and replied.

13

OVERWATCH

TURNER; SAENZ

"'ma tell Aunt Angie." Slade gasped, sounding like a little kid on the playground who just got pushed off the seesaw by an older cousin.

"I could eat a bowl of alphabet soup and shit a better response'n that. Stop complaining." Turner inspected Slade's forehead. "You're not even bleeding. 'Sides, why do you think you're out here with me?"

Slade heaved against Turner's grasping paw, which moved not an inch. The kid's eyes drifted to Turner's thick forearm, tracing the lake of scars swimming under the tattoo ink. Turner bounced Slade's head off the dash again. The pink fuzzy dice hanging from the El Camino's rearview mirror vibrated.

Slade moaned. "Stop it, OK?"

"Let go of the piece."

Slade nodded jerkily. Turner loosened his grip enough for Slade to slide his hand out of his pants. Once his fingers were free, Turner took the Glock and dropped it into the door cubby behind him. "Ready to listen, or'm I gonna have to bobblehead you again?"

"You are *toast*, mother—"

Turner tightened his grip on the back of Slade's neck and drove his head forward, but stopped halfway. The kid nearly flinched out of his pants. He raised both hands, palms up. Supplicating.

THE GUILTY SLEEP

"OK, man, OK."

"Are. You. Ready. To. Listen." Turner said gently, squeezing Slade's neck with each word.

The boy nodded, glaring. Turner released him. Shifted back in his seat, giving Slade some personal space back.

"I'm going to say this once and then my font of wisdom is dry forever. Your Aunt Angelita cares about three things," Turner said, ticking the items off on his fingers. "The business, the Bible, and her blood. Seeing as you're the only Cooke other than her dear departed husband she's ever mentioned, means you're important. Tracking so far?"

Slade nodded. Kept his mouth shut, a point in his favor.

"From what I hear and see, you care about exactly three things too," Turner continued, ticking this list off in the same way. "Chasing girls, playing video games, and smoking up with your little crew of wannabe gangsters. But that's not gonna cut it for your aunt. You're out with me because she wants you to learn the business. Think about it."

Slade stared at him from under his eyebrows, face as stony as he could make it.

"Look, I'm her best bag man for a couple reasons. I don't rock the boat, meaning she can trust me not to do something stupid like dropping a body that'll be tied back to her. I'm dependable—never missed a pickup in all my years. Finally, I watch and listen and report back. I got this thing I picked up out West. California prison firefighter program," Turner said, nodding at his burn-scarred arms. "I can sense the wind change, smell smoke before we see flames. Metaphorically. Still with me?"

Slade nodded again, his expression softening from outright fury to sullenness, leavened with growing interest.

"For example, lately I've had the feeling someone's been watching. Not law, not a rival organization. But someone. Makes my ass itch, you get me?"

"Yeah," Slade mumbled.

"I track that stuff, report it to your aunt. Take independent action when needed, because she trusts me. Now. Why would your aunt want you to stop knocking around Inner Harbor tourists to get a close-up view of what I do on the daily?"

Slade shrugged and peered at his reflection in the visor. He fingered the growing lump above his left eyebrow. Turner shifted in his seat, barely enough to make the leather squeak. Slade jumped so hard he bounced his own head off the side window. He snarled a curse, but carefully didn't direct it Turner's way.

Turner needed to get the boy back, bring him along. Angie had been clear about what she wanted.

"Why, Slade?" Turner said, his voice as soft and kind as he could make it. "Let me paint you the picture I see. Then I want you to tell me if I'm right or if I should go juggle rocks. Can we do that?"

"Whatever."

"I think you've been taking chances lately, with that stoner crew of yours. Maybe flashing your pieces too much, knocking the marks around too hard when you take their iPhones. Pawning at the wrong shops. Ripping off corner guys, my dude. Risky stuff. And in spite of your little performance tonight, I think you're smarter'n that. I think"—Turner paused, letting it sink in—"they're looking for a little attention from your aunt. What do you think, should I go jump through my own ass or'm I on to something?"

"I don't know, man. Maybe."

"Come on, Slade. Do better."

The kid looked at him, then away. Seemed to make a decision and set his jaw. Kept looking out the window, but said, "Yeah. I wanted her to notice . . . what I was up to. I asked her before, you know. I . . . uh . . . went away for a bit when I was a kid. When I got back, I asked her to bring me in, let me work with her. She said I could apprentice with the foreman down at the latest build site. I told her she knew what I meant, but she laughed it off, said I should show her I could hack it on the straight and narrow."

"And it wasn't for you, was it?"

"Naw, man. Was it ever for you?"

"No," Turner said, stifling a chuckle.

THE GUILTY SLEEP

"Did it work? Did she notice?"

"Oh yeah."

"You're not my babysitter," Slade said, lips pursed.

"Follow that thread, bright boy."

"She . . . grooming me?"

Turner nodded. "She's thinking about the future. About retirement maybe, what comes next. Your aunt's built something here. Something real. I've been around long enough to know. And maybe she's thinking that if the long, narrow road to the peaceful valley ain't for you, maybe the crooked path to the bloody mountaintop is. And so we'd better keep you from getting rolled up for some stupid-ass nonsense, so you can take the reins of that real thing. Someday."

Slade stared out the window, but was seeing something much farther away.

"I didn't think she'd change her mind."

"I know. But we are who we are."

"Blowing my mind, big man." Slade's tone had slipped all the way to calm introspection. Kid wasn't a genius, maybe, but he had a low cunning. Things were falling into place in his mind. Balances shifting, dynamics altering. He looked at Turner, really looked at him. Met his eyes, then looked back out the window. Chewed on it for a few seconds.

"Sorry I tried to draw on you." It wasn't sincere, not totally. The voice was too flat. Disaffected. There was still a long way to go with the kid.

"Forget about it."

"I can keep riding with you?"

"Just need one thing."

"What?"

"Take back what you said about 'Mandolin Rain.' Bruce Hornsby's the man."

Saenz and Sunny Porter were slumped low in the front seats of a navy-blue sedan—a Golden Oak company car. Winkowski sprawled in the back seat, blowing vape steam in the direction of the cracked window behind his head. Saenz and Porter were looking at the two men in the brown-and-cream El Camino across the parking lot in front of the coffee stand.

Saenz lowered the detached ACOG rifle optic he was using as a monocular.

"What do you think, Sunny? Really gave the little guy a pounding there. Lovers' quarrel?"

"Does not appear so, but certainly a disagreement. They seem to have settled things for now," Porter replied, still peering through his own binoculars.

"Who cares," Winkowski groused. "Don't mean anything unless Frogger's in."

"Yes," Porter said, nodding once, his large, block-shaped head moving like a statue reluctantly come to life. Then he sighed. "I wish we did not need him."

Saenz didn't reply at first. He raised the optic and watched the car pull slowly out of the parking lot, heading in the direction of Pine Hill Bank.

"I wish we didn't either, Sunny. You know me, I'd rather plan it to death a year out and run it by the numbers. But we don't have much of a choice, not if we're going to pull this off. And what are the odds, right? Still working at the bank. The stuff he talked about in Oman, still happening?"

"Call it fate, then," Winkowski said. "You made the approach, and he told you to stuff it. You gave him a drive-by yesterday, and he told you to stuff it again. What are the odds he changes his mind now? With everything in the balance like this? I say we set up a meet with the port guy, then close him out and dump him in the harbor."

Saenz pinched the bridge of his nose and breathed deep.

"Trying to limit the attention on this one, Wink. You think disappearing a senior homeland security lawman's a good way to do that?"

"At this point, we're mission-committed," Winkowski said. "Collateral's collateral."

"Shut. Up." This from Porter, his voice low and calm. Wink muttered something, blew some steam toward the front seats.

"I'm going to try again," Saenz said. "Mea culpa, cuppa coffee. Bring your charming asses to bear. If I can get him to sit down with us, I think we can close it. Or he gives us something we can use at least. Better'n even odds, I think. Frogger . . . he's looking for something to make right. And if we sweeten the pot, yeah. I'd say better'n even."

"Text him, then," said Winkowski. "Sweeten the pot. Let's go for it. Meet for coffee and reel him in."

"What say you, Sunny?"

Porter tilted his head again. "More potential collateral. But I agree. We have no other good options."

"OK," Saenz said, digging out his phone and passing the scope to Porter. "Let's give it a go, Blackbirds."

14.

GROUP

DEX

Terrence's group met in the basement of the Unitarian Universalist Chapel half a mile up the road from the bank. Dex walked it, the last of the storm blowing away ahead of him, moving east toward the northern tip of the Chesapeake. A mocking, incremental respite from the heat. The pavement steamed and wavered uncertainly. By the time he got there he was a mess, his work shirt rumpled and sweat-soaked.

From the outside you might think it was an AA meeting, at least until you took in the scars and missing limbs. It was a bigger group than last week. Several people Dex had never seen before, or only once or twice. All the newbies were his age or near enough, which tracked. Iraq and Afghanistan vets, watching half the peace they'd built collapse like a tissue house in a tornado. Seeking comfort in the presence of others who'd seen what they'd seen, done what they'd done. Or maybe looking for a place to explode.

The basement was cool and dim, all fake wood paneling, industrial carpeting, and fluorescents buzzing like the tap-tap-tapping of a fly. Bulletin boards full of bright posters with Bible verses on them. A painting of a brown-skinned, dark-eyed Jesus, his carpenter's hands cradling a lamb with surprising gentleness. Dex didn't want to be there. He wanted to be anywhere else. Almost anywhere else. Not the compound. Not the women's room.

There was something in his hands. He looked down, surprised to see he was gripping the back of one of the chairs. Plastic orange, straight out of the eighties. His knuckles ached, and he fought the urge to heave the thing across the room.

"Hey, Dexter, good to see you." The voice was deep, mellow as old leather. Dex forced a smile, forced himself to release the chair, forced himself to stand upright and walk around it.

"Hey yourself, Terrence."

The man rolled over, held out his hand. He was Dex's height—or would have been, standing—but bigger. Solid. Huge through the arms and shoulders. The handshake, as always, could've powdered his bones if Terrence *really* squeezed.

"I mean it," Terrence said, his voice low. He motioned for Dex to sit and, when he had, Terrence leaned forward. "I was hoping you'd be here. Got some new folks this week, no surprise, and most of them are from your theater of operations. If you're open to sharing tonight, there are folks who need to hear what you have to say."

Dex looked away. "I don't know, T."

"Brother, if you want to talk, go ahead—I'll make sure we leave the floor open. You don't, that's fine. I'm just glad you're here." It was the kind of genuine encouragement that made Terrence such a magnetic guy. Warm, honest, light on the pressure. Dex hadn't opened his mouth in months, so T was pushing without pushing. A natural leader, like Saenz.

T was a Gulf One guy. Lost his legs when one of Saddam's retreating Fedayeen blew a supply depot as T's dismounted cav scout troop was coming in to secure it. Three of his squadmates were killed, vaporized right in front of him. He spent the next decade figuring out how to piece himself back together. Somehow, he'd cracked the code. Released the anger, the guilt, and the loss. Decided to give back, start something for veterans like him. Founded the group in 2003, just as the first wave of Afghanistan vets was coming home.

"How *are* you doing?" It wasn't a throwaway.

"Truth?" Dex pushed a hand through his hair.

"Truth."

"Tired," he said, then coughed a short laugh. "And . . . looking for the next right thing."

It was possible Terrence had saved Dex's life. Six months ago, with the world falling apart around him, fresh off moving into his open grave of an apartment and facing the prospect of losing his family, drowning in a bottle every night, Dex's mind kept coming back to the black plastic case on the top shelf of his closet. He thought about where to do it to ensure no collateral damage. Wondering where to put the bullet—temple, t-zone, or roof of the mouth. He'd started to imagine the taste of cold metal and oil on his tongue. He showed up at Terrence's door at midnight, handing over the pistol case without a word. Terrence took it, looked Dex in the eyes, and nodded. That was it, that was all.

In the basement of the church, Dex couldn't meet those eyes. Couldn't say anything else. Terrence clapped him gently on the shoulder—for him, anyway; any harder and he'd have knocked Dex across the room.

"That's all we can do, right?"

Dex nodded. "I wish it was . . . more."

"Being here's a good step, my friend." Terrence dapped him up and wheeled away, going from person to person, cluster to cluster, making everyone welcome. Now that Terrence had spoken to him, Dex couldn't leave. He shifted the chair back a few inches, barely out of line with the rest of the circle, and waited.

■

"I guess the whole thing feels . . . inevitable. Didn't matter if we stayed a year or twenty, this was always gonna happen." The speaker a couple years younger than Dex. Melanie something, he thought. She'd only been at group a couple of times.

"'At's because the stupid mission never made any sense inna first place," said a burly, bearded guy sitting two places over.

THE GUILTY SLEEP 95

"What do you mean, Leo?" asked Terrence.

"Don' get me wrong, we needed to be there. After 9/11, we had no choice. 'At part made sense. Had to go after bin Laden. Taliban, too, for shelterin' him. But the nex' bit?" Leo scoffed. "Spreadin' Western-style democracy in a place 'at never knew it, never wanted it? Come *on*."

"It might have worked," someone else said. "If we'd actually tried."

"Sure," Leo scoffed. "If we'd poured a trillion dollars into, uh, infrastructure. Hunnert thousand doctors and teachers and engineers and lawyers and whatever else. In perpetu-ality. Naw, we should have left when we schwacked the Taliban. Hunted UBL from a distance. Spooks 'n' drones, not infantry divisions."

"We could have done it," said a Latino guy in a sleeveless T-shirt, 101st Airborne tattoo on his shoulder. "Beat them for good, made the place work. Made peace. I heard there was this underground lake in the north, you know? Enough freshwater to irrigate the country for five hundred years. Turn it green."

"So what, Froylan?" Leo scoffed.

"Clean water and good crops bring peace. If we'd fought with any kind of sense of purpose or direction, if we could've trained up the ANA better, cleaned up some of the corruption—"

"Starry-eyed idealism right there, my man," said Leo. "Sure you was even over there?"

There was a chorus of *heys*—the loudest from Terrence—with a few *come on, mans* sprinkled across the top. Leo put up his hands in the ancient gesture of surrender.

"Sorry," he said. Took a deep breath. "I'm . . . I'm all messed up 'bout this right now." Froylan nodded, his mouth a flat line.

"I think that's a fair statement for a lot of us," said Terrence, who always seemed to know the right time to step in, to keep things moving in a productive way. "It's what we've all been hearing today. But what do we always have to acknowledge? The number one thing?"

"I am not the enemy," the group unisoned, "and my brothers and sisters in arms are not the enemy." Dex didn't add his voice. Speaking felt like too much effort. Even being in the room felt like too much, but he held Rowan's face in front of his mind. Clenched his teeth and breathed through his nose.

"What did we bring home?" Terrence asked.

"We brought the war home," the group responded in a low chorus.

Terrence let the silence lie for a minute. Then he nodded at Melanie, who'd stuck up her index finger.

"S'my point. Regardless if we stayed forever or left right after we took out the Taliban," she said. "My LT used to say, 'We have the watches; they have the time.' Makes a lot of sense to me. They outlasted the British, the Soviets—shoot, they outwaited Alexander the friggin' Great. They had no problem waiting us out too."

"More'n that," added Treshaun, a slim, one-armed guy who'd been at every single meeting Dex had ever attended. "Taliban, AQ, all those guys, they had *belief*. They knew—"

"We had it too," said Froylan.

"Listen," said Treshaun. "Those guys are *true* believers. Their system—I don't mean Islam in general, I'm talking that hardcore fundamentalist stuff—like it or not, they believe in that way more than the average American believes in spreading a 'Western-style democracy' around the world," he said, punching finger quotes in the air.

"Speak fer yourself," Leo muttered, but if Treshaun heard him, he ignored it.

"S'what kept them going," Melanie said.

"Right," Treshaun said, drawing the word out and raising his chin at her.

"Didn't help we had a bunch of politicians sticking their noses in all the time," Froylan added. "Never let us fight the war we needed to fight."

"Yeah, I can get with 'at, Froy." Leo spit dip juice into an empty Mountain Dew bottle. "And the generals more concerned 'bout getting their next star 'n' a book deal than winning the war. No real goals beyond 'at."

Froylan nodded. "Only way we could've won was to fight the war we needed to fight. If we'd—"

THE GUILTY SLEEP

"We were never going to win, though, *that's* what I've been trying to say," Melanie cut in. She was sitting up now, hands clenching her knees. Veins stood out in her neck. Terrence put up his hand, but Froylan put his up first, patting the air. *It's OK*, the gesture said.

"We just weren't," she continued. "All that stuff, everything you're all saying. We. Couldn't. Win. And we *still* stayed there for twenty years. Two decades of blood spilled, ours and theirs. How many of our friends got blown up? How many families were . . . were *annihilated* in the crossfire?"

She looked around the room, searching. Treshaun gripped the bottom of his opposite bicep, where his arm ended.

Dex saw Ahn, his heels carving channels in the gravel of the ANA compound, his life fountaining from his neck. He saw the blue door and what lay behind it. The tap-tap-tapping of the fly.

"While the Afghan government an' a bunch of contractors lined their pockets," Leo added.

"Now we pull out, let the Tallies take it all back . . . I know I'm saying it was inevitable, it was going to happen no matter what . . . but . . ." Melanie trailed off, shrunk in on herself again. Someone coughed.

"But it still feels awful," Dex said, without realizing he was going to open his mouth. "Like everything we did, everything we lost, was for nothing."

"Exactly," Melanie and Leo and Treshaun said at the same time. Melanie choked a laugh, grimacing.

"And it feels like we're abandoning the ones who tried to help us. The people who wanted us there," Dex added, not sure why he was still talking. "They're going to be tortured and killed. Their families too. We're sending an entire country back to the dark ages. We spent twenty years chasing our tails and watching our friends die. And now we're all wondering what the hell it was for."

"Got-*daing*, yinz sound like a buncha poly-sci majors fighting over the last wine cooler at the world's sorriest frat party." Vernon. A heavyset guy with white stubble across his jowls and a huge, red-veined nose. He was one of the OGs. He wore a blue cap with *Vietnam Veteran* in gold stitching across the front.

"Care to elaborate?" Terrence said.

Vernon cleared his throat. "Here it is, young bloods. End of the day, gotta learn one thing. Same every war, since men first started jabbin' each other with pointy sticks. Both sides think they're righteous. Rich old men send poor young men—and women"—he glanced at Melanie—"off to die. Corporations, politicians make their money. No one back home gives a wet fart unless someone they know comes home in a bag. After a while everyone gets sick of it and packs up their toys and goes home. No different in the modern world, 'cept ten years later, everyone starts getting sick. My generation, it was Agent Orange. Terrence's, Gulf War Syndrome. Yinz, it's the damn burn pit cancer. Either way, when it's all said and done, there's a bunch of new stones at Arlington, bunch of plaques in towns like ours all over the country. Bunch of grunts waiting for their turn at the gotdaing VA." Vernon took a raspy breath and wiped his mouth. Looked around the room, meeting the eyes of anyone who'd meet his. "And it don't mean a thing, young bloods. It don't mean a thing."

Silence sat over the room like a weighted blanket for ten seconds, until someone delicately cleared their throat and said, "Bullshit."

It was Saenz. He was sitting in the back, in the shadows, just outside the circle. Dex hadn't seen him come in. The group shifted, turned, silently took him in. Terrence nodded in welcome, pushed a couple locs behind his ears, and raised his eyebrows. *Continue, newcomer.*

"The blood we spilled, the people we lost, it wasn't for nothing," Saenz said, his voice even. "They killed three thousand Americans. So we went in there and toppled a hostile government in about twenty days, then spent the next couple decades bringing the bloody vengeance of the almighty American colossus down on the heads of anyone who even looked at us funny. We took twenty thousand tangos off the board and rendered Al Qaeda a shadow of itself. They've ceased to exist as a coherent, ideological entity, and they'll never threaten us again. It's what we do. It's why people like us exist. To show the world

THE GUILTY SLEEP

that you don't get away with something like that. *That's* what it means."

■

Afterward, Dex met Saenz in the church parking lot.

"Think you made an impression, Sarnt."

"Yeah, sorry about that," Saenz said, running a hand through his thinning hair. "I got here early, thought I'd poke my head in. I was only going to listen, see what it's all about. I just can't abide that nihilistic garbage."

"It's how a lot of us are feeling."

"Is it how you're feeling?"

"I don't know."

"Fair enough, and I'm your friend, not your shrink. Thanks for texting me back."

"Thanks for meeting me. I just wanted to say—"

"Don't worry about it. I would've reacted the same if someone pitched me cold on something like that. Must be out of practice." Saenz shrugged and smiled slightly, turning it into a joke. "Sunny and Wink are gonna meet us at the place."

"Give me a ride?"

"Sure thing."

15

CAST AND RETURN

SAENZ

"Sorry to disappoint you," Frogger said, and looked like he meant it. He also looked like warmed-over dog vomit. Bruised, scraped, dark circles under his eyes. No tread on his tires. A good thing, far as Saenz was concerned. Frogger was trying to present like he had it together, but Saenz saw through him like cut crystal. Guy was shattered, and here was his old boss and friend, bearing broom and dustpan. Ready to put him back together and turn him to a purpose.

They were clustered into a small booth in the back of the Minuteman, the town's only 24-7 restaurant. It was a throwback, all chrome and red plastic padding and black-and-white checkered floor tiles. Little jukeboxes on the tables that took a quarter and played songs from the '50s and '60s.

"Ain't surprised, frankly," said Winkowski. He gestured with his fork, and sausage gravy spattered his plate. "Told Stu you didn't have the stones for this jawn."

Saenz shot a look and stilled him. Frogger took a perfunctory poke at his cherry pie, eyes on his plate.

"Ignore Winkowski. Thanks for meeting us." When Frogger had texted him back, asked him to meet up after his touchy-feely vets group, Stu figured he had him. It was just a matter of adjusting the

THE GUILTY SLEEP

levers, rigging the fulcrums. Never should have left him an opening. Only way to win was to not play.

"Yes. It is good to see you," added Sunny. "You look . . . well."

Grant spread his hands apologetically, looked around at them. Got right into it. "Guys, I can't. Look, I'm not going to say anything to anyone about this—"

"Never even occurred to us," Saenz lied.

"—but I've got to figure my stuff out," he finished, then chuckled wryly.

"Something funny?" This from Winkowski.

"Just something my wife said."

"Separated though, right?"

"Shut up, Wink," Saenz snapped as Frogger's eyes flicked up and bored into his former teammate's face.

Saenz mirrored Frogger, spreading his hands regretfully. Creating a subtle mental match with the physical movement. *See: We're the same, Frogger—you're one of us.* "I had to bring the guys up to speed so we could start working up an alternate plan." Another lie, of course. This was it; no time, no angles anywhere else.

"Separated," Frogger said, dropping his fork and pushing his over-long hair back from his forehead. Rasped a hand over the stubble on his chin. "I'm ate up as a soup sandwich, boys, and trying to get right. Trying to get my family back, trying to do right by them. I can't go to jail and I can't get myself dead: I've got a mortgage and school loans and my daughter needs surgery on her eye, and"—he paused, gathering himself—"I need to be there for her."

"How's things working out so far?"

"Shut up, Wink," Saenz and Sunny chorused. Frogger shrugged it off. The script was playing out just how Saenz had told Sunny and Wink that it would, and everyone was playing their part to a tee.

"Not well, but I'm gonna keep trying. Above dirt and free, I got a chance. This thing of yours goes sideways, that's the whole bushel of crabs right there. The cops or the robbers are coming after us."

"Come on, Grant." Saenz slapped the table softly. "Your small-town flatfoots aren't gonna even sniff this. And since when is a low-rent wannabe kingpin better than the Blackbirds doing what they do? No way some Carroll County redneck is going to figure out what happened to their cash. Remember, this is exactly the sort of background I came from, back in the day. I know the sort. Come after us? We'll be ghosts, man."

"Ghosts."

"Poor choice of words," Saenz said, although it was exactly what he'd meant to say. Let Frogger feel like he had some power, some agency. Give him an opening here and there for pushback, let him feel like he was still resisting. "Look, this whole thing is just like recruiting a source—you can move anything with the right lever and a perfectly placed fulcrum."

"Which am I?"

"Hell, Dex, you're both," Saenz said, tuning his smile to half-chagrined.

Saenz's eyes darted to Porter. His move. The quiet, taciturn rock of the team. Logical, rule-bound, unemotional. The least likely to speak up with what came next, and therefore the best choice.

"I think . . ." Sunny began, ponderous as a glacier, "this could be just what you need."

"What?" Frogger said, fork halfway to his mouth.

"You are a mess, as you say. Spiraling. You are trying to help yourself and failing. What if what you need is to help someone else? Someone in worse straits than you?"

Grant chewed, watching Porter from the corner of his eye. Saenz flicked his eyes to Winkowski. Step two.

"And here's the thing, Frogger," Winkowski said, "what if you could help someone else *and* help your family at the same time?"

Helping Jalal wasn't enough, Saenz had realized. The envelope from *Dean and Morris, Family Law*. Divorces were expensive. And the stack of bills. The surgery estimate from *Associated Ophthalmologists of Central Maryland*. Monday night, Dex had drunkenly thrown the whole mess on top of his fridge. But Saenz had already rifled through them the previous week, when he'd let himself in to the crappy little apartment during one of Frogger's predawn runs. Pre-op intel

THE GUILTY SLEEP

collection, familiarizing himself with the details of Frogger's weak points. Leaving nothing to chance.

"What're you saying?" Dex said, voice wary.

"What Sunny and Wink are getting at, I think," Saenz said, easing into it, "is you've got hard times going. You want to get your wife and kid back, but . . . you've got trouble on the money side too."

"Comes with the territory," Frogger said, his eyes never leaving Saenz's. Almost daring him to say what came next.

"It doesn't have to," Winkowski offered, off script and out of turn. Saenz pushed down annoyance.

"We can't do this without you," Saenz admitted. "But we'll limit your involvement. I've got the whole op figured, plug and play."

"Almost," Frogger replied.

"Almost," Saenz said, nodding. "A little inside information, the kind only you can provide, maybe one little piece of the action, and that's it. Almost zero risk. A few minutes of in-depth conversation tonight and five minutes of work tomorrow. Takes us to a hundred percent chance of success, reduces odds of collateral damage and detection to zero. You're never directly involved. Or implicated."

"Uh-huh," Frogger said, flatly incredulous.

"And here's the thing, Grant. The kicker. Based on what you told us back in Oman, I bet we're talking about more than what we need."

"Two hundred forty thousand, you said."

"That's right. And I'd wager everything we already put into this, there'll be more than that. A cushion."

"And we—" Winkowski started but Porter cut him off with a look.

"We talked it over, Dex," Saenz said. This was it—the second boot, dropping feather-light into a field of eggshells—the moment where it would all come together or explode in his face like a supernova. He loved it with every atom of his soul. "Anything extra, anything off the top—we want you to have it."

"What?"

"Maybe if you can solve some of the money troubles, it'll help you solve some of the family troubles. Seems like a pretty good overlap there."

Frogger stared at him. Looked at Winkowski, then Porter. They looked back. Winkowski even managed to keep his trap shut.

"Do something good," Saenz said, almost whispering. "Save some lives. Maybe it helps get your head right. And pay some bills, take care of your family. Buy yourself some time and space to get them back. All for a few minutes of operational background."

"And five minutes of work tomorrow," Frogger quoted, and Saenz knew he *had* the bastard, had him *hooked*.

"Max. Click of a button."

Frogger stared into space, considering. The pause lasted an eternity.

"What does it look like?" he asked.

Hooked indeed.

16

BEST LAID PLANS

DEX

Dex forked a bite of cherry pie, followed it with another sip of coffee. The pie should have been sour, the coffee bitter. Saenz had played him and he knew it, but like the pie, it was unfair to hate it for being perfect. Saenz knew his levers and fulcrums, and it only took him two approaches. Dex saw it, but it didn't matter because it was what he'd been looking for: the Next Right Thing. A few minutes of conversation, maybe a minute or two of work. Pushing a button, whatever that meant. Save some lives, maybe save his family. Maybe save himself.

Dex looked around the table. Saenz sipped his Diet Pepsi, turkey club forgotten in front of him. Sunny had ordered two skinless chicken breasts, steamed broccoli, and a large water, room temperature, no ice. The waitress, a tired woman who walked like her shoes were filled with gravel, looked at him like he was crazy, but Porter'd always eaten clean. Given he still looked like he could crack walnuts between bicep and forearm, he'd never stopped. Maybe it was a cosmic offset for Winkowski, who'd put on at least forty pounds since Afghanistan. Not being able to run anymore certainly wasn't doing the big guy any favors, but when you order biscuits and gravy, extra gravy, with a slab of scrapple on top and a side of tater tots, you're taking matters from bad to myocardial infarction.

They were in the back corner, a sea of open tables around them for privacy. The waitress seemed like she resented the walk, but Saenz had insisted with an easy grace that was impossible to refuse. Stu had directed them all to their seats with subtle gestures and looks, but Dex still saw it for what it was. He'd seen it too many times before to miss, even in his current state. Saenz with his back to the wall, facing the entrance. Winkowski on his right, easy to corral with a poke or a touch. Dex was straight across from Stu, for ease of engagement and reading of expressions, with Sunny a steady bedrock to Dex's left.

The team. He was part of something again, something bigger than himself.

"Can't go inside," Saenz said, getting right into it. Not leaving him time or space to second-guess.

"Right." Dex nodded, pulled along in Saenz's inexorable current. "Looks too much like a bank job."

"Cameras, silent alarms, cops," Porter added.

"Collateral," Dex added, thinking about Marty and Fred.

"Stu already said no road hijack," Winkowski grumbled, shaking Old Bay over his tots.

Dex had been thinking about it since he texted Saenz to meet him after group. Knowing what he was walking into and determined to say no, but he couldn't stop coming back to what it might look like. Saenz would have a plan, even late in the game with Dex a desperation heave as time expired.

"The parking lot," Dex said, then stopped. The waitress shuffled up with a carafe in one hand, a sweating pitcher of Diet Pepsi in the other. Saenz winked at him.

"Top yas off?" she said. "Coffee or Diet?"

Dex held out his mug, forcing a grateful smile. Stu did the same with his chunky plastic cup. His smile looked real.

"Want another wooder, hon?"

"I am fine, thank you," Porter said.

THE GUILTY SLEEP

"'Nother Flying Dog when you get a chance," Winkowski said, clinking the empty bottle with his fork. The waitress nodded and shuffled away.

"That's your third. Maybe after these refills, we do not keep inviting the potential witness back to the table," Porter said, glaring.

"Tchawant, I'm thirsty."

"That salty slop is the reason, and water rehydrates better than beer."

"Thanks for the advice, Billy Blanks—"

Saenz placed his hand gently over Winkowski's beefy forearm and the guy went quiet like someone hit his personal mute button.

"As you said, Grant. I'm thinking the parking lot's the place."

Winkowski looked away from Porter and set down his fork. He drained the dregs of his Flying Dog, gulping noisily. Porter bayoneted his last piece of broccoli like it insulted his grandmother.

"But you'll want to know about the cameras, right? Security?"

"That's one of the things only you can talk to," Saenz agreed.

Winkowski: "Give us the good stuff, bro."

"Easy," said Dex, moving the last sliver of pie crust around the plate with his fork. "Shopping center's fifteen years old. Due for a retrofit, so property management's been letting some things slide, pending the full revamp."

"Security system?" This from Saenz, hopeful.

"Exactly. Hasn't been right in over a year. Heard the super talking to Freddy about it: Family of squirrels made a nest in the junction box, chewed through the main feed. Whole parking lot's a black hole. No video. Even if the cops do get involved, or if the . . . you know . . ."

"Criminal organization?" Winkowski supplied.

Dex rolled his eyes. "Parking lot it is. What's next?"

"Former Specialist Winkowski here," Saenz said with a smile, "is Golden Oak's law enforcement support branch quartermaster. He's got a warehouse full of goodies and keys for a fleet of vehicles."

A detail clicked in Dex's head. Winkowski had always been intense, bordering on scalpel-edged. Given to unchecked outbursts, not that Dex was one to judge. You don't want a wildcard like that on the team when you're planning a significant (and significantly illegal) operation against a dangerous adversary. But if he was the supply guy, it was a no-brainer to bring him in.

"And good ol' Wink," Saenz continued, "has procured a van for us. One of the surveillance jobbers we lease to the feds. White or beige? I forget."

"White," Winkowksi replied. "Innocuous."

The waitress was back with a new beer for Winkowski. She'd brought the water pitcher, too, no ice. She topped up Porter's empty glass. He gave her a brilliant smile and she patted at her apron, flustered.

"Anything else for yas?"

"We're good, thank you," said Stu.

"Well then, here ya go, hon." She set the ticket on the table, face down in front of him. "Pay at the counter by the door, OK?"

"Thank you," said Sunny, his voice as smooth and soft as velvet. "Have a wonderful night." She blushed, the red rising from the neck of her striped shirt all the way to her cheeks. When she walked away, there was a noticeable pep in her step.

"What?" Porter said, meeting Winkowski's gaping stare. "She was nice. Water with no ice."

Stu slid a quarter into the tabletop jukebox. Pressed C/1 and Roy Orbison came on, warbling about how only the loneliest people knew how he felt. Saenz slouched back and looked at his plate, seemingly startled to find his sandwich untouched. He picked it up, took a huge bite, then pointed it at Dex.

Dex picked up the thread, extrapolating Saenz's next question. Still not fully believing he was having—*participating* in—this conversation. "Fred parks right in front of the bank. F-150, moonrock gray. Nondescript, but you can't miss it. It'll be in a reserved space. Light pole right in front of the space."

"Easy enough to pick out," Winkowski muttered. He shoveled a heaping forkful of scrapple and biscuit and gravy into his mouth.

"And every third Friday is casino Friday."

"Lucky us," said Winkowski. Of course, luck had nothing to do with it. They'd scoped this from every which way, three and four and eight dimensions—a typical Saenz op.

THE GUILTY SLEEP

"Destiny," echoed Saenz, and gave Dex another wink. "You close at three on Fridays, right?"

"Yup. And five minutes later, Freddy's out the door with a suitcase. He's in the vault before that."

"Emptying the safety deposit boxes of whatever proceeds have arrived the previous month," said Porter.

"How big?" asked Saenz.

"Rolling suitcase. Hard-sided. Not small. Magnitude bigger than the bags the courier brings in."

Stu closed his eyes, rubbed the bridge of his nose. "Wink?"

"Could be"—Winkowski closed his own eyes, sucked his teeth—"four, five hunnert?" He smiled like he'd done a half-decent party trick. Dex, who'd studiously avoided thinking about it for half a decade, was still surprised. Half a million a month in illicit proceeds moving through his bank. And he'd kept his head down, asked no questions, invited no lies. None of his business. Do the work, build a future for Daria and Rowan. Pay the bills, keep a roof over their head.

Now, maybe half that bag would be his. Pay for Rowan's surgery, pay off Daria's loans, pay down the mortgage too. Breathing space. All for this conversation and the push of a button—whatever that meant.

"Enough to pay the port guy and get our boy Frogger on a new path," he said.

"He puts the bag in the passenger compartment with him," Dex said.

"Right," said Stu. "Wouldn't trust it in the bed."

"We hit him when he's puttin' the truck in the bag," Winkowski muttered around his final mouthful of scrapple. "Er, bag in the truck."

"We don't hit him at all," Dex said.

"Figger of speech."

Roy Orbison finished, and Stu slotted another quarter. D/6. Frankie Laine came on, crooning "Moonlight Gambler."

"I mean it," Dex said. "We don't want to 'hit' him when he's putting the bags in the trunk. Freddy's a big guy. Out of shape and not as big as, say"—and he nodded at Porter, whose Under Armour polo stretched like a second skin across his chest—"but big. And he's got a custom horn in the truck. Loud. Could cause problems."

"Which is why—as you say—we aren't hitting him at all. Pardon Wink's enthusiasm." Winkowski belched. "Variables," Saenz continued. "We don't like those."

"We do not," agreed Porter. Winkowski looked disappointed, like he'd welcome all variables, wilder the better. Like he'd enjoy the opportunity to hurt someone if things broke bad.

"That's where the van comes in," Saenz said. "Freddy puts the bag in the truck, climbs in . . ."

"Van pulls up behind, blocks him in," Dex finished. "With the light pole, he won't be able to drive over the curb. He'll be blocked in."

"Exactly. Porter's wheel. Wink and I hop out the side door."

"You're on point, Sarnt?" Dex couldn't believe how seamlessly they'd slid back into operational planning mode. He could almost smell the burning trash, feel the heat of the sun, hear the call of the muezzin.

"Oh yeah." Saenz chuckled. "I knock on the window, get his attention. Doors unlock, Winkowski's on the passenger side to grab the bag, and we're off."

"Easy peasy Japanese-y," Winkowski added, popping the last tater tot into his mouth with a look of regret.

"It's going to get messy if Freddy lays on the horn. Or throws it in reverse and punches it."

"Yeah." Saenz nodded. "But what if," he said, picking up the dinner check and turning it over in his fingers with a small smile, "I planned for that?" The old team leader shone through in that smile. The consummate CI agent, the one whose greatest joy was educating junior troops on the finer points of elicitation, interrogation, counterintelligence indicators, and operational planning.

"What do you mean?"

"Your five minutes of work. The push of a button. You up for it?"

Dex looked up from his empty plate. There was something about this moment: the team, working together to solve a complex problem,

THE GUILTY SLEEP

execute the plan. It felt like being back in K-town before it all went wrong. The quiet question, the expectation, the confidence in response. There was only one reply he could give, the one they'd always given when Saenz looked to the team to get the job done. Their motto, their moniker, their identity. The team, together again.

"Blackbirds."

17

INTERLUDE: KANDAHAR, THREE YEARS AGO

DEX

On Dex's first excursion outside the wire, he almost shot a kid in the back.

They were mounting up for a quick run to the airfield to resupply. Sergeant Porter had put him in the bed of the last Hilux pickup of three.

"Watch the roofs on either side and do not let anyone drive up on us from the rear," Porter grunted. "If they get too close, draw down."

"Roger that."

Porter stared at him, motionless.

"Um . . . roger, Sergeant?" Dex tried.

Porter nodded. "If they keep coming, light them up."

"Got it." And then, a split second too late, "Got it, Sarnt."

"Enunciate."

"Got it, Sergeant." Sunny was a stickler, even downrange. The opposite of Saenz, who seemed willing to run a relaxed shop as long as they got results. Modeling the Special Forces team who occupied the ground floor—a bunch of tanned, rangy dudes with gray-streaked beards and still, calm eyes that saw everything.

They exited the governor's palace, passed the Shrine of Muhammad's Shirt, and it was immediately apparent Dex wasn't

THE GUILTY SLEEP

going to be able to keep anyone from pulling too close. The traffic was insane, worse than D.C. or Baltimore by a circus tent mile. Old Russian compacts, slightly newer Mercedes sedans, and ubiquitous Toyota pickups vied for space with brightly painted jingle trucks. Orbiting these, remoras among sharks, flowed streams of motor-cycles, scooters, donkey-drawn carts, bicycles, and even pedestri-ans who danced fearlessly with death at every step. Surging wildly through this sea of color and noise were the omnipresent tuk-tuks: small, three-wheeled taxis built on a motorcycle frame; driver sat in front of a small, covered passenger compartment, big enough for two but usually holding three or four. There were stop signs and stop-lights and sweating, blue-shirted traffic cops standing at the occa-sional corner, ostensibly enforcing rules that surely existed but were routinely and extravagantly ignored.

The Afghans paid the American convoy no regard. Half a dozen near-collisions before they'd gone half a mile, horns an unrelenting chorus. Dex sat with his back against the cab and braced one foot against a wheel well. He kept the barrel of his rifle generally angled behind, but up at the sky. His eyes roved from rooftop to rooftop, up one side of the road and down the other, then swept across the arc behind the truck. His sinuses ached with the constant repetition.

He understood why Porter put him back here. He was supposed to meet the insanity face to face, see how impossible the situation was. A microcosm of their position in the city. Most of these people only wanted to live, take care of their families. A small subset wanted to actively help the Americans, and a very few wanted nothing more than to kill Dex and his friends, preferably via torture. It was impos-sible to tell which was which.

"Hey, America!" yelled a kid on a bright purple bike. Anywhere from twelve to an undernourished fifteen. He was pedaling behind the truck, steering with one hand and waving with another, smiling wide and gap-toothed.

"Hey!" Dex yelled back, smiling and waving. Hearts and minds.

"Candy?" the kid hollered hopefully.

Winkowski had mentioned this as a certainty before they headed out, rolling his eyes. "Ignore 'em and they'll give up after a bit," he'd said. Dex had stashed a roll of MRE candy in one of his vest pockets.

"Yeah, hang on," Dex said, digging for it. One friend at a time. The boy pedaled harder, getting right alongside the truck.

"Allahu Akbar!" the kid shouted, and dropped something dark and oblong into the bed. It skittered toward Dex's boots.

Dex pounded his free hand against the window of the cab behind him. "Grenade!" he bellowed. He lunged for the thing. The truck slammed to a halt and it slid between his feet and thumped into the Kevlar padding behind him. He was never going to get it in time. He flung himself over the edge of the bed, hearing the truck's doors opening behind him. With luck, the guys would clear the explosion in time and the Kevlar-padded bed would contain most of the blast.

The arterial push of traffic arced around and away from the truck as they scattered. Dex caught a glimpse of dust-colored shirt and a flash of metallic purple. The kid was across the street, heading for an alley. Dex ran after him. There was a high, thready beep and a scrunch of tires as a tuk-tuk swerved to avoid him, coming up off one of its back wheels and nearly tipping over, the driver spewing a lively stream of emphatically uncomplimentary Pashto.

There was another honk, deeper and more assertive, and Dex skidded to a halt; a pickup slashed by him, the side mirror nearly clipping his elbow. Soon as it was past, he was on the move again. The kid was well down the alley. A packed minibus blazed by right in front of him, blowing hot diesel grit in his face.

He made the side of the road and the alley opened up before him, miraculously deserted except for the rapidly shrinking figure of the bomber and his technicolor ride. Clear as a lane at the shooting range. There was no time to think about whether he had it in him to kill someone, much less a boy, much less shooting him in the back as he rode away. There was no time to think about anything except sight picture, breath control, and trigger squeeze. Dex raised the rifle, socketed it into his shoulder, and aimed at the kid's back. Started pulling

THE GUILTY SLEEP

the trigger just as the little punk ripped a hard right and disappeared around a corner.

The whole thing had taken seven seconds. Which, he suddenly realized, was double the average fuse time of a hand grenade.

He turned, suddenly and acutely aware he was a soldier in a foreign land, someone had just tried to kill him, and he was alone—separated from his friends by a zipping chaos that halted for no one. He repeated his dancing, stutter-step journey back to the trucks. Porter and Saenz were conferring at the bed of Dex's Hilux. Saenz was holding something behind his back. He beckoned Dex over with a lifted chin. His mouth was all twisted up and for a second Dex thought he was furious—Porter's face was stony as a biblical altar—but when he got closer, he realized Saenz was suppressing a grin.

"Saw you crossing the street in my rearview. Some moves there, Specialist Grant."

"Kid got away, Sarnt."

"Probably for the best," Saenz replied, holding up the grenade. Only it wasn't. It was an ovoid rock, painted drab green and crudely marked up with black lines like an old-school pineapple grenade.

"I almost plugged that kid in the back," Dex gasped. He bent over, hands on his knees.

"Heya, Grant," Sully hollered from the next truck up, "can't believe ya made it across and back in one piece—some wicked footwork theah." He giggled.

"Looked like Frogger," added Winkowski. "You know, 'at arcade game. Lil' guy hoppin' across mad traffic, tryna not get hisself splatted."

Ol' Dirty Le Batard hooted approval. "Think we found your call sign, Grant!"

◾

Dex is thinking about that moment—the kid and his purple bike, the painted rock, the death-dance in the street, starting to pull the trigger, almost sending himself to hell—as he climbs out of the pickup at the ANA compound.

This op is a fresh start. He can do some good work with Fatima and the women at the compound. Get everyone calling him something other than Frogger. The nickname caught on fast, but he might get out of it yet.

Saenz strides forward, flanked by Jalal and Porter. The dagarman holds out one massive hand, the other over his heart. He smiles broadly and shakes Saenz's hand. Dex and the rest of the crew gather round and Saenz—via Jalal—introduces everyone. There are smiles and nods and the dagarman beckons them inside. The Blackbirds climb back into their trucks, and one of the ANA soldiers points toward a long, low-slung building in the middle of an acre of dust and gravel. They park in front of it, all in a line.

The dagarman and his deputy, a little guy with a wispy beard, confer with Saenz and Jalal, then the Afghans head toward the building and Saenz huddles the Blackbirds.

"He's going to show us the cache. Shipping containers buried on the other side of the main building," Saenz says.

"They discovered it when they were digging the trench for a new toilet," Jalal says and chuckles.

"Found more than they bargained for," Saenz agrees. "Everyone look suitably impressed, OK? Then, to work. Jalal and I'll sit for tea with the boss and make nicey-nicey, arrange for EOD to come out and blow the cache. Frogger, take Fatima and Ahn and see what you can get from the women. Everyone else gets to watch the ANA boys empty the cache and be impressed with their martial prowess."

"Photos and inventory, too, not just smoking and joking," adds Porter, ever the killjoy. "Sullivan, camera duty."

From the corner of the building, the dagarman's deputy chatters something at Jalal, gesturing.

"Hey-hey-hey, we better go, you guys," says Jalal. He never calls anyone by their names. It's always "you guys" or "hey, man" with him, but there's no malice behind it. Only a slightly soft befuddlement that would spell doom for anyone even slightly less competent. As it goes, he's become some combination of friend, coworker, and mascot. According to Saenz's briefing when Dex first arrived, they've had nothing but wins with Jalal as lead interpreter. He's got good instincts and his own stable of highly reliable sources.

They follow the deputy around the main building, and they don't have to act impressed. Dex isn't sure what's more amazing, the size of the cache or the fact it's been here almost two decades without being discovered. The hide is three shipping containers side-by-side-by-side, buried under two feet of lifeless Afghan dirt.

The ANA have dug out a broad entryway down to the container entrances, probably by hand; there's no heavy equipment to be seen. That's all the better—between the likelihood of old booby traps and even older munitions, the whole thing's a literal powder keg. Sooner EOD can get out and safely blow the ordnance, the better for everyone.

The Afghans have formed a human chain and are casually passing the contents up to a huge pile against the wall of the compound. Right now, they're hauling old 107-millimeter Chinese-made rockets out of the middle container and the Afghans are making light work of the forty-five-pound munitions. Next to the growing pile of rockets are a dozen teetering stacks of Vietnam-era American claymore mines and a pallet of 7.62 rifle ammunition crates blazoned with Cyrillic lettering. A rusty melting pot of destruction, waiting for a hard jostle to go off. The skin on Dex's forearms stipples in spite of the heat. He won't be sorry to head in the other direction.

"Grant," says Sunny Porter, who steadfastly refuses to use nicknames, "peel off with Ahn and Fatima. Jalal said he"—Porter nods at the deputy—"will take you to the women's room."

"Roger, Sergeant," Dex and Ahn chorus.

"Frogger, take lead. Show me something," adds Saenz softly. Dex hasn't realized he'd been listening. He and Ahn head toward the deputy, who's standing in the shade of the main building, smiling and nodding as they approach. There's another ANA soldier with him, a young guy. His face is pocked with acne scars and his eyes are that startling green you sometimes see in the south. Probably the babysitter,

118   **JEREMY D. BAKER**

the ANA troop who'll sit with Dex and Ahn to make sure the American barbarians don't exceed the bounds of honor.

The deputy leads them across the dusty open field of the compound's center toward the opposite wall. The young soldier follows, and, via Fatima, introduces himself as Habibullah.

There are rooms built out from the compound wall, and the deputy leads them to the biggest. It juts from the corner and is dug a few feet into the earth to help keep the interior cool. There are a few horizontal windows near the roof, and just one door. It's painted UN peacekeeper helmet blue, but as they get closer Dex sees an earlier paint job showing through, a kind of whirling underpattern the color of dried seaweed.

The deputy motions to the door, smiling and nodding like a marionette. Fatima thanks the deputy in Pashto and opens the door. Dex lowers his head and steps in, Ahn on his heels. He feels the deputy's eyes on him, and then the shadows and still air swallow him up.

The first thing he hears is a fly buzzing. Tap-tap-tapping at one of the high windows.

THURSDAY

18

PLACEMENT

DEX

It was a workday like any other, except it was about as far from a typical workday as you could get. A perspective shift of interplanetary proportions. Still, at this moment, it was all talk. Planning and conjecture. War games. Nothing more than a fistfight in a parking lot and a conversation of hypotheticals between some war buddies over coffee and pie. Plausibly deniable.

Later today, it would become real. Action would be taken—*Dex* would take action, let's not sound passive about it—setting the stage for tomorrow. New horizons, and Dex would be a different person having crossed that terminus. A criminal, if ripping off criminals was a crime. A betrayer, if betraying a man who launders money for criminals counts as treachery.

It was a wonder he could function. Start with exhaustion: They'd been at the Minuteman until after midnight, finalizing the operational plan, looking at every angle, holding the thing up to the light and turning it over in their hands and looking for flaws.

Laying out the middle game, the part where they go to ground with the money. Sunny and Wink and Stu laying up and lying low with the cash at a safe house, counting out the future. Holding tight until the next day. Dex, apart from the others. The inside man staying inside the parameters of usual behavior, drawing no attention from Freddy or the organization behind Freddy.

After the diner, back at his apartment, he'd tried to sleep. It was a losing game. His mind was a mechanical rabbit racing around a greyhound track. He couldn't stop thinking about what came next. The predicate success for the entire op. His five minutes of work, which would keep the critical moment—the actual money grab—static and controlled. It would eliminate the possibility of Freddy smashing his truck into the van or sounding his horn for help.

The push of a button, for a chance to save Jalal, redeem himself, help his family, earn half a suitcase of cash. Two hundred thousand dollars, maybe more.

Finally, somewhere in the lost, inchoate hour between three and four, sleep crept up on him and pulled him under.

And Dex did not, for the first time in three years, dream.

■

The alarm hit at seven thirty and brought him up out of the calm nothing he'd been chasing since he got back from K-town. He was thankful for two things: the untroubled sleep—he trembled with the wonder of it—and that he'd remembered the timer on the coffeepot before he went to bed. The smell did as much to wake him as the alarm, and he was going to need the caffeine.

This wasn't the exhaustion from a slow, grinding slog of another day in an endless cycle, followed by drinking too much to try to fall asleep, only to lie awake staring at the shadowed corners, only to find eventual sleep haunted by visions of blood and blue mesh and the sound of a tap-tap-tapping fly. Waking in a silent scream, tearing at his covers. Rinse and repeat until he couldn't think of anything but going to Terrence and getting his pistol back.

No, this was different. This was an exhaustion from too little sleep, colored with exhilaration that the sleep he'd had was clean and clear,

THE GUILTY SLEEP

and steeped in the fact he had a job to do. Something that wasn't a holding pattern. Something that *mattered*, would help someone who needed to be helped. Would help his family. The next right thing.

He finished the pot before he left and gratefully drank the coffee Marty brought as they waited for Freddy to pull in. Tried to focus on their usual banter. Tried not to give off any "hey, I'm about to help my old war buddies steal a load of cash from the criminal organization you didn't know our boss is money laundering for" vibes.

The bells of Saint Patrick sounded and Freddy presaged his presence with a long, triumphant blat of the air horn. Dismounted and sauntered up with the typical soggy quips.

Dex went through the motions. Counting out his drawer, firing up the computer, chatting with Marty. Serving the occasional customer.

There were the other things, though. Watching Freddy. Walking by his boss's office and making sure the truck keys ended up where they always did, a waist-high row of pegs on the wall just inside the office door. Checking *BurnR*, the secure comms app Saenz'd installed on his cell, to see if Winkowski had come through on his end yet.

"What's up with you today?" Marty asked. It was midmorning and he'd checked his phone, he thought surreptitiously, for the fifth time. "You're a million miles away."

Dex pushed his hair back from his face, rubbing at his eyes. "Guess I am."

"Still waiting to hear back from Daria?"

She'd thrown him a lifeline. He liked Marty, didn't want to lie to her. "Yeah. Trying to see if she'll meet up after work. Community Pond Park."

"Good spot, 'specially since Rowan's so into animals."

"The ducks, yeah?"

"Uh-huh. 'Manda got all into bird watching during lockdown, right? Heard there's some kind of rare duck been spotted at the pond. Down from Central Park in New York, maybe, 'cause that was the last place anyone saw one. Her Discord's *all* blown up on it."

"Ro would love that."

"You should bring something for her to feed them with. Not bread; never feed a duck bread. Bad for their digestion. Get a bag of frozen peas or a head of lettuce."

Dex nodded, and felt his phone vibrate. Two quick buzzes, the *BurnR* calling card.

"Sounds like a plan."

"And, you know, be chill." She nodded at his pocket. He wondered if she'd heard. "You know how he gets if he thinks we're on our phones all day."

Dex wasn't thrilled the next part depended on Winkowski. The guy was clearly in loose cannon territory—not that Dex could throw any boulders around his own glass sandcastle. Only, he'd feel more comfortable with Saenz on the other end, or even Sunny Porter's brooding stone façade. But Saenz and Porter were Baltimore-bound to meet with the bent port director. Laying the foundation for the payoff to get Jalal and his family off the boat and through the port. And it was Winkowski who had the Golden Oak supply end locked down, from the van to the thing they needed for this morning.

"Dex?" Marty thumped his shoulder. "She'll come."

He smiled back at her, hoping it looked real. If he could get this next bit right, he'd have the bandwidth to think about whether Daria would bring Rowan to the park—she still hadn't texted him back. He was trying to keep things compartmented. So far it was holding. Barely. He was vibrating from caffeine and tension and the disbelief it was all happening.

"Freddy wants a coffee and a donut before he tackles the weekly. You want anything?"

"I'm good," Dex lied. "Thanks, Marty."

The door had barely closed behind her and his phone was out, *BurnR* open and displaying the message.

Winkowski: It's a go.

19

FOLLOWING FIRES

TURNER

"How does the money side work, anyway?" Slade asked. "Not the collection piece, but after? Like, so five-oh don't catch on or whatever."

They were en route for Turner's regular check-in with Angie at Sunrise Vista. It was his first time with Slade in tow, and the kid was continuing to surprise him by showing an interest in the business.

"Five, ten years, this stuff'll all be cryptocurrency and, whatever it's called, chainblocks. We're gonna need to change with the times," Turner said. He was warming to this whole Obi-Wan Kenobi thing. "Young buck like you should be able to help with that, but for now . . ."

Money laundering 101, as Turner explained: An illicit cash business needs a licit cash business to hide the capital flow from the G. There's a dozen ways to do it, but Angelita had done what Turner considered the best—get in tight with a legit financial institution from the jump. Pine Hill Bank and Freddy House. The bank keeps your cash pickups in its safety deposit boxes. Informal escrow and instant security, courtesy of a concrete vault no competition can touch and no lawman's looking into.

That's the hold. Next comes the wash.

Once a month, your pet bank manager takes the money to one of four different casinos in Maryland, Delaware, or New Jersey. Buys four hundred K in chips, give or take, and gambles ten percent. That's his cut, win or lose. After a day at the tables, he cashes out. A check for the remaining ninety percent. Three hundred and sixty K, or thereabouts. Deposits said check to the Cooke Construction Solutions business account, tagged as receivables, well, received, for any one of a dozen construction projects underway in central Maryland at any given time. Five untraceable million a year, on top of legit construction profits. Give or take.

The bank manager's a play-dumb kind of guy, but not as dumb as he plays. Doesn't invite undue attention. He's been cleaning for them half a dozen years with nary a whisper of detection. It's turbocharged the growth of CCS, which has in turn turbocharged the ability of Angie's syndicate to spread its drug and gun business south all the way to Wheaton and east to the outskirts of Baltimore, with a planned push up to Pittsburgh in the coming days.

"You're not just the bag man," Slade said. Turner chewed that one for a minute.

"Guess not. S'where I started, so it still feels right."

"You're like a . . . consigliere or something."

"Sure."

"A trusted lieutenant. Redneck Paulie Walnuts."

"Fine."

"If I'm going to take over for my aunt someday, I have to pay attention to you." Slade was staring out the windshield, but also watching Turner from the corner of his eye.

"You're learning," Turner said, though there was something about the boy's tone he didn't like.

He was going to have to pay attention to Slade too.

■

They arrived at Sunrise Vista in late morning, and as he drove out from the tree-covered approach into the open wound of the

THE GUILTY SLEEP

construction site, the sun beat at Turner's eyes like he owed it money. There was a CCS trailer at the edge of the meadow to the left, where it could catch a modicum of shade from the forest until almost midday. Turner parked at the demarcation line between sun and shadow. As they approached the trailer, he didn't look toward the main pit. The foundation, poured two days ago.

"Still think your music sucks," Slade muttered, but there was no real heat in it.

"And I despair for your generation," Turner replied equably. "Annie Lennox kills."

The trailer door opened and Florencio's cousin Lael stepped out on the small wooden landing. Angie'd personally recruited the two former Kaibiles from the Guatemalan diaspora down in Aspen Hill. Where Florencio was tall, almost willowy, with jet black hair slicked back into a ponytail, Lael was thickset, with a shaved head set directly into his heavy shoulders, no neck to speak of. The guy's work shirt was halfway unbuttoned, revealing the Kaibil pendant he always wore. Turner and the cousins knew each other, had all worked for Angie for years, but they didn't *know* each other. Like vicious dogs in a pack, they sniffed around each other and occasionally bared their teeth, but they watched and followed Angie, the alpha.

"Miz Cooke here?"

Lael raised his arm and pointed at the wrought iron archway to their left. It was ten feet tall, pitted with age and rust and listing to port. Near the top of the curve, the line of the arch split in parallel, and the words *Sunrise Vista* were worked into the metal between the lines. There was a dirt track under the arch leading up into the woods.

Turner set off, feeling the Kaibil watch him. Slade scrambled to keep up.

"Where we going?"

"Your aunt's up the hill. At Sunrise Vista. She likes to go up there sometimes."

"I thought Sunrise Vista is the place we're building here for the oldens."

"She named the retirement home after the landmark."

"Never heard of it."

Sunrise Vista waited a half-mile up the shadowed trail. Turner's back was giving the occasional twinge on his longer strides, so he slowed—he hoped imperceptibly—and told the story.

In the late nineteenth century, there was a steel baron from up Pittsburgh way, name of Silas Verritt. Rich as Croesus—"Who?" "Never mind."—and twice as eccentric. Deep into spiritualism, deeper into secret society stuff. Skull and Bones at Yale, Freemasonry until he decided it wasn't esoteric enough, on to Rosicrucian mysticism and its fringiest elements. A man given to lust for wealth and an avid consumer of conspiracy, yes, but devoted and loyal to his wife and six children. Used to come south to take in the clean air on the downslope of the Alleghenies, away from the smog and soot of the steel town. Bought a thousand-acre swath, including this exact spot. Rumor had it there was once a mineral spring nearby, but Verritt's will stipulated it be filled after his death so no one else could use it.

Ol' Silas was a firm believer in the afterlife, and he wanted to ensure his family stuck together in the great beyond. That's why he built Sunrise Vista. Half temple, half mausoleum, all Rosicrucian symbolism. Turner pointed out the first set of stone steps heading up the front slope of the ridge. Eight stairs, corresponding to the eight-point compass rose, part of the order's hallmark rosy cross sigil. Nine more steps after a switchback, lined with rose-colored quartz imported from who knows where, corresponding to the nine strata of the Rosicrucian Well of Initiation in Sintra.

At the top of the ridge, in a small clearing Angie re-cleared when CCS purchased the site, a rotunda fifty feet in diameter, cast in concrete. Open to the air, with sculpted cement pillars at regular intervals around the circumference. Ten pillars, corresponding to the ten fruits of the Tree of Pansophia, a representation of the catalogue of universal hidden knowledge.

"How you know all this weird stuff, man?"

"Your aunt figured it out," Turner said.

"But, like, why?"

THE GUILTY SLEEP

"She bought this land three years ago. We found this spot together, when we first walked the site. Her first order of business was to clear all the brush out; second was to learn what it actually was."

"Uh-huh."

"We looked into the old land records, found Verritt, and the rest was research. She does a lot of business planning up there. Told me it focuses her on the important stuff."

Slade was unmoved, at least until the last chapter of the story. The part about how Silas Verritt loved his family so much he demanded they all be buried together. In Sunrise Vista. He'd put it in his will. After he died, his wife, two sons, and four daughters would each receive access to a substantial trust so long as they filed their own wills stipulating they be buried at Sunrise Vista too. See, in the center of the rotunda there was a dais, also cast from concrete. Around the dais, organized like the seats at a dinner party, were eight concrete chairs framed in steel from one of Verritt's mills. One was larger than the rest—the patriarch's, of course. One was slightly smaller, for the wife, and six smaller still for the children. The frames started out empty. When Silas passed, he was cremated and his ashes mixed into concrete, which was poured into his frame. And so it went for each family member. First for the oldest son, who was killed in the Great War, then the youngest (Spanish Flu), the wife, and so on, until each chair was filled.

"You're saying my aunt likes to do her deep thinking in a graveyard."

"I think she considers it a monument to family and to will."

"I do," Angelita said. She appeared from behind a tree at the top of the slope, looking down as they climbed the final few feet. She looked like she belonged in the woods, with her soft flannel work shirt and brown eyes and dark hair piled messily on top of her head. The warm, chubby-cheeked grandmotherly smile. A forest sprite who'd guide lost and weary travelers to a safe homeward trail. Or the stony bottom of a riverbed, if you crossed her.

There was a flicker of movement to the left. Florencio, stepping back into the dappled shadows, holstering a pistol.

They reached the top and Turner watched Slade take in the rotunda and the chairs. He seemed, at last, suitably impressed. One of the chairs, Verritt's by the size, had Angie's insulated tea mug set in front of it. There was a green hard-covered notepad—her business book, and *not* the one for CCS—sitting perfectly angled with a mechanical pencil keeping her page. A bible, leather-bound and worn, set just so next to the notebook. It was open somewhere in the middle. Old Testament, no surprise. The thin pages stirred in a breeze that whispered through the trees.

Angie returned to the table and beckoned them to take seats. She pointed Turner to the wife's grave, not, he thought, because of any order of preference but because trying to fold himself into one of the smallest chairs would have been impossible. Slade fit just fine, and, watching Turner out of the corner of his eye, he took the one on the other side of his aunt.

"Nice spot, Aunt Angie," Slade said. She patted his forearm and gave him half a smile, then looked at Turner. Her gaze was a physical weight flitting across his face.

Turner glanced at Slade, then back to Angelita.

"Report, Melchizedek."

Angie waited, an eyebrow raised. An implicit question. He knew what she was asking, and he bowed his head in assent. "I think it's something. I didn't want it to be, but I can't shake it."

"What're you talking about?" Slade asked.

"Listen to advice and accept instruction, that you may gain wisdom in the future," Angie intoned. Something from Proverbs, probably. Slade looked down at the table. Angie slammed her palm flat on the cover of her business book. It made a sound like a gunshot, and Slade started so hard he would've fallen out of his chair if it weren't for the armrests.

"Pay attention, nephew of mine."

Slade bobbed his head, eyes wide.

"You know how long Melchizedek has worked for me?"

"Yeah."

"You know where he was before?"

"Out West. California, he said."

THE GUILTY SLEEP

131

Angelita inclined her head toward Turner. "But you're a Maryland man, aren't you, Melchizedek?"

"Eastern Shore, originally."

"Why were you in California?"

"I guess you'd call it trying to make my way. Staying mostly legit. Had some trouble back home, see," he said, directing his words to Slade, "and I was trying to keep my nose clean. Unfortunately, I never was much good at that."

"Good at plenty else, though, aren't you," Angie said.

Turner inclined his head again. *I suppose*, it said. And *thanks, I guess.*

"And things broke a certain way, and Melchizedek ended up a guest of the state."

"Lompoc," Turner added.

"What for?" Slade asked. The wrong question.

"Irrelevant," Angie replied. "What's relevant is California's inmate fire service program."

"He said something about that."

"Now listen," said Angie. "Whoever is wise, let him attend to these things."

Slade nodded. His eyes flicked to Turner's arms, the burn scars swirling under the prison ink.

"Melchizedek was a part of that program. For seven of his eight-year sentence, if memory serves."

"Yes, ma'am," Turner said. That final year didn't bear thinking on; it had been a long and painful recuperation.

"You were good at it, weren't you? A commendation from the warden and a referral for early parole."

"Yes, ma'am." He didn't like talking about it, and willed her to reach the point.

"The point is," Angie said, reading his mind as always, "Melchizedek developed a second sense when he was fighting those California wildfires. He doesn't like to talk about it, and I'm guessing he doesn't like to think about it all that much," she continued, shooting him a smile, "but I dragged it out of him during his probationary period with the business, and I've seen it borne out over time. And because of that sense, he usually makes the right decisions to help protect the business, to move the organization forward in accordance with my vision."

"OK, I get it," Slade said. He tried to look chagrined, but it came on more like constipation.

"He also," Angelita continued, "seems to have a sense of when things are coming around that might burn us in the ass. A carryover from the firefighting days. Is that fair?"

"Sure, boss."

"How would you describe it?"

"Hard to say. Change in the wind, a shift of scents. A feeling the fire's turned, maybe reignited in an area you just cleared. Behind you, yeah? Something that says you're about to be trapped in a ring of flames."

"What did you call that?" Angie took a slow sip of tea.

"A following fire."

"Yes, that's right. I like that," she said. "I will send a fire upon the walls, and it shall devour all strongholds." Her smile was a little more genuine this time. She stared at Slade, and while her expression didn't perceptibly change, it somehow did. Colder and harder, without a single twitch of a muscle. "Tell us, then. Is there a following fire?"

"I think so, ma'am. I've had this sense, last couple weeks. Bein' watched. Nothing too solid until yesterday, and even then . . ."

Angie made a *continue* gesture.

"When we were picking up at the coffee stand, there was a car. Behind us at the edge of the parking lot, half around the corner. Where I'd watch from, if I was watchin' me. Think there were a couple guys in it, maybe three. Saw a cloud of smoke come out the back window. No one got in or out while we were there."

"What kind of car?"

"Sedan. Not one of the county unmarkeds though."

Angie made a scoffing noise. The county sheriff was so deep in her pocket he could sublet space for a tidy profit. "Feds?"

THE GUILTY SLEEP

"Don't think. It was older, a little more beat up than they like to use on a mobile trail team, but not so beat up as ones they use for static observation."

"One of the Bawlmer gangs, then. Making a move."

"If I saw aright—and it was only a glimpse, mind you—at least one of them was a white boy. Be highly unusual."

"Hmm."

"Might be nothin', boss."

"But it might not be nothing."

"Yes."

"And if they were by the coffee stand—your last stop before the bank?"

Turner nodded

"They're after the collect, if they're after anything."

Slade caught up. "You think someone's trying to rip you off?" Angie doled out a soft look and a nod, a miser clinking a gold coin into a beggar's palm. Slade smiled gratefully.

"OK." She clapped her hands together, rubbed them briskly. It sounded like a piece of wood being sanded. "I can't spare Florencio and Lael. We're starting the push up to Pittsburgh tonight, so they'll be out of pocket. And we must be wise as vipers. Nephew of mine. Are you serious about being more involved in the family business?"

"Yes, ma'am," Slade said. His voice was an echo of Turner's respectful responses. He was trying.

"Your crew of dime store hoods—any of them dependable enough to provide a little muscle?"

"Oh, sure," Slade replied eagerly. "There's Mike—" Angie cut him off with a gesture.

"Spin up a couple you trust. No more than four. They'll stay under your direction."

"I'll—"

"—and *you* will stay under Melchizedek's direction. Understood?"

Slade deflated slightly, but attempted a recovery. "Yes, Auntie."

"Good." And then she murmured, "If a thief is caught while breaking in and is struck so that he dies, there will be no bloodguiltiness on your account."

"What?"

"We do what we need to do," Turner said.

Angelita's eyes were still as a forest pond. "With the Pittsburgh expansion, there's no room for shrinkage unless we dip into the emergency fund, and I refuse to do that. Keep on the money. Keep on Freddy all the way to the casino and back. And keep me posted," she said.

Slade followed Turner down the hill. He waited until they were halfway and started regaling Turner with tales of his crew and their exploits. Mostly chasing girls and rolling tourists at the Inner Harbor in Baltimore.

"These're just the guys for this," Slade said for the third time as they reached the El Camino. His face was alive with excitement at the prospect of what he'd surely consider action, but Turner only considered a pain in the ass.

"That's as reassuring as a warm seat in a porta-john," Turner said. He climbed in, slammed the door. Eased back in his seat and turned the key. The engine rumbled to life. Slade said something, but Turner gunned the engine, drowning him out. The El Camino shot across the brittle summer grass and down the path through the trees, falling into shadow.

20

ACCESS

DEX

The next *BurnR* message from Winkowski read, In possession. And then, En route.

ETA? Dex replied.

45

30 is better. Best chance then.

Winkowski replied with a cannibalistic anatomical impossibility. Dex slid the phone back in his pocket, resolving to not touch the thing until the next double buzz, which would tell him Winkowski was in the parking lot, ready to go.

Next for Dex: Billy Ripken and the keys, but not yet. Everything had to follow the usual flow of events. That meant coffee and a donut and Freddy starting the weekly report, *then* Billy and the keys. He straightened the already razor-sharp counter space around him. Filled his stapler. Did a quick count of his drawer. Twice. Marty came back with the coffee and the donut for Freddy, a frosted eye roll for Dex as she delivered the goods.

He looked at the clock on his computer. Then the one in the corner of the lobby, an honest-to-goodness grandfather clock, all stained oak and brass and brontosaural pendulum. Ten thirty. Freddy would drink his coffee and eat his donut for the next half hour, scrolling through Drudge and Barstool and TMZ on his desktop. Fortifying himself for the books, which he ran every Thursday between eleven and noon if it went smoothly, eleven and sometimes up to closing if it didn't. Always with muttered curses and general sturm und drang. He'd be distracted, even more so if Billy cooperated.

"Marty!" he hollered from his office. "How many creamers?"

"Three," she shouted back. Then, in normal volume, "Like always, you ingrate."

"It's too strong," Freddy said, sticking his head out. "Will ya go get me another?"

"She just went. I'll get it," said Dex, over the start of Marty's caustic reply, hoping he didn't sound too eager.

"Long as *someone* does. Got heartburn, and coffee this strong's gonna sting. Need to smooth the edges off."

"No worries, Fred. Be right back."

As soon as he was out the door, he broke his promise to himself and whipped his phone out. Sent a *BurnR* note to Winkowski.

Bought you 7 mins.

He kept the phone out as he walked down the strip mall to the little coffee place next to Villa Maya. He could have skipped the line and grabbed a creamer from the basket by the register, but he waited. The phone buzzed, but it wasn't Winkowski. It was Daria.

We can do 4:15 at CP park.

It took him three tries to get his fingers to cooperate.

Great! Allegedly there's a rare duck.

Ro will love that.

Can't wait to see her. How was the eye doc?

Good. She's excited to see you too, so
don't flake on us.

THE GUILTY SLEEP

> I'll be there. Promise.

He waited, but she didn't respond. Not even the three dots.

"What can I get for you?" asked the teenager behind the counter, professional boredom lacquering his voice. He'd reached the front of the line without realizing it.

"Can I grab a couple creamers?"

"Sure," the kid replied, nearly asleep.

He was almost back to the bank when the double buzz tripped. Twice. The first message was from Winkowski, a simple k. The other from Saenz.

> Status?

> In progress, Dex replied. Stand by.

Another message, Winkowski again. 9 out.

> 10-4. Watch the truck.

He could make it work. He stowed the phone, nodded at Marty, and brought Freddy his extra creamers.

"Wasn't sure, so I got you plain, hazelnut, and vanilla."

"Lookit you, gunnin' for promotion."

"Assistant manager?"

"Assistant *to* the manager." Freddy never got tired of that one.

"Pretty sure Marty and I already fill the role."

"Marty and *me*. Now leave me in peace for a few. Gotta center myself."

On his way out, Dex glanced at the hook by the door to make sure Freddy's keys were still there. The fob was black, blazoned with the blue Ford oval. House key, bank front door key, vault key, safety deposit master key, and a couple smaller ones. Make a jingle if he muffed it.

He turned right, headed to the break room instead of his station. Billy Ripken brooded in the middle of the dim space, a fat plastic altar to the commerce gods of the olden '90s. The printer-scanner-copier was marginally effective and often broken, and they pretended this was why they'd named it as they did. And because Freddy insisted it be kept around, much like Cal Senior had protected his real-life son, the machine's namesake Orioles second baseman. The real reason they called it Billy Ripken was because every time the monstrosity sprung a toner leak, jammed, or otherwise broke down, Freddy bellowed the infamous two-word phrase that mysteriously appeared on the knob of the real Billy Ripken's bat in the first, uncensored run of his 1989 baseball card. Marty had found one of the second-run cards online, which had a small black square superimposed over the notorious words. She'd taped it next to the "start" button.

They all hated Billy, but Freddy's hate was tinged with the grudging respect of a familiar adversary. Probably like his marriages. And in about five minutes, Freddy was going to print the weekly.

Dex knelt before Billy. Put his hands on *Tray 1 | Letter*. The air-conditioning hummed and ticked. The refrigerator gurgled. Enough background noise, probably. He put his thumbs against the front of the drawer, index fingers behind the corners, prying at the gaps. Barely enough pressure to ease the drawer open a crack without the usual twang of tired springs. Once it came free, he inched it forward. Licked his thumb and forefinger and eased out the top piece of paper. Slowly, he folded it against his chest. Slipped it inside his shirt to soften the noise, then crossed his arms and hunched forward. The paper crinkled and crunched, the sound muffled against his skin. He pulled the sheet out and unfolded it. It was creased like the surface of a dry lake bed. He slid it carefully back into the tray, a cellulose time bomb. He pressed the drawer closed, flinching when it latched with a rheumy clack.

Back at his counter, he listened to Marty talk about the Central Park duck that had been spotted at Community Pond, and all the associated drama on her girlfriend's Discord channel. *Bird people*. His eyes darted between the clock on his computer screen and the venerable grandfather in the corner of the lobby.

Exactly two minutes later, he felt the *BurnR* double zap against his thigh, which could only mean Winkowski was in place in the parking lot. Exactly two minutes after that, he heard Freddy's empty coffee cup *thunk* into the trash can in his office, and exactly two minutes after *that*, Freddy screamed the infamously foul phrase from the knob of Billy Ripken's bat.

"Oh, here we go," Marty muttered.

"Martyyy!"

"You bellowed, boss?"

"Billy's on the fritz again!"

"Never would've guessed."

"What are the odds?" Dex added at the same time.

"I gotta get these reports printed," Freddy whined, poking his head out his office door. "Gimme a hand, wouldja?"

Freddy considered himself a Billy Ripken whisperer and Marty his faithful sidekick-slash-apprentice. Dex had a bad run of luck with ol' Bill a few years back—a loose toner cap that cost Freddy his second-best (worst) tie and a built-in stapler misfeed that had the repair guy nearly in tears, so he was no longer invited to the corrective action parties.

"Wish me luck," Marty sighed, and followed Freddy around the corner. Dex waited until he heard one of Billy's access panels being opened, followed by more curses from Freddy. He sent a message to Winkowski.

One minute.

"Now that's a paper jam if I ever seen one," Freddy hollered. "You oughta come see this, Dex. It's dang near a worka art."

"I'll keep an eye on things up here, boss," Dex called, already sidling around the counter and making his way to Freddy's office. He paused at the opening, trying to watch the hall to the kitchen on one side and the front doors of the bank to the other. Wouldn't do to be seen going in or coming out. He reached inside the doorjamb, feeling for the keys. Slowly. If he grazed them, it'd jangle like a tambourine. Chanced a quick peek around the frame, saw he was a couple inches low, then just went for it. Closed his hand around the fob, trapping the keys against each other and his skin. Hardly any noise, and what there was couldn't have been heard over the banging and curses coming from down the hall.

"Pull it, Freddy."

"I *am* pulling it. Whaddaya think I'm doin'?"

"Straight through, though, not like that or you'll—never mind."

". . . It ripped."

"Tried to tell you."

"Well, tell me *faster* next time, wouldja?"

Dex raised the fob and pointed it at the front doors. Hit the unlock button, watching the pickup through the glass. Nothing. The running lights should've flashed. Hit it again. Same. He wasn't close enough.

"Get the rest of it."

"I did, Freddy."

"Naw, there's a scrap in the back left roller. Can ya reach it?"

Dex took five quick steps down the hall, keeping the key fob aimed at the truck. Every step he clicked the unlock button. Every step, nothing.

"*That* got it, I think. Thing was way back there."

"Lemme look, see if you got it all."

Dex was halfway across the lobby. Same pattern. Step, click, nothing. There was a plasticky thump from the direction of the break room. Billy's access panel closing. Three more steps, almost running. Step. Click. Flash. Then a double flash as he hit the button a second time.

Footsteps, coming around the corner.

"What's up, Dexter?" Freddy asked from behind him.

Dex pivoted to his left, sliding the keys into his right pocket.

"Uh, checking the sky. Wondering if it's going to storm this afternoon," Dex said, walking toward Freddy. His boss made a hard left into his office and Dex quickstepped behind him as Marty came around the corner, wiping her hands on a paper towel. She quirked an eyebrow. *Sure you want to follow the gorilla into his cage? He's cranky.*

Dex gave an upwards nod. *I'll brave the beast.* He went in after Freddy, before his boss reached his desk and had a chance to turn

THE GUILTY SLEEP

141

around. He positioned himself half in the doorway, blocking the empty key peg with his body.

"Not supposed to," Freddy said.

"What?"

"Rain this afternoon, ya knucklehead."

"Right. Yeah, sorry."

"You OK?"

"I'm OK, Fred. Just thinking," Dex said, watching his boss but trying not to look like he was watching him. Freddy didn't sit, just leaned over and braced himself on the desk, looking at his monitor. Getting ready to print the weekly again. Dex slid his right hand into his pocket and gripped the fob, gathering the disparate keys together into his fist like the metal legs of a recalcitrant spider.

"Thinking what?" Freddy said, glancing up. Dex'd just started to pull the keys out. He shifted his weight, trying to look natural and feeling anything but.

"About ol' Billy the Rip back there."

"What about him?" Fred said, looking at the monitor. He fumbled with his mouse, then double-clicked something. Dex pulled the keys out, staring at Freddy's eyes, willing him to stay locked on the screen. The fob came free and Dex shifted again, putting both arms behind his back, a casual approximation of *at ease*.

"You sure it's not time to upgrade? We could move into the twenty-first century. Get ourselves a Trey Mancini instead."

Freddy was studying his screen. Probably watching the print indicator widget, verifying the reports were spewing forth from Billy's maw as intended. *Now or never.* Dex leaned back slightly, feeling for the peg with his empty left hand. Found it as Freddy looked up, his brow furrowed.

"Trade in ol' Billy? Not on your life. Only thing that gives us any excitement around here. Besides—*aha!*"

Dex was mid transfer, trying to loop the key ring over the peg, when Freddy slammed his hand on the desk. The keys dropped. Only one thing to do. He slid a half step backward, bumping into the wall as the keys hit the ground with a jangle.

Freddy looked up, saw the keys on the floor.

"Sorry, boss, you startled me." Dex bent over, gathered the keys, and nonchalantly hung them on the peg. Put his hands in his pockets to hide the shaking.

"Geez, man, take it easy," Freddy said, pointing at his monitor. "It was just Billy. Printing like a charm. Grab it for me, wouldja?"

"Sure thing."

Back at his desk, he turned to Marty. "Our fearless leader is now firmly ensconced within the comforting bounds of his weekly report."

Marty's hands fluttered, fanning herself with faux relief. "All shall be well, all shall be well, all manner of things shall be well," she intoned. "And we," she continued, pulling her phone from her purse, "have a little time unbothered."

Dex pulled out his own cell, saw a message from Winkowski, tagged two minutes before.

Moving.

Dex chanced a surreptitious glance through the front windows at the F-150. The midmorning sun poured molten light across the windshield, but if he squinted, he thought he could see a humped shape ducking behind the wheel. Winkowski, doing his thing. His *thing* being the insertion of a small black box into the truck's under-dash OBD-II port. It was a proprietary Golden Oak doodad designed for law enforcement, still in late prototype stages. See, the ODB-II was intended for diagnostic purposes—outputs only. But with the right software, you could turn the ODB into a two-way street. You could plug Golden Oak's little box into any modern vehicle's port and do a number of things from a distance, outputs like downloading the vehicle's telemetry and geolocation history, sure, but also *inputs*, from adjusting computer-controlled settings like climate or fuel mixture, or—as it would be used in this case—creating an engine kill switch and door unlocker.

"Daria get back to you yet?"

"Sorry, what?" Dex wanted to punch himself in the face. He was jumpy as a preacher's kid cutting Sunday school.

"Man, you are *miles* away today," Marty said sympathetically. "The park. You going?"

Over Marty's shoulder, he saw the door of the pickup crack open.

"Ah. Yes. They're coming."

Marty smiled. "Good news. How're you getting there?" The door was wider now, wide enough to let Winkowski's bulk through. Dex willed him to hurry.

"The number three has a stop by the park."

"But the number three doesn't go by the Safeway, does it?"

"For what?" He saw the low hump of Winkowski's back as the guy rolled out of the driver's seat. The door eased closed.

"For the frozen peas, dummy. To feed the ducks?"

The truck's horn gave a short, almost plaintive blat. Winkowski had remembered to hit the lock button before he closed the door. Dex wanted to collapse in relief.

"Hey, you guys hear my horn go out there?" Freddy called, sending a cold fist into Dex's guts. Of *course* the guy would recognize the sound. It was his love language. "Anyone messing with my ride?"

Dex made a show of stepping from behind his counter and peering out the front doors.

"Nah, Fred, I don't think so. All clear."

"Must be hearin' things."

"Come on, boss, the weekly isn't going to balance itself. We've got it under control out here," Marty called. She turned her attention to Dex. "I'll give you a ride. Safeway first for the peas, then the park."

"You're a lifesaver, partner."

She gave him a wink and turned back to her phone.

BurnR was waiting for him.

Complete, from Winkowski.

10-4, Dex replied. Nice one.

No response, not that he'd expected one. He opened up a new message for *Contact #1*—Saenz—and sent a quick good to go.

Roger came back immediately; then, Outstanding work.

He allowed himself a deep breath. Every step, every move took him deeper. The waters of the Rubicon washed across his hips, but he'd take that over the black river any day.

21

MEAT AND GREET

SAENZ

The port director had a Hollywood name: Jim Phoenix. He had a Hollywood look: sleek and deeply tanned, with a full head of thick hair swept back from a high, shiny forehead. A classic cop mustache. Bespoke frameless glasses, and an Omega Seamaster Bullhead on his wrist. His navy blue uniform fit him like a tailored suit and his black leather gun belt was polished to a reflective sheen. His look was like his name—if you were casting a corrupt fed, you'd laugh the guy out of the audition for being too on the nose.

They met at a Brazilian steak house on the Inner Harbor. Phoenix had what must have been a regular table on the second floor. It was the middle of the afternoon and the place was dead, and by rights the second floor should have been closed off to save the staff the journey up and down the steps. The table was by the windows and overlooked the water. Phoenix sat facing the stairs so his face was the first thing anyone coming up would see. There was another officer sitting to his left, watching Stu and Sunny approach. Her hands were out of sight under the table. Phoenix didn't stand, only nodded to the two empty chairs.

"You can tell our mutual friend he can consider the favor returned," Phoenix said as they sat. His voice was like the rest of him, so slick

146 JEREMY D. BAKER

and smooth it had to be a put-on. "I don't usually do follow-ups, let alone in person."

"I appreciate you taking the meeting," Saenz said.

"Thank *her*," Phoenix said, nodding at the other officer. His deputy, judging by the fact she had a single star on her epaulets and Phoenix had two. Nordic blonde hair pulled back so tight it made Saenz's face hurt just looking at it. Her nameplate read *Osorio.* "She's a little more . . . forward thinking than I am. Willing to entertain new ideas."

"Our mutual friend said you'd make it worth our while," Osorio murmured, "so I suggest you take the chance."

Phoenix smiled indulgently and gestured to the waiter by the steps. The man snapped his fingers and thirty seconds later, a squad of guys in white linen shirts marched up the stairs with skewers of steaks, sausages, chicken, and shrimp. Baskets of bread and bowls of salad, pitchers of water and tea. The staff did their thing with practiced precision, a fragrant and meticulous tornado. Phoenix got a dozen slices of filet mignon and Osorio's plate received a pile of shrimp the size of a sand dune. Saenz took a sausage and a steak. Porter grudgingly accepted a salad and some chicken, and immediately set to working off its skin with his fork. All the while, the guy who'd snapped his fingers flitted around Saenz and Porter, giving them a professional pat-down. When it was over, the waiters receded like a flood; the head guy nodded the all clear at Phoenix on his way out, and everything was still again.

Osorio did something under the table that sounded exactly like a handgun sliding back into a plastic holster. Then she pulled a small plastic box the size of a deck of cards out of her breast pocket and put it on the table. Flipped a switch, and watched a small LED cycle through red to orange to green. A whisper-box. Not a Golden Oak product, but they were in the middle of acquiring the small Israeli firm that made them. Killed any frequency or Wi-Fi in a fifteen-foot radius. No cell coverage, no wiretaps. Even an old-school microcassette recorder would only play back static from here on out. She nodded to Phoenix. "All clear."

THE GUILTY SLEEP

"You do keep me out of trouble," Phoenix said, then made a beckoning gesture at Saenz.

"As I said, we appreciate the in-person follow-up," Saenz started. "You're an important man with a full schedule, so I'm not going to waste your time—"

"Which is usually what someone says when they're about to upend a dump truck full of buffalo patties at my feet, son," Phoenix said, slicing a piece of filet into neat cubes. He didn't look up.

"You put us in a bad spot with the mid-stream price increase. We had an agreement."

"We had an agreement in principle," Osorio corrected. She popped a shrimp in her mouth.

Phoenix gave Saenz a wink. "I don't exactly sign a contract for this type of proposition, Ace. Your price doubled when I found out you were movin' Afghans and not something more . . . mundane. Cameroonians or whatever. Call it a hazard fee. Now. Why are we here?"

"We were able to secure coverage of the increase."

"Then I reckon this'll be a short meeting. Leave it in the car?"

"It's not with us."

Osorio put down her fork and put her hands in her lap under the table. She cleared her throat with a sound like a glacier calving.

Phoenix leaned forward, leather gun belt creaking. "Where is it, fella?"

"Why we asked for the meet. I want to work out the details of the payment. We'll bring it Saturday, to the dock. Give it to you there."

Phoenix lifted a desultory hand. "That mine ain't got no ore in it, sport. You know the drill, and I know you know it, because our mutual friend made sure you understood the drill right from the jump, right?"

"That was before you raised the price."

"You've got three seconds before this meeting concludes in a very unpleasant way," Osorio said. Something metallic happened under the table.

Saenz was ready for this, because of course he was. Guy like Phoenix was sharp and savvy, laid his groundwork. Cautious. Wouldn't have gotten as high up as he had, corrupt as he had, if he weren't. Saenz laid out the offer. It took a while, because the waiters kept coming with fresh skewers of meat, and because Phoenix had a lot of questions. Some about the payout, but mostly about what Saenz called a continuing service.

Golden Oak supplied a number of digital investigative file management systems for law enforcement customers. One of those customers happened to be the Homeland Office of the Inspector General, the internal affairs program overseeing investigations into corruption in the department's various agencies.

Phoenix's eyes positively iridesced at the idea of a passive back door into the OIG intake system. An early warning trip wire if anyone was even hallucinating about taking a look under the covers at the Port of Baltimore.

"Gotta say, champ, you have my attention," Phoenix drawled. Osorio fiddled under the table for a second, then brought her hands up and pushed her plate away. Phoenix slid a small silver case from his pocket and drew out a metal toothpick shaped like a railroad spike. "But that's a two-edged sword o' Damocles danglin' over your bright little head."

"People don't always like it when they've got his full attention," Osorio said with a shark's smile.

Phoenix dug at one of his molars with the toothpick, then dabbed at his lips with a napkin. Osorio wiped her own mouth. Phoenix sipped at his ice water, and Osorio sipped at her iced tea. Phoenix steepled his fingers in front of his chin, and Osorio fiddled with a strand of hair that had dared escape the gulag of her bun. Saenz and Porter waited.

"Ayuh, sometimes I turn my full attention to something, I spy an angle that gets me ornery as a bear woke up halfway through hibernation."

"What do you want to know, Director?"

"My title is Chief. My role is Port Director."

"No offense, Chief."

"None taken. But words mean things. We're gonna speak plainly, right?"

THE GUILTY SLEEP
149

"That's right," Saenz said, with a firm nod. The guy was a *caricature*. If it weren't so deadly serious, it would be seriously hilarious.

"I get the OIG back door. That's a hell of a sweetener," Phoenix said, toying with the toothpick. Osorio swirled the ice around her drink. "Plus our fee."

"Including the increase."

"For one afternoon's work. That the sum of it?"

"That's the sum of it."

Phoenix's eyes lasered in on Saenz's from across the table and he set down his glass with a thump.

"So what," Phoenix said, "is the story?"

"The story?"

"Why are you doing this?" Osorio said. "Why's this cargo so important to you?"

"Easy," Saenz replied. "It's the most precious thing in the world."

"And what might that be, bright boy?"

"Keeping my word."

Phoenix crossed his arms. "Sweeping pronouncement like 'at might work in the movies. Next scene. Fade to black. Roll credits, whatever. I live in the real world, sport."

"Do better," Osorio added, arching an eyebrow.

It's what Saenz expected. People like these two would never go for the simple, thumbnail sketch. So he laid it all out. The story of Jalal Hamidzai and how he'd saved the Blackbirds and how Saenz owed him. Chapter and verse, soup to nuts, as they liked to say in the government. Almost everything. He didn't expect to tug any heartstrings. But he didn't expect Phoenix to laugh at him.

"Slappy Sam, you're 'bout as full of mierda as a constipated bull steer." Phoenix dabbed at the corners of his eyes with his napkin. "All this effort to pay back some hajji kite runner? You Army boys are softer'n I thought."

Saenz was keenly aware of Porter next to him. Unlike Osorio, his own deputy had remained silent throughout the meal and the show. But now, without saying a word or seeming to move, he loomed like a thunderhead. The port officers felt it. Phoenix's eyes flicked back and forth between them. The muscles in Osorio's throat stood out as she swallowed.

"Awright, Ace, don't take offense now," Phoenix said. His words were placating, but his tone was hard as steel. The man was emperor of the largest roll-on/roll-off facility in America, supreme lord of a square mile of real estate gatekeeping seventy billion dollars of commerce a year. The most important economic facility in the eastern half of the United States. Saenz let the moment hang, let Phoenix see the weight of his words being felt.

"None taken."

"Good. Would hate to think I hurt your feelin's."

"I was supposed to have feelings, Army would've issued 'em."

Phoenix smiled at that. A real smile. White as snow and perfectly straight. A large piece of peppercorn nestled between his front teeth.

"We have a deal, Chief?"

"We do," Phoenix said. "When you tell me the rest of it."

Saenz almost smiled himself. The guy was a shaved gorilla with a god complex, but he wasn't dumb. Saenz leaned forward, speared a piece of filet mignon from Phoenix's plate, and told them.

22

BALLAD OF THE CENTRAL PARK DUCK

DEX

Dex proposed to Daria at twelve hundred feet. She'd always wanted go up in a hot air balloon. It was something to do with a movie or TV show she'd seen when she was three; not old enough to remember the details, but old enough to know she wanted to get up into the sky under a big, brightly colored floating globe and see the world spread out before her like an eternal diorama.

Dex, never a fan of heights, spent the first few minutes sweating and gripping the edge of the bamboo basket with one hand and the ring box in his pocket with the other. He nearly broke the box before he'd had a chance to bring it out, but he got it together long enough to get down on one knee (something of a relief) and hold out the ring with a shaking hand. After she said yes, after she pulled him to his feet and kissed him, she'd pressed her back against his chest as he held on to the railing, enclosing her in the half-circle of his arms. They drank deeply of the endless October horizon, and suddenly he wasn't afraid of heights.

He remembered the way the town looked that day, spread like an inverted V, legs angled southeast and southwest, pushing into the valleys that framed the boundaries of the municipality. State Route 97 ran the right-side leg. If you followed 97 all the way south, you'd graze

Sykesville, cross the Patuxent—where 97 added the name Georgia Avenue—then hit small towns like Sunshine and Brookeville before running into larger exurbs like Olney and Rockville, which blended seamlessly into the endless churn of the outlying suburbs. And then, before you knew it, you were at the tip of the broken diamond that was D.C. Back in town, at the inverted V where 97 split the tip and headed northwest for the Pennsylvania border, was a trapezoidal shard of grass and trees and dirt paths. There was a green-blue basin sparking in the sun, shaped like a child's drawing of a fish. Community Pond. A last jewel cowering in the rust-eaten heart of his town.

In his memory, the balloon's burner roared and they rose another twenty feet. His stomach dropped and Daria pressed even harder against him. His body thrummed like a plucked guitar string. The breeze stirred, blowing Daria's hair back, tickling his neck. He could smell jasmine and heather.

"Daddy!"

Dex turned his back on the pond and the memory. Rowan ran to him, little legs pumping. Her mouse-brown hair, defiant of all brushes and ties, bounced away from her forehead and the eye he could see was as wide as her smile. She wore a bright pink adhesive patch over the other. A piece of paper flapped in her hand. He knelt and she crashed into him. He almost went over and would have been fine with it. *Fall forever, baby girl, long as Daddy can hold you.*

He picked her up and she giggled, high and free, and he was transported instantly to the infant days, when he'd tickle her tummy and she'd grin that toothless grin and bubble up laughter that made the world perfect.

"I almost knocked you over," she squealed into his ear.

"You sure did."

"Put me down, Daddy."

He did it, reluctantly, and she squirmed back to arm's length and held up the paper.

"I made you this!" she said proudly. Rightly so, he thought. A crayon masterpiece: a blue blob on a field of green, three colored splotches sporting stick-like, y-shaped feet that could only be ducks.

THE GUILTY SLEEP

A happy sun, inverted Ms of birds in flight. An honest-to-goodness rainbow. Three stick figures, large, medium, and small. A long brown blob with four legs that could only be *Bradypus variegatus*. All of them smiling. It was the best thing he'd ever seen, and he told her so.

"Can I keep this? Please say yes."

"Daddy, you're silly. I drew it for you. You *have* to keep it. Do you like the sloth?"

"The sloth is amazing. And I'll keep it forever, promise."

"Will you lock it up in a big box at your bank? To keep it safe?"

"That sounds like a perfect idea."

"And then you can take it out and look at it whenever you want and remember today."

"But what if I want to look at it all the time?"

Rowan's little face scrunched up as she thought about it. She put a hand to her lips. It was pure Daria.

"Maybe you should keep it with you, then?"

"I think that's it. I'll keep it with me. Always."

"That sounds good," she said, smiling.

"Thank you so much." His heart tried to claw its way up and out of his throat. Rowan saved him by hugging him again, squeezing him harder than he remembered she could. She was growing up too fast, growing up without him.

A flash of an image in his mind, Freddy with that rolling, hard-sided suitcase, off to another casino weekend. Another flash, another photonegative ghost, Jalal standing over him in the blazing August sun, raising his pistol and saving Dex's life. A flash of color in the present, the bright pink of Rowan's eyepatch.

He was about to take a massive risk, and in any other circumstance he'd have admitted it was insane. But when the chance at hand had a payoff like *this* on the other end—getting his head right by saving a man who'd saved his life, saving that man's family, getting his family right with a life-changing amount of money . . . And with his old team leader at the helm, the finest op planner and counterintelligence mind he'd ever known, a man he'd trust with his life? It was the sanest thing he could do.

He looked over Rowan's head and Daria was coming from the parking lot, and now the heart that was trying to explode out of his body went still and slow and calm. Brown eyes, the exact shade of Rowan's. Hair halfway between firelight and rose gold, a cascade of brown freckles across the bridge of her nose and cheeks. She was wearing clompy Doc Martens, lived-in jeans, and a black tank top. Black-framed glasses, hair desultorily corralled in a loose ponytail, sunlight painting her shoulders. She moved with force and purpose, like a natural law. Even with the fights, the tears, the fury, the packet of papers from *Dean and Morris, Family Law*, Dex thought she was the best thing he'd ever seen.

Rowan ran to her, and it was all he could do not to hang on, pull her back, never let her go. He stood, staring at his wife and blinking away tears, more certain than ever he was doing the right thing.

"Mommy, he loved it! 'Specially the sloth."

Daria took the girl into her arms and gave him a tired half-smile over their daughter's head. "We knew he would, didn't we?"

"Uh-huh, we sure did."

"Don't forget to give it to him, though."

Rowan pulled back and looked at the paper still in her hand. Her face was the picture of surprise: *How did* that *get there?* Dex and Daria laughed and Rowan joined in. It was a perfect, unexpected moment and he wanted to hold on to it with the same intensity he'd wanted to hold on to his daughter, even as he knew it couldn't last. She ran back to him and held out the paper.

"Thank you so much," he said again.

"Daddy, there are ducks," Rowan said gleefully, pointing.

"There sure are. I counted about ten before you got here."

"Wow, *ten?*"

"Yep. And my friend Marty said she heard somebody spotted a special duck around here."

"For real?"

"They think it flew all the way from Central Park in New York. City."

"Is that far?"

THE GUILTY SLEEP   155

"Super far."

"Wow," she breathed. "Did you see it?"

"Not yet. It has a tan body and an orange head. I've never seen a duck like that before, have you?"

"Never ever."

"Well, look," he said, holding up the small, sweating bag of frozen peas. "These are a certified favorite duck treat." He handed the bag to her, and she took it like he'd handed her the keys to a real-life princess castle. "You can throw some by the edge of the pond if you want. See if you can spot that Central Park duck."

"Can I?" she said, looking at him and then her mother.

"Of course," Daria said, smiling. "But hang on a quick second." She checked her phone. "It's been eight hours; we can take off your patch."

Rowan sighed expansively. "Thank *goodness*."

Daria slowly peeled the patch away from her eye. Rowan blinked and Daria kissed her softly on the eyelid. "Now go throw some peas. Just don't go too close to the edge of the water, OK?"

"OK, Mommy. Thanks, Daddy!" She hugged him again, hard and fierce, and then she was running. Dex picked up her drawing and watched her. Locking her into his brain. The ducks scattered at first, but when she started throwing peas, they came clustering back, cackling and flapping their wings. His daughter stood fearless, sowing the peas in a wide arc and chattering back at the birds.

"She's amazing," he breathed to himself.

"She is," Daria agreed, moving next to him. "Nice call on the peas."

"Marty's idea. Apparently Timanda's bird group highly recommends."

"Who knew?"

"I bet you did."

"Yeah, I did."

Dex smiled. He couldn't help it. She caught him out of the corner of her eye and smiled back. A little.

He didn't hate his wife. Couldn't. He wasn't angry at her—not all the time and not right now. He understood what she was doing and why. He was the one who'd blown up their marriage, but he was still drawn to her. Iron filings to a magnet, compass needle to the North Pole. She was the primary, preeminent force in his life. He couldn't shake her.

"It was a good appointment?"

"Clarity at least. Doc Feuchtbaum says we've gotten as far as we can with the patching, keep it steady at eight hours a day, but we need to schedule the next step."

"The surgery."

"I hate the thought of her having to go through it. The sleeping gas and the . . . how they're going to have to cut our girl."

He fought the urge to move closer, put his arm around her. It was pure instinct. "I hate it too," he managed.

"I'm just trying to remember it's a common procedure. Ninety-nine point six percent effective. It worked for me, after all."

"And she won't remember a thing, right?"

"I didn't," Daria agreed.

"But we will."

"You're telling me," Daria said, taking off her glasses and rubbing the bridge of her nose. Rowan had inherited her strabismus from her mom. One more thing that tied them together in a perfect matched set. She wiped the lenses on the hem of her shirt, held them up to the light, then put the glasses back on. It was a gesture as familiar to him as any of his own. Once upon a time, he was the one who'd swipe the glasses off her face and clean them on his shirt.

"Thank you for coming," he said.

"Thank you for being here."

"Wouldn't miss it." It sounded hollow and flimsy as wet cardboard. It sounded like a lie. He'd missed plenty from inside the bottom of a bottle, the well of exhaustion, the derelict edifice of his sleepless nights. He angled his head like he was avoiding the high, hot sun, but it was an excuse to watch her. The line of her jaw, the delicate half seashell of her ear. The tattoo running from the top of her left shoulder to the middle of her forearm. Green vines of ivy woven in an intricate design, interspersed with red calla lilies and the single, red-berried branch of a rowan tree. Ten flowers, one for every year they'd been together, going back to senior year of high school. It was a living artwork, up until six months ago. She'd never add another flower, and they'd never add another branch.

"What?" she said.

"Nothing." Rowan was walking slowly across the grass now, doling out peas one at a time by throwing them as far into the water as she could. "Kid's got a good arm."

"She's got a good everything."

"Yeah, she does."

They watched her, the silence building like a tsunami into what he knew was coming.

"Dexter."

"I know."

"You need to sign the papers."

"I can't."

She turned, facing him. Gearing up. "This isn't fair. Rowan keeps asking if you're coming home. She needs closure. I need closure."

Dex chewed on the words, looking for the perfect response. He was so good in the interrogation booth, had been brilliant in training. Why did every word taste like wet ash in his mouth? He managed: "What if I could come home?"

"We've been over this."

"I still love you." It wasn't a hard admission. It was the easiest thing in the world to say, because it was the truest thing in his life. The love for his wife, for their child—it was the only thing he had left that felt real. And maybe—just maybe—the idea that he could get it all back.

"I know. And . . ." Daria paused, looking at Rowan. Her neck flexed with effort. "I still love you too." It came out in a rush, almost whispered.

"You see why I can't sign?"

She half-turned away. "We can't go on like this, Dex. Look, feeding the ducks . . . the drawing . . . the way you seem today, that's not what we are. Not anymore. It's a veneer. It's what we could have been."

"We could still be, Dare."

"No, we *can't*. How many times have you said that? Acted like everything's OK? And then—"

"I know I've been—"

"—you have a week where you can't sleep—"

"—struggling, seems like forever, but I really think—"

"—and then it's the stupid bottle but it doesn't work and you're exhausted and drunk and we fight and—"

"—there might be something—"

"—Rowan gets caught in the middle and I can't *have* that again, Dexter."

"—I might be able to do something here, though. If I could—"

She grabbed his arm, staring up into his eyes. "*Stop*. I grew up in that family, remember? Why do you think my mom's taken this so hard? She saw what was happening with us. The fighting, the yelling. The drinking. Throwing plates."

That one slashed his guts to pieces, but it was a fair blow.

"And the hitting. I know. But I'd never hit you. Never hit Rowan."

"Not on purpose, maybe. I can almost believe it. But I look at you and I remember the stupid plate and her *face*, Dexter, her face, when it happened!"

"I—"

"And I wonder if this is what it looked like at the beginning, with my parents." She wiped a tear from her cheek. "I told myself I wasn't going to do this with you today," she said. Her voice was tight. "I wanted it to be fun for her."

Rowan laughed and threw a huge handful of peas into the pond. The ducks floomped together in a mass of flapping wings and a spray of water.

"What if I told you I stopped drinking?"

"When?"

". . . well . . . since Tuesday, but—"

"That's one day. Are you telling me you're so deep in the bottle a full day without a drink means something?"

THE GUILTY SLEEP

"What I'm getting at is, I haven't wanted a drink since. And here's the thing—last night, I slept. Not long enough, but still real sleep. No nightmares."

"I'm glad for you. I am. That's good. But it doesn't change anything."

"But what if it could? What if I found something I could do to get better, and what if this is the start of it? Quit drinking, totally. Keep going to group every week. A VA shrink again, and maybe I'll find one who listens. Try new meds, different doses, whatever it takes. And if I'm sleeping, not drinking, not running on fumes all day every day, wouldn't that make a difference?"

Daria was silent for a long time. Dex stared at Rowan, burning her movements, her smile, her joy into his brain.

"What makes you so sure it's different this time?" she finally said. "A day without a drink, going to Terrence's group, and a good night's sleep is not exactly a pattern."

"There's this thing inside me, Dare. Ever since Afghanistan. Since what happened."

"I know."

"The root of what went bad in me. It was getting worse, especially this month, especially with what's going on over there. The drawdown and the Taliban coming back . . ." He choked on it. "Like nothing that happened even mattered. Like Ahn . . . like they died for nothing."

"It's awful."

"I think I found something that's going to help."

"Group and sleep and no drinking. How do you keep it going, though? That's the problem, Dex. Consistency."

"The nightmares, the anger, the booze, those are symptoms, right? I think I found the disease. The thing that happened there when we got hit. That's where it all came from. It's like a tumor that's been growing inside me. And maybe I can cut it out."

"How?"

"I have to do something."

"Do what, Dexter?"

"I have to help someone."

"Help someone with what?"

"I—"

"Mommy, Daddy, look!" Rowan's scream was Christmas morning and cuddly sloths and every good thing all at once. She pointed at the cluster of ducks congregated in front of her like a group of expectant churchgoers on Sunday morning. In the churn of gleaming green and drab dun heads, he saw it. A cream and tan duck, slightly bigger than the others, with an orange-red head. Bright red eyes. The other ducks took no notice, but it strutted among them like a king. "It's the Central Park duck!"

"Yay!" Daria yelled, waving at her.

"Throw him some peas!" Dex added.

Rowan upended the bag in front of her and the ducks crowded forward, croaking and flapping. His daughter danced back, laughing deep from her belly. He wouldn't let this go. Couldn't.

He took Daria's arm at the elbow. Gently. His thumb over one of the calla lilies.

"I have a chance to make a difference," he whispered to her, still watching their daughter. "To make something right I never thought could be made right. It's . . . a job opportunity."

"I don't understand."

"I know. I can't tell you any more right now, because it's all still pretty notional. But it gives me the chance to help people who need help and . . . it pays pretty well. I'll be able to take care of Rowan's surgery and—"

"I'm not sure I like the sound of this."

Rowan was running back to them, singing at the top of her lungs. "I saw the Central Park duck! I saw the Central Park duck!"

"It'll be OK. It'll be better than OK. And soon. Like, maybe this week. All I'm asking is . . . don't give up on me yet. Please? Let me see about this job and then let's look at where I am. If I'm not feeling better—getting better—I'll sign the papers. I promise."

His wife was silent, but she didn't pull away from his hand on her arm. She bit her lip, looked up at him.

THE GUILTY SLEEP

"One week, Dexter. Figure this thing out and we'll talk again. Or you'll sign. One week."

And their daughter was there and they knelt in front of her and she tumbled into their arms, laughing. Dex held her as tight as he could, leaning against Daria's side, the sun baking the back of his neck.

Any doubts he had about what Saenz wanted to do, any worries about the consequences, wisped into shadow. This was his chance to fix everything.

They walked to the parking lot holding hands, Rowan in the middle. He watched them drive away, then folded Rowan's picture carefully, creasing it into four even rectangles. He slid the treasure into his pocket.

23

INTERLUDE:
KANDAHAR, THREE YEARS AGO

DEX

In the shadowed dimness of the women's room at the corner of the Afghan National Army compound halfway between Kandahar and the Pakistani border, something is wrong. Details matter, Saenz always says. It's not the noise of the fly against the window. That's a common enough sound in-country, near ubiquitous, although this one seems to persist in Dex's awareness more than it should—an atonal, off-tempo pizzicato fluttering around the edges of consciousness and refusing to be shunted into the background. It's not the sun, streaming in thick bars through the windows near the roofline. It's not the soft warble of the Pakistani ballad on the radio. But it's something.

There are seven women in the room in addition to Fatima. Three are wearing full, deep blue burqas, their faces obscured and silent behind thin mesh. The rest are in hijabs, a spray of vibrant color complementing the carpets covering the floor.

Fatima is already engaging the women in rapid-fire Pashto, gesturing widely and smiling. She's pulled on her own hijab, a reddish-orange cloth with blue and green paisley swirls. The Afghan women have pulled back in a cluster that can't seem to decide whether it wants to shuffle left or right, the hijab-clad women together in one

THE GUILTY SLEEP

163

tight huddle, eyes downcast, faces turned away from Dex and Ahn. He can't tell which way the burqa wearers are looking.

Dex pulls off his baseball cap, folding the brim and stuffing it in his back pocket. He gestures at Ahn, who removes his own glasses and blinks against the dimness. Habibullah, the ANA soldier, has already parked himself on a small stool next to the steps leading up to the door.

Fatima introduces them, smiling even wider. Dex nods, almost a bow, hand over his heart, stepping forward. The women, almost imperceptibly, shuffle back the same amount. If he takes another step, he'll drive them into the walls. He retreats, still smiling. He looks at Fatima and she nods reassuringly. Just need to warm them up a bit. Saenz has thought of this already, because of course he has. Ahn has a small bag, which he passes to Dex. It's full of gifts. Boxes of tea, packs of tissue, a sack of sugar cubes, three tubes of oat cakes, and a carton of Marlboro Reds. Dex opens it, passes it to Fatima, and she doles the gifts out to the women. There's an increase of chatter then, but none of the smiles he's hoped to see. Habibullah shifts in his chair, eyeing the goods. Chances are, he'll angle for a cut after the team pulls out.

One of the women, the oldest unless there's a wizened great-grandma under one of the burqas, says something to Fatima, and Dex catches the word *chay*. Tea, then, which is a good and necessary beginning. Fatima agrees enthusiastically. She turns to Dex.

"They would like to offer you some tea."

First thing they drilled into you about the proper use of the interpreter was to always talk directly to the other party and let the terp's mouth do the walking. Avoid the trap of "tell them" this and "ask them" that. Muddies the water and invites too much supplemental input and color from the terp. He nods at Fatima to let her know he understands, then faces the older Afghan woman. He looks in her direction, but not at her face, and does the nod-to-bow, hand-on-heart gesture again.

"Thank you very much," he says. "We are honored to share tea with you." Fatima relays his response with a smile and subdued gestures, and Dex watches obliquely as the other woman replies with a smile that doesn't reach her eyes. The woman turns to the others and barks a curt order. The two youngest hop to it along the far wall, where there's a propane tank with a burner mounted on it and some shelves of pottery and supplies.

From there it's a matter of tradition on both sides—the Afghan ritual of tea and guests and hospitality, and the Army practice of trying to remember your training, field manuals, and the instructions of your team leader. As a sign of respect, they lean their M4s against the wall out of reach; it's largely moot since they still have their pistols. The younger women bring a platter with a huge metal teapot and a dozen small glass cups and they settle on the center carpet, a brown and green pattern hearkening a windy day on the Chesapeake. The older Afghan woman puts out one of the tubes of oat cakes, and one of the younger ones pours the tea. The tip of the spout rattles against the rim of Dex's cup, but he keeps it in place and prevents a spill. One point for diplomacy.

Dex hates tea but they're looking at him expectantly and he knows the drill, so he sips it and smiles broadly, like a scalding cup of herbal lemon water is just what he needed on an August day in Afghanistan. Ahn sips noisily and smacks his lips in real pleasure. One of them brings a cup to Habibullah, who murmurs something that makes the girl blush. The Afghan women—except for the three in burqas, who remain against the far wall—settle around their side of the carpet and help themselves as well. For a moment, all the communication is nonverbal. Averted gazes, pouring and sipping tea, reaching for an oat cake, smiles that don't reach the eyes. The Baloch pop song's wandering jangle from the radio provides soft counterpoint to the persistent tapping of the fly.

Dex takes the lead and works through Fatima. "Thank you for the tea," Dex says. "It is the best I have had since arriving in your country." It's the truth, because it's the only tea he's had since arriving in their country. Fatima relays it and the response from the older woman.

"You are welcome to our place."

"The tea and your place are very welcoming."

"Thank you, and honor once again to our guests."

THE GUILTY SLEEP

165

Silence reigns in a kingdom of downcast eyes. Dust motes dance and swirl in the beams of sunlight from the windows, seeming to move in time to the beat of the Pakistani power ballad.

In CI training, they taught that silence was your friend. Get someone talking, whether a source or an interrogation target, and let them go. As a rule, humans don't like silence and want to fill it. Ask an open-ended question and let the quiet do the work. But the quiet here isn't doing any work at all, partly because Dex hasn't asked any questions and partly because of the cultural divide. He needs to get things moving.

He starts by asking about the type of tea, where it comes from and how it's prepared. He compliments the tea set, which, in fairness, is beautifully made. He admires the carpets and asks where he might find one to purchase and ship home to his wife. The standard gambits for establishing rapport, something he's done a few dozen times in the real world, mostly during his previous tour in Kurdistan, and hundreds of times in training.

His seeds fall on dry sand. Even through Fatima's deft lips, the answers come back short and clipped, full of reserve and implied distrust. What you'd expect, perhaps, in the first weeks after the fall of the Taliban when the Americans and their allies were still an unknown quantity. Not what he'd been led to expect these days, almost two decades later. He's going to have to think on this later, and deeply.

He drains his tea and is instantly offered a refill, which he politely accepts. One of the younger women approaches the dozing Habibullah with the pot and he opens his eyes and sits up alertly, raising the empty cup from his lap as she nears. He takes the tea and smiles at the girl, who looks away as she retreats.

Dex shares a look with Ahn, who stares back impassively. Waiting for Dex to show him something. The answers should have been more fulsome, even to the basic foundational rapport questions. He considers going hard, right up the middle, and asking about the cache buried in the yard. It would be a breach of etiquette, but it might shock them into revealing something. He nearly goes for it but decides on another tack first, with the nuclear option in reserve.

"Is there anything you need here? What can we bring you on our next visit?" He's calling an audible; this is usually the conversation closer. But it's also a crowd pleaser, universally expected when meeting with a team of Americans for the first time, and according to Saenz it's the best way to seal a deal. There's always a list, even if it's just the basics: a pallet of water and a stack of clean blankets. No one ever says no. Ever.

"No." the spokeswoman says. In English, after Fatima has finished relaying his words. "Thank you very much," she enunciates carefully. Dex blinks. The beat stretches forever. The Baloch vocalist wails, the dust dances, the fly bumps out the rhythm.

"Your English is excellent," Dex says, smiling widely.

The woman nods. She looks at one of the younger women and says something fast and clipped. The girl hops to, starting to clear the tea service. Fatima catches his eye and her lips purse for a split second, and then her face carefully returns to neutral. The chay should have lasted an hour at least, and the host never makes the first move to bring it to a close. This is a gobsmacking breach of protocol.

As Saenz had once said: The greatest events in history sometimes turn on the smallest chance.

During a visit to Sarajevo in 1914, an Austrian archduke's car stalled out in front of a delicatessen where a Bosnian student, himself a would-be assassin, was morosely grabbing a sandwich after an earlier assassination attempt failed. The guy couldn't believe his luck. Fumbled his gun out, stepped forward, and fired two shots, killing the archduke and his wife. Sentenced Europe to a half decade of carnage that killed millions.

Big events, small fulcrums.

In the case of the Blackbirds, they figured out later, it came down to the short-range walkies. Ahn's handheld hadn't seated correctly in the charging station the night before. It had enough charge left over to last through radio checks and the ride out to the compound. But now, when Dex begs the pardon of the Afghan women and turns to Ahn and mutters at him to check in with the team and let them know

THE GUILTY SLEEP   167

all is purple at their location—which is Blackbird code for *something's hinky*—Ahn's walkie is as dead as the hospitality in the room. The PFC hits the squawk button, then again, but there's no squelch, no blip. He shakes his head.

Dex is disappointed. He wanted to prove he could bring something to the team, but Saenz always said that while he didn't demand perfection, he did expect them to ask for help if they needed it. And something feels off. Something *is* off. Flagging that's going to count for something, but the important thing right now is to let the rest of the team know.

"There's no way forward here," he whispers to Ahn, who nods in agreement. He's felt it too. "Let's pull back, see if the boss has any ideas."

Dex stands carefully, avoiding the personal space of the young woman clearing the tea service.

"I'm sorry," he says, hand over heart and head inclined. "We need to get something from the truck. We may have some more cigarettes there as well. We will be back in one moment."

Ahn grabs his M4 and clomps up the steps, but Fatima leans in as Dex moves. She doesn't touch him, mindful of impressions and decorum, but she gets as close as she can.

"This is weird, man. Something's got them rattled," she whispers.

"Come with us. We'll talk with Saenz and Porter, get some ideas for a redirect. Come back with a new angle."

"I'm gonna stay," she says. "Might be you big strong American men make them uncomfortable." She grins. "Let me see if I can shake something loose while you're gone."

Dex thinks about it, listening to the fly tapping against the window. Ahn opens the door. A thick shaft of light pierces the gloom. The radio wails softly.

"Yeah, OK. Good idea. Thanks."

Fatima gives him a smile and turns back to the women. Dex follows Ahn up the stairs into a daylight so full and hot it settles like a weight around his shoulders.

168   JEREMY D. BAKER

Dex catches up with Ahn, quickly settling his own M4 behind his back. The gravel crunches under their feet. It feels as lifeless and dry as the moon.

"That was weird, man," Ahn says, and the fact the high-speed PFC noticed it, too, makes Dex feel better.

"Yeah, usually you get them with the gift bag and a spot of tea, right?"

"Way they do hospitality in this country. I never seen it fail."

They're halfway back to their trucks.

"I wonder if there was something with the ANA guy," Dex says. "Habibullah."

"That one girl wasn't a fan, if that's what you mean," Ahn replied. "Things looked awkward when she brought him the tea."

"Exactly. He said something, and she kind of tensed up."

"If that's what passes for flirting here, maybe I should—hey!" Ahn is a step ahead of him and has just walked around the bed of the closest pickup. Dex almost crashes into him when he stops. Ahn reaches behind him, pushes Dex away, and grabs the stock of the M4 slung around his back. He starts to slide it around and Dex steps to his right and sees one of the ANA guys kneeling by the front wheel well of the middle pickup.

"What are you—" Ahn starts, and the ANA guy raises his hand and there's a sharp clapping sound and something wet sprays across Dex's face. Ahn coughs and staggers back. Dex grabs him under the arms, but Ahn's gone to jelly and he takes Dex to the ground with him. The sun hits him full in the face and he realizes he hasn't put his sunglasses back on. Between that and the wetness on his face, he's blind.

"Ahn!" Dex shouts, worming out from under him. His hindbrain is thinking faster than the rest of him, and the weight of his pistol appears in his hand as if by magic. "What happened, man?" His mouth is the slowest runner in the race. "You OK?" There's a puff of wind, and now there's sand and grit in his eyes too. He blinks, squinting. Ahn's throat is a mess of blood and burst flesh. The blood bubbles and sprays every time Ahn fights for breath. That's the wetness, then,

THE GUILTY SLEEP

some part of him thinks, trying to be clinical and sane. *Private First Class Ahn has been shot in the throat and the wetness on my face and in my eyes is his blood.*

Dex raises his pistol, fighting the sun and the dirt and the blood. There should be someone in front of him. The ANA guy who was kneeling by the truck. *Nice of you to catch up*, his hindbrain has time to sneer. *Now why don't we shoot the bastard?*

There's another thunderclap and something hits Dex in the chest like a freight train, right over his heart.

FRIDAY

24

THE GUILTY SLEEP

DEX; TURNER

Saenz told a story once. This was back in the world before Dex's first tour in northern Iraq teaching the Kurds to interrogate ISIS nicely. Before Dex made Spec Four and before, of course, the compound. It was during one of their National Guard training weekends out at Fort Meade, and it was the first time Dex realized if he ever had a chance to work for the lanky staff sergeant, he was going to jump after it like a dog going for prime rib.

They were executing a timeless and time-honored military tradition, probably instituted by von Steuben himself at Valley Forge: inventorying the supply cages. Dex thought they didn't need to bother. Saenz allegedly never forgot a detail, and he was the one who'd stocked the cage the previous month. He could've stood in the doorway and known if something was missing with a glance. But this was Maryland's well-regulated militia, so it was clipboards and pencils and a barcode scanner and four hours in an unheated warehouse.

The thing happened during one of Saenz's earlier tours in Afghanistan. He was in Kabul, working out of the embassy on loan to the Defense Intelligence Agency. There'd been an attempted VBIED. Media called them car bombs, but this improvised explosive device was borne via motorcycle.

174 JEREMY D. BAKER

"Across the street from a Canadian-Afghan checkpoint, guy pulls up on one of these ancient Honda CT90s. They're all over the place—you'll see when the unit goes back. Cargo box mounted behind the seat, probably three feet square. Typical delivery bike." Saenz paused, watching Dex from the corner of his eye. Making sure he was paying attention. "Driver fiddles with something between the handlebars. There's a little explosion from the rear of the bike—barely more'n a puff of dust—and the guy dismounts and legs it. Couple of ANA bubbas chase him down."

"Good," Dex said, more to show he was listening than anything else.

"A start. Anyway, Canadian EOD takes a look at the bike and finds an IED. Twenty-five pounder."

"Yikes."

"Yikes is right. Had a layer of bolts and rusty nails in the casing. Would've shredded the checkpoint and everyone in it if the secondary trigger ticked over like it should've when the first stage igniter blew."

"Oh man. Good guys got lucky."

"Skill is a beautiful thing, but we'll take luck any day, PFC Grant."

Saenz and a Canadian intel sergeant took a run at the motorcycle driver, who claimed he knew nothing about any bomb on his motorcycle. He was supposed to make a delivery to the shoe merchant right past the checkpoint, only his bike stalled out. He was checking the ignition when something exploded behind him, scared the balls off him, and he scarpered. EOD confirmed the IED was hidden in the cargo box under a dozen layers of sandal leather. The driver, when asked who placed the order, gave the extremely helpful response of Hamad no-last-name. But he continued protesting his innocence. Either the guy's a suicide bomber who had a change of heart immediately after realizing he hadn't arrived in paradise after all, or he's a witless dupe.

They hold him overnight. Saenz and the Canadian trade off watching the security feed. Slugging coffee (Diet Pepsi for Saenz), smoking cigarettes (dip for the Canadian), going for quick walks in the cold night air, anything to stay awake. The Afghan sleeps like a sawn log. It's all they need.

THE GUILTY SLEEP   175

Next morning, they take another run at him. Tell him they've pulled fingerprints from the shoe leather (they haven't) that proves he packed the crate (it doesn't). Tell him they're going to bring his family in for questioning (they won't), and they'll turn him over to the Afghan intel boys next (they might).

Guy cops to everything right then and there, in the first twenty minutes of the day's session. It was him, yup, and he was supposed to blow the checkpoint, sure. Orders from the local AQ cell leader—you guessed it—Hamad no-last-name.

"The point," Saenz said, adopting the semi-casual, laconic tone he slipped into during his frequent teaching moments, "is this. Innocent people toss and turn all night, pace the room, do PT, whatever. They're fuming about being wrongfully accused and terrified they won't be able to prove it.

"Not so the others. The guilty ones did it, they know they did it, they know you probably know they did it, or are gonna work it out. They know they're caught, and they'll either go down for it, or you won't figure it out and they'll walk. Either way, their fate is decided. Nothing to lose. They sleep. You're ever on the fence about someone in custody, you keep 'em overnight and watch what happens. Got me?"

"Gotcha, Sarnt. The guilty sleep."

"Thus endeth the lesson, PFC Grant." Saenz nodded with satisfaction and checked the final set of night vision goggles off the inventory sheet.

Dex sat at the sad, wonky table in his sad, dingy little kitchen, sipped his coffee, and wondered what Saenz's story said about him. Because he'd slept like a dead man the night before. Went to bed thinking about Jalal and his family and the life they could have. Thinking about Rowan feeding frozen peas to the ducks and her song of triumph when she'd spotted the Central Park duck. Thinking about the money in Freddy's suitcase and changing his own family's life. Last thing he saw before he closed his eyes was Rowan's drawing, carefully unfolded and propped on his bedside table. The pond, the ducks, the sloth. All of them together. Remembering Daria's face when she'd said *one week*.

No need for the Catoctin Rye. No tossing and turning. No nightmares for the second night in a row, just the seamless, dreamless rest he hadn't known could still exist behind his eyes.

He woke without his alarm. Refreshed. The black river nothing but a memory. The four-and-a-half-mile run from his place south to the community college and back. The stopwatch read 27:30; not his personal best per-mile time, but it was within shouting distance and he didn't even feel like he was going to die.

Maybe there was something to this whole life of crime thing.

He sipped coffee and spread Rowan's drawing on the table, working it flat with his palm. Couldn't take his eyes off it.

He ran into Mariam's husband, Dawit, on his way out. Dawit was wearing faded dickies and a blue button-down with *Inner Harbor Parking* sewn over his breast pocket. He smiled when he saw Dex, his little mustache blooming.

"You feeling better?"

Dex had a vague memory from earlier in the week. Dawit, poking his head out when Saenz had brought Dex back to his apartment after the fight at Thievery Collective.

"Much. The tsebhi helped, you know."

"Mariam, she is a miracle," Dawit said. His eyes shone with pride.

Showered and dressed, time for one more coffee. Rowan's drawing folded back up into a neat rectangle in the front pocket of his pants.

Thinking about what he was going to have to do. The hard part was over—for him. He'd done his push of a button, gotten Winkowski into Freddy's truck so he could plug the kill switch into the OBD port. All that was left was to have a normal workday. That, and send a *BurnR* message to Saenz when Freddy was getting ready to leave for the casino.

Five minutes after three: Freddy stows the suitcase, levers himself into the driver's seat. The team rolls up, Porter driving. They block Freddy's truck from behind, Saenz and Wink dismount. Courtesy of the takeover box Winkowski installed into the OBD-II port of Freddy's truck, assisted by Dex and his key fob tango, Porter uses an app on his smartphone to kill the engine. Saenz knocks on the window, distracting

THE GUILTY SLEEP 177

Freddy. Porter unlocks the doors, again with the app. Winkowski opens the opposite door, grabs the suitcase, throws it in the van, the team rolls off. Fifteen seconds, in and out. Nobody gets hurt; Jalal and Dex get new lives. An easy op.

He should have been twisted into a rusted, Gordian knot of misfiring nerves. Instead, he was sipping coffee and feeling like a new man. The echo of Rowan's song. Daria saying *one week*.

If this was how the guilty lived, let him be condemned.

Turner was worried.

It started early, the moon still low and fat and yellow on the horizon. Half an hour before they started the collect, Slade introduced him to the guys he was bringing on for extra security. It did nothing to ease Turner's unquiet mind. Bunch of yellow-belt ninjas if ever there were. Two skinny meth heads: a white guy named Cody with his arm in a cast and a Black guy—Jay—who was wearing an Army jacket and whose nose had recently been pushed in a new and exciting direction. They looked like they'd been stuffed in an industrial clothes drier with a couple of cinderblocks and set to high tumble. A jacked Asian kid with a shaved head who Slade introduced as Mike, and a jacked white kid with platinum cornrows Slade introduced as Chauncey, which Turner hoped was a nickname because otherwise: poor kid—Melchizedek Turner knew all about challenging first names. Mike and Chauncey rode those Japanese motorcycles with the fiberglass body that could go a million miles an hour in a straight line but weren't exactly inconspicuous. Turner made them leave the crotch rockets where they met, parked between the dumpsters behind Villa Maya at the Pine Hill shopping center.

"You four take Slade's car," Turner said. "Follow us everywhere, but not too close." He passed out the walkies. One to Slade and one to Mike, who on the surface seemed like the sharpest bowling ball on the rack.

"What is this, bro?" Cody mumbled. "We playin' secret squirrel?"

Turner looked at Slade, raised an eyebrow.

"Shut up and listen to the man," Slade said.

"Stay on channel two. You see anything unusual, you give Slade a holler. We see anything unusual, he'll call you. Otherwise stay off the air after comms test."

"What's unusual?" asked Jay, as Chauncey said, "Comms test?"

Turner rubbed his hand across his eyes and fought the urge to bounce their skulls together like a couple of billiard balls.

"If someone's following us, watching us, that sort of thing. Something don't look like it belongs," Slade said. At least he was trying. "And a comms test is exactly what it sounds like. You get in my car," he said, handing his keys to Mike, "and I'll call you on the walkie, make sure you can hear me, and then you'll call me to make sure I can hear you. Geez, guys."

Slade had to show them how the walkies worked, and had the good sense to look embarrassed. Turner walked them over to Slade's car, a lowered Honda Accord that was half black matte spray paint and half gray primer. Somehow they made it with no one tripping over a shoelace.

"Look," Turner said, motioning them all into a half circle. "You're a bunch of all-stick corndogs, but Slade's vouching for you to his aunt. You should know what that means. Stay behind us, stop when we stop, pay attention. Use the walkie if anything looks weird. We'll end up back here, 'bout nine thirty. From that point, we watch the bank. Rotating shifts until it's time for the next leg. I'm gonna have the bank manager leave early, just in case. If something's amiss—"

"Amiss?" said Cody.

"—we'll be ready."

He looked at the group clustered around him. Wondered if they had half a dozen brain cells to rub together between them. Probably not enough to start a fire. It wasn't a good feeling. "I'm assuming everyone is strapped?" He almost dreaded the answer.

There was a chorus of troglodytic assent and chest thumping, and Chauncey proudly lifted his sleeveless undershirt to show the chromed .45 jammed in his waistband.

"What do I say about guns, Slade?"

THE GUILTY SLEEP

"You pull a piece on the job, you've already failed."

"In other words, nobody draws unless Slade says to, or you see one of us with a heater out. You get me?"

There was a round of disappointed grunts and some additional chest thumping, but he stared at them until they settled.

"You guys should come with a warning label. If you put a monkey wrench into this, it'll be out of Slade's hands and it'll be out of mine. You dig?" He looked each one in the eye, searching for comprehension. Mike looked like he got it. The rest of them, he could've been speaking Mesopotamian. He wasn't satisfied, but there was nothing else to do.

He climbed into the El Camino and Slade eased into the passenger seat.

Turner reached out, touched the picture of the little blonde girl taped to his dash. Slade started to do it, too, and Turner slapped his wrist, not gently. He didn't like the way Slade was looking at her.

"What? I thought we did that for luck."

"Not you."

"Still haven't told me her deal, but I'm guessing that's your kid, right? An old picture, so she's gotta be . . . she even eighteen yet?"

Turner ignored him. Said: "That's your crew."

Slade closed his door with a sigh. "They might not be pros—"

"It's impossible to underestimate them."

"—but they're loyal. Those four, they've never run from a scrape and they do what I say. I wish they were better, but they're the best I have."

Slade seemed sincere, and slightly surprised at himself. Like he realized he'd been playing Double A and the rest of his teammates weren't good enough to sniff the majors. Like he was wondering how good that made him, and maybe he needed some extra batting practice.

"If you're right, we've got a chance."

"Really think someone's coming after us? After the collect?"

Turner stared at the moon. Rubbed the scar tissue on his forearms and thought about fire season in Northern California. Volcanos of smoke creating a mockery of dark clouds in the low, blue sky. The echoing thunder of hundred-year-old pine trees exploding like artillery shells as the sap inside superheated to steam. The scent of ash and burning brush. Of roasting meat. The sense that something had circled around behind him and closed off the only way out.

"Hope not, kid. Nothing ruins a nice day like a run and gun."

25

PRIVATE MURPHY, REPORTING FOR DUTY

DEX

Dex picked up a bag of bagels and spreads from the deli and had them waiting, plus coffee for everyone. Four—count 'em, four—creamers for Freddy. He was sitting on the concrete planter in front of the bank a full ten minutes before Marty arrived, and another five before Freddy blatted in. Dex was showered and shaved, wearing the best of his three pairs of khakis and the clean blue button-down—freshly ironed, no less. Making an effort.

"To what do we owe this bounty?" Freddy asked around a mouthful of onion bagel with chive and onion cream cheese. He waved the bagel vaguely, taking in the food and perhaps Dex's appearance.

"It's a beautiful day, boss."

"Gotta love a Friday, that's for sure." Freddy was always in a good mood on casino weekends. Dex almost hated to imagine his boss's face when his pickup refused to start. When the van pulled up behind him. When Saenz knocked on his window. When the doors unlocked and Wink snatched the suitcase.

"*I* for one say thankee sai, Dex. Hits the spot," Marty said. She sipped her coffee and fired up her computer. Cinnamon raisin bagel for her, with pineapple cream cheese. Freddy'd had a near conniption over the combo.

"One a yas wants to come along this weekend, get away from it all, offer's still open. I know Marty's gonna say no, but how 'bout it, Dex? Might do ya some good."

"I'm OK, Freddy. Really," he added at Freddy's look.

"Sonny boy," Freddy replied, his voice low, "you've looked like a rat on a sinking ship the last six months."

"I . . . I know." *This much emotional intelligence from Freddy House, of all people, today of all days.*

"Well, then, let Uncle Freddy hook you up. We'll do the thing— dice and cards and booze and a little Bolivian dancing powder, maybe see if we can't scrounge coupla cocktail waitresses. Get all that," he said, waving vaguely at Dex, "right out of your system."

What he had in his system right now he didn't want out. Rowan singing about the Central Park duck. Daria saying *one week*. The drawing in his pocket. The waters of the black river receding into nothing. The next right thing.

"I'm good, boss, but thanks."

Turner came through the doors like a graceful avalanche. He carried one of his nylon satchels. Faded black jeans, faded black Duran Duran T-shirt, sleeveless leather vest.

"Heya, Turn', that time?"

"That time all the time, my dude," the big man replied in his incongruously high, gentle voice. He looked tired, washed out. Bruised purple bags under his hangdog eyes. He needed a shave. Until a few days ago, Dex could've related.

The ritual greeting complete, Freddy led the big man into the vault. Dex pulled out his phone and threw Marty a wink at her warning glance. He'd told her about the lake and the Central Park duck. The frozen peas. Let her think he was texting Daria. He pulled up the *BurnR* app and sent a message to *Contact #1.*

Morning deposit today.

We have eyes, Saenz replied immediately. Tx.

Turner and Freddy were bantering in the vault as usual. Turner said something, too soft to hear. Closer, Marty murmured something, probably to her computer. The ancient CPU was fifty-fifty to boot up on the first try.

"You sure?" Freddy said, just loud enough to make out.

Turner said something affirmatory, but Dex still couldn't make it out.

"OK." Freddy again. "Sure."

"I said, she gave you a whole week?" Marty said, her voice slightly raised.

Dex fought the urge to shake himself as he snapped his attention back in place.

"A week."

"A week to do what?"

Dex smiled. "I'm not exactly sure. To show I've gotten it together— or I'm trying to get it together, maybe?"

"What then? Sunshine and rainbows, happy family all over again?"

"I don't know. I don't think she's gone that far in her own mind. What I'm hoping is, another week."

"And then another week after that."

"Et cetera and so on."

"And then maybe sunshine and rainbows."

"I'm trying not to go that far in *my* own mind."

"One day at a time, my G-maw used to say."

"Bye everyone," Turner said. "See you next time." He waved casually at Dex and Marty as he pushed through the doors.

"Later," Marty said. Dex nodded and gave a half-wave of his own, keeping his face neutral. *Nothing to see here.*

"Yeah," he said. "One day at a time."

The sound of a door slamming. Freddy, disappearing into his office. Marty quirked an eyebrow. "Hope there's no trouble in paradise. He'll take it out on us."

"No kidding," said Dex, thinking the same about the first part, not worrying at all about the second.

Freddy stayed in his office the rest of the morning. Dex drank his coffee and ate his bagel and occasionally glanced out into the parking lot, wondering where Saenz and Porter and Winkowski had parked the plumber's van.

The day danced forward on a knife's edge and in slow motion. The clock on the corner of his monitor and the one in the corner of the bank mocked him with their glacial, epochal graduations. He waited on the rare customer: a kid on a bike hefting a coffee can of coins for the counting machine, and the manager of Strosnider's Hardware brought his weekly cash deposit.

Dex was white-knuckling sanity, and three was never coming.

But the waiting became moot because at a quarter after twelve Freddy House blew the whole plan to absolute smithereens.

The door to Freddy's office opened in a rush of air, but by the time Dex looked that way, his boss had disappeared into the vault. He slipped his hands into his pockets, felt the hard edge of his phone in one and the sharp crease of Rowan's drawing in the other.

"Someone's in a weird mood today," Marty said.

"Say true, partner." Dex hoped his voice was steady. It sounded frayed to his ears. *Something's wrong.*

"Maybe he should grab a margarita at Villa Maya."

"You tell him. I'm keeping my mouth shut."

Marty smiled, like he was daring her. "Boss," she called, "you copacetic? Maybe you should grab a 'rita at Villa Maya." She stared at him, *you really thought I wouldn't do it?* written in her eyes, grin spreading. She did love to wind Freddy up.

Freddy came around the corner, his hard-sided suitcase rolling behind. From the expression on his face, Dex was positive he hadn't heard a word.

"Hey, guys—"

"Guy and girl," Marty said.

Freddy steamrolled. "—I'm heading out early. You can handle things here, close up at three."

"Everything OK?"

"All good, Dexter," Freddy said, but his face belied it. "Figgered I'd take a little personal time today. All work, no play, et cetera."

Turner had said something to him in the vault. Spooked him. Which meant the big man suspected something. Had seen something.

THE GUILTY SLEEP

185

"Sure thing. Got you covered, Fred."

His boss didn't even do that thing where he forced a scowl when Dex called him Fred. Dex slid his phone out, held it against his thigh underneath the counter.

"Thanks, guys. See yas Monday." And he stepped through the doors out into the light.

Dex couldn't let Marty see him send a text right before this went off, not when the plan was falling apart. It'd be too easy to correlate.

"I'm gonna grab a bottle of water. Want one?"

"Nah, I'm good. Thanks."

He moved as quickly as he could while trying to not seem like he was hurrying. His shoulders tightened. Last time he'd felt something like this had been at the compound, just before Ahn spotted one of their supposed allies doing something suspicious by one of the Blackbirds' trucks.

Soon as he made it around the corner, Dex whipped his phone out and sent a message to *Contact #1.*

Zero.

It meant they were closing up for the day and Freddy was getting ready to come out with the money and they should move the van into place.

Only thing, he was sending it three hours too early and three minutes too late.

For a millisecond he saw three dots cycling in a reply bubble. Then they went away. It probably meant Saenz had seen his message, started to reply—asking for a confirmation—but they'd seen Freddy coming out with the money. Dex let out a breath he hadn't realized he'd been holding. He walked back out, breathing deep.

"You weren't thirsty?"

"What?"

"The water."

"No, I was. I drank it in there."

Marty looked at him, eyes narrowed. "You and Freddy both. Weird today."

"I'm in a strange place, I guess. After everything."

She shrugged. Started to say something. There was a screech of tires from the parking lot.

26

FIRST CONTACT

DEX

From where Dex was standing, he had a straight shot out the glass double doors into the parking lot where Fred's F-150 was parked on the other side of the through lane. In the noon sun it was a blurred pool of gray topped by the poured silver of the windshield. Winkowski's white Ford Transit skidded to a stop behind the pickup. The side door slammed open and two figures got out. One tall and lean, the other shorter, stocky, and limping. They were wearing dark blue painter's jumpsuits and balaclavas. Saenz glided up to the driver's-side window of the truck, and Winkowski stepped around the other side, ready to open the passenger door and grab the suitcase. Saenz tapped on the window.

For a few seconds it was a frozen tableau. Some kind of modern art take on a Renaissance painting. Then Saenz knocked on the window. Again.

"You OK, Dex?"

He should've been walking back to his station like nothing was happening. Instead, he was standing in the middle of the lobby like an idiot.

"Yeah, sorry. Like you said, I'm off today." He shook himself like a dog coming out of water and walked back to his station, trying not to stare out the front doors. Last thing he saw: Saenz knocking on the window, pulling on the door handle with his other hand. Gesticulating. Winkowski looking left and right, shifting his weight. Getting impatient. The takeover box they'd plugged into the OBD-II port was controlled by smartphone app. Porter, behind the wheel of the van, was supposed to kill the starter and unlock the doors.

Dex lost sight of the full scene. He could only see the corner of the truck, an impression of color through the windows of the bank's vestibule.

A horn sounded. A short, grunty blast. Then a longer one. Like a tugboat grounded on a sandbar. They knew the sound well. It usually signified Freddy House, on the move.

"What's up with that?" Marty said. She left her station, moving toward the front doors. Dex followed, his body moving without any conscious direction. He wanted to catch Marty and pull her back, but he couldn't, not without giving up the game. She froze and gasped. Everything came back into view around her shoulder.

Something had gone wrong. Saenz was yanking on the door handle with one hand, pounding on the window with the other. Winkowski had his phone out. Probably trying the app himself. Dex couldn't hear what Saenz was screaming, but clearly something with the controls had gone sideways.

"They're carjacking him," Marty gasped.

Outside, Winkowski walked back around the truck, pocketing his phone. His hand came back out of his jumpsuit, filled with a gun.

Marty wheeled, heading for her station and the panic-button silent alarm just under the lip of the counter.

Wait! Dex wanted to shout. *Don't push it. Don't bring the cops down on us.* Which would have been game over for his cover, so he swallowed the words as he watched her reach under her station and punch at the alarm.

"They'll never get here in time," she said. "What do we do?"

Dex ripped his eyes away, looked back out the window. Winkowski shoved Saenz aside and smashed Freddy's window with the barrel of his gun.

THE GUILTY SLEEP

"They're gonna kill him!" she gasped. It was possible. Winkowski was wound tighter than an eight-day clock. There were too many ways for this to go south, for someone to get hurt. That wasn't the plan.

"Stay here," Dex said. "Wait for the cops."

"Don't be stupid, Dex!"

She said something else, but it was lost in the explosion of the bank doors as he burst through into daylight. He was in a full sprint in three steps.

Winkowski leaned through the shattered window, grabbing at Freddy. Saenz pulled at Winkowski, but the bigger man pushed him away. Saenz stumbled over the curb and went down.

"Unlock the doors. Do it now!" Winkowski bellowed.

"Help, somebody help!" Freddy screamed, pounding the horn.

"Man, *forget* this," Winkowski snarled. He stepped back and raised the gun. Dex crashed into him and they stumbled back toward the van. Winkowski had Dex by sixty pounds, but the bigger man was soft and unsteady on his feet. Dex drove him back until they slammed into the sliding door.

"No one gets hurt," Dex snarled, trying to keep his voice low. "Remember?"

Winkowski shouted wordlessly in his ear, grabbed him by the shirt, and threw him to the side. "Stay out of this," he grunted.

Dex had to get them away before Freddy got hurt, before the police showed up, before the thing spiraled even further into chaos. "Get out of here," he shouted, layering fear and indignation across his voice. A foolhardy bystander, too dumb to know the danger he was in. "Cops are on the way." A warning and a *warning*.

"Dex, help!" Freddy screamed. Saenz was inside the window now, wrestling with him. Dex could see Freddy thrashing, legs pistoning. He was holding on to the steering wheel with a one-handed death grip, punching the starter button with the other.

"Give us the case," Saenz said, almost pleading. "We don't want to hurt you."

Freddy cursed and thrashed. Something in the passenger compartment broke with a snapping sound and suddenly the pickup roared to life. Freddy must have kicked the takeover box. Broken it free. Saenz stumbled away as the F-150 lurched forward and thumped into the base of the light tower just in front of his parking space.

"Break contact," Porter called from the van, his voice booming through the open panel door. "Time to go."

Maybe Dex had gotten through to him. Or maybe he'd seen something, or multiple somethings, to make that call. People watching, certainly. Marty was outside now, standing in front of the bank doors, her face a mask of shock.

"Oh, forget this," Winkowski muttered and stepped forward, raising his pistol. "I'm going to *cap* this motherf—"

Dex grabbed him around the collar and yanked back as hard as he could. The gun boomed and the back window of the truck shattered. Winkowski bellowed, his fury deep and wordless, and swung his elbow, catching Dex on the bridge of the nose and sending him reeling. The back of Dex's knees hit the bottom of the opening to the van's passenger compartment and he fell against the edge. Saenz and Winkowski were converging on Freddy's open window. Dex could hear his boss's high, plaintive screams over the roar of the F-150's engine. Through the back window, he could see Freddy heaving at the gearshift. The truck's backup lights came on, a pair of ghost-white eyes.

The pickup's tires screamed and Dex yanked his legs up, rolling the rest of the way into the van. Freddy's truck smashed into the side of the van where Dex had been a second before. The van rocked on its springs and the truck skidded sideways. Everything went still. Dex met Porter's eyes in the rearview. They widened as Sunny saw something past him, out the back windows.

The world came apart at the seams, an explosion of metal colliding. The van lurched forward, sending Dex tumbling against the rear doors. Porter stood on the brakes, but they were pushed ahead on squalling tires. Dex smelled burning rubber. He lurched to his knees and looked out the rear windows.

It was Turner, in his vintage brown-and-cream El Camino. Well, not vintage anymore. Its crumpled hood was merged with the van's backside. A hula dancer on the dash vibrated madly. The El Camino's

THE GUILTY SLEEP

engine roared and the van slid forward another three feet. Dex scrambled on hands and knees toward the side door. Dragged himself forward. He had to get out.

"Break, break, break," Porter bellowed. It was the right call. Everything was in shambles. Only thing to do was get everyone out of there. Regroup, go to ground.

Dex's fingers found the open doorframe. He heaved himself the rest of the way into the opening just in time for Winkowski to come barreling into the van, knocking him over. Saenz followed right behind and landed on top of them both.

"We can still get it," Winkowski screamed, waving his gun. "We can still get it!"

Another crushing impact from the rear and the van skidded forward again. Dex looked out the side door and couldn't see the gray pickup anymore. They'd been pushed past it. He caught a glimpse of Marty. She was ducked behind one of the concrete posts supporting the shopping center's overhang. Smart lady. Their eyes met. Dex reached out toward her. It was a gesture that said he was stuck. Had tried to save the boss and instead had gotten himself trapped with the bad guys.

The back double doors of the van ripped open and sunlight flooded into the compartment. The El Camino reversed away, pulling the doors wide where they'd caught in what had once been a beautifully-chromed bumper. Turner leaned out the window, pointing a sawed-off double-barrel. Dex made himself as flat as he could, pulling at Saenz and Winkowski. The shotgun roared, a massive twin boom. A constellation of holes appeared across the inside of the roof of the passenger compartment. Winkowski yipped.

There was a higher engine roar. The burly V8 in Freddy's truck. Another squeal of tires and another crash at the rear of the van, shoving the back end aside. The open rear doors banged and clashed and stuck together, nearly closed. Freddy had reversed into the gap between them and Turner's car, knocking the van the rest of the way clear of his path. Freddy looked over his shoulder through his shattered window and, like Marty's, his eyes bored into Dex's.

The pickup lurched forward like a nervous stallion fighting the reins, tires spewing black smoke. It slewed to the left, grazing a parked minivan, then overcorrected and swerved to the right. Freddy clipped the front end of Turner's car and tore off the El Camino's bumper. The collision righted the ship and the truck tore down the lane of the parking lot, skidded left, and disappeared. For a breath there was silence. Then, in the distance, the rising wail of at least two sirens in counterpoint. Marty's panic button had done its job.

"Go," Saenz barked, and the Transit leaped forward.

"Where am I going?" Porter asked. His voice was calm and even. Like everything was normal.

Saenz heaved the side door closed, fighting against bent runners. "Follow," he said. The world shifted as the van skidded into its own turn, and Dex was thrown against the side wall.

"You bastard," Winkowski snarled at Dex. "This is your fault. If you hadn't—"

"Shut up, Winkowski," Saenz said, his voice calm. "No battle plan survives first contact with the enemy. We can do this." Then to Porter, "You have eyes on?"

There was a long silence, broken only by the roar of the Transit's engine and the bark of its tires as they slid through a hard left. Finally, conversational as a comment on the weather, Porter said, "I see him."

27

GONE FUGAZI

DEX

"Up front, Wink," Saenz ordered. Winkowski heaved upright, bracing against the roof for balance. He lurched forward and slumped into the passenger seat next to Porter. Saenz sat on the bare cargo area floor across from Dex and pushed his back against the side of the van. He pulled up his balaclava and wiped his face with his sleeve.

"*That* could have gone better, Specialist Grant."

"SNAFU, FUBAR, and TARFU all in one, Sarnt."

Saenz smiled wearily. "This," he said, waving at Dex, "was not part of the plan."

"I didn't want to get stuck back here either, but someone shoved a big angry man on top of me just as I was climbing out."

Porter heaved at the wheel and slammed on the brakes. The van slid sideways, felt like it was going to tip, then righted itself and blasted forward. Winkowski hollered. Dex looked at what he could see of Porter. Shoulders and half a profile. The man's face was calm and untroubled as a frozen pond. There was a blast of siren and a flash of blue and white. A county cruiser, blowing past them to the scene of the crime.

194   JEREMY D. BAKER

"We can make this work. We'll let you out after. Anyone asks, you never saw our faces. You begged us not to kill you. Showed us pictures of your little girl."

"What's the new plan?"

"We're going after him," Saenz answered, his voice pitched to carry. "This thing has a police interceptor package. Standard Golden Oak law enforcement mod. We can catch him."

"Maybe," said Dex. "Got a big ol' engine in his truck too." He clambered to a kneeling position and duck-walked to the front. He grabbed the handles on the rear of the seats, steadying himself. "But I know this town as well as he does. High school days, nothing to do but drive around. I can help."

Dex saw Porter's eyes flash up into the rearview. Looking back at Saenz for approval.

"Frogger's on nav," Saenz said, and Porter nodded.

"Hate that nickname, Sarnt," Dex said, getting his bearings. The shopping center, now three miles behind, was on the northwest shoulder of the inverted V of the town. They were heading west on 140, passing the outskirts in a blur. A shallow ring of suburbs and trailer parks next, then flat forestland that stretched unbroken until Taneytown thirty miles up the road. Freddy was a raincloud dot in the distance.

"OK," Dex said. "We've got—" He glanced at the speedometer over Porter's shoulder. The needle was pegged at 120 but they were surely going faster. The van juddered and shimmied like a half sail in a high wind, but the engine thrummed steadily. "—about thirteen minutes before he hits the next town. If he—hold on."

They blew by a minivan like it was standing still. The gray dot had vanished.

"Next exit on the right, Sunny. There-there-*there*!"

Porter slammed on the brakes and the speedometer needle dropped to ninety, eighty, seventy.

"Now!" Dex barked, and they shot down the exit ramp. "Slow to fifty or we'll flip. Then turn right. Open her back up, maybe eighty-five if you can hold it there."

"I can," Porter said. He might have been answering someone who asked him if he could do a single push-up.

"What are you doing?" Winkowski snapped. "Didn't get off here— he hit the next one."

"Right," Dex said. "He got off on Avery, which means he's heading north toward Stone. It's a secondary cut-through. Barely two lanes. No cross streets. Only one other road hits Avery before Stone and we're on it. We'll intersect three miles south of Stone. Best chance to catch him. If he gets to Stone, he can go east or west. Suburbs to disappear into in one direction, or he can open it up and run for the hills in the other. Either way, we'll never catch him."

"In other words," Saenz said, "shut up and let the man work."

Winkowski grumbled something and checked his gun. Ejected his magazine, inserted a fresh one. Checked the chamber.

"No one gets hurt," Dex said. "Still the plan, right?" There was a pause that went on way too long.

"Not if we can help it, Frogger."

"Still hate it."

"Fine, don't get all jumpy on us now."

"Too far, Sarnt, too far."

Saenz laughed, and for a moment everything felt just like it had. Far and away, back in K-town before it all went bad. Blackbirds in flight, operation underway. Bad jokes and ammo checks.

Dear God, have I missed *this?*

There was a sudden dip and he felt himself rise off his knees as the van bottomed out. He knew the spot well. He used to run his old beater down this road, and that drop was the best. Send your stomach a bit into your throat, make Daria hold your hand a little tighter. Maybe lean into your shoulder. Turn the music up a little louder. Windows down, warm summer night air streaming through like a jet stream.

"Merge'll be in a mile," Dex said, blinking against the memory. "We'll need to look both ways, see if we can spot him. Should come out just ahead if we hold this speed."

"Any sign of the car that hit us in the parking lot?" Saenz asked. "Or the cops?"

"I do not see anyone, but there is limited visibility behind us," Porter said.

"Ain't seen nothin'," Winkowski mumbled, peering into the side mirror.

"Keep your eyes open. The big guy with the boomstick in that car, he's the bag man, right?"

Dex nodded. "Someone else in the car too. A younger guy. I think he was with him on the last drop, but I hadn't seen him before that."

"Means the bag man—"

"Turner."

"—Turner, he made us somehow. Brought backup."

"It's gone fugazi," Dex agreed, "sure as sure." So easily he'd slipped back into the old terminology, the old feelings. *This* was why it was so hard for some guys to let go. The adrenaline. The camaraderie.

No, he hadn't missed this, he told himself. It was a means to an end, a means to *one week* and we'll see what happens. That was all. It was still the next right thing. It had to be.

A yellow diamond-shaped sign whooshed by on the shoulder.

"Brakes!" Dex said. The van's nose dipped and they screeched to a stop just into the T-shaped intersection.

"There," Porter said, with as much excitement as Dex had ever heard. He let out an explosive breath. They'd done it. The gray dot again, flickering through the trees. Freddy was a half-mile south and booking hard. Right toward them.

"Probably won't see us for another few seconds," Dex said.

"When I call it," Saenz said, crowding forward, "ease out, Sunny. He'll stop."

"And if he doesn't?" Winkowski asked.

"Then we'll either have bigger problems or none at all."

"Or he'll turn around and go back," said Winkowski.

"That's why we're going to time it right. Get out and wait in the grass. He stops, you can be on him before he turns around."

Winkowski grumbled and climbed out. Dex pushed the rear doors open, dropped to the road, and followed. Winkowski looked back resentfully, but Dex wasn't about to let him put a bullet in Freddy's

THE GUILTY SLEEP

head. They could still do this without anyone getting hurt. He could hear the roar of the pickup's engine, screaming like a war cry. *Now*, he told himself. *Now, Porter.*

Porter read his mind. The Transit shot forward, spraying gravel. There was a bark of brakes, and the pickup's engine noise spun into a throaty growl as the truck sloped into view around the last bend. Freddy was doing his best, but the speed, the road, the truck's high center of gravity, and the sudden appearance of the van, were too much.

The pickup slid right, overcorrected left, then went into a skid that carried it past the Transit's nose and into the grass of the soft shoulder, shedding speed and shreds of rubber from its abused tires. The truck flew off the road, rotating in midair like the world's biggest Frisbee. It caromed into the trees with a deafening tsunami of glass and plastic and metal. The trees swayed with the impact, the leaves dancing and scattering shadows on the pavement that swirled and writhed like dervishes.

"Stay here," Winkowski sneered. "Wouldn't want to blow your cover."

Porter got out, joining Winkowski and heading toward the side of the road. The pickup was in pieces, like a bomb had gone off in the engine. Chunks of bodywork were scattered everywhere. Smoke and steam rose among the trees. Here and there a gleam of shattered chrome or glass reflected the high August sun. Saenz joined the other two. Dex looked past them, scanning the wreckage for signs of life. Aside from the slowing dance of the trees and waving grass, everything was still.

"Oh, Fred."

28

THE SUDDEN STOP
IS WHAT GETS YOU

DEX

Quiet descended save for the occasional tick-ping from the Transit's engine as it cooled. Dex looked up and down Avery in both directions, then back up the road they'd come down. Nothing moved.

"Hello the truck," Saenz called. "Anyone hear me?" No response.

Saenz pulled his balaclava back down and motioned to Porter, who did the same. "Let's find the suitcase. Wink, watch the roads. Any civilians come along, wave them off and tell them we're from the county, clearing the scene."

Dex watched Saenz and Porter move down the embankment and through the high grass into the trees, watched Winkowski watching the intersection, and made a decision. He scrambled after Porter and Saenz. The chassis was twisted like a soggy pretzel and nearly naked, pieces of body and trim scattered everywhere. The engine was smoking and little fires were starting to spring up in the summer-dry underbrush. Dex stamped them out as he got closer. Got to what was left of the driver's area and saw Freddy slumped over the deflated airbag.

"Freddy," Dex said. "Can you hear me?" He reached out, touched a still shoulder. Freddy twitched and heaved and pushed back from

THE GUILTY SLEEP

the dash with a gasp. He had a cut across his head where his hairline had been twenty years ago, and blood was pouring down into his eyes. The scars on Dex's own forehead burned in sympathy and he remembered the feeling of hot blood cascading into his face, blinding him and leaving only the sound of a fly tapping against a closed window. He pushed it down, pushed it away.

"Dex, that you?" his boss mumbled, slushy and indistinct.

"I'm here." He leaned in and unsnapped the seat belt. Freddy groaned. "Let me get you out, boss."

"What're you doin' here?"

"They grabbed me at the bank when I came out. Made me come with."

"I'm all busted up, man."

Smoke rose around them, stinging his eyes. The flames were starting to spread.

"I'm going to get you out. Hang on to me."

"Leg stuck, unner th' pedal. Think's broken." Freddy was right. The ankle was bent the wrong way, foot twisted half around. Dex crouched, coughing against the smoke, and tugged at Freddy's pant leg, gently as he could. Freddy screamed, voice high and reedy with pain. It was getting hotter as more of the grass caught fire. He heard the sound of liquid spattering into the earth, and the smell of gas hit like a wave.

"Got it," Porter said, conversationally. He was twenty feet into the woods, hefting a much-scuffed but intact hard-sided rolling suitcase.

"I'm going to pull it sideways. See if you can move it."

"Y'gotta get me outta here, Dex."

"I'm trying, boss."

"I don' wanna die . . ."

"Ready? Now!" He yanked and Freddy shifted. There was a wet, grinding pop and the foot came free. Freddy's scream faded into a whisper and his head slumped to his chest. Dex levered him forward, got his arms around his chest. Heaved back, and they tumbled into the grass. Flames licked at his elbow. He forced himself to his knees and began dragging Freddy's bulk toward the side of the road.

"Back to the van!" Saenz called triumphantly.

Porter dashed by, parting the grass like a freight train, cradling the suitcase in his massive arms.

"Come on, Fred," Dex panted. "Wake up and help me out here. Flames hit the gas, we're toast." The man didn't stir.

Saenz went past, following Porter's path.

"Stu!" Dex grunted. Saenz saw him, slid to a stop. Came back.

"I'll get this one, take the other," he said, grabbing Freddy's left arm. Dex slid around, took the right, found it covered in blood from a gash in Freddy's shoulder. "Pull, Frogger!"

Together they heaved Freddy toward the road, at which point things went from worse to an absolute pile of fertilizer.

The flames from the grass hit the fuel pouring out of the ruptured gas line and there was a breathless whump as the main body of the wreck was wreathed in a high, blue corona.

"Company!" Winkowski shouted.

"What we got?" Saenz called.

"Fast movers times two, way we came. First one's that El Camino."

"Come on, Grant, we gotta go!"

"We need to get him away from the fire."

Saenz didn't respond, just pulled, grunting. And then Porter was there, shouldering them both aside. He bent, shoving his arms under Freddy's, then stood and dragged him the rest of the way up the hill. Saenz and Dex staggered after him. Saenz grabbed the suitcase from the roadside as Porter lay Freddy on top of the embankment with a surprising gentleness.

Past the Transit, the smashed-up El Camino came tearing down the road, followed by a black and primer-gray Honda. Winkowski whooped, high and wild, and stepped into the middle of the intersection, limping toward the oncoming cars. He raised his pistol in a sure, two-handed grip and started firing. One shot every half second, fifteen rounds until the slide locked back. In two more seconds, he'd dropped the magazine and swapped a new one and started firing again.

Dex reached the van just as the cars skidded to a stop twenty feet away. The El Camino went sideways and right, its headlights shattered and one of the tires going flat. The Honda banked left, barely missing the rear of the El Camino. In the distance, Dex could see two brightly colored dots smaller than a car, closing fast. The high, revving whine of motorcycle engines rode over the wind.

"Go!" Winkowski screamed. "Get in the van!" He kept firing and the Honda's windshield buckled, then shattered.

Dex felt a hand on the back of his neck, gripping his shirt and twisting it tight. The muzzle of a gun pressed into the back of his head.

"Act scared," Saenz whispered, which wasn't hard. He dragged Dex around the front of the van, giving the occupants of the cars plenty of opportunity to see the performance. He shoved Dex into the cargo area, keeping the gun pointed at him and then throwing the suitcase on top of him for good measure. As Dex fell into the van, Porter tumbled out like a boulder rushing down a mountainside. He was carrying an H&K G36 assault rifle.

No one gets hurt is a fine plan. A worthy goal. But when it comes down to the moment, there's always plenty of hurt to go around.

29

CORDITE PSALMS, PROVERBS OF LEAD

DEX

Turner's shotgun boomed and the passenger-side mirror of the Transit exploded. For a split second, Dex could've sworn he heard his daughter singing the ballad of the Central Park duck, her notes high and clear. Then Porter opened up with the G36 in a shattering roar. Saenz climbed over Dex and into the driver's seat. Winkowski followed, forcing Dex back as he went by with a shove that felt deliberate.

"Sunny, come on!" Winkowski shouted. He leaned out the side door, squeezing off shots with his pistol. There was return fire from outside, and three holes appeared halfway up the side of the van. If Dex had been on his knees instead of lying under a suitcase full of money, he'd have taken at least two of the rounds center mass. There was one more burst of automatic fire from Sunny's G36 and then Porter dove headfirst through the open door. Winkowski screamed for Saenz to punch it. The van leaped forward and hung a hard left.

"Dex, with me," Saenz said.

He crawled forward and slid into the passenger seat.

"Good call on the left turn. Spared us a broadside, Sarnt."

"You're no good to me dead," Saenz snapped, then softened it with a twisted smile. "Gonna be on us in a second," he continued. "Work your magic again."

THE GUILTY SLEEP

"We're heading back the way Freddy came," Dex said. "Toward 140—"

Winkowski hollered from the back, "Saw coupla bikes comin' behind the chase cars. Even if we make it to the highway, those two horsemen of the apocalypse'll catch us easy. Or, way things've been going, we'll blow a tire or get spotted by the State Police."

"Same ol' Wink," Saenz shouted over his shoulder. "Never change, man."

"Ain't cynicism if bad shit keeps happening!"

Porter said, "They are right behind us now."

"Just the little car and the bikes," Winkowski added. "Sunny blasted that El Camino to hell. Too bad—the thing was cherry."

"Wink's right—highway's no good," Dex said. "Another mile and a half, we'll jog right and then left, and cross a little bridge over Bear Branch. Just past that's an old logging trail. Right side. Soon as you see the bridge, stand on the brakes, take the turn. Might be able to get on the trail before they see us. If we can buy some space."

"Hear that, Sunny?" Saenz said. "Buy us some space."

"Stand by," said Porter. Dex watched in the mirror as he slid to the rear of the van. "Hold speed, please."

"You got it," Saenz replied.

Porter braced his feet against the rear doors, assault rifle at the ready. Winkowski knelt behind him, holding on to his collar. Porter slammed his feet into the van's rear doors and they flew apart. He opened fire with the G36. Inside the enclosed space of the van, even with the back and side doors open, the sound was deafening. Porter emptied a mag at full cyclic in three seconds, then called over his shoulder, "You have space."

"Wink, get the side door closed and secure that suitcase."

"On it."

"Half a mile, Sarnt."

"Tracking, Frogger."

"I hate that nickname."

"I know."

The van leaned left as they hit the rightward jog, then dipped right as they slid left. The narrow little bridge came into view.

"Now!"

Saenz slammed on the brakes, the nose of the van dove, and the tires screamed in fury. He heaved the wheel and the Transit slid hard, rear end whipping around. Then the wheels bit and they shot forward off the road, down the slope and under the trees, jouncing over the ruts of the dirt trail. Branches thumped and scraped over the roof and the side panels. Dex looked out the still-open rear doors.

"Stop," Dex said, and the van skidded to a halt. Porter, still seated on the floor of the passenger compartment, slid forward until he thumped into the back of Dex's seat.

There was a booming roar and a crotch rocket shot by like a cannon shell, heading for 140 and the horizon. There was another blur as the Accord went by, then a squeal of brakes and the sound of atomizing rubber. Split second later, the second motorcycle slid into view, also slowing.

Saenz sighed a soft but vehement obscenity. Then, louder: "Sunny, Wink—out on the flanks." Turning to Dex, he said, "Tried to keep it pacifistic for you, Frogger. I really did." Saenz reached into his jumpsuit, drew a handgun and opened the door, shimmied out and looked back at him. "Stay here, stay low." Then he was gone.

Dex slid down as far as he could. Reached up and angled the rearview so he could see out the back. Winkowski hopped out the back, following Saenz. Porter slid out the side door and disappeared into the trees on his side of the trail.

Up the trail, the Honda pulled into view, reversing hard and almost smashing into the stopped bike. It turned and nosed up the track until it was in the shade of the trees. The bike pulled in behind it. The rider lifted his visor, peering into the shadows. The Honda's doors opened and a skinny Black guy in an Army jacket and a skinny white guy with a cast on one arm tumbled out. Turner emerged from behind the driver like a bear coming out of a too-small hibernation cave. Another guy got out from behind the front seat passenger. Thin kid with a round face. Tightly manicured beard, baggy

THE GUILTY SLEEP

clothes. The guy who'd been in the El Camino with Turner back at Pine Hill.

The two skells looked back. The round-faced guy nodded and motioned them forward. The guy in the camo jacket was carrying a pistol and the guy in the cast had a Tec-9 with an extended magazine. Neither looked too comfortable.

"Go back!" Saenz's voice rang out from the trees. "Last chance."

Arm Cast cut loose with the Tec-9 and emptied his machine pistol wildly into the trees, shredding bark and leaves about ten feet in front of him. The echoes faded quickly into silence, muted by the foliage.

"I tried to tell you," Saenz called. He sounded disappointed.

There was a sound like a buzz saw. Sunny, opening up from the other side of the trail with his assault rifle. Arm Cast took half a dozen rounds in the back. His knees buckled and he slammed into the Honda's fender and slid to the ground, keening breathlessly.

Then it all went a little crazy.

Turner lifted the sawed-off double-barreled shotgun and let fly in Porter's direction. Two handguns opened up from the opposite side of the trail, Winkowski and Saenz. Camo Jacket and Turner's partner returned fire, ducking behind the open doors of the Honda for cover.

And the guy on the motorcycle decided to be a hero. He throttled up and the bike roared down the trail, blowing past the car, heading straight for the van.

Camo Jacket took a hit to the gut and folded against the car door, clutching the wound with one hand. He raised his pistol, groaning, then his head snapped back in a spray of red and he tumbled to the ground.

The guy on the bike got within ten feet of the Transit and locked his brakes, sending the bike in a spinning slide into the rear of the van with a gnashing scrape of metal. The rider spun around on his back and popped to his feet, running forward. He pulled a handgun from the small of his back and climbed into the cargo area.

Dex slid down in the seat, holding his breath. Tried to watch the guy from his peripheral vision in the mirror without staring at him. Felt like if he looked at him too hard, he'd be inviting return eye contact. He sent every ounce of will screaming the other way. *Don't look up. Don't see me.* He needn't have worried. The rider only had eyes for the suitcase.

"I got the money!" he yelled, grabbing the pullout handle. "Cover me!"

The rider hopped out of the van and the side of his helmet exploded in a spray of plastic and blood. He dropped like a pile-driven fence post. Winkowksi stepped from around the side and lowered his smoking pistol. He bent and when he came back up, he had the suitcase. He threw it in the van. Same time, there was another round of gunfire from the direction of the Honda. There were half a dozen sharp impacts to the rear of the van, and a hole appeared in the middle of the windshield. Winkowski yelped and tumbled away. Dex looked in the driver's-side mirror and saw him crawling into the woods.

Turner fired his shotgun again and the G36 answered, shredding a tree just past the Honda. The thin dude with the little beard fired back over the roof of the car. He started to dart forward around the sedan like he was going to make a run for the money too. But Turner came up behind him like a mama grizzly, enveloped him, and threw him in the back seat instead. The big man followed, covering the smaller guy with his body, which was just as well, because Porter dumped a whole magazine into the Honda, shredding the driver's door and blowing out most of the windows.

This was the chance, then. To press the advantage and maybe bring the whole thing to a close. Same principle as when you're running an interrogation, Saenz would've said. Find the opening and exploit it, drive the wedge home, don't let up, and thus endeth the lesson.

Dex threw himself across to the driver's seat, cranked the key, shifted into reverse. There was a thump and a bounce as he ran over something he hoped was the motorcycle and not the body of the rider. He pressed the pedal the rest of the way to the floor. Gritted his teeth for the collision.

The van smashed into the front of the Honda. Dex bit his cheek with the impact and his mouth flooded with the taste of hot iron. He

THE GUILTY SLEEP

207

kept the pedal down and the whole grinding mass skidded backward up the trail, the van pushing the little sedan. They hit the edge of the road, the rear tires of the van coming up off the ground and jouncing back down, grinding against the Honda's front bumper. Dex kept pushing, heading for the opposite bank.

There was a blur of motion and the throaty, high whine of an engine as the first motorcycle shot by across the bow of the van, heading in the opposite direction. *Poor guy keeps missing the action.* Then the van tipped backward and he hit the brakes. Dex watched the Accord slide down the slope in the driver's-side mirror. The front end was crushed in, steam rising through the gaps. He could see the outline of Turner's great bulk in the back seat, thrashing around.

Dex shoved the shifter into L and climbed the van back onto the road. Sunny and Wink were there, waiting for him. Porter had an arm around Winkowski's waist, holding him up. Arm Cast, the skell who'd emptied his Tec-9 fruitlessly into the trees and took a half-dozen rounds in the back for his trouble, was somehow still alive. He crawled up the trail behind Porter and Winkowski, blood dripping from his mouth. Saenz strode past the skell and, without stopping, he shot the guy in the back of the head as he passed. The man collapsed, his dirty cast brushing the edge of the tarmac.

Porter half carried, half dragged Winkowski through the side door, then forced it closed with a squeal of tortured metal. Saenz climbed in the passenger seat, staring first at Dex and then looking past him to make sure the suitcase was still in place behind the seat.

"You don't mind, Sarnt, I think I'll drive."

"Sure thing, Frogger."

Dex buried the gas pedal all the way back to Route 140, watching the rear and side view for pursuit. Nothing, not even the day-late and dollar-short motorcycle. Porter pulled up the left leg of Winkowski's jumpsuit while the latter moaned, "Not again, not again."

Porter grunted. "You are going to need a new leg."

Winkowksi was furious. "I *know*. This sucks. S'was favorite prosthetic."

Saenz chuckled. Reached across, gripped Dex by the shoulder.

"Nice work. Now see if you can get us to the safe house without this rattletrap drawing the eye of every five-oh in a hundred miles."

"I know just the way."

"Then drive, Frogger. Drive on."

30

COMMAND, CONTROL, COMMUNICATIONS

SAENZ

To Frogger's credit, he kept the shakes at bay until they'd reached the safe house. Well, safe rooms. The motel was pepto-pink, a low-slung cinderblock apology. Probably designed by a prison architect. A buzzing neon sign advertised VA ANC and C BL TV. The nearly deserted gravel parking lot told the VA ANC story well enough. The place was at an intersection, where 97 hit a seldom-used maintenance road half a dozen miles south of the Pennsylvania border. A county water tower glowered over the place like a tired giant rusted into place millennia before. Time and customers had both clearly passed the place by. Perfect for their needs. Anyone else showing up would stand out, and they had their pick of rooms. The two at the end, least visible from the road, with quick access to the maintenance road if needed. Saenz had gotten them the day before. He paid cash.

Frogger parked the battered van between the corner of the hotel and the ratty chain link fence encircling the water tower. Saenz had him back in, so the rear doors were facing the bathroom window of the last room. Porter disappeared around the corner with Winkowski leaning on him for support. No way was Saenz leaving Frogger alone with the money, not when they were so close.

A minute later, Porter unlocked the bathroom window. Saenz passed him the suitcase and turned around to find Frogger had vacated the driver's seat and was slumped against the wall of the cargo area. There were three bullet holes in the side of the van above his head. The kid was holding his hands in his lap and shaking so hard he looked like he might shatter into pieces. His pants were streaked with dirt and grease and smoke-blackened around the ankles, and his light blue dress shirt was torn at the collar and speckled with blood. Sweat-soaked hair hung over his face.

They were going to need him to keep it together, or the whole thing was going to vibrate apart. Saenz sat down opposite. Didn't say anything for a while. Just sat. Lit a cigarette and took a drag, then offered one to Grant.

"Trying to quit."

"Me too," Saenz said, then chuckled as he took a long, deep pull. "Some things I just can't give up."

Frogger lifted the corner of his mouth, still staring between his feet.

"So," Saenz said, blowing a stream of smoke toward the rear doors, "things didn't exactly go as planned."

"Smorgasbord charlie foxtrot," Frogger said, his voice as shaky as his hands. "Quite an accomplishment."

"It was all a blur once your boss came out early."

"The op plans of the great Stuart Saenz don't usually go wrong, not that I've heard."

"With one notable exception, Grant," Saenz said, keeping his voice low and injecting the ghost of a tremble at the tail end. Frogger, well-trained as he was, would pick up on it, read it as a deep and barely controlled grief.

"That wasn't your fault."

Saenz sniffed, knuckling an imaginary wetness from the corner of his eye, ever so slightly angling his face so Frogger would pick up the motion in his peripheral vision. "Tell that to Ahn, to—"

"How's Winkowski?" Grant interrupted, which was good. He was deflecting, trying to change the subject, make Saenz feel better. Focusing outward.

THE GUILTY SLEEP

"Grumpy about his leg, even for him, but he has a spare."

"Gotta be the world's unluckiest appendage."

"You ain't kidding." Saenz chuckled. Ran his hand through his thinning hair. Projecting a rueful exultation. "I can't believe we pulled it off. When it broke bad at the bank . . . I thought it was over."

Frogger didn't respond. He stared at his hands, like he was willing them to stop trembling. One more thing Saenz needed to address, to keep things on track and get Grant under control for the next phase. "I'm sorry your boss got hurt."

"Me too. Wasn't part of the deal, Sarnt. None of it was."

"No, it wasn't," Saenz agreed, adding a pinch of regret and resolve in equal measure. Taking responsibility, letting Frogger hear it. "That's on me. Should've had the van closer in case things went off book. Could've moved in quicker. Shoot, when the door unlocker failed, I could've smashed the window then and there. Yanked him out, hit the locks myself."

"Yeah. What happened there?"

"Didn't work."

"No kidding."

"The thing's a prototype." Saenz shrugged. "We tested it on the van and it worked fine. Must have been an issue with the F-150's system or something. They didn't talk right. It shut down the engine, but that was moot once he knocked the thing out of the port. I wish—"

"If wishes were ponies, we'd have a stable of horses."

"Hm. Haven't heard that one."

"My mother-in-law's, believe it or not."

Time to bring it home. Saenz reached across the space between them, gripped Frogger's forearm. His palm almost covered the Blackbird tattoo. "It wasn't your fault," Saenz said, bedrock in his tone. "When it counted, *you* were the one who kept things on track. You got us off that logging trail. You saved your boss's life. And now, because of you, we're going to save Jalal's life too. His whole family. That's a lot of good. A lot of making things right."

"By doing wrong, you mean."

"By doing one wrong thing, yes."

"People died today. I counted three men in the dirt."

This was an easy one, and Frogger's voice had no heat in it. "Enemy combatants. And you never pulled a trigger. What you did was save lives. You kiboshed the gunfight, got us out of there without more violence."

Grant pulled his arm away. Rubbed his hands on his thighs. Saenz was watching the kid pull himself together in real time, which was good. They needed him to keep it together until after the *Antares* arrived.

"You ready to help me ditch this van, Sarnt?"

Victory. Nearly as good as getting free and clear with the suitcase full of drug cash. They needed Frogger for two more things, and this was the first.

Saenz smiled, let him read the relief in it, let him read the relief as care. "You know it."

Frogger drove up the maintenance road three miles. Saenz followed in his company sedan. The cut-through was right where the map said it would be. They followed it to an abandoned farm, reclaimed as an environmental set-aside according to the signage. They parked the van in a clearing a hundred feet from the rotting barn, and doused the cargo area and engine block with gasoline. Saenz had Frogger light it. Another irrevocable psychological tie to the operation. Another invisible shackle binding him to the group. They watched it blaze down to the chassis, making sure the fire didn't spread.

The second thing: Heading back to the motel, Dex pulled up the *BurnR* app and selected phone mode. The app created a traceless VOIP using a bounceNet VPN to obscure origin and metadata. He turned up the volume so Saenz could hear the full conversation.

"H—hello?"

"Marty, it's me."

"My sweet Lord, are you OK? I've been trying to call you."

"They made me turn off my phone."

"Did they let you go?" The words spilled out in a rush. "I couldn't believe they grabbed you. Oh, Dex, I was so scared."

THE GUILTY SLEEP

"I'm OK, promise. They let me go a few minutes ago, threw my phone into the woods. I just found it."

"The police got there like a minute after you guys drove off, and I told them what happened."

"Good. Grabbing me wasn't part of their plan. I kind of got . . . caught up. I don't think these guys really knew what they were doing."

Frogger looked at him as he said it. Saenz rolled his eyes and Grant fought a smile. Good.

"The cops were putting out a bulletin. Trying to find them, find you. What *happened*, Dex?"

"After I fell into the van, they put a bag over my head. Never saw a thing. One of them said they didn't want to hurt anyone, and I should tell the police that when they question me. They certainly weren't looking to kidnap me."

"Was this . . . some kind of gang thing?"

Saenz nodded, and Dex nodded back. It was heading in the right direction. Frogger'd remembered the comms plan and was sticking to it, true blue. Saenz was almost proud of him.

"I think so. A carjacking crew. I read somewhere that F-150s are super popular for that."

"I thought that might be it. Or they were looking to get the bank keys and alarm code from him, rob the bank."

"Yeah, that could be it too," Dex said, his voice threaded with doubt, "only they didn't say anything about that. One of the guys said something about it being a shame about the truck . . ."

"Well, I just told the cops what I saw and they didn't ask me to extrapolate. I said it looked like our boss was being jumped by some guys and you went out to help him and got caught up, and then some other guys showed up with guns and crashed into the first group, and then everyone drove away. Dex, that was *crazy*."

"Are you OK?"

"Ha. Nice of you to ask. I'm not the one got kidnapped." She was all business now, either past the emotion or pushing it down to get the job done.

"Any word on Freddy?"

"Got off with the hospital right before you called. They brought him to county med about a half hour ago. Some Good Samaritan came across his truck all broken up out on Tyrone Road. He was pretty hurt, but they said he was going to make it. Was . . . was that your guys?"

Frogger glanced over again, and Stu nodded at him. A lie with the biggest dose of truth in it is the easiest to maintain. Thus endeth the lesson.

"It was. Felt like we were chasing him for a while. Back roads, from the turns and dips. They stopped when he wrecked. I made them—begged them—to let me try and help. I got him out of the car, but after I did, they put the hood back on."

"Hooooly schnikes."

"You ain't kidding."

"And they let you go?"

"I still can't believe it. I think they were trying to avoid that potential kidnapping charge."

"Where are you? I'm going to the hospital to check on Freddy—I'll come get you."

"I . . . I can't, Marty. I'm a mess. Not in a good place to see anyone, or to talk to the cops yet. I'm almost home. They dropped me off a couple miles from my place. In the woods by the college."

"Are you sure?"

"I'm sure. Go check on Fred. I'm not in the best headspace, and I think the rest of the walk back'll do me some good. I need to get myself together."

"Are you *positive?*"

"Hundred percent."

"Cops'll want to talk to you."

"Soon as I collect myself, they're the next call, I promise."

"I appreciate you called me before the cops."

"You're my friend." Frogger said it like he had a mouthful of broken glass. He didn't like lying to his friend. Saenz could read it like a

THE GUILTY SLEEP

billboard on his forehead. But he was doing it. He was too far in to turn it around now. The idea of saving Jalal, the idea of half a suitcase of cash free and clear, were twin anchors.

They pulled into the motel parking lot as Frogger hung up.

"Excellent," Saenz said. "Some real Blackbird stuff right there. Do that with the cops and we've got nothing to worry about." Frogger managed a nod, but seemed like he was all talked out.

Inside the room, he sat silently on the spare bed and watched Porter and Winkowski finish counting the money. There were two piles—a jumbled mess and a neat, rectangular stack. They pulled bundles from the jumbled mess and sorted the bills by denomination, then ran the sorted bills through a money counter. Porter re-banded the bills and placed them in his meticulously straight pile while Winkowski sorted the next batch. Saenz sat at the table by the window, smoking. Watching the fruits of his labor.

Four cigarettes later, Winkowski sat back with a groan and Porter placed the final stack of bills into his cubic masterpiece.

"How much?" Saenz asked, pitching his voice to pierce the dark cloud that seemed to be circling Frogger's head.

"Four twenty-seven," Winkowski said.

"Four hundred and twenty-seven thousand, two hundred and fifty-eight dollars," Porter added.

Saenz stubbed out his cigarette and deflated into his chair. Put his hands over his face. "We did it, boys."

Winkowski whooped. He rolled off the bed and thumped Saenz on the back before limping around to give Frogger an awkward, one-armed hug. He finished his victory tour by forcing Porter to give him a fist bump. And Sunny Porter actually smiled. Slightly.

"Plenty for the port director, plenty for our inside man," Saenz said, nodding at Frogger, who nodded back with a deep breath that lifted his chest. A look on his face like he was coming out of a bad daydream.

"Plenty all around," Winkowski shouted, pulling a beer from the fridge and cracking the can.

"Throw me one of mine," Saenz said. Winkowski tossed him a Diet Pepsi, and Saenz drained it in three long swallows. The tension bled out of the air, seeping through the cracks in the cinderblocks, disappearing into the muggy late afternoon air.

Twenty minutes later, Saenz dropped Frogger off in front of his apartment building. They drove by in both directions first, to make sure no county cops were waiting.

"Still out looking for you, probably," Saenz said. "You ready?"

"Yeah. Gonna call them in the morning if they don't show up before then. Tell them I made it home and the shakes hit," he said, looking ruefully at his hands. Saenz gave him a look that said, *I hear that, brother.* "Then I passed out and called them as soon as I woke up and pulled myself together."

"Same story you told your work friend, same as she told the five-oh."

"Same story. Carjacking gone bad, got stuck in the van, never saw any faces or distinguishing marks, Freddy wrecked, I pulled him out, you let me go. Don't know who the other guys were. They ask me to speculate, I'll say probably just a couple locals trying to play vigilante. No way Freddy'll tell the cops about the cash."

"It all holds together. Solid cover. Even if they don't believe you, there'll be no inconsistencies for them to pick at."

"Simpler the better, like any cover story."

"Thus endeth the lesson," they said in unison.

"We lay low. You lay low. And tomorrow night, after we get Jalal, we'll meet back at the hotel and I'll deliver your cut. A hundred and eighty-seven Gs, Frogger."

"Turned out to be more than a button push and a conversation, Sarnt."

"Yes it did, Frogger."

"Least you can do is stop calling me that."

"For a hundred and eighty-seven thousand dollars, maybe we can make an allowance every now and again?"

"We'll see," Frogger said, but with a half-smile that told Saenz this was all going to work. Hold together long enough to do what needed to be done, and do it in sequence. Just like he'd drawn it up. It was better than the rush of combat, better than the first cigarette of the day, better than anything.

He was God.

31

THE LAST THING

DEX

Dex sat at the crooked kitchen table of his moldering apartment and unfolded Rowan's drawing. Flattened it gently, stared at it forever. The sun and the pond. The ducks. The three happy stick figures. The sloth. He picked it up, held it under his nose. Breathed in the unmistakable crayon scent and, he imagined, a whisper of his daughter's shampoo.

He thought about the bottle of rye, thought about it for too long. Started the coffee maker instead.

One thing was left. The thing he needed to do most of all. He called Daria's cell phone but it went to voicemail. He reluctantly scrolled to his mother-in-law's entry and called her.

"Hello, Dex."

"Carleen, how are you?"

"How'm I?" His mother-in-law chuckled, her voice dry and yellow as old paper. "Fair to middlin'. Thanks for asking."

"You don't have to sound so surprised." He kept his tone light. Tried to.

"You looking for the girls?" Was her own tone lighter than he remembered from their most recent conversations? She'd been guarded then, bordering on hostile.

THE GUILTY SLEEP

219

"If they're around, yeah. I tried Daria—"

"Outside, watering the garden, both of them. Gotta get it done before sundown. Left her phone on the counter a-course."

In their neighborhood, you didn't go outside after dark and you didn't stand in your yard with a cell in your hand or pocket. You'd be inviting trouble. He couldn't wait to get them out. And now—the idea swelled, warring with the guilt and shame of what he was going to have to do next—he could.

"Could I talk to them?"

"Sure, hang on."

It wasn't his imagination. Some of the hard, brittle edges had been smoothed away. They'd always gotten along fine, even after Carleen had moved in with them when the tire plant died. Until they didn't. Until the plate smashed against the wall. Until Daria kicked him out. Until *Dean and Morris, Family Law.* But now, there was an actual note of . . . not quite softness, no, but a softening. He wondered what Daria had told her mother.

"Dex?"

"Hi," he said. A warmth settled in his chest. He paced around the table, looking at the picture, then decided he needed fresh air, to see sunlight.

"Everything OK?"

He pulled the door closed behind him, navigated the worn carpet to the lobby, and burst through the front doors. The muggy evening air cradled him like damp wool, but it was better than being inside.

"Everything's good now."

"Now?" A note of concern slid into her voice.

He paced back and forth along the flank of his building, holding on to the phone and his wife's voice as hard as he could.

"I wanted to check in. Let you know about something. Is this an OK time?"

"It's fine. We're just working in the garden."

"Hi, Daddy!" Rowan called in the background. "The hallapeenoses are coming!"

"And hallapenoses they shall be henceforth," he whispered.

"And forevermore. Hang tight, I'll put you on speaker."

"Wait, please. Just us for a second."

"What happened?" That concerned note deepened.

"There was a thing at the bank today. You might hear about it."

"Oh no, did you guys get held up? Are you OK?" She was whispering and muffled. He could almost see her, turned away and cupping her hand over the phone to keep Rowan from hearing.

"I'm fine. We didn't get held up, but some guys tried something with Freddy in the parking lot. Carjacking, I think. It got a little . . . chaotic. But everything's all right."

"Are you sure? Are you hurt?"

"I'm OK. I wanted—I needed to hear . . ."

"Dex?" she said, after a few seconds.

He fought the hitching in his chest, focused on catching his breath. "I'm here, Dare."

"I'm putting you on speaker," she said. "Rowan, tell your dad all about our garden."

It was a mouthful of cold, clear water in the middle of a desert. Rowan took him through everything and he listened and walked and breathed. Hallapenoses and tomatoes and peas (yay) and green beans (ick). And this shiny green beetle on the cucumber vine and they would take a picture and text it to him and Grandmama Car would teach them how to pickle things, and maybe that might be . . . shhh . . . *gross*, but she would still try it.

"That was exactly what I needed," he said, when Daria was back.

"I figured. Seriously, though, are you OK? I'm worried."

He knew what she meant, and the fact she was being so gentle about it had to mean something. It did, he realized. It meant *one week*. And it meant: *Are you going to drink, are you going to get angry like lightning from a cloudless sky, are you going to yell and throw a plate across the room if a neighbor fires their stupid shotgun into the air?*

"I actually am," he said. And meant it. "Thank you." And meant that too.

"Do you want to talk about it?"

"I do, but not right now. Right now, I'm going to sleep for twelve hours and then I'm going to check on Freddy and talk to the police, but yes. I want to talk about it."

"Come over. Tomorrow."

"Yeah?"

"Let Rowan show you the garden. She'll have her nap and we can catch up. Talk about things. If you want."

He wanted to ask her how she could still be so kind after everything he'd put them through. How broken he was. How she could ever have decided to take a breath, to give him a week to see if he could hold the line. Instead, he said, "Carleen be all right with me coming by?"

"If I say it's OK, then yes."

Dex reached the end of the building and stepped out of shadow and into the light of the evening sun, which was diving toward the horizon like it was running from something. The western clouds were a crown of gold and purple flames. He pulled the damp air deep.

"Then I'll see you tomorrow."

32

INTERLUDE: KANDAHAR, THREE YEARS AGO

DEX

Dex is slammed flat next to Ahn. His ribs are crushed in an invisible vise. Can't breathe, which pairs nicely with not being able to see. If the bullet went through his ballistic plate, he's a dead man and his body doesn't know it yet.

He thinks of Daria and her wry, secret smile, and the scatter of freckles across her nose. Her gold-flecked brown eyes and the way her hair never wants to stay out of her face. He thinks of his daughter and the way she gurgles with laughter when he tickles her tummy. The part of his brain that controls his emotions finally comes awake and whines about how unfair everything is, how he's going to die here in the dirt and never hold his girls again, but the other part of his mind, the instinctive, sarcastic lizard brain, shuts it down viciously and decides if he's going to bleed out next to Ahn in the lunar dust of this compound, he's going to take the other guy with him. He raises his pistol.

Ten feet away, a shadow materializes by the row of trucks. The shape snarls at Dex, pointing at him. Dex blinks, and the shadow resolves into the ANA guy. The one who'd been doing something to one of their trucks, the one who'd shot Ahn in the neck. Shot Dex in the chest. He points a small pistol at Dex, getting ready to put one in his head for the coup de grâce.

Someone looms over Dex from behind, shouting in Pashto. Their shape is squat, rounded, limned around the shoulders with a river of fire from the August sun. A pistol barks twice, right over Dex's head. The ANA shooter tumbles backward against the truck, slumping to the ground. The new silhouette leans down over him and becomes Jalal.

Jalal, holding a smoking pistol. He has just killed the man who shot Ahn and Dex.

Another shadow, taller and leaner, joins the first.

"Frogger," this one shouts, the tone identifying him as much as the shape, even though the sound quality is off, all high and tinny-sounding. Saenz. "You hit?"

"In the plate," Dex gasps, and adds, "I think." He blinks rapidly, and Saenz comes into focus.

The staff sergeant slips his hand between Dex's vest and his shirt, then pulls it out and holds it in front of Dex's face. The fingers are clean. "Didn't go through," Saenz says. "Try to get up. I've got to get Ahn." He turns. "Jalal, give me a hand!"

Jalal lowers the pistol he's not authorized to carry. The one that has saved Dex's life. There are pounding footsteps. Curses and shouts. The rest of the team arrives in chaos. Schoepe-Dogg pulls him to his feet, grunting. "Come on, Frogger, up you go."

Chonk is crouching over Ahn, pressing on his neck and shouting at him to hold on.

"What happened?" Sully screams.

"Green on blue," Saenz mutters, and then repeats it so everyone can hear. "Give me a perimeter, now. Anyone see the ANA commander?"

Dex rubs his eyes, clearing away the gelid crust of sand and grit and blood. The guy they'd stumbled into at the truck is sprawled against the rear wheel well. There's a splash of red on the white paint behind him. The guy's pistol is on the ground next to him. Porter kicks it away. There's something else by the body. Three metal tubes bound together with duct tape. Wires, too, red and black and white, and an ancient cell phone. Porter picks the whole mess up and calmly heaves it as far as he can in the opposite direction, out into the open gravel scree of the compound.

The rest of them are clumped around Ahn and Chonk and Saenz and Jalal. It's a perimeter only in that they're facing out, although everyone keeps looking back over their shoulder at Ahn's body. They shift from foot to foot, shouting over each other, trying to make sense of it. Ahn is their first casualty. They haven't heard or processed Saenz's command. Only Winkowski seems alertly focused, peering toward the gatehouse and raising his rifle. Porter starts to chivvy them into some kind of order.

"We should get out of here," Dex says, but it comes out in a whisper. He can't get the breath. He tries again and gasps, "There was something wrong, something off, back in the women's room."

Saenz doesn't hear him, and says, "Sunny, find me the ANA commander right now." Porter nods crisply and turns, but there's a shout from the other side of the trucks. The dagarman has found them instead. He comes around the trucks like a killer whale breaching the ocean, trailing his deputy and a few other ANA soldiers. His voice is angry, questioning, face dark as a funnel cloud. Jalal is muttering into Saenz's ear, translating, but Dex can't catch it.

There's a gunshot and they all flinch back. The ANA commander cuts off like a paused song and staggers around the middle Hilux, one of his great bear paw hands pressed to his chest. There's a spreading stain against the olive green of his uniform shirt. He's staring at Dex, his eyes wide and confused. Then the front of his face blows out in a spray of blood and bone and he thuds to his knees in the dust.

Dex screams, the sound tearing out of his throat, emptying his lungs. The dagarman's deputy, behind the hood of the truck, is holding a pistol in one outstretched hand. The barrel is wide and dark as midnight.

Winkowski fires a crisp three-round burst that takes the deputy square in the chest and drops him straight down.

"What the fa—" Sully starts, but the front of the Hilux shudders with the impact of automatic rifle rounds, followed a millisecond later by the unmistakable sound of an AK-47. It sounds like reams of paper being ripped in half by a chain saw. Someone is shooting at them from around the corner of the central building to their left, by where the weapons cache had been found. Something zips over Dex's head like an angry wasp.

"Contact left!" Winkowski yells, and he and Le Batard open up. Others join.

"We've gotta get out of here," Dex says, fighting for breath.

More incoming fire, this time from near the compound entrance off to the right. There's a muzzle flash from the small gatehouse that abuts the entrance. One of the taillights on the Hilux in front of him shatters in an explosion of plastic.

"Contact right!" Sully screams, returning fire.

"We need to get somewhere safe," Jalal shouts, pulling at Saenz's arm. "The women's room should be dug down into the ground. Good cover!" Saenz nods curtly. Decision made.

"Broken arrow, Blackbirds! Covered withdrawal in pairs to the northeast corner," Saenz barks. "Porter and Chonk with Ahn. Go!"

Dex claws at Saenz's arm. "Sarnt—" he begins, but Saenz cuts him off.

"Get me some fire on the gatehouse, Frogger. Now!"

Dex holsters his pistol and slides the carbine around from his back, kneels, flicks the safety, and starts firing single shots toward the gatehouse, quick as he can.

"Boss," he calls over his shoulder without looking. "We need to get out of here!"

There's no indication Saenz has heard him, because he shouts, "Wink, Jalal, go!"

Now everyone is shooting. A sideways orchestra of chaos. Someone's grabbed Chonk's squad automatic weapon, pouring controlled bursts at the corner of the main building. The rounds chew up the side of the façade, bricks exploding in a shower of brown dirt. Dex keeps shooting at the gatehouse until his mag runs dry. He drops the empty, swaps it with a full one from his vest pouches, resumes firing. The motion is from muscle memory. The rest of him feels like it's slowly coming out of a fog.

More bullets zip in from the direction of the gate, and the dirt in front of him kicks up. He screams breathlessly and fires again.

"Sully, Frogger, go!"

He gives up trying to convince Saenz they need to leave. The incoming's too hot; they're too exposed. Cover is better. The women's room at least offers that, dug into the earth like it is. Jalal's suggestion makes sense. They can dig in, call in the QRF from the palace. Couple squads of Green Berets will make short work of whatever this is.

Dex fires three more rounds. His final shot splinters the center of the gatehouse guard shack door. He sprints after Sully, catching and then passing him despite the burning fire in his chest. He's always been a runner, usually in the top three finishers in the two-mile run portion of the quarterly battalion PT test. Even with only half his wind and the lightning-strike pain in his chest, he's fast.

Winkowski and Jalal have passed Porter and Chonk, who are dragging Ahn between them. Ahn's heels catch and bounce in the dirt, kicking up a trail of dusty gravel. Dex can't bear to look at Ahn's too-pale face and the bright redness painting his neck and upper chest. He can't bear to look but he can't look away, can't stop seeing it, even as he passes them.

The mud brick wall of the compound rises above them. He's almost caught Jalal and Winkowski, who are both faster than he'd thought. But Jalal stumbles over nothing, goes down in a heap. Dex hurdles him cleanly to avoid tripping over him, then skids to a halt. He heaves Jalal to his feet, and carries-drags-shoves him forward until they've got momentum. He pushes the terp ahead.

Hold the door from whatever's out there and call for backup, that's what they've got to do. Let the snake eaters come out, scour the place, and then they can pick up the pieces. AQ and the Taliban have both pulled this kind of thing before, a green on blue insider attack. He's read up on it, scanned the intel reports before deploying. Usually, it's

THE GUILTY SLEEP

only one guy though. Pulls a gun, shoots as many coalition troops as he can before he's taken out. This, the shooting and the bomb and the multiple hostiles, feels like something else. Maybe all the Blackbirds' operational successes have made them a top-tier target, something worth expending a passel of resources and operatives.

Winkowski charges on, but Jalal peels off and stands to the side, shooting back the way they came. Stupid brave. Screaming at him to *go go go*. Beyond Wink, the wooden door. The bright paint, blue as the sky, but with whorls of a seasick green underneath from a previous paint job. Cheap metal handle with a knob-turn lock, cracked wood around the edges, dark with dirt. Three more steps and he'll be caught up. Two more. He could almost reach out and grab Winkowski by the canvas drag loop on the back of his vest if he wanted to.

There are footsteps behind. The rest of the team. There's more enemy gunfire from back by the trucks. The wall above the blue door explodes with impacts, fountains of brick and mud cascading over them.

Dex pushes hard, one last burst.

Winkowski crashes into the door, flings it open, and disappears into the dark. Dex trips on something and his feet slide in the loose soil.

Eyes appear in the shadowed doorway. Luminous, brown, huge. An open mouth, calling him. A hand reaches out of the black. It's small and delicate, nails painted bright red. A thick Bronx accent, screaming at him. Fatima. She grabs the front of his vest and pulls him inside.

Down into the dark.

Dex stumbles down the rickety trio of steps, tripping over someone's feet and sliding to the floor on his knees. The women are huddled in the far corner. Seven of them, three in those full, deep blue burqas and the rest in hijabs. His ears ring now with a continuous, whistling hum. Habibullah, the Afghan soldier, is shouting questions at Fatima, who's ignoring him and trying to pull Dex to his feet.

Schoepe-Dogg crashes through the door next, manages not to fall down the steps, turns back, and fires into the courtyard. The room's in deep shadow, but light flares every time someone else crashes through the door. Even with the high, naked aftertone of gunfire ringing he can somehow hear the tap-tap-tapping of the fly. One of the windows shatters and he wonders insanely if the poor bastard will finally be able to escape. He gets to his knees, Fatima's hand on his vest, when the door flies open again and there's a tangle of limbs and the sound of grunts and cursing. Three double thumps as they stumble down the steps and crash into him, taking him down again.

The world blooms bright. Shadows sharpen into knives.

It's Porter and Chonk, Ahn still between them. Dex is trapped under Ahn's body, and he starts to scrabble free. Porter gets up first, gracefully, and heaves Chonk to his feet.

"Ah, no," Chonk groans, looking at his left forearm, which is shattered and gaping, dripping blood in a stream that spatters into the dirt floor. "They got me. I can't believe it."

Dex looks at Ahn. The PFC's sunglasses are askew and his eyes are open, staring at nothing. His skin is the tone of wet dust in the blade-edged light.

Another pendulum of dark into light, a chiaroscuro of gloom and white-hot gold. He makes out Saenz, shoving a shouting, struggling Jalal down the steps into the room ahead of him. Jalal screams like a wild man, waving his pistol. He trips and falls over Ahn's legs, crashing over Dex. He surges insanely back toward the steps, and Dex snatches at his belt to hold him back.

"You need a tourniquet," Porter says to Chonk, matter-of-fact like he's reading a weather report, and pulls one out of his med pouch and gets to work. Saenz bellows something. Sully and Le Batard are crouched on the steps, shooting out the door into the courtyard. Saenz stands behind them, adding his own fire. Jalal pulls free of Dex's grip and hunches behind Saenz like he's looking for an opportunity to charge back up the steps into the fray. Everyone's there.

"I counted eight—maybe ten—hostiles," Saenz calls. "Wink, you have the radio?"

"Got it, Sarnt. Calling for QRF now."

THE GUILTY SLEEP

"Oh no, oh no," Fatima is saying, and it comes out like a mantra, *ohno-ohno-ohno-ohno*. She leans down to help Dex free of Ahn's prone form.

There's movement from the far side, where the women are clustered. The three in the burqas are striding forward and the others scatter and their brightly colored hijabs flutter with the sudden movement. Like butterfly wings. The burqa-clad women are moving in a tight, tactical triangle that suddenly spreads, and the ones to either side bring short-barreled AKS-74Us out from the folds of their deep blue burqas, smooth and slow, like they have all the time in the world. They shout Allahu Akbar with deep, rough voices. Male voices.

Jalal screams, high and desperate.

Dex's rifle is trapped under Ahn's body, but once again his lizard hindbrain has taken over and his pistol appears in his hand. He points it past Fatima's head, trying to somehow yank her behind him, pull himself the rest of the way up from the floor, and squeeze the trigger all at once. He only manages the third.

Fatima howls as the concussion destroys the air beyond her ear. It's a good shot, better than any he's ever made at the range, and it takes the figure on the right square in the burqa's mesh facemask. The man goes down, spasmodically pulling the trigger of his AKS. His rounds smash into Fatima and she shudders under the impacts, slumping into Dex's arms.

The women in hijabs—the real women—are screaming. The Blackbirds are shouting and turning and raising their rifles to face this new threat. Jalal shrieks again. It sounds like the same thing he shouted before. He seizes Habibullah by the front of the shirt. The kid struggles, beating at Jalal's hands.

"Wait . . ." Fatima gasps in Dex's ear, her lips worming against the skin of his cheek. The life is draining out of her, but she's putting everything she has into it. "You have . . . to stop. It's . . ."

Jalal hurls Habibullah into the burqa-clad man at the center of the triangle. The one without a rifle. The one holding something small and square in his right hand, which is raised as if in triumph. There's a button under his thumb. He pushes the button just as Habibullah crashes into him and knocks him back, and the room disappears in a flash of light hotter than the sun, a tearing boom louder than thunder, a concussive blow like the hand of almighty God has reached down and smashed them all flat.

SATURDAY MORNING

33

THE PARABLE OF THE REAVER

TURNER

"And the bodies?" Angelita asked, when it was just the three of them in the elevator.

"Chauncey and me . . . buried them," Slade said. "Off the trail, deeper into the woods."

Angie looked at her nephew, measuring him. Her eyes were the color of a grizzly's fur and sharp as the claws. Slade didn't shrink back under that gaze like he might've done the week before, Turner noticed. Your first gunfight, provided you live through it, makes the things you might have been scared of before seem about as terrifying as a game of tiddlywinks.

"Can they be tied back to me?"

"No. Took their wallets, their phones and stuff, and burned it all. And we buried them on pine needle mulch and powdered sulfur."

Angie raised an eyebrow and Slade trailed off. Turner waited a beat, let him hang to see what the boy would say.

"Turner's idea. Make the soil more, um, alkaline—"

"Acidic," Turner murmured.

"—help them decompose faster. In, like, two days they won't be able to pull any prints even if they do find the bodies."

"They won't, boss," Turner added. "Grave's way off the beaten track. Inside a week, even a cadaver dog won't hit on the spot."

"And none of 'em got their DNA in the system, far's I know," Slade added.

"It's good you buried them in the woods," Angelita said, clipped and spare as frostbite. "Saved space in the foundation at Sunrise Vista. We're going to need it."

The elevator dinged and Turner remembered a sound, one he'd first thought was maybe birdsong, but was actually the cries of a couple street dealers, boys who'd pressed their foreheads together as the cement cascaded down.

Everything was gleaming white and antiseptic and quiet. A recovery floor after midnight usually is. There was a reception area to the right, with a scattering of chairs and vending machines. One person seemingly asleep there, wearing sweats with the hood up, legs curled underneath. Slumped over in a way that made Turner's lower back twinge.

They walked past the call station and the night-shift nurse pretended she didn't see them. There was a cop waiting at the end of the hallway, Sheriff Pittman himself. From a distance, the man cut an impressive figure in his starched blue uniform. Four stars on the collar, like a general. Closer in, he was less impressive. It was the eyes. Small and pink-rimmed. They darted nervously between Angie and Turner, like a fox in a cage. It was the hands too. They turned his smokey bear over and over, rapidly deforming the brim. A single nose hair poked out of the chief's left nostril, and Turner wondered if Pittman felt it tickling his top lip.

"Miz Cooke," Pittman began, then coughed and cleared his throat. He sounded like a preacher's son who'd been caught with a fifth of Jack and the neighbor's daughter. "What do you need from me?"

"What I need from you, Arn, is to stay the hell out of my way."

"I'm sorry?"

"This is my problem, and I don't want your little collection of pisspots mucking up the works."

THE GUILTY SLEEP

Pittman wiped his mouth. "Miz Cooke—ma'am—near's I can tell, we just had an attempted bank robbery, three gunfights, and car chase in the middle of the county seat . . ."

Angelita lasered him with her eyes and he wound down like a toy robot whose batteries had quit.

"It was an attempted carjacking gone bad," Turner said quietly, leaning in and letting his bulk do some work. "Word on the street, some bangers came up from Baltimore, looking to score a set of wheels. I hear they've got a network of slice and dice shops out there. Big money in parts or even wholesale. Or maybe they wanted it for a drive-by—you never know. Once Mr. House wrecked out, they booked it. Wasn't worth the salvage—all the leftovers were too small."

"Or burnt up," Slade added helpfully.

"Or burnt up," Turner confirmed.

Sheriff Pittman rotated his hat around in his hands some more, surely mirroring the solitary wheel turning in his head. His eyes bounced from Turner to Slade to Angie. Whatever he was thinking, it was no contest versus what he was being told.

"I understand," he said. "Gangbangers. Probably gone back Bawlmer way. We'll close it out." He shuffled around them to escape, settling the bent-brimmed smokey back on his head like a helmet. Turner watched him all the way to the elevator, and Pittman never looked back.

"Money well spent, boss," he murmured. Angelita gave him a tight smile and tipped her head at the door on their left. "Wait here, Slade."

Turner followed Angie into the room. Freddy was sleeping. His right leg was in a cast from toes to hip, elevated in a complex harness that looked like a medieval torture device. A bandage circled his forehead. His eyes opened when Angie touched his hand, then opened wider when he saw it was her. Turner put his hands on the rail at the end of the bed and leaned forward, which loosened his back somewhat. That was nice, at least.

"Hey, Freddy, how they hangin'?"

"Hey, Turn'. H . . . hello, Miz Cooke."

"Fred. They taking good care of you?"

"Pretty good, all things considered. Leg's broke in three places. They put in a bunch of screws and rods and stuff. I gotta have physical therapy."

"I'm glad to hear it wasn't worse."

"Miz Cooke, I'm sorry about this. I tried to get away."

"I know you did. Turner told me."

"They chased me down, wrecked my truck—"

"You did everything you could."

"—but I almost made it." Freddy hadn't seen it yet, what was coming.

"You almost did." Angie smiled down at him. Her hands were on the bed rail. The black stone necklace was coiled around her left hand, cross dangling over her thumb. Which meant it was all over but the crying. Turner buried a sigh.

"Listen, I think I can help."

"How's that, Freddy?" Turner asked.

"It was an inside job." Freddy whispered, like he was worried someone was listening in.

"The girl? Wassername, Mary?"

"Not Marty, no."

"Wait—not the guy who ran out," Turner said. "The war hero? Looked like he was trying to help you, Freddy."

Freddy nodded, his face hangdog with sadness. "Dex. Dexter Grant."

"Doesn't make sense, Freddy. He jumped those guys. I saw it. They tossed him in the van. When we caught up to 'em, they had him at gunpoint."

"No, listen," Freddy insisted. "When I wrecked out, I got stuck. Truck was in pieces around me. On fire. Dex was there. He pulled me free. With my leg an' all, I kinda passed out."

"Go on, Fred," Angie encouraged, smiling softly.

"He was draggin' me away from the car, an' I was kind of in and out of it, ya know? But one of the other guys came to help him pull me away from the fire. Dex knew his name. Called him Stu. And that guy, I heard him call Dex *Frogger*. Like a nickname."

THE GUILTY SLEEP

237

"They knew each other."

"They did. He was with 'em. Must've brought 'em down on us."

Turner glanced at Angelita and her eyes held him like a bug pinned to a card.

"Where can I find him?" Turner asked.

"He an' his wife split up, few months back. He's got some crappy apartment. It's only like half a block north of here on Old Washington. The white building with the maroon awning. I don't know which apartment." Freddy blinked and a tear rolled down his ruddy, weathered face. "I just can't believe it."

Angie nodded at Turner. He stepped around to the head of the bed.

"Moreover, it is required of stewards that they be found trustworthy," she said.

"Ma'am?"

"Madre de Dios, you're *compromised*, Fred. I can't use you or the bank anymore."

"I'll hire a full-time guard. Bring them with me when I do a casino run. An' I won't tell anyone. I promise."

"It's the talents, Freddy."

"The talents?"

"Shhh," she whispered. "A talent, worth six thousand denarii—a single denarii being a day's wages. Long time ago, see, there was a terrible master. A reaver, Fred, feared by all. He gave five talents to one servant, two talents to another, one talent to a third. The first two took care of the money and doubled the investment. The third was afraid of his master and buried it. Some versions of the tale say he lost it altogether. The terrible master comes back, looking for his money. Rewards those who safeguarded and grew his investment. But to the third one, the master says, 'You wicked and slothful servant, you knew that I reap where I have not sown and gather where I scattered no seed. Then you ought to have taken care of my money. What you have, I will take, and you are a worthless servant who shall be cast into the outer darkness.' You see?"

Freddy looked up at Angelita and realization finally dawned.

"No. Please, Miz Cooke. Angie. It's not fair."

"Dios le da pan al que no tiene dientes, Fred." She fingered her cross necklace. The black stones tapped against the bed rail.

Turner didn't much care for this part, didn't much care for his part in it. But it was inevitable as an avalanche once the first echo rumbles the snowfield. He slid the pillow from under Freddy's head and put it over his face. Pressed it down. Freddy's hands flapped around the pillow like a pair of bird's wings. Angie took the hypodermic out of her back pocket and uncapped it. The liquid was clear, just a hint of gold. She slid the needle into the IV port and pushed the plunger. The heroin flowed. A hot shot, triple dose of pure H. Thirty seconds later, Freddy went still and his breathing slowed. Turner held the pillow down until it stopped.

They walked out of the room and pulled Slade into their orbit as they moved down the hallway.

"A day of darkness, a day of gloom, a day of blackest night."

"Auntie?"

"The prophet Joel, boy." Her voice was low and dry, a copperhead sidling through the brush. "Beat your plowshares into swords and your pruning hooks into spears, oh men."

"Yes, ma'am," Turner murmured.

"I recalled Florencio and Lael from Pittsburgh. They'll be back in two hours. A fire devours before them, and flames burn as they ride. I'm putting them on this inside man. I want to see him face to face. You two, sit on his place until they get there."

Turner slid the envelope of cash to the nurse as they passed the station at the far end of the hall. The woman took it without looking up. Smart.

"Then what?" Slade said as the elevator doors closed.

"You and Turner are going to take care of the other part."

"What's that?"

"Leverage."

THE GUILTY SLEEP

Turner hadn't yet mourned the El Camino. The last thing he'd done was unstick the picture of the little blonde girl from the dash and enshrine her gap-toothed smile in the folds of his wallet. The car itself had been transformed into a block of compacted metal, four feet to a side, courtesy of Junior's Junkyard and Wrecker Service, a proud if off-the-books subsidiary of Cooke Construction Solutions. Along with a slightly smaller black and primer-gray block that had been Slade's Honda, it was just another cube in the crushed-car wall that encircled Junior's yard. The soulless, anodyne white pickup he was sitting in now only made the loss sharper. They'd pulled the CCS-branded magnetic decals off, of course, but those were the only character the thing had. And the stereo sucked.

He and Slade were outside Dexter Grant's apartment building, waiting for the Kaibiles. Poor guy didn't know what he was in for.

"Gotta hand it to you," Turner said. "It was a good idea."

Slade froze, Mountain Dew halfway to his mouth. "What?"

"The Google. Social media, whatever. Smart call."

"My generation has its weaknesses, right? But that stuff is useful too. Once we had his name, it was just following the links."

Slade looked down at his phone, thumbing through the pictures in Grant's ex's feed. He used a pair of fingers to expand one photo, zooming in on the little girl's face. Touching her eyes.

"Like any other breadcrumbs, huh?"

"You don't have to look so surprised."

"You're learning, my young padawan. That's all."

"We hosed it up. Let the money get away. My guys didn't carry their weight."

"Three of your guys carried their weight right into the dirt. Their side had bigger guns. It happens. Angie knows it—how do you think she got control of what she's got, her and the Motherchucker? Wasn't through diplomacy and pretty speeches, tell you that."

"And this Grant guy, he was in the war, right?"

"Yup."

"Means the other guys . . ."

"Probably his old Army buddies," Turner finished. "Which means we went up against a buncha dudes who were better armed *and* trained. We gave it a go and we lost. But we tried, we're not compromised, and we're part of the solution. Which is why we're not in a hole next to your friends."

Slade breathed out, long and slow.

"Well, maybe not you. You're family, after all."

"That's reassuring."

A car pulled into the parking lot. Turner slid low in his seat and thumped Slade on the thigh and the kid followed suit. The car backed into the space next to the truck. The passenger window descended. The Kaibiles. Lael riding shotgun, shaved head gleaming in the sodium overheads. Turner levered himself upright and lowered his own window.

"Go now," said Lael. "Do the next part. La Jefa is waiting."

"Happy hunting," Turner said. The guy didn't respond.

Slade put in the address, propped his cell in the cup holder so Turner could see it.

"Let's go, yeah?" he said. Eager as a hound on a leash, scenting blood.

Turner sighed. He pulled out of the parking lot and made the first turn. "Yeah. Let's go."

34

RUN

DEX

It was New Year's Eve in the little yellow-framed house with the white front door and green shutters. The one in the neighborhood their lying realtor swore was on the way up, the home they shared before it all exploded like, well, a dinner plate thrown against a wall.

And it was the women's room in the ANA compound in Afghanistan, before it went up in a tornado of flame and rock and vaporized flesh. Dinner time, tea time.

Ahn's blood spurting red, and the early winter sunset coming through the kitchen window and firing the wall above the sink. Dex's pistol bucking in his hand, a hole appearing like magic in the burqa facemask of the assassin on the right. Fatima shredded by the return fire, collapsing against him, gasping words that will haunt him until he, too, is dust: "Wait . . . you have . . . to stop. It's . . ."

Jalal, throwing Habibullah into the middle attacker just as he detonates. The next-door Weavers, those drunken hillbillies, smashed up early for New Years Eve and shooting into the air at five in the evening like lunatics. Sending him back to that room and the guys in the burqas and the thunder of the explosion. The Weavers' shotguns roared and Dex hunched over the sink clutching the plate, head splitting, vision narrowing to a pinprick. Daria's concerned hand on his shoulder as he shook. The shame and fear turning to rage at his weakness. Fury erupting, the shout of *leave me alone*, the thoughtless hurling of the plate.

It sailed through the air toward the far wall as Rowan toddled around the corner, bright green strabismus patch over her eye, a smile on her face, and her favorite stuffed animal, a worn sloth named Brownie, trailing along behind.

He tried to pull the plate back. To save his daughter.

He tried to shoot the assassins. To save his friends.

He failed.

He failed.

The plate detonated into a thousand pieces above his daughter's head. Habibullah and the suicide bomber exploded into a thousand pieces at the far end of the room. Rowan's face crumpled in terror and Dex's heart ripped in half. The back half of the women's room collapsed, burying the enemy kill team and the Afghan women. Rowan fell to the floor. Her face was bleeding.

Daria ran to their daughter, picked her up. Dex followed, willing frozen limbs to respond, moving like he was wading through an icy swamp. Rowan screamed and sobbed and bled into his wife's shoulder. He reached for his little girl and Daria wrenched away, keeping him at bay while she looked at their little girl's face. She turned, staring at him. *Look what you did*, his wife said with her eyes and maybe her mouth. *Look what you did*, he said to Jalal in the ghost of his memory, looking at two severed feet in their sandals, all that was left of Habibullah. His daughter had a deep cut on her cheek, welling blood. A shallower one on her forehead above her right eye. The strabismus patch she wore over that eye was scored, showing the white padding beneath. If she hadn't been wearing it, he'd have put her eye out.

This was the moment. These were the moments. The ones that changed everything. As his wife pressed a wet paper towel to his daughter's face and screamed at him to grab her purse. As the women's room vanished in fire and smoke. The Blackbirds were destroyed.

THE GUILTY SLEEP   243

Shattered by the ambush. His family burned to cinders around his feet. And he was holding a smoking match in his hand.

Look what you did.

He sat up, drenched in sweat, fighting the sheets. Back to this again. The twin nightmares held him, pulled at him with icy claws. *Come back*, they whispered. *Wade into the black river. Sink beneath the waters and breathe deep.*

His guts twisted. He'd thought he was past this, but he should've known better. After the way things had gone down, was it any wonder?

He blinked, images strobing behind his eyes. The motorcycle kid jumping out of the van, his head exploding. Dragging Freddy through the flaming grass. Smashing into the little Honda with the van, pushing it across the road. Saenz walking by the crawling tweaker at the edge of the road and blowing his head off.

He tore his way loose from the sheets and stumbled to the bathroom, wondering what woke him. Nearly the eternal buzzing of the fly, but not. There it was again. His phone, on the kitchen table where he'd thrown it next to Rowan's drawing. He staggered over, reached for it, knocked over the empty bottle of rye. The bottle rolled across the crayon masterpiece and he fumbled for it and knocked it to the floor, where it shattered like an icicle. Like the plate. Like the women's room. Like his life.

He shoved it all down, swallowed the mustard sourness at the back of his throat, and answered the phone.

"Marty, it's five thirty in the morning—"

"Freddy's dead."

Dex worked his misfiring mouth until a jumble of words tripped free. "That's impossible, he—"

"Shut up and listen. I've been calling—"

"I was—"

"*Listen*, Dex. I was at the hospital. Waiting for Freddy to wake up. Turner came in. He was with some lady and a younger guy. The lady and Turner went into Freddy's room. After they left, I went to see if he was awake, and he wasn't. He was *dead*, man."

Something settled in his chest, sliding like a tumorous weight from his throat to his lungs. "You think they killed him." It wasn't a question.

"I . . . don't know. It's all so messed up. The stuff at the bank, and now this?"

"Marty, I'm—"

Dex breathed a curse.

"What?"

"Marty, I've gotta go."

"Dex, what's—"

"I'm sorry," he said, and hung up.

Ran to his room and pulled on a pair of worn black jeans, a dark T-shirt, and his running shoes. Back through the kitchen. Looked through the peephole, the door flimsy as cardboard under his palms. He wished he hadn't given Terrence his gun. If Freddy came out of his visit with Turner and his people with flatline status, he had to assume they were tying off loose ends of their operation. And it was possible Freddy had figured out he was involved somehow, or suspected him. Which meant they'd be coming for him next.

No movement, not that he could see through the fisheye. But if they'd gotten to Freddy, he had to assume they knew where he lived. Since it was a ground floor unit, the windows in his bedroom were barred. The door was his only way out.

He slid the security chain loose and slowly turned the lock. Eased the door open, peered both ways. Started out, froze, turned back to the kitchen table, grabbed Rowan's drawing. He pulled the door closed behind him until he heard it click.

Moved toward the lobby, folding Rowan's drawing back into its neat rectangle, trying to keep his gait free and easy. He slid the paper into his pocket, and it felt like a piece of totemic protection falling into place.

Out into the early morning, still dark but the air already sopping. Brain still waking up, the gears starting to turn.

Saenz. The safe house. He had to warn the others.

35

ANGELS AND DEMONS

DEX

At the edge of the parking lot, under a sickly haze of sodium light, Dex saw Mariam's white Toyota. There was a red smear on the trunk and quarter panel. A handprint, dragged across the bodywork. He crept to the car, every striation of his muscles tugging him in the opposite direction. The driver's door was cracked. There was red on the handle. He opened the door and Mariam looked up at him through heavy-lidded eyes. Blood soaked her shirt. Her skin was the color of putty. A flash of Ahn's face over hers. Cold and gray, eyes dimming.

Not again.

He whispered her name.

She took a shuddering breath. "Dex."

"It's gonna be OK," he said, thinking it was a lie. "I'll get help."

She muttered something, but he couldn't make it out.

"What?" he said, leaning down. She turned her head to look at him, revealing a deep gash in her shoulder, welling blood. The white of bone gleamed.

"Can't breathe," she whispered. She reached out, arms ribboned with deep defensive wounds. He put her hands behind his neck and lifted her up out of her seat. The waist of her pants caught on the key ring dangling from the ignition, and he freed her as gently as he could before pulling her the rest of the way out. Laid her on the grass at the edge of the light cast by the overheads.

"What happened?" he asked, though he already knew the answer. It chewed at the back of his neck, waiting for the words to come out of her mouth.

She held up a hand and pressed something into his. A medallion on a broken chain. He angled it, catching the light. It was a sword inside a black-and-white oval. There was a word along the upper arc: *KAIBIL*. Military insignia.

"Looking . . . for you," she said. "I tell them . . . you live on the third floor."

"I'm sorry, Mariam. I'm so sorry." He dragged out his phone. Cycled through his contacts until he found Dawit's number. "Mariam, stay with me." He repeated it like a mantra as the call rang.

"Hello?" Dawit answered on the third ring, the sound of a running shower in the background.

"Dawit—" Dex said, looking back at the apartment. There was a guy standing under the entrance awning. Short and thick, shaved head, holding something long and metallic. A machete. He was staring at Dex.

KAIBIL. The word snapped in his brain, meeting the medallion in his hand. Guatemalan Special Forces. He'd learned about them at Fort Huachuca. Hardcore bastards, trained in the jungle for months at a time. *Heart of Darkness* stuff. History of war crimes and working sideline for the cartels. Which meant the guys who'd done this to Mariam were working for the people who'd killed Freddy. And, looking for him, they'd caught her on her way to her early shift on the custodial crew at the college.

"Hello, Dexter?" Dawit said.

The guy with the machete started toward him. The blade glinted in the dim light, but it was stained along the edge.

Dex needed to draw the Kaibil away so it was safe for Dawit to come down. But if he retreated, he'd lead the guy right past Mariam,

THE GUILTY SLEEP

and maybe he'd decide to finish what he'd started. Dex thought about Mariam's blood, her dimming eyes, Ahn's feet drumming in the Afghan gravel.

He slid his phone into his pocket and held up the medallion. It dangled from his fingers, catching the light. "This yours?" he said to the advancing Kaibil. Then, more softly, he called back over his shoulder, "Hang on, Mariam. Just hang on."

"Dexter?" Dawit crackled from his pocket.

Dex backed up a step as the guy came on, swinging the machete in playful little arcs at his side. There was a car next to Mariam's Toyota, and the Kaibil came between them like water through a funnel.

"Where's the money?" the guy said, his voice flat and low. Dex flung the medallion into his face, and got a smile and nod in response, as if to say, *That's what I thought.* With no seeming transition from stillness to violent motion, the Kaibil swung the machete in a vicious arc that would've taken Dex in the neck if he'd still been standing there. But he'd seen it coming. It was the only move to be made, hemmed between the two cars. Dex stepped back and yanked the Toyota's door open. The blade scythed and Dex shifted right and the machete clanged, sliding between the door and the frame and cracking the side mirror. Dex slammed the door, smashing forearm and trapping blade. Same movement, he stepped forward and punched the Kaibil as hard as he could, flush on the chin.

The guy only smiled and blocked Dex's next right, then crashed a left into Dex's side. It felt like someone hit him with a baseball bat. Dex bounced into the side of the car, the radio antenna thwapping him on the back. The Kaibil started to pull the machete free and Dex kicked the door as hard as he could and it slammed on the guy's hand. The window shattered and the Kaibil let go of the machete with a grunt. Pulled his hand free and stepped forward, still smiling. Dex waded in, raining kicks and elbows, trying to keep him in the narrow space between the two cars, limiting his options. The Kaibil blocked everything and countered with another left, this one a straight shot below the sternum that stole Dex's breath and sent him reeling. He spun into the side of the car and his face went into the antenna. Mariam rose from the ground like a ghost, pulling on the fender to lever herself upright.

The Kaibil slammed into Dex's back, whispering something dark and prophetic in his ear. His breath was hot on Dex's neck. Mariam, her arm dripping blood on the hood, grabbed the antenna near the top, pulled it toward her, and let it go. It whipped past Dex's head and slashed across the Kaibil's face. The guy cursed and let go. Mariam grabbed the antenna's base, groaning. Her groan turned to a scream, desperation and rage in equal measure, and she ripped the antenna free. Pressed it into Dex's hand, then stumbled away around the front of the car. Dex wheeled and swung the three-foot metal wire like a lash. It caught the Kaibil flush on the face again, opening a cut across his chin.

The guy stumbled back and Dex kept slashing, opening cuts on the side of his head and then forearms as he raised them to protect himself. The passenger door of the Toyota creaked open and the cabin light came on. Dex caught a glimpse of Mariam fumbling in the passenger well.

Dex hit the Kaibil with the antenna again and the guy hunched up to protect his face. Dex aimed a kick at his head but the Kaibil slipped to the side and thundered an uppercut into the outside of Dex's thigh. Dex reeled back, windmilling for balance, and caught the blade of the machete where it was still trapped in the door, felt it graze his palm. The Kaibil grinned through bloody lips and smashed his body against Dex's, pinning him against the car. Mariam's arm flashed over Dex's shoulder. She was holding a plastic spray bottle. She misted the Kaibil in the eyes, and the powerful odor of ammonia washed over them. The Kaibil screamed and pulled away, wiping at his face.

Dex snatched the blade and yanked it free of the door. The Kaibil snarled and closed in, blinking furiously.

Dex flipped the machete, caught the handle by a miracle, and swept the blade out as hard as he could, trying to force the guy back. The Kaibil lunged for Dex's throat. Blood sprayed across Dex's face. The Kaibil grunted. Something thumped onto the hood of the other car.

THE GUILTY SLEEP

The guy stared at the thing. So did Dex. It was the Kaibil's hand, palm up. Like a monkey's paw ashtray and twice as cursed. A finger twitched.

The Kaibil stumbled back another step, holding his left hand over the spurting stump of his right wrist.

"You like to cut people?" Dex hissed, raising the machete. "I'm gonna carve you like shawarma."

There was a loud cough and the back window of the car next to Mariam's shattered. Another guy was striding across the parking lot. This one was tall and slim with a slicked ponytail, but he, too, was wearing a work shirt with rolled-up sleeves. He was carrying a blocky pistol, tipped with a suppressor. Dex kicked the first Kaibil in the guts, driving him back into the parking lot. Threw the machete at the second guy, making him sidestep, then turned, looking for Mariam. She was slumped against the hood of the car, holding a hand over the bloody gash in her shoulder, head down. Dex dove toward her, bearing her to the grass, gasping *sorry* as they went.

There was another muffled gunshot, and something thumped into the Toyota's trunk.

Dex pulled Mariam around the front of the car to give her cover, then took off in a sprint parallel to the parking lot. Giving the Kaibil with the gun something to see between the cars, something to aim at away from Mariam, hopefully too hard to hit.

He'd made the length of ten parking spaces when the Kaibil materialized a dozen feet ahead of him, stepping into a pool of vomit-yellow light from the overhead light.

Dex skidded to a halt and raised his hands. "Wait—"

The Kaibil smiled and raised his pistol.

A squat shape blurred from the Kaibil's left, cannoning into the guy and smashing him headfirst into the light pole. There was a muffled *bong*, and the Kaibil slid to the ground like all his tendons had been cut.

Dawit panted, looking down at the man. He nudged the gun away from the Kaibil's hand with one bare foot and stepped back. Stared at Dexter like they were strangers to each other and themselves. Dawit was still dripping from the shower, wearing a damp undershirt and soccer shorts. His mustache drooped.

"Where is Mariam?" Dawit asked. "Is she hurt?"

Dex led him to his wife. Dawit knelt, cradling her. She stared up at her husband, eyes wide. Dawit touched her forehead, then snapped his gaze to Dex.

"No time for ambulance. Help me get her to my truck."

Dex got an arm around her waist and helped lift her up. She gasped in pain.

"I'm sorry, Mariam, I'm so sorry," he said as they carried her to the other end of the row of cars and Dawit's little pickup. A powerless litany. An inchoate invocation to a universe-spanning guilt. They eased her into the seat. Mariam whispered something to Dawit, who looked up at Dex with shadowed eyes.

"They were here for you." It wasn't a question.

Dex nodded. "I'm sorry."

Dawit ignored him. Turned his back and ran around the front of the truck. He climbed in, stared at Dex with eyes hard as tungsten, then shifted his gaze to his wife as he turned the key and slammed the gearshift into reverse. The sorrys kept spilling out, poisoned water from a broken dam.

Dex danced aside as the truck launched backward. The side mirror would've taken him out otherwise. He turned and ran back the way they'd come, watched Dawit's truck skid on to Old Washington and speed toward the hospital. Still gasping his worthless apology. He slid to a stop in front of Mariam's car, stared at the light stanchion ahead. The Kaibil was gone. He looked around, didn't see the one-handed guy either.

Dex needed to get gone too. Go to ground, warn the others.

Dex slid into Mariam's seat and, with a final apology, wrenched at the keys. The Toyota sputtered to life. He shifted into reverse, slammed the gas.

The car shot backwards and Dex heaved at the wheel. There was a shout. Dex looked in the rearview. The tall Kaibil with the ponytail stumbled into frame. He'd found his gun. The guy raised the pistol

THE GUILTY SLEEP

and Dex ducked, slamming on the brakes. There were two more gunshots as the car skidded. The back window shattered and the rearview mirror exploded, spraying Dex with the shards. There was a thump as Dex hit the guy, and a grunt and the sound of a body hitting the pavement behind the car. Dex shifted into drive and slammed the accelerator down again. The Toyota's engine protested and the tires spun.

The Kaibil with the shaved head and missing hand staggered in front of the car, painted white in the Toyota's headlights. He was reaching behind his back with his remaining hand. The little beater lurched forward like a horse being spurred. Dex hit the guy square on. The Kaibil rolled up the hood, adding new cracks and a spray of blood to the windshield before bouncing into the air with a scream.

Dex slewed to the right, lining up with the parking lot entrance. He let up on the gas just enough to make the turn on Old Washington. The rear of the car slid around and nearly spun out, but he steered into it, righted the nose, and tore off down the street. Looked to his right, caught a glimpse of the tall Kaibil on his knees, huddled over the broken, crumpled body of the first.

The street was deserted. He didn't think they'd be chasing him now. Even so, the principles of vehicular surveillance detection were inseparably ingrained—time, distance, direction. Dex made a hard right at the next intersection, then an immediate left. Kept parallel to Old Washington for a half mile, then another right, followed by a right and a left. He reached a red light and coasted to a halt. Checked the mirrors. All clear. The palm of his left hand stung where he'd grabbed the machete. He swallowed, thinking of Dawit, racing his wounded wife to the hospital.

He needed to warn the others. He pulled his phone out and opened the *BurnR* app and mashed out a message to *Contact #1*:

broken arrow broken arrow broken arrow

[The user *Contact #1* is no longer in the chat tree] came back instantly. He tried *Contact #2*—Porter. Same message, same auto response. *Contact #3*, Winkowski, better than nothing. Same. There was no chat tree anymore, no text contact with the team via the app.

The light turned green and he accelerated, switching to voice call mode. Waited three seconds while the bounceNet VPN navigated TOR to an anonymous call node, then tried to call Saenz.

[No telephonic connection for *Contact #1* found]. Saenz and the others had already gone dark. No surprise there. In counterintelligence, OPSEC is key. If he'd been halfway himself the night before instead of fighting his nightmares at the bottom of the bottle of rye, he'd have remembered to delete the app himself.

Going straight, he'd be heading for the pepto-pink safe house. He could warn them in person. But there was a creeping coldness in his gut. 'Cause here was the thing—if they knew about him, knew where he lived . . .

He turned right instead, slamming the pedal to the floor. Heading for the little white house with the black shutters and red door and terrible neighbors. He had to get to Daria and Rowan and Carleen, get them out of town, somewhere safe where no one could find them and hurt them to hurt him. Then he'd go to Saenz and they'd figure all this out. The sky ahead was turning pink with the promise of sunrise. The color of a wildfire, just over the horizon.

36

SOW THE WIND

TURNER

It was a small house in a lousy neighborhood. Turner could see what might motivate an ostensible good citizen like Dexter Grant to take a run at Angie's collect, if his cut meant getting his family out of the place. The sidewalks were cracked and weed-riven. Most of the front yards were overgrown, strewn with abandoned toys and rusted appliances. Broken glass sparkled in the gutters under the light of two surviving street lamps. The whole town had been going to ruin over the last decade, but this place was the suppurating edge of the rot.

The small house with the green shutters looked like the occupants were still trying. Inside the waist-high chain link fence, the grass was cut and the yard was trash-free. There were flower boxes in the two front windows and a small garden of raised beds along the side. The front door had an iron-framed security screen.

"We'll have to try the back, yeah?" Slade said.

"Yeah," Turner said. "You got the thing?"

Slade nodded, exasperation scrunching his round face. He held up the olive drab plastic box. Military surplus, retrieved from the ogre who maintained Angie's arsenal in the back of the abandoned tire shop at the closed-down mall on 140.

"Good. And remember: slow and quiet, minimal disruption."

"Said that already. Not that anyone on *this* street is calling five-oh."

They climbed out of the truck and Slade eased aside the front gate. They moved through the shadows to the backyard. There was a trio of steps leading to a kitchen door. They creaked ominously under Turner's weight. He pulled out his set of picks and started to unzip the pouch when the kitchen light came on. An older woman with the straw-dry hair and skin of a lifelong smoker trudged into the room, yawning. Turner froze.

The woman walked toward the back door and made a left at the last moment, reaching into a cupboard and pulling down a coffee mug, rubbing at her eyes with her free hand. Slade moved, easing off the lowest step. At the minute shift in weight, the half-rotted wood beneath him groaned.

The woman looked up, looked out the window. Her eyes widened. Turner grabbed the handrail for balance and blasted his foot through the door just below the dead bolt. It was a heavy, high-quality lock, but the doorframe was as weak with dry rot as the steps. The door exploded open. It knocked the mug out of the woman's hand. As it shattered on the floor, she opened her mouth to scream and Turner put his hand over her face. Slade stepped past Turner and showed her his gun.

"Not a sound, lady," Turner whispered, though kicking in the door had been louder than a Harley backfire. The woman nodded, eyes wide.

"Gotta be quick," Slade muttered.

"Sit down," Turner said, and the woman backed into a chair and collapsed, still staring at Slade's gun.

"Be chill and we'll be gone in three minutes," Slade told her. "Make it hard and we'll kill everyone here." He sounded like he meant it. The woman—Grant's mother-in-law, based on the pictures Slade had found—nodded, stifling a moan.

"Give me the thing and zip her to the chair," Turner said. Slade stuffed his pistol into his waistband, dug out the green plastic box, and tossed it to Turner. He turned back to the woman and pulled out a set of plastic ties.

THE GUILTY SLEEP

Turner went through the kitchen doorway and found the stairs. Came around the newel post and found Grant's wife on her way down. She was wearing sweats and a Furiosa & the Toecutters concert T-shirt. Carrying a wooden baseball bat, sleep-wild red hair waving around her freckled face. She saw Turner as he saw her, and her face twisted in a grim snarl. She leaped for him, brave as hell, bringing the bat down with all her might.

Turner caught the end with his left hand and pulled, yanking her forward. His right hand found her neck, caught her in midair and shoved her sideways, smashing her head into the wall. He pulled it at the last moment, trying not to kill her, but the impact still cracked the drywall and knocked a trio of family pictures smashing to the floor. Her head lolled, and Turner bore her gently to the floor.

"What—" Slade started from the doorway, but Turner silenced him with a wave.

"Finish with grandma, then zip her up," Turner said, nodding at the prone redhead. He leaned past Slade and looked at the older woman, who was secured to the kitchen chair with zip ties around both feet and—so far—one hand. "Any other adults in the house?"

He watched her face pale as she took his understanding. She shook her head.

"Please," she whispered, "don't hurt her."

"Last thing I want to do," Turner said, then headed up the stairs. The fourth creaked loudly. The girl's room was at the end of a short hall. There was a sloth poster on the door, and the name *Rowan* in bright green letters. He pulled the olive drab box out of his pocket, opened the casing, and pulled out the cannula and tubes. He made sure the three small metal canisters were firmly seated in the delivery nozzles, then started the flow. He sniffed the end of the cannula carefully, got a whiff of cotton candy and vanilla. A hint of vertigo caressed his inner ears. He shook his head and huffed out a breath to clear his airways.

He opened the door and found the little girl sitting up, rubbing her eyes. Stirred awake by the sound and fury he'd unleashed. A flash of memory: his little girl woken by a thunderstorm that rattled the walls of their trailer, calling for her daddy.

The girl saw him filling the doorway and screamed. "Mommy!"

He strode to the bed and clamped a hand across her mouth. It covered nearly her entire face. She struggled and he stifled her as gently as he could. Hating himself.

"Don't worry," Turner whispered. "Mommy's coming with us." He slipped the tubes behind her ears and put the cannula into her nose. She wriggled, eyes wide in terror. He held the cannula in place, and in three seconds the halogenated enflurane had her limp and snoring. He wrapped her in the blanket and cradled her against his chest.

A father's muscle memory lasts a lifetime.

He carried her down the steps and found Slade had dragged the wife into the kitchen and had zipped her hands together. She was still out. The older woman was staring at Turner and, now that she was fully secured to the chair and gagged with a rag, seemed to have found her fury. Her eyes lashed Turner's face.

Slade put the ancient cell phone on the table in front of her. He held out his hands. "Gimme the kid, wouldja? Take Mommy."

Turner laid the little girl in Slade's arms and stared at the older woman in the chair, not breaking her gaze. "When he gets here," he rumbled, "have him call the number on the paper. You know what happens if anyone calls the police, right?"

He stared at her until she nodded, and then he crouched and pulled Daria into a sitting position. He heaved her torso over his shoulder and stood slowly, knees popping and obliques twitching ominously. She stirred, mumbling something indistinct into his back.

Slade stood at the gaping back door. He cradled the little girl, staring down at her closed eyes like he was in another world. Slowly, he touched her chin with his thumb. Brushed his fingers across her forehead.

And Turner had a flash of Slade climbing into the El Camino, running his thumb over the photo of the little blonde girl taped to the dash. And Turner was back at Sunrise Vista, Tuesday morning, just before Angie opened the spigot and buried two young men alive in the foundation. "You know he had to go away before, right? When he was fifteen?" she had said. And then: "Sixteen months. And for a while I thought maybe that would get things out of his system."

Turner nudged Slade's foot with his own. Slade's eyes snapped up, transitioning from furious to preternaturally still in the time it takes a scorpion to sting.

"Gotta go, sport," Turner said, trying to push down the frozen lead weight in his throat. "We gotta go."

37

REAP THE WHIRLWIND

DEX

Dex called Daria three times on the way, and Carleen twice. No answer. It was possible they were still sleeping, but PFC Best Case Scenario had been AWOL all week. He buried the accelerator and tried not to think about alternatives.

He skidded to a halt behind Carleen's old pickup, scattering gravel and trash like shrapnel. A fingernail of sun was scraping the bottom of the sky, painting thick stripes of shadow up the front of the house from the power lines across the street. He killed the engine, thinking about Mariam and Dawit. They'd shown him kindness like he might be an angel in disguise, when in the end he'd been a devil. He hoped they'd made it to the hospital in time.

Dex hammered on the metal security door so hard its hinges rattled like tambourines. He waited a few seconds, peering through the glass, then pounded again. Called for his wife and his mother-in-law. No movement, no sound. Dread welled up in his guts like oily groundwater.

He went round back and found the door hanging drunkenly on one twisted hinge. There was a massive, muddy boot print below the lock, and the jamb was splintered to pieces.

THE GUILTY SLEEP

Carleen was zip-tied to a chair with a cloth in her mouth. Pieces of a shattered mug littered the floor. Her eyes rolled at him. The ties were thick plastic, unyielding against his fingers. Carleen made noises behind the gag. That, at least, he could undo.

"What did you do, Dexter?" she said when she'd gotten her breath back. He knelt behind her, sawing at the ties with a knife from the block on the counter. "They knew you were coming, so what did you *do*?"

"I screwed up, Carleen. Bad." The tie around her left hand separated under the blade, but she didn't seem to notice.

"THEY TOOK MY GIRLS!" she screamed, voice scraped raw.

The second tie gave, and her right hand snapped free. She tried to stand, but collapsed back into the chair.

"Hang on, your feet are still tied. Daria and Rowan, are they OK? Did they . . . hurt them?"

He cut the final tie and Carleen lurched to her feet. He stood to help her, and she slapped him across the face.

"Are they OK? The big one threw Daria into the wall, knocked her out. They put some sort of gas into Rowan's nose and carried her out like a tranquilized animal. You want to know if they're OK? You bastard . . ." she breathed. "What. Did. You. Do?"

Dex stared at the floor. There was nothing but to own it. He'd owned it ever since the diner, when he'd said yes to the whole stupid, deadly thing. "I helped some buddies from the Guard rip off a drug dealer to pay for our former interpreter and his family to get to the States so the Taliban wouldn't kill them." The words came out in a rush.

"You—what?" Carleen sank into the chair. Stared at him. He repeated it. She reached for her smokes.

"It sounds crazy, I know."

Carleen put a cigarette in her lips and raised the lighter. Her hand was trembling so much she couldn't flick the wheel. Dex took it and her hand fell limply to the table. She stared at him as he lit her up. Took him three tries.

"It *was* crazy. And stupid."

Carleen took a long drag. "They figured out it was you," she said, blowing the smoke in his face.

"Yes."

"And they came and took your ex-wife and daughter."

Dex stepped on the automatic response. *My wife. Still.* The words were wet ash.

"You said there was a big one. Graying mullet, handlebar mustache? Like that TV bounty hunter, but more tired-looking?"

Carleen nodded.

"Another guy with him? Younger, skinny, but with a round face and little beard?"

She nodded again.

"I'm sorry. I tried to get here."

"Well, you didn't. So what're you going to do now?"

"I'm going to find them. Bring them back."

"Start there," she said, pointing at a phone on the table. An old brick of a Nokia. There was a rubber band around it, holding a piece of paper. "You're supposed to call that number. They said if you call the cops—if you . . ." She looked away, shoulders shaking.

Dex reached for the phone. Carleen grabbed his wrist and trapped his hand on the table. She sucked at the cigarette until the cherry glowed. She ground the butt into the back of his hand. The pain shot all the way up his arm, but he held his hand still and flat on the table and took it. Met her eyes, didn't look away as she burned him.

"That's what I'm feeling right now, Dexter, you understand me? My whole body. When I think about my girls—" She broke off again as the shakes took her. Dex squatted next to the chair and put his arm around her and she stiffened, but after a few seconds she leaned into him.

"I feel it, Carleen. The burning," he whispered. "I'll call them. Figure this out. I'll bring them home. Promise."

Carleen looked at him. Her eyes were orbs of wet steel. The black river swirled at his feet, the depths calling. He'd been blinded by the money, the opportunity it presented. And he'd gotten so wrapped up

THE GUILTY SLEEP

261

in trying to save someone—to make something right—he'd put the most important people in the world into mortal danger.

His chest grew tight, and he was on his back in the Afghan dust, shot in the vest and unable to breathe, lungs crushed in a vise.

"I need air," he said, picking up the phone. Carleen stood, reaching for her smokes. They went to the concrete steps at the front, sat side by side. Carleen lit another cigarette.

Dex pulled the rubber band off the phone and ripped the paper free. Called the number. Kept the Nokia angled so they could both hear. Someone answered on the second ring. He spoke into the silence.

"Do you have my wife and daughter?"

"Dexter Grant?"

"Do you have my wife and daughter?"

"Do you know who this is?"

"Answer me."

"Death and life are in the power of the tongue, and those who love it eat its fruits."

"What?"

"It means if you want me to cast lots and kill one of them, by all means, keep talking."

Carleen's eyes widened and she clutched his free hand with a grip that dimpled his skin and turned her knuckles white.

"Do you know who I am?" the woman on the other end said at last.

He remembered Marty telling him about the hospital. Turner and a woman going into Freddy's room, and when they came out his old boss was dead.

"No," he said.

"I'm the woman whose money you stole." Dex leaned against Carleen, or maybe she leaned against him, still holding his hand. "Do you deny it?"

"It was me."

"Look what you have sown."

"Are they hurt?"

"Whoever troubles his own household will reap the whirlwind."

"*Please*. Did you . . . are they alive?"

"They are, for now. Your wife's scared to death but your daughter is sleeping—we've seen to that. Such a precious little girl. How could you do this to them?"

"What do you want?"

"Come to me."

"Where?"

"There's a construction site off Uniontown Road past the intersection with Springfield. Sunrise Vista."

"I can find it."

"I'll give you credit," the woman said, her tone almost conversational. "You got away from my Kaibiles somehow. They're hard men, so maybe now you're thinking you're a hard man. But I promise, you're not harder than me. I got a jar on my mantel, Dexter. Full to the brim with the balls of men who thought they were harder than Angelita Cooke. You understand?"

"Yes."

"Let me hear you say it."

"I understand."

"You have one hour. Keep the phone. You know what happens if you call the police. If you bring *anyone*, I'll sew your wife's eyes open and make her watch while I carve your daughter into pieces."

The call disconnected with a click. Carleen exploded into a string of blasphemy that quickly gave way to great, heaving sobs.

"I'm going to bring them home, Carleen. Swear to God."

"I don't care what you have to do, Dexter. You just do it. Whatever it takes."

"I promise."

"Even if you have to . . . give yourself up. You do it."

"I will."

His mother-in-law stood, holding on to him for support. She pulled back, wiped her eyes, stared at him. Taking his measure, making sure he meant it. Then she nodded out at Mariam's car. There was blood on the windshield and something more substantial where the glass met the roofline. Chunks of bone, maybe. Brain matter. Cracks radiated from the spot like an asteroid impact. Holes in the back and front window, rearview mirror in pieces and dangling.

"You came in that?"

"Yeah."

"Take my truck."

38

SPARKING EMBERS

DEX; TURNER

Dex found Sunrise Vista right where Cooke said it would be. Made it in forty minutes. He wanted to do a dozen things instead. He wanted to go to the police, the FBI, whoever; turn himself in and ask them to get his wife and daughter back. He wanted to go to the pepto-pink safe house and beg Saenz for help. He considered each in turn and knocked them apart. All were selfish at the root, and all ended with his girls dead. This was on him.

The path through the trees was a tunnel. A rising breeze swirled the branches, creating a strobe-flash dappling as he went through. He blinked against disorientation. He came out into blazing sunlight and pounded the brakes. Carleen's big pickup lurched to a stop, stirring a cloud of dust. There was a construction trailer off to the left. He drove toward it slowly, barely faster than a walk. Let them see him coming, nice and easy. He stopped twenty feet away. Opened the door and stepped out. Sweat sprang up on his forehead instantly. It was going to be a hell-hot day.

As he walked toward the trailer, the door opened and a woman came out. She looked like someone's grandmother. Battered work jeans and a loose canvas shirt, messy hair piled in a gray-brown bun atop her head. A soft, round-cheeked face, deeply tanned with grooves

THE GUILTY SLEEP

at the corners of her warm brown eyes that spoke to outdoor work. Just needed a plate of cookies and a smile to complete the picture.

"Hello," Dex said, cautiously. "I'm Dexter Grant, and I'm looking for—"

The woman held up a hand.

Two guys came out from behind the trailer, one on each side. Both with handguns. The one on the right was a muscly white kid with bleached cornrows. The one on the left was the tall, ponytailed Kaibil. The one with both hands. He had a black eye, courtesy of Dawit and a parking lot light pole.

"I know who you are," the woman said, and her voice was the voice from the phone. "Lift up your shirt and turn around slowly."

Those eyes, Dex realized, weren't warm. They were as muddy and dangerous as a sudden desert flood.

Dex did what she'd asked, moving deliberately.

"After we spoke," Cooke continued, "I learned you killed Lael." She sounded almost impressed. "Explains why my boys didn't bring you to me directly. Good thing I went for leverage."

Leverage. That was what his family was to her. He pushed back against the rage. Being fair, he should be pointing it at himself, but this woman had his girls. His life.

"I'm here now," he said.

"That you killed a Kaibil is not insignificant," she said. "Florencio would really, *really* like to take you apart with his bare hands. They were cousins, but closer than brothers." Dex looked at the guy, who stared back, his face impassive except for the vein throbbing in the middle of his forehead.

"I'm here for my wife and daughter."

Cooke laughed. The sound was dry and chill, wind stirring fallen leaves.

"And I want my money back. But before I let Florencio have you—" At this, the Kaibil shuffled forward. His mouth changed shape infinitesimally, from a straight, flat line to something that was suppressed eagerness. A horse at the blocks, ready to race. "—I want you to satisfy my curiosity. Melchizedek tells me you've worked at

Pine Hill Bank for years. You're some kind of war hero. Why throw it all away? A greedy man stirs up strife like a dog with a mighty appetite. What got you so greedy you'd burn your life to ashes?"

He had no reason to lie. Only a hope there was something after, something he could do to save Daria and Rowan and, if he somehow got luckier than he had any right to be, maybe there'd be a chance to say goodbye.

"I was in the National Guard."

"I know."

"When I was in Afghanistan, we were attacked. Ambushed by a squad of assassins and turncoat Afghan troops. We had an interpreter named Jalal. An Afghan. He saved my life. Saved a bunch of us, when we were about to be blown up. He was trying to get to the States, but couldn't get a visa." He stared at the woman and watched for a reaction. Her face was stony and her eyes never left his. "Soon as it became clear Afghanistan was going to collapse, he took his family and ran for it. He was at the top of the Taliban hit list. He's trying to come here, almost *is* here, actually. The money was to pay the smugglers."

Cooke stared at him. The silence stretched. The guy with cornrows passed his gun from one hand to the other. There was a flicker of motion at the corner of his eye, coming from the windows in the trailer. The blinds were down and mostly turned, but something had moved there.

"No one who utters deceit shall continue to draw breath before my eyes."

"It's the truth."

"That simple?"

"Yes."

The woman laughed again, and this time there was a touch of actual feeling in it.

"And you thought you'd rob from me, because it wasn't like you'd be breaking the law. Probably thought you were doing the right thing."

Dex spread his hands slowly, palms out. "You got me."

"How noble. And yes, I do. The others in your crew?"

"Friends from the Army."

THE GUILTY SLEEP

"Bread gained by theft tastes sweet, but afterward your mouth will be full of stones. Do you understand?"

"Sounds biblical."

"I want you to grasp the gravity of the situation."

"I know I'm a dead man—"

"Yes, you are."

"—no matter what I do. But is there a scenario where you let my wife and daughter go?"

"Why do you think you're here?"

Dex held his tongue again. He was doing barefoot ballet on a razor's edge.

Finally, she said, "You want to free your family?"

"Yes."

"What are you willing to do?"

"Anything."

Cooke walked down the steps. As she reached the ground, the Kaibil and the kid with cornrows came forward to flank her. She stopped ten feet away.

"Here's the thing, Dexter. You and your friends picked a lousy time to steal from me. Bad for me, anyway, maybe good for you. Last year this time, I would've just killed your family in front of you, let Florencio torture you to death, and buried your pieces in that foundation over there. Lucky for you, my expenditures right now are higher than usual. Business expansion comes with operating costs. Overhead. Payroll. Utilities." She waved her hand vaguely. "Miscellany. Instead of writing off what you stole from me as the cost of doing business and wiping the slate clean, you actually have a chance. You stole somewhere in the neighborhood of four hundred thousand dollars from me."

"Four hundred and twenty-seven thousand, two hundred and fifty-eight dollars."

Cooke stared at him, stony faced. "I want it back. Will you get it?"

"Every dollar."

"Even if you have to steal it back from your Army friends?"

"Yes."

"Even if it means betraying this interpreter? And *his* family?"

Dex swallowed. The sweat was stinging his forehead. A drop slid down his neck and trailed along his spine. "Yes."

"Bring the money here by sundown. Twelve hours from now."

It was an artificial deadline, because the money would be in the hands of the smugglers and corrupt port people long before then. His real deadline was going to be much shorter. But he wasn't about to tell her that.

"I will."

"Better get going."

Dex took a breath. Held it. Pirouette on the razor's edge. "I want to see my family."

"You're not in position to ask me for anything."

"I know. But if I'm going to do this, I need to know . . . I need to see they're alive. Otherwise, you can kill me now and you'll never see your money again."

"You're that confident you can get it back."

"Yes," he lied.

Cooke smiled, cold and lightless. He couldn't believe he'd ever thought those eyes had seemed warm. Grandmotherly. "I'll meet you in the middle, Dexter. Split the baby, as the saying goes. No? Too close to home? How about this—you can see your wife, and she can tell you if your daughter is alive. You can see your little girl when you bring my money back. To say goodbye."

Without turning, she raised a hand over her shoulder and made a beckoning motion. The door opened and Daria came out. The young, round-faced guy with the pencil beard was behind her. He pressed a gun into her neck.

"Dexter!"

His wife pulled at him with an impossible, solar gravity. He wanted to run to her, drag her away. Kill them all with his bare hands and take her and Rowan and just *drive*. He must've started forward, because suddenly Florencio and Cornrows were pointing their guns at him. The Kaibil looked like he was praying Dex would take another step.

"I'm here," he managed, stupidly. "Are you OK?" He winced at the inanity of it.

THE GUILTY SLEEP

269

"No. Not by a long shot," she said. Her voice trembled. Exhaustion and fear, but that wasn't all. He'd known her almost his entire life. The others may not have heard it, but white-hot fury coursed through every syllable. It was a plumb line dragging through his chest.

"Is Rowan . . ."

"Asleep in the back. They've got her on some kind of sleeping gas."

"Did they hurt you? Either of you?"

She started to say something, then bit back the words with what he could tell was a subvocal snarl. She angled her head slightly and pushed her hair back so he could see the bruise growing across the entire side of her face. Her eye was nearly swollen shut. Dex clenched his jaw so hard his temples felt like they were splitting open. She nodded over his shoulder in the direction of the truck. Gathered herself. "Is my mom OK?"

"She's . . . pretty mad. But she's OK. Just wants you home."

Daria stared at him, eyes like supernovae. "Then you better get going. Do what you have to do."

"I love you. I love you both."

She turned away, let the kid with the beard lead her back into the trailer. As the door closed, she turned her head and said, barely loud enough to hear: "We know."

Turner listened to the roar of the receding engine. Eight cylinders, loud exhaust but not showy. Something big, but a working vehicle. A van or a truck. He turned his attention back to the girl, who was curled on the couch next to him. He checked the cannula to make sure the nasal inserts were fully seated. Checked the green plastic box and the small dial showing the gas flow level and remaining pressure. All systems go.

The door to the front office opened and Slade came in with the mother. Daria. Her eyes did their best impression of his double-barrel.

"Lady, if those pretty eyes of yours were laser beams my brain'd be boiling like a pot of crabs."

JEREMY D. BAKER

She ignored him, just stalked to the far end of the couch and eased herself under Rowan's head, gathering her daughter into her arms. He made sure she didn't try to remove the cannula, then looked at Slade. The boy nodded and gave a quick thumbs-up. Turner stood. Daria stared up at him.

"Wish I'd split your skull back at the house."

"I know. You nearly did. It weren't hardly a fair fight."

She told him to do something physically impossible. He didn't take it personal. He'd have told her the same, standing in her shoes.

He glanced pointedly at Slade. "I'll be right out." The boy left, and he squatted so Daria could look in his eyes. "I'm a dad too. I was. Your little girl," he said, ". . . she reminds me very much of my daughter."

"What does that have to do with anything?"

"Listen." He kept the smile on his face with all his strength. "You have any chance to get out of here, it comes with your man doing what he promised to do, and with you not doing anything stupid."

"I figured."

"Stay put. Don't touch the cannula, the tubes, or the box. Let her sleep through it all. Everything goes like we want, she wakes up tomorrow and doesn't know nothin' 'bout nothin', you dig?"

She didn't say anything. Just stared at him with considering eyes. Like he was a smear on the bottom of her boots, and he couldn't blame her one ant's fart for that.

His knees popped like firecrackers as he stood. "I'll come back in a bit to check on you. Need anything?"

"You know what we need," Daria said, her voice flat and hard.

He left them, locking the door behind him and leaning against it. Put the key in his pocket. Wouldn't do to let Slade get into the room, he thought. No, that wouldn't do at all.

Angelita and Slade were waiting in the shade, standing beneath the iron archway that marked the path up to the Sunrise Vista monument. The sarcophagus.

"It's a real shame, boss," he said. "Never talked to that boy much, but he seemed nice enough."

"Don't worry. You won't have to kill him."

THE GUILTY SLEEP

"You're going to let the wife and daughter go?"

Angie's eyes were darker in the shadows. Her hands were in her pockets, and he figured she was running her fingers over the black stone cross of her necklace.

"I can't believe you'd ask me that, Melchizedek, after all these years together. But if he brings my money back, I might make it quick." She smiled. "I must be getting soft."

He held his sigh. Wouldn't do to let her see any cracks, or one day soon he'd find himself in the foundation taking a concrete shower.

"Think he has a chance?" Slade asked.

"They pulled it off the first time," Turner said, "and it sure feels like he was in the middle of it. If he's telling the truth about being in this with his old Army buddies, I doubt they'll see him coming."

"We'll know by sunset."

"Yes, ma'am."

Turner ran a hand across his forehead and flicked the sweat into the trees, wishing it hadn't come to this. Wishing he didn't hear the crackle of the flames, smell the smoke and ash. The rising heat on the back of his neck. The flesh beneath the burn scars on his forearms twitched.

There was a shifting wind and the inferno was on the move. He hoped it wasn't coming from behind.

39

A LOW, FLICKERING LIGHT

DEX

The urge to do everything at full speed, chasing instinct and pure reaction, was overwhelming. It was seven thirty in the morning and sunset was at ten minutes to eight. Twelve hours to get the money and get it back to Cooke, but the deadline meant nothing. The ship was docking today and Saenz had to deliver the money today, surely before nightfall. Which meant Dex needed to get to Saenz and convince him to give up the money with a quickness. To help him come up with some other plan to get Jalal and his family into the country. Take the money back to the construction site.

Say goodbye.

First things first—get to Saenz. The plan had been for Dex to lie low and keep out of contact. Talk to the police, feed them the story. Create no patterns, give nothing for anyone to go on. Link up back at the safe house later tonight, after Jalal's arrival, to pick up his share. *That* ship had made like the *Titanic* and disappeared beneath the waves. A cold approach, then, made direct and in person with no warning.

He cranked the A/C to high. The dashboard fans wheezed in protest. He was back in Afghanistan, riding in the dusty heat to the compound, Ahn humming tunelessly behind the wheel. He blinked and it went away. He gripped the steering wheel so hard his hands cramped.

The truck roared out of the tree-lined track and back onto paved road. He was at the low, hopeless pink hotel in twenty minutes. One car in the lot, a rattletrap slumped across two spaces by the office. He parked at the rear, by the sullen water tower. Walked around the corner like he belonged and tried the near door first, then the second. Both were locked. He knocked and put his ear to the doors and heard nothing.

He went to the office and a guy who could have been physically distilled from the word *squirrelly* looked up from his magazine with supreme disinterest.

"Help you?" he said, like he fervently wished the opposite.

"Hope so. I'm looking for my friends. They were staying here last night, and I accidentally took my buddy's phone with me when I left," Dex said, holding up his phone and waggling it apologetically.

"Hm. Don't ring a bell."

"You sure?"

The guy sighed and laid his magazine flat, rolled his shoulders. Licked the tip of his finger, turned a page. "Can't say's I 'zactly remember. Brain's so dang foggy these days. Musta got that long COVID."

"This is important."

"So's my time, man."

Dex stood outside his body, like he was watching a movie scene play out. He watched himself detonate, snatching the clerk's collar and jerking him forward, grasping the back of his head and slamming him face-first into the counter. The guy squealed, and the piteous sound snapped Dex back into himself and he let go, vibrating.

"What's your problem, man?" the clerk shrieked, reaching for the phone.

Dex grabbed it first and yanked it off the counter so hard the cord ripped out of the wall. He heaved the phone across the lobby, and the clerk cowered in the corner. He'd lost control, but he could turn it to his advantage if he could ride the lightning long enough. He shifted into an interrogation approach he'd been trained on back at Huachuca, a natural fit for the scenario, given he was there already:

fear up. He loomed over the guy, who was bleeding profusely from his nose and looking up at Dex like he was some kind of monster.

"Don' hurd be, ban."

"I don't want to. I'm just looking for my friends."

"Th . . . three, wadn't it? Tall, thid guy, 'nother who looged like a marble stadue, and the third wid a limp?"

"That's them."

"They left."

"That can't be right," Dex said. The clerk flinched.

"It's true. Three hours ago. Tall guy turned in the geys."

"Both rooms?"

"Yeah. You busted my nobe, ban."

"I think I did," Dex said. "He say anything about where they were going?"

"Nod a thing."

This was wrong, and not just what he'd done to the poor clerk. The guys shouldn't have checked out, not if they were going to meet him here later to give him his share of the money.

"They all left together?"

"I thing tho."

Dex deflated. Stepped back. The clerk watched him warily.

"Give me your wallet."

"Huh?"

"Your wallet—give it here."

"Aw ban," the guy said, "you're robbing be?"

"No," Dex said. "You're leaving. I'm taking your license; you get in your car and drive. You call the cops, I'll see them coming, disappear before they arrive. And then I'll reappear at your place, sometime down the road when you think you're safe."

"I won' call no cobs," the guy said, handing over a battered Velcro wallet. Dex believed him. He looked like the kind of guy who'd had a scrape or two with the law. Probably didn't want to go down that road again.

"Good," Dex replied. "It'll be on the counter when you come back. Give it an hour."

THE GUILTY SLEEP

"I'll gib it a day," the clerk said, then beat feet in his jalopy, spinning a cloud of dust and gravel in his wake.

Dex grabbed the room keys off the pegboard behind the counter, trying not to think too hard about smacking the clerk around, about using fear up. The guy was a civilian, a bystander. He was losing control. This wasn't him.

Or maybe it was. It was the him who'd made a series of devastating choices and was faced with the prospect of losing the only good things in the world that still mattered. This was him, backed into the darkest corner, waters of the black river swirling around his neck, out of all options but the bad ones.

He walked to the far end of the motel, keys digging into his palms. He unlocked the first room, the closest to the office. Empty. The bed was rumpled. Slept in, but not restfully. He moved to the next. Nothing there but an ashtray overflowing with butts and a trash can overflowing with Diet Pepsi and Natty Boh cans.

If Saenz and the others had checked out, left the scene already, then the plan had changed and they hadn't told him. Maybe they were planning to come back tonight and meet him at the hotel to give him his cut, but if that was the plan, why check out? Why not keep the rooms, so there was a safe place to do the handover, so Jalal and his family had somewhere to sleep their first night in a new homeland? Why not keep the rooms, so they had somewhere safe to settle in, link back up, recap the operation, swap war stories, and give Dex what they'd promised? No, Saenz would have said if this was the plan. Something had happened.

Or . . . something else was going on.

And he was sitting on the edge of the bed, biting his fist, breathing raggedly. He screwed his eyes closed, but he could still see Daria's face. The silvery trails of dried tears over the freckles on her cheeks.

Not by a long shot, she said, when he'd asked if they were OK. And saying now in his mind what she hadn't before: *We deserve to live. Do what you couldn't for your friends in Afghanistan. Save us.*

He forced his eyes open and splashed water on his face. Stared at himself in the mirror. *Save your daughter, Dexter. Save your wife. Do that and save yourself, no matter what else happens.*

The next right thing.

He remembered what Saenz always said during training: *Thorough keeps you safe. Thorough gets the job done. Half-assed gets you killed.* He was pinballing around like a crab in a pot and he needed to slow down, think things through.

He felt like a lousy detective in a forgotten noir. There should be a pad of paper on the desk. He could rub a pencil gently over the page and see a clue impressed on it from the page above, since torn away. Only there was no pad and no pencil, and he was no Bogart.

What was left? *Take it step by step.*

Saenz was a planner. *The* planner, best Dex'd ever known. Which meant when they checked out it was deliberate. And not telling Dex they'd be checking out in the morning, that was deliberate too.

Dex shook his head. First things first. Where were they? Saenz wouldn't leave anything to the last minute, which meant they probably went to set the stage. With Jalal's ship arriving today, they'd be meeting with the port director to pay him his share. Best place to do that, and to set up for Jalal's arrival, was the port.

He pulled out his phone. First principle of modern intelligence work—forget SCIFs and Top Secret databases. For practical purposes, you can find out almost anything via open-source searches and social media.

Saenz had mentioned the name of the ship that first night, a lifetime ago back in Dex's sepulcher of an apartment. The internet helpfully told him the *Antares* was due at the Port of Baltimore at eleven and would begin unloading cargo at noon. Saenz wouldn't give anyone their cut of the cash until he had eyes on Jalal. It was his way. *Trust but verify? Forget* that, *Blackbirds.* Never *trust and verify twice. Thus endeth the lesson.*

The payouts would be between eleven and noon, probably in the back half of the hour, closer to unloading time. The captain would want to get any human cargo off before the rest of the containers, and he and the port boss would surely want their money up front. He had to get to Saenz before the ship arrived, before the payoffs. But here was the thing: Would Saenz give the money back? The early checkout, the seeming change in plan, wasn't giving him a warm fuzzy.

It was already eight thirty, the minutes slipping through his fingers like greased bearings. Baltimore was ninety minutes away, maybe more in traffic.

As Carleen's truck roared out of the parking lot, Dex ran his hand over his face, feeling the stubble scrape across his fingertips, and made a decision. If Saenz wouldn't give the money back, he'd take it.

That meant two more stops. He needed to *move*.

He knocked on the door, trying not to pound, then rang the doorbell. Knocked again. Two minutes later, it swung open. Terrence looked up at him and blinked in surprise, then tried his best to conceal the concern that flickered like a shadow across his broad face.

"Dex! It's nice to see you, brother. All good?"

Dex had cleaned up best he could on the road. He'd wiped Lael's blood from his face with some napkins and a water bottle he'd found in the glove box. He found a tattered work shirt behind the driver's seat of Carleen's truck. Tore one of the sleeves off and tied it around the shallow gash in his left palm from the Kaibil's machete. But he was all too aware of the figure he presented. Dirty T-shirt, ripped at the collar. Black jeans spattered with what he hoped Terrence would think were oil stains. He looked like a hobo having a bad day on the rails.

"I'm a mess, I know. But yeah, I'm OK. Thanks," he said, trying for sincerity. Putting on the mask, like they'd taught him at CI school. Be who you need to be to get what you need. He hated it. One more sin on his infinite list. "Been doing some work at the apartment, trying to get myself settled."

"Want to come in? *Die Hard* marathon's on in a bit. Treshaun and Leo are coming over, picking up some breakfast on the way. Plenty to go around. Got some iced tea too."

"Thank you, no. I, uh . . ."

"Oh," Terrence said, his eyes going somehow hard and full of gentle concern at the same time. "You're here for your gun."

"Yeah."

"Remember why you gave it to me?"

"I do. I'm not here for that. Farthest thing from my mind."

I'm not going to kill myself, because I'm already dead. But I'm going into a situation with some bad people, many of whom will be armed. I may have to steal almost half a million dollars from three men who trust me, men I've called friends, men I've bled with. Money I already stole from a drug queenpin, so she doesn't murder my family before she kills me. That's all.

"I'm actually, like, feeling pretty good. I'm figuring stuff out. Starting to put things back together."

"Uh-huh."

"It feels . . . symbolic somehow. I've put those thoughts behind me, haven't thought them in months." That much was partly true. Kind of. *More like a week.*

Terrence was still looking at him. Letting his silence do the work. He might've been a former cav scout, but he would've been at home in the interrogator's booth.

"Can I trust you with it, Dex?"

He met the other man's eyes. Didn't look away. Let him see what he needed to see. The mask.

"You can trust me with it."

Terrence backed up, spun his chair, and disappeared around the corner. Three minutes later, he was back. Dex only checked the clock on his phone four times in the interim. Terrence handed him the hard plastic case. "No ammo. Sorry."

"All good, Terrence. Thanks. You're a lifesaver."

The other man barked a surprised laugh. "You don't say."

"I do say."

THE GUILTY SLEEP

"See you at group on Tuesday?"

"Count on it." Dex put the pistol case under his arm and reached out and shook Terrence's hand. "Enjoy John McClane's bon mots."

"Yeah, right," Terrence said, rolling his eyes. "Team Hans Gruber all the way. Guy had *panache*."

"Thanks again, T."

"Tuesday!"

"Tuesday."

It was nine on the dot. Terrence's place was ten minutes from the Walmart. In twenty minutes, he'd bought everything he needed.

He put the bag with the clipboard, hard hat, Day-Glo safety vest, and magnetic yellow light bubble on the passenger seat, then opened the plastic gun case and took out his pistol. A Beretta PX4 Storm, an updated version of the 92F he'd carried in his early National Guard days. Two magazines, seventeen rounds each. He loaded them both, plus one more in the pipe.

And he was on his back in the dust, the sun blinding him and his chest crushed in an invisible vise. Ahn's legs scrabbling in the gravel as he kicked and died. Dex lifted the pistol, looking for a target and blinking through the blood and the sand and waiting to die.

Someone honked a couple rows over, and he was back in the cab of Carleen's pickup. He fought down vomit, gasping. He was losing control. Everything was coming down around him.

Dex didn't want more violence. More blood, more death.

But if it came down to that or his family, he'd wade into the black river and never look back.

He caught a low, rumbling echo through the cracked driver's-side window. Like the pounding of distant artillery. There was a roll of clouds off to the west. High and dark, like a mountain range. Deep inside, something flickered and flashed.

40

FIFTEENTH BRIGHTEST STAR IN THE NIGHT SKY

DEX

Carleen's truck rumbled like a dyspeptic locomotive. Dex headed southeast, pushing the big pickup hard as he dared. The first twenty miles were farmland and scattered forest, then the outer suburbs, tony and whitebread. East on the 695 Beltway, and for a wonder and a mercy, no traffic on the Saturday morning, no orangeworkers laying miles of barrels to slow him down. Then a slashing dive straight south on 83, through ever tighter and dingier outliers, the tenements brooding like gangrenous mushrooms.

The worst part was the grinding slog through the dirty, beautiful, beating heart of the city and toward the inner harbor. Construction ever-present, every road squeezed to a single lane, not that any work actually seemed to be getting done. The labyrinthine, gentrifying snarl of Canton and Brewers Hill, all cracked sidewalks and narrow brick row houses, held and mocked him as he eased the big truck through narrow gaps, threading the needle ever forward, ever winding. The cranes of the port were visible from miles out, sprouting in neat white ranks like a collection of massive alien trees, mocking him by never seeming to get any closer. The sun was always in his eyes. The smell of the harbor—wet garbage and fish guts—rose on the hot

THE GUILTY SLEEP

summer air. The pavement steamed, though there'd been no rain. The storm was still chasing him.

You can get into just about anywhere, restricted or not, long as you carry a clipboard and a harried look. They'd trained on the concept during counterintelligence school at Fort Huachuca. One of the principal tasks of the Army CI corps is red-teaming military installations to verify the right force protection protocols are in place, executed the right way by the right people. Most of the time they found things TARFU across the board. When a base's local contract guard force, or worse—the MPs—actually caught a red-teamer, chances were they'd drag you into the guard post for wall-to-wall fisticuffs as a show of appreciation for your hard work and dedication to the mission.

In other words, sometimes a clipboard and a harried look weren't enough. Especially in a place with supposedly better-than-average security, especially if you wanted to avoid a beating.

Dex pulled over a block past the port entrance and pulled on the bright yellow vest. Plugged the magnetic yellow revolving light bubble into the cigarette lighter and stuck it on the roof of the cab. Pulled some paperwork out of the glove box—registration, insurance, the last few oil change receipts and mechanic's invoices—and stuck it on the clipboard in a fat stack. He put it on the passenger seat, easily visible from the driver's-side window, but far enough away that it'd be hard to tell exactly what was on it. Looked official, though. He put the hard hat on the dash in front of the steering wheel where it couldn't be missed. He did a quick search on his phone for public-record maintenance contracts associated with the port.

Last thing he did was transfer Rowan's drawing to his left pocket and take the small folding knife he found in the center console and cut the seam of his right front pocket until it was hanging open.

He blinked, and saw Chonk sitting with Schoepe-Dogg kneeling behind him. The women's room was half-collapsed, sparks and ashes tracing death-sigils on the swirling smoke. There was so much blood.

Dex opened the door and vomited into the gutter. He wiped his mouth and spat. Slammed the door. Then he looked both ways, banged a U-turn, and, fifty yards later, a hard right into the Port of Baltimore's access control point.

It was seven minutes after eleven.

The guard at the shack was young. High and tight haircut, dark shades, cheeks smooth as a baby's belly. Shirt pressed, badge shined, massive pimple on his chin. Looked like a boot Marine on shore leave, trying on a rent-a-cop's uniform for a costume party.

"Good afternoon, sir. What brings you to the Port of Baltimore today?"

"Good afternoon, Officer . . . Montrose," Dex said. "Jim Crumley, Charter Mechanical. Got a buzz about the primary crane on dock seventeen." He held up the old Nokia from Cooke's people. At the right angle it looked for all the world like a walkie-talkie.

"No problem," Montrose said. "ID?"

Dex made a show of patting at his thighs. "Look at this, man," he said, pointing at the ripped pocket. "Caught this on the door of the truck this morning. Didn't even realize it until I stopped for gas. ID's probably sitting on my driveway right now."

"Sir, there's no entry without ID."

"I understand the policy, but you can make an exception, right?"

"I'm sorry sir, I sure can't."

"Officer Montrose, we're talking the *primary* crane on dock seventeen. The balance control gyro lost a stabilizer bearing and I'm the tech on call. I'm the only guy in the *state* today who can fix this thing. And dock seventeen just had an arrival about . . . eleven minutes ago," he said, making a show of looking at the clock in the truck's dash.

"Mister . . . Crumley, was it? The policy—"

"You have any idea how much the cargo on that ship is worth, Officer Montrose?"

"I—"

"—because the dockmaster screamed it in my ear about an hour ago: two hundred and thirty-seven million, six hundred and forty-four thousand, nine hundred and twenty-two dollars."

"But—"

THE GUILTY SLEEP

"I know I'm the one who screwed up here, Officer Montrose. Or more accurately, the fickle hand of fate saw fit to ruin my day *and* a fat chunk of today's economic motility balance for the entire East Coast—"

"Economic motility balance—"

"—at the same time, but I need to get in there and fix the balance control gyro stabilizer bearing on the primary crane of dock seventeen or you and me both are collectively *hosed*."

"You and me . . . both, sir?"

"Well, whose name do you think I'm going to have to drop to the dockmaster when he files a formal complaint about Charter's non-response to this emergency repair order, which subsequently cost the American economy two hundred and thirty-seven million, six hundred and forty-four thousand, nine hundred and twenty-two dollars in one day? You seem like a squared-away guy, Montrose, but listen—and I say this with all due respect to the rules and your position—if I get boned on this, I am *not* getting boned alone. I don't go for that. Unless you want to be held responsible for the loss of—"

"Two hundred and thirty-seven million, six hundred and forty-four thousand, nine hundred and—"

"—and twenty-two dollars, Officer Montrose—"

"—in one day?"

"—you'll let me in."

Montrose's Adam's apple bobbed like a stuck elevator. He looked left and right, then pushed his sunglasses up his forehead.

"That's not necessary, OK? How about—just this once—you sign in on the visitor's sheet?"

Dex smiled. "That'll work, Officer Montrose. That'll work just fine."

It took another two minutes for the paperwork, then Montrose raised the gate.

The port was imposing, though he tried not to show it while Montrose could still see him. It was a city within the city, its streets defined by rows of shipping containers and low-slung cargo warehouses.

The stacks of containers made the skyline. The streets were painted with a mishmash of arrows and dotted with stop and yield signs. The massive white cranes loomed over all, slowly tracing their mysterious paths.

Even on a Saturday, the miniature city was awash in traffic. Trucks large, small, and semi rumbled in every direction, and dockworkers scuttled around like ants in the world's largest metallic hill. He crossed a rail bed queuing an empty line of flatbed cars, a loudly beeping loco-tug slowly backing into position on the rails. He rolled his window the rest of the way up—the noise was insane.

He'd never have found dock seventeen without the map on his phone. It was at the far end of the port, through a series of turns that ran a gauntlet of abandoned containers fused into a rusting maze. It felt like an afterthought to the workings, a seldom-used hinterlands. The chaos faded. If you were going to sneak a family into in an otherwise busy port, this was the place to do it.

He rounded a particularly high stack of containers and Saenz's gray Golden Oak company sedan was there, parked against one of those long, low buildings. Past the warehouse, a wide finger of concrete jutted out into the harbor. A half-mile down the jetty, the *Antares* was bellied up to the pier like a sidelong skyscraper. A huge crane was slowly rolling along a set of tracks into position athwart the containers stacked amidships. Other than the ship and Saenz's car, it was deserted.

He drove past Saenz's car without slowing down, the hard hat pulled low over his eyes. Just another dockworker on an errand. *Hope for slightly better than the worst and plan for a flaming disaster, and thus endeth the lesson.*

The worst-case scenario looked like screaming out of the port with his ass on fire, chased by corrupt port cops or cargo ship crew. Or both. So he kept going to the end of the row of containers, then looped around the other side. He stopped at the end of the aisle, the nose of the truck just shy of the leading edge of the stack, pointing back the way he'd come in. Straight shot out and away, but with a wall of containers between him and the building.

He dismounted the truck and threw the yellow vest and hard hat back inside. A gust of wind pushed up the alley of containers and he could have sworn the smell of the harbor was replaced for a moment with the scent of cooking lamb, kerosene, and dust. There was a faint echo, perhaps the warble of muezzin calling prayers. He closed his eyes, pressed his fists against his temples. Leaned against the truck and tried to breathe. The past had its claws in him now, dragging him deeper into the black river. Any farther and he'd be breathing the chill, oily waters.

Another draft, stronger this time, pushing a devil of dust and trash. He'd raced the afternoon thunderstorm all the way to Baltimore, but it had caught him. The cooling air blew across the skin of his arms and neck. He reached under the seat and pulled out the Beretta. Tucked it against his spine and flipped the tail of his shirt over the grip. He stuck the tips of his fingers into his pocket, touched the edge of Rowan's drawing. Imagined the smiling stick figures, the fat yellow sun, the happy sloth.

There was a slight gap between the first two stacks of containers. He eased up and looked through. Recon. He had a straight shot at the back window of Saenz's car, and in the dimming storm-light, the sun's glare was gone. Dex could see three heads inside. Two in the front, one in the back. The heads were moving, the one in the back bobbing back and forth. A pair of hands came into view, gesticulating.

The back door shot open and Winkowski climbed out. His movements were wild, jerky. The wind blew his words across the lot.

"—not a chance in hell!" His voice was heavy with fury.

Saenz or Porter must've responded, but they were still in the car and Dex couldn't make it out. Winkowski leaned down and said, "I don't care, man, I'm out."

The other doors opened and Saenz and Porter got out. Winkowski paced between them in agitated, limping strides behind the car. Saenz patted the air placatingly and said something Dex couldn't hear.

"No," Winkowski said, chopping the space between them with the flat of his hand. "I'm an asshole. Grade A, first-class promotable. You know it and I know it; the whole world knows it. An' I never liked Frogger, smart-ass that he is. But doin' *that* ain't me, Stu. I'm not—"

Saenz gave a quick upward nod, and Porter's arms snaked out and one pinned Winkowski's arms behind his back, and the other hand clamped over the bottom of Winkowski's face. Porter arched his back and pulled Winkowksi's chin up. Something flashed in Saenz's hand and Winkowski's neck opened like someone had drawn a zipper across it. Saenz danced back, deftly avoiding the spray of blood. The gouting redness painted Winkowski's neck, his chest. His legs kicked and spasmed. For a lightning flash, Dex saw Ahn in Porter's arms, being dragged toward the darkness of the women's room. Dex chewed the inside of his cheek to keep himself from screaming and tried to tear his eyes away. Failed.

Winkowski's chest rose and fell, rose and fell, slowing. One hand fluttered at the sky, then sank to his side.

Saenz popped the trunk, then leaned forward and closed Winkowski's eyes. When he spoke this time, it was loud enough for Dex to hear.

"A conscience. Who knew?"

Porter murmured something, still holding Winkowski's slumped form upright. Saenz reached into the trunk and pulled out the hard-sided suitcase. Then Porter's G36, which he slung around his back.

"He served his purpose," Saenz replied. "On to the next step."

Porter said something else, nodding at Winkowski's feet.

Saenz bent, grabbed, and stood. With a grunt, he helped Porter heave the body into the trunk.

There was a massive double boom, followed by a slow, rolling echo. Dex flinched, squinting against a remembered flash of fire, the women's room disintegrating in a flood of stone and blood.

The storm wasn't coming. The storm was here.

"What do you think?" Saenz said, stretching and knuckling his lower back. "Room in there for one more, Sunny?"

Porter sighed, wiping his arms with a Golden Oak–branded golf towel. He threw it in the trunk and it landed over Winkowski's face. "Grant will fit, yes. But tall as he is, I may have to break his legs."

41

DARK DEEDS AT HIGH NOON

DEX

Saenz and Porter disappeared into the building with the suit-case. There was a dark puddle on the ground behind their car. In the fading stormlight, it could've been an oil spill. Dex pulled the PX4 from his waistband and eased the slide halfway back, making sure a round was chambered. The movements were rote, wooden. His brain was still trying to process what he'd witnessed. He'd watched a man he admired—someone he considered a mentor, a *friend*—open the throat of one of their own. Quick and cold and callous as carving an Easter ham.

And they were coming for him next.

The whole thing fell apart like a house of cards in a hurricane. There was something deeper going on, more to Saenz's plan than he'd let on to Dex.

He thought about how he'd found his apartment door open the previous week, and the flash of Saenz leaving that first night, how he'd pulled the door shut until the lock clicked. How his former team leader had seemed to know exactly the right buttons to push with him. He thought about the all-night diner, sitting at the table with Saenz and Sunny and Wink, and everyone said just what they needed to when he needed to hear it. He thought about how the other three had checked out of the safe house early, before it made any sense to do so, and how they wouldn't give him his cut of the money right away.

Only one thing fit. Saenz had run an intel op on him. Spot and assess, look for weak spots to exploit. Break into the guy's apartment if need be, get the pieces you need to recruit the asset and run him once you've got him. The flophouse apartment and the packet of paper from *Dean and Morris, Family Law* had given him plenty to go on.

I never liked Frogger, smart-ass that he is. But doin' that *ain't me, Stu,* Winkowski had said, just before they killed him. So: Saenz wasn't going to give Dex his cut of the money; he was going to cut his throat and put him in the trunk of the car. Burn off a loose end that could tie Saenz to the rip and run. But Winkowski wouldn't go for it, so they killed him. Like Dex, they'd needed Wink; the job would've gone nowhere without his access to the Golden Oak supply warehouse. But if he wasn't on board with killing Dex, there was no reason to keep him around. They'd squeezed Dex, dry too, for his inside track at the bank and Cooke's operation. They'd gotten what they needed. Now he was collateral. They were going to kill him.

Get in line, fellas.

He stuffed the pistol back into his waistband, rubbed at his mouth, and was surprised to feel a snarl curling his lips. His anger snapped him back into focus. Time to get the money back. And he wasn't going to feel a smidge of guilt about stealing it. *Re-stealing it. Whatever.*

Dex started past the containers, but ducked behind Carleen's truck when a white and navy Yukon squealed around the corner. The SUV nosed in next to Saenz's sedan. A beefy guy with slicked hair and glasses slid out of the passenger seat, adjusting his gun belt. Couple stars on his collar. A slim, severe blonde woman climbed out of the other side and led the way into the building. Two other guys in uniform slid out the back. One was tall and thin, hatchet-faced. The other was just as tall, but looked like he lived in a weight room. The port director and his top people, then, probably. Here for their cut. Whatever Saenz was really up to, *that* at least was the truth.

THE GUILTY SLEEP 289

He was too late to confront Saenz and Porter alone. One-on-two with the element of surprise could work. But one-on-six, all the others armed? Suicide wouldn't help Rowan and Daria.

He backed away from the stack of containers and looked down the pier. The crane had just lifted the first container off the *Antares* and was rolling slowly toward the building in front of him. There were dots at the base of the crane that might have been people. Time to move.

There was a strobing flash, with an instant crash of thunder loud enough to rattle his teeth. The hair on his forearms stood up and did a little dance. The wind railed, suffused with ozone and damp metal. Fat splats of rain hit the back of his neck, the top of his head. The sound of the rain vibrating across the city of shipping containers rose like a wave. In three seconds, he was in the middle of the deluge.

He smiled.

Dex ran across the open ground to the building, just another dock-hand hustling out of the storm. He pressed himself under the shallow overhang next to the door the others had gone through. Put his ear to the metal, but couldn't hear anything over the reverberation of rain on the metal roof. Moved to the corner of the building and peered down its length. A series of rolltop doors pierced the wall, evenly spaced and facing an expanse of concrete to accommodate the movement of containers in and out. Halfway down, one of the doors was open. The crane tracks ran right in front of it, parallel to the building. If this was still about Jalal, he and his family were in the shipping container heading his way right now. Which meant Saenz and Porter and the others were gathered by that open door, looking out at the rain. Dex could go through the metal door without being seen. Maybe.

Lightning flashed and he put his fingers on the handle. Thunder exploded like angry gods doing battle, and he levered the door open and slipped inside, closing it behind him before the echoes had faded.

"Oo-*wee*," someone called, their voice echoing. Dex froze. "That was a big 'un."

He was in a massive, open space. It was a microcosm of the port itself, a cavernous labyrinth of containers and boxes and crates, organized according to some madman's fever dream. Some of the stacks reached the ceiling thirty feet overhead. Others were head high or shorter. The door Dex came through opened into an artificial antechamber formed by a dozen hip-high wooden crates. He ducked, but not before he caught sight of a cluster of people in front of the open rolltop. Couple hundred feet away, looking out at the rain. They'd stayed in separate cliques, forming a loose semicircle. Stu and Sunny were at the far end of the arc, with the four port cops closer to Dex. In the middle of the semicircle, barely inside the opening to the outside, they'd set up a folding table. The hard-sided suitcase was sitting on it.

Dex started forward, then froze when his foot bumped into a fire extinguisher in a metal bracket mounted just off the floor next to the door. He bit his lip and cursed himself, listening for any reaction to the soft clank. When none came, he dropped into a crouch and wormed through the maze of crates, keeping to the shadows and working his way closer. Plenty of cover. No one looked his way. It had gone evening-dark outside thanks to the storm, and the bulbs overhead were scattered and dim. He circled slowly to the right, overshooting the open rolltop door and keeping it to his left. If he could make a run for the suitcase, he could head straight back to the door he'd come in.

Dex reached a spot at three o'clock to the open door's twelve. Thirty feet away.

There was empty space between Dex and the group. If he went any farther, he'd be seen. He went prone, peering out from between an open crate of automotive parts and another of rubber tubing.

"In here!" Saenz called, facing the open door and the storm.

There was a rumble deeper than thunder and the base of the crane rolled into view on the tracks. Four figures swept in out of the rain. The first one through was short and stocky. He shook his head, flinging droplets of water from his hair and beard. Saenz was on him immediately, hugging him fiercely and pounding his shoulder.

THE GUILTY SLEEP

They stood back, gripping each other by the forearms and smiling. It was Jalal. He looked like he'd aged two decades in the last three years—no surprise. Porter stepped forward and Jalal shook his hand. The other three came in, shaking water from rain slickers. They each had a Kalashnikov strapped to their chest.

"Gentlemen—and lady," Jalal boomed, nodding to the blonde woman. "My sons, Ilyas and Fahad." He indicated the two younger men who'd come in after him. He then indicated the third. This guy was older, with a long beard and thick build. "And representing our patrons, my cousin Gulbuddin Haqqani." Unlike his sons, who'd smiled and nodded as Jalal introduced them, Haqqani just stared at the rest of the group. His hand was resting casually on the stock of his AK. No sign of Jalal's wife and young daughter. Another piece of the puzzle, along with the AKs Jalal's crew were carrying. Not to mention the presence of Jalal's cousin. Whatever this was, if a Haqqani Network member was involved, it was bad news. *State Department made the right call on Jalal's visa.*

Saenz moved with Jalal to the center of the semicircle, next to the table with the money. Saenz was doing a round of introductions. Beyond them, the bottom edge of a container appeared, slowly moving toward the ground.

Jalal, quieter now, was speaking to the group, his hands moving in grandiose gestures. The Haqqani cousin stood at his side, stone-faced. Jalal spoke for a solid three minutes, too low for Dex to hear, with occasional interjections from Saenz. The container reached the wet asphalt with a clang that echoed through the interior of the warehouse. His sons stood by the container, just out of the rain. They, too, now had their hands on the stocks of their Kalashnikovs. The blue-uniformed guy with the slicked hair and glasses leaned forward, staring at Jalal. Doubtfully at first, but with growing interest. Once he put his finger up and conferred with the blonde woman, who whispered fiercely in his ear. Lighting flashed in frozen white fire, followed by an artillery salvo overhead. Everyone flinched and then Saenz laughed.

"Sign of things to come," he said.

"Proof's in the pudding, Hoss," the port director said.

"Let us see the pudding, then," Jalal intoned. There was a chorus of assent, and a half dozen umbrellas snapped open. "Ilyas, stay inside for now. With the money."

The group made their way out into the rain, their backs to the warehouse entrance. Ilyas, the shorter of Jalal's two sons, stayed by the table. He'd turned his back to Dex and was splitting the difference, halfway between the table and the open door to the outside. The best chance to go for the money was right now.

Dex brought his feet up under his hips and slowly eased into a crouch. The group outside was bunched in front of the shipping container. He took a dozen steps, shading to the right so he could come at the table on the run, grab the suitcase, and haul ass straight to the side door.

Ilyas took a few more steps forward, craning his head to see what everyone else was seeing. He was almost out of the warehouse. It created another five feet of space for Dex. A buffer. The guy with the glasses was cutting the customs seal on the container's doors with a pair of wire snips. The blonde held an umbrella over his head. The port director stepped back, pulling the woman with him, and Jalal moved into the gap, seized the container doors, and flung them wide open.

There was another strobe of lightning and an answering crash of thunder. Everyone flinched and Dex froze. The brief burst of white light illuminated the interior of the shipping container. Jalal's wife and daughter weren't inside. There was no living space in the container. The entire volume was filled, top to bottom, front to back. It was full of plastic-wrapped, tape-bound parcels, each the size and shape of a ream of paper.

"As I said," Jalal said, his voice pitched to carry over the storm, "half is heroin, grown from the poppies of Helmand, the best in the world. The other half—and this is truly exciting—the purest crystal methamphetamine in the world. Organic, synthesized from natural Afghan bandak, what you call ephedra."

"Artisanal," Saenz put in with a chuckle.

THE GUILTY SLEEP

"Not to put too fine a tittle on it, champ, but what's to stop me 'n' my gang here from slitting y'all's throats and taking it for ourselves?" the port guy with the mustache said, his tone light and conversational. His hands were on his hips, his right one just above his holster. His three other officers had adopted similar poses.

"Man has a point," Saenz said with a laugh.

"Two reasons," Jalal said, half turning. Dex went statue. He'd started to take another step, but the next one would put him inside a dim circle of light cast from an overhead fixture. If he moved forward, or if Jalal turned the rest of the way, he'd be seen. "Why don't *you* cover the first one, my friend?"

"First," said Saenz, "this shipment is worth three hundred million dollars, conservatively, once you step on it, distro it out street level. That's in addition to the initial entry fee and good faith cash payment there." He nodded in the direction of the table.

"You're making our point," the blonde woman said.

"We're gonna bring one of these in per *quarter*," Saenz continued, putting his finger up like a lecturing schoolmarm. "A billion in product a year, *Hoss*. Nice haircut for you right off the top, call it an import duty, and a little brokerage fee for me and my partners here. Plenty to go around, for a long, long time. In perpetuity, if nobody gets too greedy now."

"Uh-*huh*," the port director grunted.

"You wanna tell him the second reason, Jalal?"

"Because my lovely son Ilyas," Jalal said, waving in Dex's direction without looking, "is holding a dead man's switch. The roof and walls of the container are prepped with a series of incendiary devices. White phosphorus. Nasty stuff. Sticks and burns with the heat of a sun, and only stops when it burns itself out."

Dex knew the feeling.

"Anyone gets twitchy," Saenz said, "Ilyas lets go of the button and the whole thing goes up to glory. Everyone goes home unhappy. Maybe some of us don't go home at all." His smile was wide.

"Well now," mused the port director, stroking his mustache. "Can't say's I like the threat, sport, but I sure as shinola respect the hustle."

They turned back, clustering around the opening again. There was a palpable release of tension. Jalal's other son, Fahad, took his hands off his AK and squeegeed rain from his forehead. The port people were looking at the merchandise.

Dex was five feet away from the money. He strode forward through the light, heading for the table. Three feet. Ilyas took another step toward the opening. One foot. Dex reached for the handle of the suitcase.

Lightning scintillated and thunder detonated and Ilyas shrank from the door, shaking his head. He turned and saw Dex and his eyes went wide.

42

A SUPPLY OF LEAD

DEX

Jalal's son opened his mouth to scream. Dex darted forward, closing the gap. He grabbed a fistful of the boy's collar, yanked him forward, brought his own head in like a wrecking ball. The forehead is one of the sturdiest bones in the human body, and the delicate bones and cartilage of the nose make it the weakest point of the human face. It was no contest. Dex's head slammed into the bridge of Ilyas's nose with a wet, crumpling sound. The boy's knees buckled. Dex, using his grip on the shirt collar, flipped him around to face the other direction. Dex drew the Beretta from the small of his back and snaked the same arm around the boy's chest, holding him upright and pinning the AK in place. With his left hand he grabbed the kid's left hand, pressing on the thumb and keeping the dead man's switch depressed. It took two seconds, after which the boy managed a surprised-sounding *hurk*.

The sudden movement drew attention. Jalal's cousin, the Haqqani, saw something in his peripheral vision and wheeled to face him, already raising his AK. Everyone else was a split second behind, but suddenly he had nine pairs of eyes on him. His mind flashed through the options, a few of which were bad and the rest absolutely terrible.

There was no way he was getting out of here alive, not like this. Too many variables, too many hostiles.

"Let him go!" screamed Jalal's other son, Fahad. He was a tall, handsome kid and he was holding his AK like he knew how to use it. Jalal raised his hands for calm, peering into the warehouse and staring at Dex's face. Recognition dawned.

Dex settled on the least terrible option. An old axiom from counterintelligence school for those red-team probing missions of base defenses. When caught, go on the offensive. Make like a politician. Distract. Inveigle and obfuscate. Sow confusion, spread doubt, turn them against each other. Then make your move.

"Federal agent!" he shouted. "Everyone put your hands in the air, *now!*" He inclined his head to his collar and yelled, "Units one and three, move in now!"

"What is this?" the female port cop snarled.

"Dex, what are you doing?" Saenz snapped at the same time.

"Outstanding work, Agent Saenz," Dex said. "You and Porter, disarm these subjects."

"Agent Saenz?" said one of the other officers, the skinny guy with the hatchet face.

"He's lying!" Saenz said. "Sunny—"

Porter started to raise his G36.

"Wait!" Jalal screamed.

The hatchet-faced officer flinched. Dropped his hand to the butt of his pistol.

Haqqani, moving with the practiced ease of a lifelong combatant, raised his AK-47 and fired, shredding the guy from the waist up. He went over backwards, legs kicking into the air.

The blonde officer standing next to the port director dropped her umbrella and drew, quick as a ghost town showman. She fired from the hip and caught Haqqani in the shoulder and he fell back, sending a burst of automatic fire into the concrete that sent everyone diving from the ricochets.

"Hold your fire, hold your fire!" Saenz screamed, but the muscly port cop pointed his sidearm at Saenz, bellowing something. Porter

THE GUILTY SLEEP 297

sent a three-round burst into the guy's neck and head and he folded, firing his pistol. Fahad, standing next to Jalal and raising his own AK, was hit in the throat by the shot. He tumbled into his father's arms, making a terrible, watery choking sound.

Dex flashed to the compound. Ahn, his feet digging into the sand and gravel of the ANA compound. Jalal fell to his knees with his son, grasping at the wound in his throat and screaming the boy's name.

Ilyas bucked in Dex's grip, wailing. Dex wrenched the kid back toward the table. The cluster of people by the container, everyone left standing, had scattered. Haqqani backed into the warehouse to Dex's left, aiming his AK in short bursts from his off hand. The port director and his blonde lieutenant split up, shooting at Haqqani and Porter and Saenz. Sunny and Haqqani fired back at the woman, catching her in a crossfire. She screamed defiance as she died in a welter of blood and flesh.

The port director was crouched by the container, half in the rain. "Set *me* up?" he shouted, and double-tapped Porter in the back. Sunny fell into Saenz and bore him to the ground. Saenz, from under Porter's body, lifted his own pistol and shot the man in both legs. The guy dropped to his knees on the concrete, wailing. Saenz shot him in the bridge of the nose, snapping his rimless glasses in two and blowing out the back of his head. The port director toppled, leaving a brief haze of blood that disappeared into the falling curtain of rain.

Ilyas twisted again, screaming his brother's name. Dex was losing him. He let go with his right arm and pistol-whipped him in the back of the head. The kid reeled, heading for the floor. Dex ripped the dead man's switch out of the boy's hand, keeping his thumb on it. He backed toward the table.

"Ilyas!" Jalal yelled still cradling his other son in his arms.

Dex was in Afghanistan again, blinded by the sun. Running for the women's room, seeing Jalal trip over nothing—*nothing*—and tumble into a heap in the gravel and dust.

Someone screamed and Dex snapped back, gasping. Saenz, lying in the rain under Porter's body, turned his head and looked at Dex. His face was a mask of fury. Dex took another step back, then two more, raising the switch. The edge of the folding table butted the back of his legs.

"What have you done?" Jalal screamed. Saenz raised his pistol, trying to get an angle around the stumbling Ilyas. If the boy took another step or fell the rest of the way to the floor, Saenz would have him dead-bang.

Dex lifted his thumb.

43

BLUEPRINTS

DEX

Dex released the button and the inside of the shipping container went supernova. The fire sprayed out from the open end, spitting and steaming in the rain. Saenz screamed as the heat reached him. Dex turned and grabbed the suitcase. He heaved it off the table and ran for the door.

There was a gunshot from behind him. Two more. A round smacked into the suitcase and he stumbled from the momentum shift, then something laid a hot crease of fire across the outside of his left thigh and he tripped, going headfirst over a waist-high wooden crate. He landed face down, smacking his cheek on the concrete floor.

The world dimmed, like he'd just fallen down the steps into the dark of the women's room. Fatima's huge brown eyes swam in front of his face.

He shook his head and looked up and the metal entry door was in front of him. He crawled toward it, feeling the pull and the heat in his left leg. Reached for the handle and yanked his hand back as a trio of bullets slammed into the door, showering him with sparks and hot metal shavings.

"I'm gonna kill you, Frogger!" Saenz screamed from somewhere behind him.

"I'm already dead, Sarnt," Dex shouted back. Without aiming, he reached over the crate and fired into the warehouse. Six rounds, quick as he could. It was the first time he'd fired a weapon since that day three years ago. The women's room. Behind his eyes, he saw the round, black hole appear dead center in the facemask of the burqa, followed by a bloom of red as the assassin fell. The image strobed in his mind with every pull of the trigger.

"Well, I'm gonna make it *hurt*!" Saenz punctuated it with another two rounds into the door. If Dex went for it again, Saenz would blow his head off. He was trapped. Even now, Saenz and Jalal, and probably Ilyas and Haqqani, were likely leapfrogging in his direction. In another minute or two, they'd have him.

He had to buy time, figure out his next move. He looked at the fire extinguisher by the door, the one he'd bumped on the way in.

"Why'd you do it, Stu?" he called.

"What do you mean, Frogger?" Saenz called. His voice was closer than it had been thirty seconds before.

"Why'd you kill Winkowski, to start?" Dex pried at the fire extinguisher. The bracket resisted him and he bit back a curse.

"You saw that, huh?" Saenz sounded tired. Disappointed. "Ol' Wink suddenly developed a conscience when I told him we were gonna have to punch your card."

"He joined me in loose end territory, huh?" The extinguisher finally came free with a loud screech.

"Whatcha doin' back there, Frogger? Sit tight. We'll be there soon enough."

Dex could hear the scrape of feet off to his left, someone trying to move quietly through the stacks of crates. He thrust his pistol over the edge of the container behind him and fired twice. Someone snapped a curse and the sounds stopped.

"Almost tagged Jalal there," Saenz said. "After everything he did for you!"

THE GUILTY SLEEP 301

Dex was again back in the heat and sand and dust. Heaving Jalal to his feet and running again toward the safety and shelter of the women's room, only for Jalal to peel off to the side, firing his pistol back the way they'd come. Providing cover.

"Why are you doing this, Stu? Why *me*?" He set down the extinguisher, trying not to make any noise with it. Thing must've weighed twenty pounds.

"You're too smart for the second question," Saenz said. His voice was close. A dozen feet away. "I trained you better'n that. Like any good asset, you had the placement and the access. All I needed was the right levers."

There was a pause, a soft scuffle. Saenz, buying time to move in.

"Which you had pegged once you broke into my place."

"Not that I needed it," Stu replied. "You were standing tippy toe on a high ledge, Frogger. Easy to read, nothin' but a little push."

"And the first question?"

"Simple. I did my time in the world's hairy nether parts, dodging bullets and picking up pieces of my friends. I paid my dues in blood. Now it's time to get rich. I was raised to this life, Frogger. The Army thought they were making me, but they were just making me a better gangster."

Saenz's voice was infinitesimally louder. He was closer, by a foot or two.

"That's all this is? Business?"

"Exactly. High time I put the skills and abilities ol' Uncle Sam honed in me to good use. Build something for me 'n' my friends, set us up for good."

Dex slid to his belly, slowly pushing the fire extinguisher ahead of him. Moved right to the edge of the crate. "And me, Sarnt?"

"And you? Nothing personal. Late addition to the workings, is all." A note of pride crept into Saenz's voice. The master planner, revealing his blueprints. "Wouldn't have wanted to involve you at all, except that port director raised the clearance fee on us. You were a contingency."

"How'd it work out for you?"

"You're about to find out, Frogger." Saenz was right *there*. Maybe five feet away. Six at the most. There was a scuffle from the right this time, either Ilyas or Haqqani. They were on him.

Dex slung the extinguisher around the end of the crate, then rolled out behind it. Saenz was, indeed, just six feet away. He took a step back, dodging the extinguisher as it skittered along the floor. Haqqani was another five feet behind Saenz. Dex sighted in on the rolling extinguisher as Haqqani raised his rifle.

Dex fired, and the extinguisher exploded in a cloud of white dust. Pieces of metal zipped through the air. Saenz screamed. Something bit at the top of Dex's head. Through the haze, Dex saw a shadow stumble back. He fired once, but couldn't be sure if he hit anything because he was already wheeling around, surging for the door.

He fought the weight of the suitcase, caught the door's handle, and tore it open. Scuttled through and slammed it behind him, just as three bullets impacted the other side.

He put two bullets each into the passenger-side tires of Saenz's company car and sprinted for Carleen's truck. His left leg was struck through with bolts of pain at each step. He managed full strides, which meant there either wasn't much muscle damage, or he was in shock and getting ready to bleed out from a severed femoral artery.

He got around the containers and flung the suitcase into the passenger side of the truck. Peered back around the corner of the containers, leading with his gun, looking for movement. Nothing.

There was a growing bloom of flickering orange light on the other side of the building from the burning shipping container. A column of dirty gray smoke and steam was rising, mingling with the rain. The air had a sweet, chemical aroma. A smell of sickness. Of death.

Dex ran to the other side of the truck, climbed into the cab, and cranked the engine. Floored it. The tires screamed and hummed on the slick pavement, then finally bit and the truck slammed forward. He wrestled the wheel, keeping the big truck straight as the back end tried to slide sideways. He backed off the accelerator and the beast evened out. He made two turns, heading for the main gate.

THE GUILTY SLEEP

There was a flash of red and white light to the right and the rising wail of a siren. Two fire trucks turned from a side alley, heading for dock seventeen and the mess he'd left behind.

Dex pulled out of the port—no sign of Officer Montrose at the gate—and promptly disappeared himself into the rain-curtained corridor streets of Highlandtown around the outskirts of Patterson Park. Making sure no vehicle followed him for more than two turns or three minutes. Time, distance, and direction, those core principles of a surveillance detection route, and thus endeth the lesson. He grimaced and barked a half-laugh. Once, Saenz might have been proud that he remembered how to run an SDR when the fecal matter had well and truly been thrown into the rotary impeller.

Satisfied he wasn't being followed, he headed for Pulaski Highway and 40. Then 83, toward the Beltway. The storm avalanched across the windshield and the wipers struggled to keep up. It pounded on the roof and bed of the truck with the roar of a freight train. The heart of the storm was to the west, and he was heading straight into it. He looked over at the suitcase. Raindrops like glass beads decorated its plastic sides.

He drove with one hand and felt at his thigh with the other. His jeans were ripped along the outside of the leg, and the tips of his fingers came away damp and pink but not red. The bullet had taken layers of skin, left him with a seeping graze, nothing more.

Plenty of blood left to pay his debts.

He reached for the Nokia.

44

INTERLUDE: KANDAHAR, THREE YEARS AGO

DEX

There's that sound again. A fly, tap-tap-tapping at the window. He shouldn't be able to hear it, because he can't hear anything. His ears are stuffed with cotton. Or he's underwater. Maybe that's why he's holding his breath. He should come up for air.

Tap-tap-tap.

He's been under a while. The water feels wrong. It's too heavy, too thick. Blood-warm. Daria, holding Rowan, smiles at him. She's pushed her glasses up to keep the hair out of her face, but it never works, not when it's windy like this.

Tap-tap-tap.

No, not a fly, not underwater.

He tastes copper and raw steak. He reaches out to touch the freckles on Daria's nose, to slide his hand around the back of her head and bury his fingers in her hair, pull her to him. To hold his girls. He can see them but his eyes won't open.

His face is wet.

Tap-tap-tap. It's louder now, and definitely isn't a fly. There's something else too. Someone singing, but from far away. Not that Baloch power ballad from before; this is far less melodic.

THE GUILTY SLEEP

He really should swim up and breathe, but the water's holding him. He opens his eyes, or thinks he does because Daria's face vanishes. He sees swirling gray and black. Red. Something moves.

He coughs without realizing he coughs, and the air burns into his lungs and he heaves and gasps uncontrollably. There's more singing, but now it sounds like shouting and it's gotten closer. Swirling gray and black, but only half the world. The other half is dark red. The same side of him that's warm and wet. He blinks and the half world of swirling gray and black disappears, but the half world of warm red stays.

Tap-tap-tap. Louder and percussive. Not a fly. A three-round burst, fired from an M4 carbine. Tap-tap-tap.

Shouting.

"Frogger, get up!" Saenz yells from a thousand klicks away.

Dex hacks and spits and rubs at his right eye and the swirling gray and black resolves to dust and smoke and bits of paper and cloth sifting through the air. Someone grabs him under the arms and heaves him to his feet.

"You're OK man, you're OK," a voice says, right next to his ear. A beard scratches at his cheek. Jalal. "Go help the boss. Don't touch your head."

Dex thinks he nods, but everything's diaphanous and loose, so maybe it was the room moving. He moves toward the greater light at the door. Falls against the steps. Crawls up until he's next to the rough, shadowed outline that's Staff Sergeant Saenz. There's a smooth metallic click and a thud. The sound of a fresh magazine being slotted and the bolt releasing, chambering a round.

"Send fire that way," Saenz says, gesturing. Dex is relieved to make out the shape and movement of the man's arm. He blinks rapidly. Half the world stays red, the other half starts to resolve a little more. The sunlight stabs at him. Saenz presses the M4 into his hands. He wonders where his own is.

"Frogger!"

"Sarnt?" His voice is slurred, lips and tongue numb.

"Shoot. That. Way. Suppressive, towards the trucks. I gotta find the radio."

"Roger, Sarnt." Dex bellies down on the steps. Points the M4 in the general direction of back-the-way-they-came and squeezes the trigger gently. The carbine pushes back against his shoulder and the rifle speaks.

Tap-tap-tap.

More sounds start to come back, slowly. A sickly, binaural underscape to his firing. Someone groans, deep and wet. A woman cries in high, wailing counterpoint. Someone else curses in a low, nonstop monotone. Dex shoots. Tap-tap-tap.

A thud on the steps beside him. A shape raises up, fires two quick shots, then ducks back down.

"Specialist Grant, are you seriously wounded?" It's Sunny Porter. He pops up, fires again—tap-tap—and drops back next to him.

"I don't know, Sarnt," Dex says. There's a brief pause. He blinks, and every time he does, the world—at least to his right eye—gets clearer. He can see the trucks now, out in the middle of the compound. There are figures moving around, half obscured by blowing dust and heat shimmer. He sees two or three bodies between the trucks and the door. Men in ANA uniforms or perahan tunban. The other side, or a few supremely unlucky mokes caught in the crossfire.

"You are bleeding from your forehead. Do not touch it." Porter shoots again, his double-tap pneumatic-smooth. "There is a flap of skin hanging over your left eye."

That explained the half-red world and the heat and wetness. His brain felt like it was still underwater, still trying to come up for air.

"It does not seem to be severe, Specialist Grant. You will be fine"— tap-tap—"provided we are not all killed in the next several minutes."

Ol' Dirty Le Batard crunches into the wall next to the door. The front of his uniform is shredded and he's bleeding from a dozen small cuts. His face is twisted in outrage.

"Used the women," he snarls. "I can't believe it." He leans around the doorframe, sights his M4, screams like he's in an action movie, and empties his magazine in four seconds.

THE GUILTY SLEEP

"Saenz says to give him a hand, Frogger," Le Batard says. "Got you covered." He switches magazines as Dex scoots down the steps and turns. The room—what's left of it—is an abattoir. A horror.

At the opposite end, the ceiling and walls have fallen in. There are bodies and parts of bodies partially buried in the rubble and scattered around the interior of the space. The oldest Afghan woman, the one who'd sat across from him at tea, is on her knees by the collapsed section, wailing. Her hijab is torn and covered in blood and she's scrabbling in the wreckage with charred fingers. She's the only woman he can see. The rest have been obliterated by the bomb or buried in the collapse. Her screams are daggers of ice. Sullivan kneels next to her, trying to pull her away, but she won't be moved. Sully's neck is drenched with blood, and there's a raw red hole in the side of his head and his ear is dangling by a thin strand of earlobe.

Schoepe-Dogg is kneeling behind Chiarelli, cradling the big PFC as he breathes in great, slowing gasps. Chonk, with his one working hand, is trying to push loops of intestine back inside the gaping rent in his abdomen. Schoepe-Dogg is weeping, whispering in his ear, resting his cheek against Chonk's face.

Fatima lies on top of Ahn, her back shredded. The Yankees cap has come loose, and dangles from one of her ears.

Dex blinks against the unreality.

"Frogger!" Saenz shouts from the corner. Dex stumbles over. Saenz is kneeling over Winkowski, putting a tourniquet on the Specialist's thigh. Winkowski's left leg is gone below the knee. There's a tangled mass of sharded bone and ropy muscle where it used to be.

"I ain't never gonna dance again," Winkowski says, laughing. "Sum*bish*, that hurts."

"Your ass got no rhythm anyway," Saenz says. Then, to Dex: "Take the radio." Winkowski holds it up, grinning. "I called broken arrow to the QRF," Saenz continues, bearing down on the tourniquet straps. Winkowski's laugh grows sharp.

"Come on, Sarnt, you don't want to *hurt* me, do you?" He giggles, then his eyes roll up and he slumps over. Saenz wipes his face absently, leaving crimson warpaint trails on his cheeks.

"Call in status updates. We've got the Group guys coming from the governor's palace, but they're sending a couple of 'Hawks from K-town airfield too. Should have backup in twenty." He says this part in a shout so everyone can hear.

"Too late for Chonk," Schoepe-Dogg says. He's kneeling over Chiarelli's prone form, pressing his fingers to the man's eyes. Closing them. Sully has left the Afghan woman at the rubble, where she's subsided into soft weeping. He holds out his bloodied hand and pulls Schoepe-Dogg to his feet.

Sunny Porter and Ol' Dirty Le Batard remain at the entryway, firing out into the compound. Sully and Schoepe-Dogg and Dex stand in front of Saenz, waiting. He looks them each in the eye, pulling them into his orbit. He sets his shoulders and smiles at them like a proud uncle.

"Hold the door, Blackbirds," Saenz says. He slams a fresh magazine into his M4, and his smile turns sharper, like a wolf's starving grin. "Twenty minutes. We can do this. Hold the door."

SATURDAY AFTERNOON

45

MAUSOLEUM

DEX

Dex made Sunrise Vista in seventy-three minutes, passing through the churning heart of the thunderstorm as he went. The summer afternoon was dark as winter dusk. Dex drove cocooned in a maelstrom of water and wind, hands clawed around the wheel. Every few minutes he checked the rearview, seeking patterns in the brightness, shape, or consistency of the rain-smeared headlights reflected behind him. Once, he reached over and undid the zipper of the suitcase enough to stick his hand inside and touch the money. The paper was rough beneath his fingers. Less than a day ago, it had been a way to save himself, save his family, save Jalal and his. Now it was a ticket to his death and a receipt for betrayal, paid in blood.

If it got Daria and Rowan free, it would be enough.

Provided, of course, that Cooke was telling the truth and held up her end. He reached beneath the seat and pulled out the extra magazine for his PX4. Ejected the half-empty one and replaced it with the spare. Seventeen rounds plus one in the chamber. He hoped to God he wouldn't need any of them, but *plan for a flaming disaster, and thus endeth the lesson.* Cooke seemed the type to make an example, crafted in death. He needed a fail-safe. He'd done it once already today and it worked better than it had any right to. To get Rowan and Daria free, he'd have to do it again.

The tree-lined tunnel was different than in the morning, here now on the ragged, trailing edge of the storm. The treetops whipped drunkenly in the wind, painting the world in shadow. The rain had mostly stopped, but the dripping from the leaves was almost as heavy as the rain had been. A low mist crept from the woods like a hesitant ghost. The path was churned mud.

Even though he was expecting it, the clearing's entrance still came out of nowhere. He eased forward in a wide semicircle, passing the cement mixer, its dispenser chute angled into the foundation pit. Came up to the trailer—but not too close—and parked with the nose of the truck facing back the way he'd come. He grabbed three bundles of cash from the suitcase. More than he'd ever made in a single month, even with combat pay.

The trailer door opened and the kid with the bleached cornrows came out. He had an MP5 submachine gun strapped across his chest, and he swaggered down the steps like it gave him superpowers. Dex slid out of the truck, locking the door behind him and jamming the keys in his pocket. The edge of Rowan's drawing brushed across his knuckles and he squeezed the crease, running his thumb over the edge.

"Hey, bruh," Cornrows said. "Welcome back. Show me your hands."

Dex slowly raised his arms beside his head.

"The money?"

"In the truck," Dex said.

"Well, grab it, numbnuts. That's the point," the kid replied, nodding at the iron archway in the trees. "We goin' up the hill."

Dex told him why he wasn't going to do that. Cornrows swallowed hard, shuffled back a step.

"Ayo, that's messed up, man."

"You're telling me. Lead the way."

"S'pose to search you for weapons."

"I'll make it easy," Dex said, keeping his hands raised and turning slowly, showing the gun in the small of his back. He pulled out the

THE GUILTY SLEEP

Beretta with two fingers, put it on the hood of the truck. The kid took it and shoved it in his waistband. He backed away from the truck like it might bite him.

Cornrows stomped to the arch and motioned Dex to the path. The shadows were deeper under the trees, blending with the low mist to make the ground nearly invisible. Dex made out the trail by the gaps in the brush. The air was cool, nearly chill enough to see his breath. The skin of his arms tightened and stippled. Water dripped steadily into the silence. If he listened closely, he could hear the tap-tap-tapping of a trapped fly, the echoing wail of a Baloch pop song.

"You guys killed my best friend yesterday," Cornrows said from behind him.

"I'm sorry," Dex said, and meant it. Another sacrifice on the altar of Saenz's greed. "You were on the bikes, right? And he's the one who made the turn."

"Yeah. Mike. He was a chill dude."

"If it helps, the man who killed him is dead," Dex said, thinking about Winkowski (*Ahn*) clawing at his throat and Stu dancing away from the spurting blood.

"You kill him?"

"No. The other guys did."

"Miz Cooke gonna be *pissed* about the money," Cornrows said.

"She'll get it."

"She better, bruh. For your family's sake, yeah?"

They crested the hill. The trees were bigger here, like the buttresses of some damp, shadowy cathedral.

There was a clearing, and in the middle of it was a circular concrete slab. A dozen stone pillars stood sentry around the perimeter, and a concrete dais brooded over the center like a dinner table for ogres. This impression was reinforced by the eight brutalist concrete chairs around the circumference.

Daria was in a chair on the opposite side of the table, with Rowan asleep in her lap. His daughter had an olive drab plastic box strapped to her chest, and there was a tube running from the box to her nose. The sight filled Dex with a sick rage.

Cooke was standing behind Daria's right shoulder, the threat to his wife and daughter clear as the gun in Cooke's right hand. Turner and the guy with the manicured beard were to Daria's left. There was a flicker of movement in the trees, the glint of a machete's edge as Cooke's surviving Kaibil disappeared between the trunks.

"Dexter," Daria breathed.

"I'm here," Dex said, remembering to breathe. He forced the words through a throat that wanted to slam closed. "You ready to go?"

"We're ready," she said.

"Where's my money," Cooke snapped.

"I brought it," Dex said.

Cooke made a show of looking around the hilltop, her eyes wide.

"It's in his truck, Miz Cooke, down at the trailer," Cornrows volunteered. "Saw the suitcase through the window."

"Why didn't you make him bring it up, dummy?" the young guy said. "That was the point."

"I—"

"Here," Dex said, pulling the three bundles from his back pocket, moving slowly as a few of the guns across the table started to come up. He placed the money on the table gingerly. Like it might bite. "To prove I have it. The rest is in the truck, like your man said."

"Best go get it, son," Turner said. He made a small motion with the hand that wasn't holding the cutoff shotgun along his thigh. *Let's move things along.*

"I don't think so."

"And why not?" Cooke asked.

"Because if I bring it all up here right now, we know how this ends, don't we?"

The woman stared at him.

"We do," she murmured at last.

"Here's the deal," Dex said. "You're going to let them go. Now. They're going down the hill. My wife will take the money out of the truck and put it on the steps to the trailer. Then they're going to drive away. She'll honk twice when they're on the path out to the main

THE GUILTY SLEEP

road. Then we'll go get your money. Together." *And you can kill me at your leisure.*

"La hostia," Cooke muttered, rubbing the bridge of her nose. "A whip for the horse, a bridle for the donkey, and a rod for the back of fools. Why on God's green earth would I do that when I can send Florencio right now?"

"Because of this," Dex said, holding up the dead man's switch, the one he'd taken from Ilyas. He angled it so they could see his thumb pressing the red button. "You know what I did in the Army?"

Cooke stared at him. Waiting.

"What?" the bearded kid asked, taking the bait.

"EOD specialist. Explosive ordnance disposal. *Bombs*," he added, when the young guy looked confused. "I've got the suitcase rigged with a three-pound ball of ANFO. I let this switch go and your expansion fund vanishes in an ammonium nitrate fireball."

Cooke's eyes flashed. He'd finally gotten to her. Cornrows and the other kid looked shaken, but the whisper of a smile appeared on Turner's mouth.

"Let them go. Right now. Soon as they're clear, we'll do the rest."

Cooke kept her eyes locked on him. He was deep enough in the game now that it didn't disconcert him anymore.

"There's a boldness to you, Grant. I almost admire it. In another world, maybe you could have been working for me." The moment held, and the decision played across her face in a microexpression that sent a surge of hope thrumming into his guts. The woman glanced at Turner. Opened her mouth.

"Only one problem with that," a voice called from the mist. "He's lying to you."

46

THE GOOD TERP

DEX

"He's lying," the voice repeated. "He wasn't EOD and he couldn't rig a firecracker. He was a counterintelligence grunt and he's bluffing you, just like I trained him. There's no bomb." Stu was ten feet below Dex on the path, G36 at his shoulder. Jalal was next to him, clutching an AK.

"Come up here, whoever's talking," Cooke snapped.

Stu limped the rest of the way up the hill. He was coated in a fine layer of white powder courtesy of the exploding fire extinguisher, and his pantlegs were blackened at the bottoms and peppered with tiny holes from the burning shipping container. Jalal came just behind, his face pale and grim. They stood behind Dex on either side, turning him into a human shield. *Not that Cooke and her people wouldn't just blow us all away.*

"I'm sure you ran a decent SDR, Frogger," Saenz whispered. "But you were never going to find the AirTags in the suitcase."

"Hope for slightly better than the worst, eh, Sarnt?"

"And plan for a flaming disaster. You *did* listen to me, once."

"Stupidest thing I ever did, and thus endeth the lesson."

Saenz slammed the stock of the G36 into Dex's kidney. A bolt of pain shot up his spine and he arched his back trying to catch it and

THE GUILTY SLEEP

317

failed. He realized he was on his knees only when Jalal gripped him by the collar and heaved him upright. He looked across at Daria, held on to her eyes, held on to the curve of his little girl's head, the softness of her cheek buried against his wife's chest.

"More to come, Frogger," Saenz promised.

"Another one from the stickup crew, Aunt Angie," the kid with the pencil beard said. "I don't know who the raghead is."

"Thank you, Slade. I gathered. King Solomon was right about honor and thieves." Then, to Stu and Jalal: "What do you want?"

"We want to parley," Stu said.

Turner slid around Daria, moving closer to Cooke. It was like a signal, because the kid with the beard—Slade, Cooke had called him—and Cornrows both started reaching.

"Everyone be still, please," Stu said.

"I don't take requests," Cooke said.

The metallic snick of Jalal flipping the AK's safety echoed in the still woods.

"Wasn't a request," Stu said, voice like sandpaper over silk.

"A thief *and* stupid," Slade said.

Jalal raised a hand and there was a sharp, flat *crack* from the woods to the right and a chunk of concrete exploded from the chair next to Cornrows. The kid yelped and whirled, raising his submachine gun. Daria flinched, pressing Rowan tightly against her chest.

"Hold!" Cooke's voice was a whiplash.

"Smart lady," Saenz said. "I've got a man in the woods on each side. With AKs. You're outgunned and outflanked. Anyone twitches an eyelash, it's all over."

"What's next, then?"

"Like I said: parley. Lower your guns, we'll lower ours, and let's sit down together and manage the situation."

Cooke thought it over, then nodded at the chairs in front of them. Cornrows, Turner, and Slade relaxed a millimeter. Saenz muscled Dex forward and pushed him into the seat in the middle. Stu sat on his left, Jalal on his right. They leaned their rifles against the table, close to hand. Dex stared across at Daria and she stared back. Cooke sat down next to Daria, laid a little chrome-plated pistol on the table. The silence stretched out, but Saenz was never going to break it first. He was going to let it work for him.

"What do you want?" Cooke said at last.

"I want," Stu said, "to take this wayward soul down the hill and paint the side of that cement truck with his brains. I owe him that, for ruining three years of groundwork. My life's ambition. More than that, he betrayed me. I don't tolerate betrayal."

"Except when you're cutting Winkowski's throat?" Dex said, the words coming out before he realized he'd opened his mouth.

"There's a longer conversation to be had about what it means to be an apex predator and what it means to be cattle," Saenz said, "but we don't have the time."

Cooke's eyes flickered between them, a flash of impatience moving across her face.

"And then," Saenz continued, his voice pitched to carry, "we're going to get in that pickup and drive away with the money. This . . . Blue Falcon"—here, he waved at Dex—"has recently undertaken actions that have wiped me out, financially speaking. We'll call this suitcase of what must be petty cash for you, a consolation prize for me. A seed pearl on the road to make me whole again. You can do whatever you want with them," he said, nodding at Daria and Rowan. "That's *your* consolation prize."

Dex's hands balled into fists. The tendons in his wrists creaked.

"What if I don't care for what you want?" Cooke replied.

"Then it's all over but the gunsmoke and pink mist thanks to the guys my partner here has in the trees. Your choice, mamacita."

"*Wait,*" Daria said. Cooke looked at her sharply. "Don't do this. You have . . . you have to stop this. There's a little girl here, a sweet little girl who loves sloths and feeding ducks and singing, and she never hurt anyone in her entire life. If you people start shooting each other, what do you think is going to happen to her? You have to *stop.*"

Daria's words fired through Dex like an explosive charge. *Wait . . . you have . . . to stop.* Fatima's words, paired with his wife's. And suddenly he knew what they meant.

THE GUILTY SLEEP   319

A slim opening, a hair's crack in the darkness. He climbed toward it.

"Your partner," Dex said, laughing.

"What?" Saenz said. Out of the corner of his eye, Dex saw Jalal stiffen ever so slightly.

"Your *partner*," Dex repeated, "who you trust so much. With Ilyas and Gulbuddin Haqqani in the trees. His guys, his blood. You really think he's not going to turn on you? Leave your body in the woods when this is done?"

"Shut up," Jalal said.

"I don't think I will." He kept his eyes fixed on Daria's and she kept hers on his. He willed her to read his intent, anticipate the moment. "Put it together, Stu, great tactical mind that you are."

"This isn't the time, Frogger."

"It's exactly the time if you want to know what really happened back in that compound. In the women's room. I can't believe you never figured it out."

"What are you talking about?"

"Jalal. He set the whole thing up."

In the seven seconds of stillness that followed, three drops of rain fell on the table with audible pops and Rowan took two deep breaths.

"You're out of your mind," Jalal said. "From what Stu's told me, I shouldn't be surprised. Shut your mouth and let the grown-ups talk." Not the hail-fellow-well-met interpreter from before, not at all. And his fingers had twitched, subconsciously reaching for the AK trigger by his knee. Dex was getting to him.

"No. I remember."

"You remember Jalal saving you at the trucks after you took that first round in the chest."

"Lucky thing I popped outside for a quick smoke," Jalal added. "Regretting it now."

"Yeah, you shot the guy who killed Ahn, who tagged me." A flash, Ahn's feet digging in the gravel, blood spurting from his neck, choking as he called for his mother. Dex pushed it down. "That was part of it, I think. Make it believable, make your part in it undetectable. But when it broke worse, after the dagarman was killed and we started taking fire, *you* were the one who told Saenz to pull back to the women's room."

"It was the safest place!" Jalal protested, and Dex knew he had him. It was there in the timbre of his voice, the slight tremble under the anger. He wondered if Saenz had heard it too.

"I was right behind you when we were running for it," Dex continued. "I watched you fall. You tripped over nothing, but I picked you up, dragged you along."

"This is nonsense," Jalal said, but Stu had gone quiet. Motionless.

"And then you peeled off, Jalal. Stepped to the side with your little pistol, shooting back the way we came. Covering us. First the fall, then the covering fire. Why? Because you didn't want to be in that room."

"Don't be stupid. I was just trying to help."

"I practically had to throw you in there," Stu said.

Cooke grunted. "This is fascinating, but I'm out of patience."

"You'll have your satisfaction," Dex said. "We're almost there." He turned, looked at Saenz directly for the first time since they sat down. His old sergeant had dark bags under his eyes, graying stubble across his cheeks. His skin hung pale and loose on his face. Suddenly ancient and tired, like he knew what was coming.

"See, when the ambush sprung, I heard Jalal screaming in Pashto—"

"I was trying to warn you."

"—and when I shot the one guy—" Dex saw the blue mesh of the burqa, the black hole appearing in the middle, the bloom of red soaking through.

"This is ridiculous, Stu—"

"—he shot Fatima, and Jalal kept screaming, and Fatima gave up her life putting words in my ear. 'Wait . . . you have . . . to stop,' she said. I thought she was asking me to save her life, to stop her from dying."

"—you can't possibly believe—"

"But she wasn't. She was being a good terp, right to the end. 'Wait . . . you have . . . to stop. It's . . .' And then she died. They weren't *her* words."

THE GUILTY SLEEP

"—this is insanity—"

"She was translating what Jalal was shouting at the suicide team. She couldn't get it all out, but I'll bet anything what came after 'it's' was 'me.' 'Wait, you have to stop; it's *me*.' Jalal wasn't supposed to be in the room with us. He was supposed to be outside when the bomb went off, but you dragged him inside with us, Stu. He didn't throw that poor kid, Habibullah, into the bomber to save us. He was trying to save himself."

"Why?" Stu said. To Dex, to Jalal, maybe to himself.

"We were the best CI team in the history of the theater. Put a bunch of tangos in the ground. You want to bet there wasn't a bounty on our heads? Or maybe it was a favor for his Haqqani cousins. But when enough of us survived, I'm thinking he realized the next best thing was to partner up with you and—"

"Enough," Jalal snarled, smashing a fist into Dex's chin and knocking him half out of the chair. Daria cried out, and Dex blinked against the spots in his eyes. He struggled upright and met Saenz's flat, weary gaze. Stu's eyes flickered to Jalal.

"Is it true, Jalal?" Saenz said. "Did you betray me?"

Cooke laughed. It was a dry sound. Like brush stirred by a high, hot summer breeze. Just before the wildfire. "Gloria a Dios. Let death steal over them," she said. "Let them go down to Sheol, for evil is in their heart."

"S'that supposed to mean?" Stu said. His voice was unsteady, riven with shock.

"It means," Cooke said, holding up a hand. There was a cross necklace in it. Black. Made of stone. "*Now.*"

47

SPECTERS

DEX

"*Now*," Cooke whispered. There was a wavering cry from the trees to the left. There was a sound like a log being split by an axe, and the scream cut off.

In the silence that followed, Dex could've sworn he heard Jalal swallow; the man's fingers twitched again, yearning for the AK's trigger.

"Ilyas?" Jalal called.

"Is it *true*?" Saenz said. His voice was low. Jalal wouldn't look at him. An admission in silence.

Across the table, Cooke smiled. Turner was gripping his shotgun so hard his knuckles were white. The avalanche in waiting. Slade's hand was at his waist, thumb through a belt loop near his pistol. He was staring at Rowan. His tongue darted out, wetting his lips.

Nearby, a bird chirped like it was coming out of its nest to assess the results of the storm. Thinking about fresh worms wriggling in the dirt.

Something the size and shape of a basketball sailed through the air and bounced across the table with a series of wet splats. Daria gasped and hunched over Rowan, turning away. The head came to a stop at the edge of the table. Ilyas's eyes were open. They seemed to look at

THE GUILTY SLEEP

323

his father. They blinked and rolled up, leaving only bloodshot whites. The head teetered, then tipped over and thumped to the ground.

Jalal moaned, low and deep in the back of his throat.

Under the table, Saenz was slowly moving his left hand toward his rifle.

Jalal raised his face to the sky and screamed. Across the table, Rowan stirred and muttered and Daria tightened her arms around their little girl.

"Daria," Dex said, voice flat. She looked at him.

"Coños, underestimated me again," Cooke said. "Know what's next?"

"End of the parley?" Saenz said.

"Get down, Dare. Now."

Saenz reached for his G36. Jalal saw it and snatched at his AK. Dex was quicker than both. He drove his legs out in a near split, kicking the rifles away. Stu and Jalal dove after them.

Turner, Slade, and Cooke were a blur of motion on the other side of the table, ducking for cover, raising their weapons. Cornrows a step behind, just starting to turn. Daria dropped, carrying Rowan out of sight.

Dex twisted out of his chair. Jalal had reached his AK and was rolling over on his back, bringing it to bear. Not on Cooke and her people across the table, but at Dex and Saenz. Dex launched himself and landed on Jalal, pushing the barrel of the AK away as he opened fire. The sound was a dragon's roar between them.

The world went double, a fade-in of grit and dust and hot yellow sun superimposed over Jalal's furious face. Dex saw Ahn, bleeding to death in the dirt. He saw the dagarman, clutching the spreading stain on his chest, his face exploding. The blue door of the women's room waited. He shook his head. He imagined his little girl, throwing frozen peas to a congregation of ducks.

Jalal spat and snarled. Dex kneed him in the balls and Jalal squealed and heaved against him.

More fire from an AK, this time from the misted trees to the right. With Ilyas dead courtesy of a Kaibil's machete, it could only be

Gulbuddin Haqqani. Bullets slammed into the chairs around them, sending shards of cement flying like shrapnel. Dex rolled off Jalal, moving under the ledge of the table. He heard the quick double-boom of Turner's shotgun. Daria screamed his name and it somehow carried through the roar of the gunfire.

Saenz grabbed his rifle on the fly and sprinted away from the table. He half-turned, firing wildly from the hip. Jalal scuttled away on his hands and knees. There was a snap of pistol fire from across the table—Cooke or Slade, Dex couldn't see which—and Saenz dove behind one of the stone columns ringing the dais.

Dex crawled around the backside of the table, away from the line of fire. Toward Daria and Rowan. He was the high point of a triangle, with Saenz behind the pillar somewhere to his left, and Jalal around the table to his right. On the other side of the table ahead of him were his girls, with Cooke and her crew.

There was more shooting from the woods, and Cornrows must have finally let loose with the MP5, because there was the sound of an industrial zipper pulled at speed.

Saenz popped around the side of his pillar, trading shots with Jalal, who was now prone behind one of the chairs. "I'll kill you!" Saenz shouted. Jalal sprayed the column with half his magazine. Saenz ducked, came around the other side, and fired over Dex's head at Cooke's side of the table. Again, Dex's vision doubled, the blinding Afghan sun stabbing him.

"Daria, stay down!" Dex called, rubbing his eyes. "I'm coming!"

Saenz leaned out from behind the column and trained his G36 on Dex's head, ready to turn him into a liar.

Cornrows materialized in front of Dex and fired another long burst from his submachine gun. Saenz flinched back, and his pillar took another pounding. He popped back out and got off a single shot. The bullet smashed through Cornrows' shin, and hot wetness sprayed across Dex's face. The double vision wavered, the yellow tinge of Afghanistan growing as Ahn's blood dripped from Dex's cheeks and nose and eyebrows. Dex screamed against it, matching Cornrows' injured howl. He pushed himself to his knees as the kid collapsed to his.

THE GUILTY SLEEP

Slade came around the table, raising his pistol, and Dex grabbed Cornrows and hurled himself backward, pulling the kid with him. Slade fired. The bullets slammed into Cornrows' chest and he screamed again, writhing under the impact. Dex reached around and found the MP5's grip and sent a burst of fire back at Slade until the slide locked on an empty chamber. Missed, but sent Slade diving below the table. Cornrows groaned and went limp.

Dex wormed out from under the body. He had to get to Daria and Rowan. Cornrows blinked up at him like he wasn't sure where he was. Like Ahn had blinked up at him. Dex knuckled his eyes, trying to force the doubling away. Cornrows' (*Ahn's*) hands fluttered weakly. His body didn't know he was dead yet. Dex pulled his Beretta free from the kid's waistband and the world started to white out, but he held Rowan's face in the front of his mind and the burning brightness receded enough to see the table. To see the trees and the low, creeping mist.

Dex did a quick scan. Saenz was ahead and to the left, behind his pockmarked column. Jalal had disappeared, probably regrouping in the trees. He turned, peered above the rim of the table.

Turner was hunched over behind a tree. He raised the shotgun and let fly into the woods. Cooke and Slade knelt behind the stone chairs on either side of where Daria and Rowan had been sitting. Cooke was shooting into the trees, and Slade was firing over Dex's head at Saenz's pillar. Dex had an angle, could have taken the kid's head off, but couldn't pull the trigger. Not with his girls on the other side, just below the edge. Not with a nightmare overlaying his vision.

Out in the trees, Jalal screamed his son's name and vowed to kill them all. Dex spun, looking for him.

Instead, Gulbuddin Haqqani knifed the mist, a specter of the woods, born in fire and smoke. He charged the dais, firing as he came, face twisted in fury. Shadows churned, and Florencio appeared, sweeping his machete through Haqqani's legs, and the man went down with a scream. Haqqani shouted defiance, and Florencio slammed the blade into his neck. Blood fountained and Haqqani's feet drummed on the carpet of pine needles. Ahn's feet kicked at the dust. Mariam gasped for breath.

The Kaibil turned, machete dripping. Dex laid his wrist against the side of the concrete chair and put three shots into the center of the man's chest. Florencio went over backwards, the machete spinning away.

The Afghan sun faded into the strobing shadows of the women's room. Mariam mouthed the words of his salvation. Fatima gasped Jalal's damnation. Blood spilled from their lips. He ducked behind the chair, willing it to end.

There was a blast of fire from the woods directly in front of Dex. Jalal. To his right, great chunks of stone sprayed from Saenz's pillar. Stu retreated toward the table, returning fire in bursts. In two steps he was right in front of the chair where Dex was crouched.

Dex surged around the chair and slammed a kick into the side of Stu's knee. Something snapped and Saenz screamed and stumbled, firing into the ground. The burst from the G36 was deep and percussive, rending great chunks of earth into the air.

From his knees, Stu spun on him, raising the rifle. Dex launched forward, sliding inside the sweep of the barrel, smashing it aside with his pistol.

With his other hand, he hit Stu in the face. Put everything into it, torquing from his hips and driving his fist straight like a pile driver. Caught him flush in the mouth, snapping his head back in a spray of blood and teeth. Saenz went over on his back, nerveless. The rifle bounced down the slope into the mist.

Dex dropped just as Cooke's crew across the table opened fire again. A hive of angry wasps tore through the air where he'd been standing a second before. He could hear Daria. Calling for him. Around the table wasn't working—it was too close. He needed a better angle. He dropped low, hoping the thin mist would cover his movements, and scrambled forward, keeping the table between him and Cooke. He crawled to the pillar just past the one Saenz had sheltered behind.

"Do you see him?" Cooke called. "Where is he?"

"Got nothin'," Slade said.

THE GUILTY SLEEP

On hands and knees, Dex peered around the column. He was close to the angle he needed. He could see the backside of the chair Slade was crouched behind. His family would be just past him. If he could—

A dump truck hit him, flipping him into the base of the pillar. Another kick, this time a wrecking ball to his face. Dex's head bounced off the stone and the pistol fell from his hand.

Jalal stood over him, breathing hard. For a second, he was a shadow, limned by a river of fire from the Afghan sun, and Dex's eyes were filled with sand and Ahn's blood. Jalal raised his AK, resting it on Dex's forehead. His finger tightened on the trigger. "My . . . boys . . ." Jalal whispered.

Saenz appeared behind Jalal, face a mask of blood. There was a flicker of dimly reflected light as Stu's hand flashed up. Saenz buried his knife in the base of Jalal's skull. Jalal arched like he'd touched a live wire, gagging and trying to pull free of the blade. Dex swatted the barrel of the AK aside as Jalal reflexively squeezed the trigger. There was a bloom of fire and the muzzle flash seared Dex's hip as he squirmed away. Then the AK fell and Jalal collapsed on top of it.

Dex wormed backward around the pillar as Saenz staggered forward, knife dripping at his side. Dex's scrabbling hand brushed something hard. The grip of his pistol.

"Frogger, you bastard," Saenz lisped. His mouth was a bloody, toothless ruin. He pointed the knife at Dex's face. "You ruined—"

There were two shots from behind Dex and Saenz staggered against the impact, his shirt fluttering. Behind the table, Slade gave a cry of triumph. Blood pouring from his mouth, Saenz raised the knife again. He screamed wordlessly and fell forward. Dex raised his pistol and shot Saenz in the left eye, smashing him back into the pillar. He slid to the base, head lolling to his chest. The mist slowly closed over him.

"I *hate* that nickname," Dex said.

48

EXIT WOUNDS

DEX

Dex's hip was on fire. He put his palm over the spot and his hand came away sooty but dry. Just a muzzle burn; another narrow, undeserved escape. He looked up at the moving branches of the trees, trying to will away the phantom Afghan sun. A fat drop of water splatted on his forehead.

"Dex!" *Daria.* Her tone told him it was over.

"Get up, man," Turner called, his voice tired.

Dex stood slowly. Stars bloomed behind his eyes, progeny of Jalal's kick and the rebound of his head off the column. The pinpricks of dancing light fought with imaginary sand blowing on Afghan wind. He staggered to the table and braced himself on the back of one of the chairs. He kept his pistol visible, pointed to the side. Daria, holding Rowan, was between Turner and Cooke, with Slade slightly behind. No more than ten feet away, separated by twenty degrees of table and a single chair. Almost close enough to touch.

Cooke held Daria's right wrist in her left hand. The black stone cross necklace dangled between them. Cooke's pistol was pointed across the table at Dex's head. His wife looked at him, eyes wide, face streaked with tears.

"Are you hurt?" Dex managed. "Is . . . Rowan?"

THE GUILTY SLEEP

329

"We're just ready to go home."

"We'll go. Soon."

"No," Cooke snarled. "You won't."

"Drop the gun, man," Turner said. He was pointing the sawed-off at Dex's belly, steady as a boulder. The barrels were big as train tunnels.

They had him dead to rights. He set his gun on the table. The concrete was somehow the color of UN peacekeeper helmets, but with an earlier paint job showing through, a kind of whirling underpattern the color of seaweed. It made Dex vaguely nauseous. But the act had moved him closer. Eight feet now. Just eight feet.

"Let them go. Please."

Cooke smiled and pointed her chromed automatic at Daria's head. Dex shut his mouth so hard his teeth snapped together. His let his knees give way and stumbled against the table, slipping a step to the left. His hand slid into his pocket, his thumb and forefinger finding the edge of Rowan's drawing. Seven feet away.

"Get up," Cooke said, gesturing with the pistol. "Stand up, Grant."

"Please," he said.

He staggered another half-step to the left. Six feet from Cooke and Slade, seven from Daria and Rowan, eight from Turner. Cooke took a step back and to her right, pulling on Daria until they were facing him in a line.

"Aunt . . . Aunt Angie?"

Cooke froze, surprised. "Slade?" she said, and the kid stepped forward. His face was pale, but there was a flush high on his cheeks. His eyes were bright. Fevered.

"I was thinking, if you really wanted to punish him . . ." He licked his lips.

Cooke looked at Daria, then at Rowan. She turned to Dex, smiling. "Tell me what you want, Nephew. Say it out loud."

"You could . . . let me take the girl down to the trailer?"

Dex felt the bottom drop out of his guts. The chill waters of the black river closed over his mouth and nose. Daria's face flashed from shock to rage.

"Don't touch my daughter!" Daria screamed, the cords in her neck standing out against her pale skin. Cooke smashed her pistol into Daria's face. She managed to keep her grip on Rowan, but crashed into the side of the table and went down on her knees. Blood spattered from her nose.

There was a thing they'd trained for, back at Huachuca. The twenty-one-foot rule. If someone had a knife, they could cover twenty-one feet at a run before you could draw your sidearm, aim, and fire. Never let a threat get inside twenty-one feet if your gun wasn't out. Of course, Cooke's gun *was* out and Dex didn't have a knife. But he had only seven feet to go and no better option.

Dex lurched toward Cooke. Or he tried to. His brain sent the message to his muscles, but they skipped and froze and all he did was shudder. He was in the women's room, tangled with Ahn's body, three men in blue burqas striding forward.

He ran his thumb along the crease of Rowan's drawing. A synapse re-fired. Taking a shuffling step, he slipped his fingers into his pocket and pulled out the paper, hiding it behind his thigh.

"Slade," Cooke said, her voice low and dry and final. "Take the girl. Do what you want. Put her in the foundation when you're done."

"No," Turner said, lowering his shotgun.

"What did you say?" Cooke asked, looking at him. Dex shook the drawing open. Looked at it, seared the bright colors into his mind.

"I said no."

"Disappointing." Cooke sighed. "You're fired, Melchizedek." She raised the automatic to Daria's head. Daria covered Rowan with her body.

Dex shouted and dashed forward. Slade stepped in front of Cooke, bringing up his pistol. Dex cannoned into him, smashed him aside.

Cooke wheeled, leading with her gun. Dex threw the drawing into the air. It flapped like a broken bird and Cooke's eyes flickered to it as she fired. Dex ducked and something drew a lance of fire across the side of his head and bit off the top of his left ear. But then he was there. He grabbed Cooke's hand, twisted her gun aside. Fingers snapped like dry kindling. Cooke screamed and Dex wrenched the

THE GUILTY SLEEP

gun away. It clattered across the table, but he ignored it and drove his hands into Cooke's throat. She was solid woman, but his hands enclosed her neck easily.

"Daria, don't look!" he shouted, staring into Cooke's eyes, squeezing as hard as he could. Her face disappeared, replaced by the shadowed mesh of a deep blue burqa. The cloth was rough beneath his fingers. Cooke clawed at his wrists. The necklace pressed against his skin. Any second, Turner or Slade was going to shoot him in the back, but he had to try. "I love you both!"

He slid his right foot behind Cooke's leg, wrenched her sideways. She stumbled over his leg and he turned with her, driving her head down into the edge of the table with all his strength, all his weight. There was a crack like a thick-shelled egg breaking. The cross necklace snapped, the beads skittering across the table like black stars.

Cooke went limp. His hands were locked around her throat and their legs were tangled, and when she slumped to the ground, she took him with her. The woman was gasping something, but the side of her head was all the wrong shape and her jaw wasn't working right. Dex's hands unclawed, releasing her throat. He sat up. So did Slade, a few feet ahead. The kid was shaking his head, looking for his gun. Dex tried to crawl forward, but his feet were still under Cooke's (*Ahn's*) and he couldn't break free. Slade rolled over, reached, came up with his pistol.

Turner blew by Dex like a hurricane, kicked Slade's gun aside, and snatched him off the ground like he weighed nothing. Slade screamed as the big man lifted him straight up over his head, then hurled him into one of the stone columns. The kid smashed into the unforgiving pillar with a squeal. His body bent into a reverse U, spine snapping with a crack. Slade tumbled to the ground, gasping and retching. He clawed at the dirt, trying to crawl, but his legs wouldn't work. Turner stood over the kid, sorrow written across his hound-dog face. He brought his huge, booted foot up. Pistoned it down. Once, twice.

Dex pulled free of Cooke's legs, scooted backwards to Daria. Her forehead and the bridge of her nose were bleeding from where Cooke had hit her with the pistol. It was an awful match to the side of her face, already bruised from the morning. Daria's eyes were cloudy, but she held Rowan tight to her chest. Turner sighed and Dex staggered upright, facing the big man. Wishing he'd held on to one of the guns.

"Didn't want to see that boy for what he was," Turner murmured. He pressed his hands against the small of his back and looked down at Cooke. She moaned wetly at him, reaching upward, trying to work her misshapen jaw. He drew the sawed-off from under his vest.

"I quit," he said, and fired both barrels.

Dex's world went gray around the edges. The blazing molten coin of the Afghan sun faded into the mist. The waters of the black river receded. Dex looked up into the cathedral of trees and drops of water fell on his face, washing Ahn's blood away.

Turner carefully laid the shotgun on the edge of the table.

"You guys should go," Turner said.

Dex pulled Daria to her feet, took Rowan, nestled his daughter's head into his shoulder. His wife leaned against him.

"Not that I'm looking a gift horse here, but—"

Turner waved at the dais, the guns and shell casings scattered over its surface. The bodies and blood. "I found my coworkers problematic."

A mad bark of laughter tore its way from Dex's throat. "They sucked."

"Truth is, it was your little girl that did it."

"What do you mean?" Daria asked.

"Last time I saw my daughter, she was the same age. Near sixteen years ago." The big man sighed. "After I clean up this mess, I think I'm going to find her."

"What about the cops?"

"Don't worry about them. Sheriff Pittman is—was—so deep in Angie Cooke's pocket he coulda knit a sweater from the lint. He'll sweep every dust bunny under the rug. Whatever he finds, anyway—he won't catch a whiff of *this*," he said, gesturing around them. "Anything pops, he'll put it on some gangbangers up from Baltimore for a weekend of mayhem."

"Town's going to pot," Dex said.

THE GUILTY SLEEP

"Ayuh. Last thing he's gonna want to do is talk to your lucky ass—you'll put a buncha holes in the narrative, and that'll point back at him."

"No loose ends."

"Right. Means you keep the money too. Reckon you earned it."

"No way," Daria said. "Absolutely not."

"Lady, you seen the price of college these days?" Turner said. "'Sides, there's a little more where that came from. Cooke's rainy-day fund. I'll call it severance."

"Just like that, huh?"

Turner peered into the mist, seeing something Dex couldn't. Then he nodded, just once, slow like a rusted oil derrick. "Just like that. Now get that little girl out of here."

49

DRIVE

DEX

Dex carried Rowan down the hill. Daria clutched his arm, nails digging into his skin. The port-liveried SUV was parked next to the trailer, doors open. They ignored it and climbed into Carleen's truck, Daria's feet on the hard-sided suitcase full of Cooke's money, their daughter in her lap.

"Dare—"

"Shut up, Dex, not a word. Just get us out of here."

She had dead center. He drove the tunnel, squinting against the shadows, but as he turned on to the main road, the sun came out from behind the clouds and painted everything in gold.

Daria pulled the tubing away from Rowan's face and stroked her hair as she woke.

"Mommy," his daughter mumbled, "I had terrible dreams. People were shouting." She paused, and her eyes cleared. "Mommy," she gasped, "your face!"

"I know, baby," Daria said, giving her a sip of water from the bottle in the dash. "Mommy got a couple of booboos today, but I'll be OK." She glared hot fishhooks into Dex's eyes.

"Hey, Ro," Dex whispered. Rowan looked at him, did a double take, and her face broke open in a smile that tore his heart in half.

THE GUILTY SLEEP

"Daddy!" She hurled herself against his side and he put his arm around her, pulling her tight against him. "Terrible dreams, Daddy."

"Oh, kiddo, I'm sorry. I don't . . . I don't think you'll have dreams like that again."

"Promise Thomas?"

"Promise bomise Thomas."

"*And* Lorenzo Lamas?"

"Him too. And to make sure, I brought you something." Dex reached behind the seat. As he turned, his daughter gasped again.

"Daddy, you have a hurt place too. Your ear!"

"I know, kiddo. Your mom and I had a rough day, but it's over now." He brought out Rowan's tattered stuffed sloth.

"You brought Brownie!" She cuddled the sloth fiercely, and snuggled up against Dex's shoulder. Whatever else happened, whatever came next, he was going to hold on to this moment. "Where are we going?" she asked, as Daria belted her in.

"We're just driving for now, Lovebug."

"Fun! In Grandmama's truck too. I'm hungry."

"Why don't we hit a drive-through?" Dex said. "Get some fries?"

"Oh, is it a special day?"

Dex chanced a glance at Daria.

"Special enough," his wife said through clenched teeth, double-checking the seat belt.

"I'm sleepy." Rowan yawned. "That's weird. I just woke up."

Daria gave her another sip of water, and then Rowan was out, snoring against Dex's shoulder.

Daria ripped open the olive drab plastic box and read the name of the gas printed on the metal cylinders inside. Dex nodded at the glove box, and Daria opened it, found his cell inside. She googled halogenated enflurane until she was satisfied that sleepiness was a normal side effect, then slumped back in her seat. She touched her cheek, wincing, then looked over their little girl's head at him. Her eyes lit with something.

"Mom!" she gasped, hand on her forehead. Daria called Carleen on Dex's phone, told her they were safe, that they'd be home soon. Told her Rowan was OK twice, three times. Dex couldn't make out Carleen's side of it.

"We'll be back soon, I promise," Daria said, closing the call. Then, to him: "Mom told me what you said. How you were going to bring us home no matter what. She said sorry she put her cigarette out on your hand."

"It's fine. I've had worse."

Daria mimed touching her ear and *hmphed* in agreement. Then she stared out the window, watching the road.

"Where are we going, Dex?"

"I didn't have a destination in mind. Just wanted to keep driving, because as soon as I stop, you're going to kill me."

"Got that right."

"No court would convict."

"No."

He touched the side of his head, grazed the new, shortened tip of his ear, and grimaced himself.

"Does it hurt?"

"A bit, yeah."

"Good." She ran a hand through her hair, sighing. He watched her in his peripheral vision, trying to imagine he saw a softening in her face.

"I'm sorry," he said. "For everything."

She stared out the window, breath fogging the glass. He switched on the defroster. The woosh of the air filled the silence.

"I know you are," she said at last. "So show me."

"What?"

Daria squared her shoulders. "Mom said you were a dumbass but you were trying to do the right thing. So, what did she mean by that?

"I—"

"Show me you're sorry, Dex. Do what I asked you to do a million times. *Talk* to me. Tell me what happened, make me understand. Don't try to protect me from the dark. You *put* us in the dark. Tell me everything." She took a deep breath and waited. Watching him.

And with their daughter sleeping safe between them, he did what he had never been able to do before. He told her everything.

Daria sat, and watched, and listened. It took him forever to get it out, and it felt like excising a black tumor from his soul.

She passed him the water bottle and he took a grateful sip. They crested a long rise, and the road spooled out ahead of them. It wavered in the returning summer heat. Dex merged onto 77 West, heading toward the mountains and the sun. The big pickup rumbled.

"Where are we going, Dex?" she said again.

"West. Just gonna drive until it feels safe. We'll bed down for the night. We can check in with your mom in the morning, make sure things seem all clear."

"Then head home?"

"Then home."

He slid into the left lane, passing a slow-moving semi. The road ahead was straight as an arrow, striking for the heart of the Blue Ridge Mountains. On the horizon there was a marshaling of dark clouds, a growing army marching the next afternoon thunderstorm forward in ragged formation. He tore his eyes away from the sky and looked at his wife. Her eyes were clear, gaze steady. Considering. He pressed the accelerator.

50

THE GUILTY SLEEP

DEX

They stopped just over the border into West Virginia. Harpers Ferry. A long, low hotel on a granite ridge overlooking the Potomac. Could have been designed by the same misanthropic architect who crapped out the pepto-pink safe house, only this one was a faded turquoise and unironically bore the honorific *John Brown's Rest*. Dex cleaned the blood from his face with water from the bottle and put on an old O's cap he found behind the driver's seat, wincing as it touched the side of his head where the bullet had clipped his ear. But he got them checked in just in time to beat the round of afternoon t-storms. They ate their drive-through food. Rowan cuddled Brownie the sloth like she was embracing an old friend.

Rain hammered at the metal roof. The room was dim, the carpet faded and musty smelling, the beds sagging in the middle. It was heaven.

Rowan was asleep again, in the bed farthest from the door, her belly full of nuggets and apple slices and fries. Daria nibbled a burger, sitting on the edge of the bed next to their daughter. Dex was on the bed across from her. They were both looking at the suitcase full of money on the floor between the beds.

THE GUILTY SLEEP

Daria tapped her feet against the hard shell of the suitcase. "So. This is what almost ended . . . everything." Her shoulders hitched as she said it, but her face was stony.

"Yeah. Almost four hundred and thirty thousand dollars in there."

"Four hundred . . ." Daria gasped.

"We'll have to be careful, but from what Turner said, I don't think anyone's going to be looking for it. Or us."

"What—what are you saying, Dex?"

"Ro's surgery. The mortgage, your loans. The Plan. I thought . . ."

Daria sighed. Rowan murmured, rolled over. Daria stroked their daughter's hair, and Rowan settled with a soft, contented sound. It was music.

Daria tapped her foot against the suitcase again. In a different world, it might have sounded like the tap-tap-tapping of a trapped fly against a window. She took another bite of her burger, a big one, finishing it off. Her eyes met his as she crumpled the paper. Her lips twitched, almost like she wanted to smile. She hurled the burger wrapper. It sailed across the room, landed square in the trash can with a muffled thump.

The rain thrummed on the roof. Their daughter breathed. Daria tapped her toes on the suitcase. Dex watched her. Daria kicked off her shoes and lay down next to Rowan. His little girl snugged against her mother's side.

He took off his own shoes, lay down on his own bed. He looked at his girls. Listened to the rain and his daughter's breathing. In the distance, thunder shook the heavens. Daria sighed again, looked at him, closed her eyes.

Dex reached down, took the suitcase by the handle, and slid it under his bed.

They'd taken the money. They knew they'd done it, and maybe someone other than Turner might know they'd done it. Come looking for it and the people who'd taken it.

Or maybe Turner was right, and they were in the clear. Maybe it would work out.

They'd either go down for it or not. If no one else knew, if no one else figured it out, no one would come looking. And they'd walk.

Either way, their fate was decided, sure and inexorable as the rain on the roof and the thunder over the hills.

Dex closed his eyes and listened to his wife's breathing deepen and slow.

THE END

ACKNOWLEDGMENTS

Writing a novel like this one is an expedition into the bloody, dangerous unknown. While much of the work was solitary, I was never alone on the journey. My wife, Sarah, and my daughter, Charlotte, were with me every step of the way, constantly encouraging. Without their unrelenting, determined support and ideas, this book would not exist. Their belief never wavered, even when mine did. I love you both! I owe my best friend, Zoltan Korossy, a significant debt. He has the mind of an engineer, and during our conversations about this book, he architected solutions to several of the challenges with which I was wrestling. My mother-in-law, Diane, has read everything I've ever written, with a keen eye for detail. She's a detective/archeologist of literature, and her suggestions land, unfailingly.

Roz Foster is the best agent an author could have. Thank you for championing this book—and for your brilliant recommendations—and for believing in me as a writer. Thank you to Keith Wallman and Team Diversion. Henry Carrigan, for catching errors large and small; Amy Martin of Neuwirth & Associates, for coordinating; Shannon Donnelly, for the great support; Anthony Morais and Jonathan Sainsbury, for the amazing cover. Clara Linhoff, Nina Smetana, Jeff Farr, Beth Metrick, all top-notch people, and all of them had a helping hand in this novel. Not least—Toni Kirkpatrick is a brilliant editor, and her attention to detail and passion for the story and its characters made this book far better than it was.

Though I've loved writing and telling stories my whole life, I started writing in earnest in early 2003, as a way to cope with combat-induced PTSD. It was the first thing that helped. In many ways, I might have been Dex if it hadn't been for the writing. Along the way,

ACKNOWLEDGMENTS

many more people than I could've imagined supported and encouraged me as a writer. Marcus Sakey, bestselling author and even better person, read some of my earliest work and told me I had *something*, and has constantly buoyed and motivated me ever since. Some of our conversations about public service and the war in Afghanistan shaped key emotional buttresses of this book. I'm grateful for those correspondences, proud to consider him a friend, and I hope someday to write with even half the pathos and brilliance he has. Zac Topping and Elliot Ackerman read earlier versions of this book and offered kind words and encouragement—I owe them a debt. They are both amazing authors, and you should buy every book they've written. Jonathan Dearman and John L. Davis were firm compatriots on the journey from almost day one.

The first person who ever encouraged my writing was, of course, a teacher. Mrs. Gill, I still have the absolutely ridiculous SFF retelling of *Romeo and Juliet* from tenth-grade English on my bookshelf at home, with your encouragement scrawled in red ink across the top of page 1.

To you, the reader, thank you for opening this book and walking side by side with me on this stage of the expedition. We survived! Our path continues, and I hope to see you along the way.